Also by Stephanie McAfee

Diary of a Mad Fat Girl

HAPPILY EVER MADDER

‹‹◇◇›

Misadventures of a Mad Fat Girl

Stephanie McAfee

NEW AMERICAN LIBRARY

New American Library
Published by New American Library, a division of
Penguin Group (USA) Inc., 375 Hudson Street,
New York, New York 10014, USA
Penguin Group (Canada), 90 Eglinton Avenue East, Suite 700, Toronto,
Ontario M4P 2Y3, Canada (a division of Pearson Penguin Canada Inc.)
Penguin Books Ltd., 80 Strand, London WC2R 0RL, England
Penguin Ireland, 25 St. Stephen's Green, Dublin 2,
Ireland (a division of Penguin Books Ltd.)
Penguin Group (Australia), 250 Camberwell Road, Camberwell, Victoria 3124,
Australia (a division of Pearson Australia Group Pty. Ltd.)
Penguin Books India Pvt. Ltd., 11 Community Centre, Panchsheel Park,
New Delhi - 110 017, India
Penguin Group (NZ), 67 Apollo Drive, Rosedale, Auckland 0632,
New Zealand (a division of Pearson New Zealand Ltd.)
Penguin Books (South Africa) (Pty.) Ltd., 24 Sturdee Avenue,
Rosebank, Johannesburg 2196, South Africa

Penguin Books Ltd., Registered Offices:
80 Strand, London WC2R 0RL, England

First published by New American Library,
a division of Penguin Group (USA) Inc.

First Printing, November 2012
10 9 8 7 6 5 4 3 2 1

 REGISTERED TRADEMARK—MARCA REGISTRADA

LIBRARY OF CONGRESS CATALOGING-IN-PUBLICATION DATA:

McAfee, Stephanie.
   Happily ever madder: misadventures of a mad fat girl /Stephanie McAfee.
      p. cm.
   ISBN 978-0-451-23805-4
   1. Overweight women—Fiction. 2. Female friendship—Fiction. 3. Florida—Fiction. 4. Mississippi—Fiction. 5. Psychological fiction.   I. Title.
   PS3613.C2635H37 2012
   813'.6—dc23   2012023780

Set in Carre Noir STD
Designed by Alissa Amell

Printed in the United States of America

PUBLISHER'S NOTE
This is a work of fiction. Names, characters, places, and incidents either are the product of the author's imagination or are used fictitiously, and any resemblance to actual persons, living or dead, business establishments, events, or locales is entirely coincidental.
   The publisher does not have any control over and does not assume any responsibility for author or third-party Web sites or their content.

To Brandon.

Your patience knows no bounds.

HAPPILY
EVER MADDER

1

<><><><><><><><><><><><><><><><><><><><><><><><><><><><><><><><><><><><><><>

I didn't think I'd be this nervous. I mean, I knew from the very beginning that this night was going to be stressful, but I didn't expect it to feel like an all-out near-death experience.

I turn away from the toilet and pick up the bottle. I don't even like champagne. I like beer. And right now I need a beer worse than I ever have, but champagne is all I've got to get me through this, so I turn the bottle toward the ceiling and hammer down.

I remind myself that this is what I've always wanted. It's *everything* I've *always* wanted, so I don't understand why it doesn't feel *anything* like I *always* thought it would. Maybe because I never thought this moment would actually arrive. But it's here. Right now. I'm about to walk out in front of a rather large crowd of people and bare my soul for their casual perusal.

Someone knocks and tries to open the door.

"Ace! What are you doing? Come on! Everyone is waiting!" A pause. "Have you got the runs? Please tell me you don't have the runs!"

"I don't have the damn runs, Lilly!" I shout at my best friend of going on twenty years. "Jeez, just give me a minute."

"You don't *have* a minute! You were supposed to be out there *ten* minutes ago, so come *on!*"

"What am I supposed to say to all those people?"

"I don't know." She pauses, then adds, "I hate to be the one to point this out, but maybe you should've thought about that already?"

"I did."

"Great—now get out here and say something before these people start leaving!"

I reach over and unlock the door. Lilly comes in and starts fussing with my hair.

"Here," she says, handing me a tube of lip gloss. She looks at the champagne bottle in my hand. "Are you drunk?"

"Unfortunately, I am not."

She takes the bottle out of my hand and sticks it under the sink.

"This is your big night, Ace Jones," she says, smiling. "Get out there and give 'em the old razzle-dazzle."

"More like frazzle-dazzle, Lilly. I'm scared shitless. What if everyone hates everything they see? What if they think it's all complete and total garbage?"

"Ace, if they think that, then they're idiots, and no one cares what idiots think," she says, taking my hand. "C'mon, now. You've waited your whole life for this."

I follow her out of the bathroom, through my brand-new office, where move-in junk is still scattered everywhere, and out into the wide-open space of the gallery, my gallery, where clusters of people are drinking champagne and looking at paintings. My paintings.

"And here she is, folks," a slick-haired fellow says into a cordless microphone. "The star of tonight's show, Miss Graciela Jones!"

Everyone claps and I smile and wave. I take the microphone from his overtanned hand, gather all my courage, and pray I don't hurl.

"Hello, everyone," I say and realize I've got the microphone too close to my mouth. "Thank you all *so* much for coming out tonight. Welcome to Mermaids of Pelican Cove."

I scan the sea of unfamiliar faces, then home in on my pals, who are congregated in the far left corner of the gallery. I see Lilly take a seat on the sofa in between her luscious lover boy, Dax Dorsett, and our mutual BFF, Chloe Stacks. Sitting directly across from Chloe is her new boyfriend, J. J. Jackson, and perched two cushions down is Ethan Allen Harwood, who is chatting it up with his best friend and my fiancé, Mason McKenzie. Mason is sitting on a rectangular ottoman, and I'd give anything to be sitting over there next to him instead of standing up here about to lose my mind. He looks at me and smiles. I feel a little better, but not much.

I look back at the crowd, take a deep breath, and attempt to parlay the speech I spent the past three weeks composing. Instead of delivering the articulate presentation I had planned, however, I sputter random words and phrases in a most disorderly fashion, then get really hot and start feeling like I might pass out. I decide to start thanking people.

"I'd like to thank my fiancé, Mason McKenzie, and all of my old friends who came down to Pelican Cove, Florida, from my hometown of Bugtussle, Mississippi. Thanks, y'all." I look at them and nod. "And I'd like to thank all the new friends that I make to meet tonight. I'm sorry, I mean, hope to make—I mean, meet tonight." I look at Lilly, and she looks nervous but flashes me a big smile, so I continue. "Thank you, Mason, for making all of my dreams come true, and thank you, Lilly, for being my BFF since we stopped hating each other the year after sixth grade. And thank you, Chloe, who's been my other BFF since we met at Mississippi State and me and Lilly moved in with her even though we thought she was a little bit weird." Then I get too close to the microphone again and mumble, "At first." I look at Chloe, and her big brown eyes are round like saucers.

I shift my gaze back to the crowd and see that more than a few people look like their underwear just started squeezing them in all the wrong places. My brain feels like it's swelling up inside my skull and I wish I hadn't drunk all that champagne. I mop the sweat off my forehead and try to remember what I'd planned to say. I don't think I meant to thank my friends individually, but since I mentioned a few, I decide to mention the others because I don't want anyone to think that I don't appreciate their driving six hours down here to watch me make a fool of myself in front of all these people I don't know.

"Thanks to Sherriff J. J. Jackson and Deputy Dax Dorsett, who came down with their lady friends, Chloe and Lilly, to see, uh, me and all this." I wave my arm around in a big circle and try to smile. "I don't know who is keeping criminals off the street in Bugtussle tonight, but since I moved out of town, I guess the crime rate has gone down considerably." I snigger and look at Lilly, who is slicing her hand across her throat. I hear a rumble in the crowd and panic. "And, finally, thanks to Ethan Allen Harwood, my best guy friend in the whole wide world and Mason's best friend in the whole wide world." I look at Ethan Allen, who is frozen like a statue. "We love you like a brother, Ethan Allen, so I guess it's a good thing that me and you never hooked up, because that would've been almost like incest."

The crowd is quiet now and staring at me like I have an alien probe sticking out of my ass. Despite my best effort not to, I start laughing hysterically. I look at Mason, who gives me a sweet "you're so pitiful" smile. He starts clapping, and others do the same. I tug at the hem of my not-so-little black dress because all of that slimming fabric has started to creep. I look around and try to remember what I just said to all these people, but I can't. "Thank you all for coming out," I say a bit too loud. "Please excuse my nervousness. Lucky for me, you didn't come to hear me speak, thank goodness—you came to see my work, so if we could please just move along to that part, well, that would be great."

I look at the tuxedo-clad slickster, who smiles at me with genuine sympathy. I verbalize my gratitude one more time and then give the microphone back to him. He gives a short and far more graceful spiel, and everyone claps and starts looking comfortable again. I stand there beside him and smile, wondering if the spotlight glaring into my face could scorch my eyeballs and cause me to go blind. I take a little bow, then walk slowly away from the brutal shaft of light, trying to project a sense of confidence that I most certainly do not feel.

Shit. No wonder van Gogh cut off his own ear.

I make a beeline for my pals.

2

◇◇◇

"Oh. Wow. That was some speech," Lilly says, pressing her lips together like she does when she's trying not to laugh.

"I don't even remember what I said," I tell her. "That was awful!"

"It was pretty awful," Lilly agrees.

"I meant having to stand up there like that."

"I meant your speech," Lilly says, providing everyone, including herself, with the opportunity to laugh off the tension.

Ethan Allen hands me a champagne glass and I take a big swig and almost choke. I don't know what in the world is in that glass, but it ain't champagne. Ethan Allen smiles at my reaction.

"Moonshine," he says. "Thought it might help your nerves."

"Ethan Allen Harwood!" Lilly says, reaching for the glass. "She needs to be calm"—I take one more swig before she takes the glass out of my hand—"not pissant drunk! We don't need her dancing on the balcony in her bra and panties."

"Has that happened before?" Dax Dorsett asks, and I can't tell if he's worried or interested.

"Yes," Lilly says. "As a matter of fact, it has."

Mason smiles at Ethan Allen. "Leave me a jug of that, would you?"

"No problem, buddy."

Lilly hands me another glass.

"What's this?" I ask.

"Water," she says. "Now, let's go mingle with your potential clientele before they leave here thinking you're a total nutcase." She takes my hand and leads me into the crowd.

After Lilly and I meet and greet what seems like six hundred thousand people, I sneak off while she isn't looking and have a seat on one of the benches. I'm wondering how improper it would be to shed my heels and walk around barefoot when I hear a commotion at the front door.

I look up to see Gloria Peacock, one of my very favorite people from Bugtussle, and her sophisticated senior citizen friends making a grand and glorious entrance. I forget the foot pain and rush over to welcome them.

"Graciela," Gloria Peacock says, giving me a delicate little-old-lady hug, "How wonderful to see you!" She looks around the place. "Magnificent!" she says, smiling. "It's positively magnificent!"

"I'm so happy y'all could make it," I say and exchange hugs with the other three ladies.

"Well," Daisy McClellan says, straightening her wide-brimmed, feathered hat. "We would've been here on time if Birdie hadn't had that altercation with the police officer who pulled us over for driving the wrong way down a one-way street!"

"Daisy!" Birdie Ross snaps. "I was going where that varmint told me to go!"

"Well, *I* told you that *I* knew exactly where this place was, Birdie. And it's a *Garmin*, not a *varmint*." Daisy rolls her eyes. "That GPS is going to get you killed!"

"Or thrown in jail," Gloria's friend Temple Williams adds.

"Trust me, ladies," I say, thankful they missed my babbling fool of a speech, "your timing couldn't be better!"

Chloe appears with a tray of long-stemmed glasses. "Hello, darling ladies," she says sweetly. "Could I interest anyone in some champagne?"

"Good holy mother of ginger snaps, yes!" Birdie exclaims, taking two glasses.

I escort Gloria, Daisy, Birdie, and Temple around the gallery, and they ooh and aah over my work to the point I start feeling giddy like I always imagined I would back when having my own art gallery was just a big, fancy dream. We wind through the gallery and back around to where Mason and the others are camped out, and since my psycho nerves are under control, I decide to make a solo venture into the crowd.

Just as I'm getting into my conversational groove, I feel a tap on my shoulder and turn to face a stout woman who looks to be in her late fifties or early sixties and would best be described as handsome rather than pretty. Her grass green dress is sparkly to the point of being obnoxious and she's wearing a shimmery gold scarf with a gigantic rhinestone brooch shaped like, of all things, a hammer.

"Miss Jones," she says with smirk, "I'm Lenore Kennashaw."

She offers a gloved hand and I can't tell if she's snarling or smiling, but I shake her hand and try not to jump to conclusions. I'm committed to turning over a new leaf here in Pelican Cove and being a normal, perhaps even pleasant person. Pretty much the polar opposite of how I conducted myself in Bugtussle.

"That was some speech."

"Uh, thank you, Mrs. Kennashaw," I say, cautiously. "I was really nervous."

"You know, one would think one would better prepare oneself for such a momentous introduction into Pelican Cove society."

"Yes," I say and feel my cheeks burning. "Well, this *one* did." I point to myself. "I actually worked on that speech for three weeks, but I was so nervous you probably couldn't tell."

"One couldn't discern that any effort whatsoever had been invested in that jumbled, incoherent discourse," she says flatly.

I wonder for a second how she might like *one* of my high heels crammed up her ass. I take a deep breath and focus on staying calm and keeping my cool. I try to remember what Gramma Jones used to say about making nice with my enemies. It had something to do with heaping burning coals on their heads. Lenore Kennashaw stares at me and I stand there and give her a big, phony smile, because I don't trust myself to open my mouth.

"So," she says and turns to the painting to her right. "Is this supposed to be some kind of Edward Manet knockoff?"

"I'm sorry, do you mean Claude Monet?" I ask, eyeballing her sparkly hammer brooch. I smile again, thinking of how she might react if I plucked that gaudy thing off her ugly-ass scarf and popped her on the forehead with it.

"I think you're mispronouncing that, dear. It's pronounced *mah-ney*, not *moh-ney*." She gives me a snide look. "If you wish to be taken seriously as an artist in this town, you might want to educate yourself on the correct pronunciation of the masters."

"I have a bachelor's degree in art history," I say, trying and failing to keep the edge out of my voice. "*Edouard* Manet painted, among other things, naked women, whereas Claude Monet generally stuck with landscapes and nicely dressed ladies." I nod toward my painting of two boats and a grassy lakeshore. "That is indeed an impressionistic rendering of the subject matter, but it's more consistent with the style and color palette of *Mo*-net. Not *Ma*-net." I really enunciate the difference in pronunciation. Her expression of shock and disdain are so pleasing that I add, "And that's a fact, Mrs. Lenore Kennashaw."

"Why, Miss Jones," she says coolly, "your conversational skills are almost as unpleasant as your oratory verboseness." She winks at me and says, "But not quite."

She turns to walk away and I stand there beside my beloved boat picture, fuming while I think of all the nasty things I'd like to say to Mrs. Lenore Kennashaw.

"Excuse me, Miss Jones?"

I turn to see a woman who is a bit shorter but way thinner than me and bears more than a passing resemblance to a wood sprite. She has sparkly navy blue eyes and short brown hair that I find immediately intriguing because it looks like she gelled each individual lock on her head, but somehow the overall effect looks tousled and unkempt. She's wearing a strapless lavender dress and a short necklace made up of multicolored stones.

"I'm Tia Wescott," she says and presents an ungloved hand. "Nice to meet you." She's smiling, so I smile back and shake her hand.

"Nice to meet you, too," I say, hoping she's as nice as she sounds.

"I'm an interior decorator here in Pelican Cove and I just wanted to tell you that I love your new gallery." She keeps smiling, so I relax a little. She nods toward the painting that sparked my nasty little exchange with Mrs. Lenore Kennashaw. "Like that boat picture. That's really nice. Is it supposed to be some kind of Eddie Money impersonation?"

"Excuse me?" I say and start feeling like I might have a Lilly Lane—style sobbing fit. "Eddie Money?"

She tilts her head to the side and says, "Or is it Eddie Rabbit?"

I stare at her and say nothing. Then she starts to laugh.

"Gotcha, didn't I?"

"Yes," I say, relief rolling over me like the evening tide. "You did. You got me."

She smiles and hits the chorus of Eddie Rabbit's classic song "I Love a Rainy Night." I start laughing and she says, "I just wanted you to know that while I've had a truly fantastic time looking around your gallery this evening"—she takes a step closer to me and lowers her voice—"the highlight of my night was definitely eavesdropping on that conversation you just had with Lenore Kennashaw." She smiles and I smile back. "Can I buy you lunch tomorrow?"

"Sure," I say, delighted to have an ally.

"The Blue Oyster at noon?" she asks.

"You've got a date." I pause and freak out because I can't remember her name.

"Tia," she says, as if reading my mind. "Tia Wescott."

"Tia Wescott," I say. "Such a pleasure to make your acquaintance."

"Let me assure you, Ace Jones," she says, patting me on the back, "the pleasure has been all mine."

The music stops and I hear the slick-haired man on the microphone again.

"Ladies and gentlemen, it's auction time!" he says with great pomp and enthusiasm. "Please grab your paddles and gather 'round!"

"You better head that way," Tia says, nodding toward the balcony, where the spotlight is beaming down on the well-groomed man.

"Right," I say. She gives me a little wave, then disappears into the crowd. I make my way to the stairwell, hoping against hope that I don't have to say a damn word during the auction.

"Where have you been?" Lilly demands as soon as she sees me.

"Meeting people," I say.

"Nice people?" she asks.

"One nice person and one person I'd like to choke with her fancy gold scarf, then stick her in the eyeball with her tacky hammer pin."

"You must mean her," Lilly says, and I follow her gaze to Mrs. Lenore Kennashaw, who is standing front and center of the crowd with her auction paddle at the ready.

"Mark my words, Lilly," I say, smiling through clenched teeth. "That woman is going to be a problem."

Lenore Kennashaw catches us looking at her and flashes a snarky grin.

"No time to worry about that right now," Lilly says. "C'mon, let's get up on the balcony and get this party started."

"Please tell me that I don't have to say anything," I whine.

"Don't worry, Calamity Jane, you just have to stand there."

"Can I take off my shoes?"

"No," Lilly says and starts making her way up the staircase.

I look back at Lenore Kennashaw and she winks at me again. She's winked at me twice in the past fifteen minutes, and in my personal opinion, that's about two times too many.

I want to wink back, then flip her the bird, but everyone would see me and I'm relatively certain that I've made a big enough ass of myself in front of this crowd tonight. So I simply smile and turn around.

I'm going to be nice. Even if it kills me.

3

◇◇◇

After an early breakfast at Round House Pancakes on Sunday morning, Mason and I see our Bugtussle friends off to Mississippi. After all the well wishes and good-byes, he heads to the gym and I go home and get back in bed. I'm physically and emotionally drained from the previous night's excitement, and my feet are swollen and achy from being crammed into high heels for six hours. Mason wakes me when he gets home from the gym and we take our chiweenie, Buster Loo, for a leisurely walk around the block.

"So, you have a lunch date today?" he says.

"Yes, with Tia Wescott. Do you know her?"

"I've heard of her," he says. "She does renovation, or restoration-type stuff or something like that?"

"She said she was an interior designer."

"You like her?"

"She seems pretty cool," I say and decide again not to mention the confrontation with Mrs. Lenore Kennashaw because that might make

Mason think I'm not trying as hard as I should be to be the nice girl I promised him I would be. Not that he would care. It's just that I don't want to muddy the waters with petty crap like that.

"Well, babe, you've worked nonstop since you moved down here three months ago," he says, draping an arm around my shoulder. "I'm glad you've finally branched out and found yourself a gal pal."

"Thanks, sweetie," I say. "Hey, have you thought anymore about where we might get married?"

"Oh yeah, I've thought a lot about that," he says, and I can tell by his tone that he hasn't. "And I've decided that wherever *you* want to get married is exactly where *I* want to get married."

"So you haven't thought about it at all?"

"Listen," he says, stopping to wait on Buster Loo, who is doing some doggie business in a shrub. "I'm a man. Men aren't picky. We could get married at Credo's Wild Wings and I'd be happy."

"Credo's Wild Wings?" I stop and turn around. "Are you serious?"

Credo's Wild Wings is a mom-and-pop joint about half a mile from where we live. It's an old fishing camp turned restaurant with a big, wide deck sprawling out to the water. The parking lot smells like dead fish every now and then, but the food is so good and the view so fantastic that you tend to overlook it.

"Yes! It's on the bay," he says, digging a doggie bag out of his pocket. "They have an awesome deck. They've got supercold beer and really good hot wings."

"They do have really cold beer," I say, smiling at him. "And great wings."

"And it's beautiful at sunset," he says.

"You're so romantic, Mason," I say sarcastically, and he starts laughing. "In a macho, wild-wing kind of way."

"I do like to wing it," he says, puffing out his chest. "Chicken wing it, buffalo wing it, wing it by the seat of my pants."

"You are so crazy!" I say, laughing.

"Really, Ace, anywhere you want is fine with me. My only concern is that, after all these years and all the stuff we've been through, we just get it done. As for the location"—he looks at me and shrugs—"I couldn't care less."

"Tell you what," I say, really wanting him to participate in planning our wedding but not wanting to nag. "I'll narrow it down to three places and you can pick the one you like best."

"Would that make you happy?"

"Yes. Very."

"Then narrow it down to three and I'll pick."

I get to the Blue Oyster at eleven forty-five and don't see Tia, so I wander up to the top deck, where every table has a spectacular view of the bay. I choose a seat that also has a view of the parking lot because, for some odd reason, I'm curious about what kind of vehicle Tia Wescott drives. I order a beer and finish it and one more by the time she arrives at five minutes past noon.

"Hey!" she says, waving. "Sorry I'm late. How are you?" She's wearing short denim shorts and a coral tank top. I can't help but notice that her short legs are very toned and nicely tanned.

"I'm great!" I reply. "Not that I'm a stalker or anything, but I didn't see you come through the parking lot."

"Oh, I walked," she says, waving toward a residential area situated to the left of the marina. "I'm working over there."

"On a Sunday?"

"Yes, on a Sunday," she says drearily. "I don't do that very often, but I've got what I call a 'dragger.'"

"A dragger?"

"Yes. That's what I call a project that just drags on and on with no end in sight." She points to the houses again. "I'm renovating one of the older places, just, you know, trying to get it up to par with the rest of the neighborhood, and I swear that everything I try to do turns up fifteen other things that have to be done first."

"Wow," I say.

A waitress appears with lunch menus and a glass of ice water.

"Thank you, Jenna," Tia says to the waitress.

"Sure thing, Ms. Wescott," Jenna the waitress says. "Do y'all need a minute?"

"Yes, please."

"So," I say after Jenna the waitress walks away. "What's good here?"

"Oh, the crab cakes are top-notch. The fried crab claws are amazing. The crab dip is good, too." She flips the menu over. "And their stuffed crab will make your eyes cross."

"I take it you're fond of crab."

"I'm quite the crab connoisseur, if you will." She looks at me and smiles. "I was born and raised in Pelican Cove and I eat all kinds of seafood, but, yes, crab is my favorite." She nods toward the restaurant. "I love this place because everything is homemade and fresh, so it's all good. You really can't go wrong no matter what you order." She looks at me. "And you can't leave here today without having a slice of key lime pie. So don't even think about trying, okay?"

"One thing you need to know about me," I say, "is that I am *not* the kind of girl who walks away from pie. Any pie. Ever."

Jenna returns and I order crab cakes and another beer and Tia orders crab claws and a Diet Pepsi.

"So," she says after we order, "what about that Lenore Kennashaw?"

"That woman is such a bitch!" I whisper. "What is her deal?"

"Just that," Tia says, sipping her Diet Pepsi. "She's an intolerable bitch. And here's the thing about her." She leans in, so I do the same. "Her husband owns all these Kennashaw Home and Garden stores all over the South, and their stuff is total *shit*! After Hurricane Ivan hit back in 2004, they kept selling Chinese drywall even after it was found to be toxic. Then when Mr. Kennashaw got sued for it, he hired Lennox Casey, a sleazeball attorney from New Orleans, to come over here and get him off the hook."

"That's horrible!"

"Yeah, but that's only part of their story," she says, keeping her voice low. "Lenore is the chairwoman of the biggest charity organization in northwest Florida. It's called Caboose Charity, and she weaseled her way into that position I don't know how many years ago."

"Being involved with charity doesn't seem consistent with her dreadful personality."

"Exactly," she says. "She and her husband are first-class scuzzy-buckets, but they present themselves in society as the world's greatest benefactors." She leans back in her chair. "I know for a fact that they give the absolute minimum required to keep Lenore on the board, which is only about five hundred dollars a year."

"How do you know that?" I ask.

She looks around and whispers, "I have a friend who volunteers for Caboose and she can't stand Lenore Kennashaw, either. A few months ago, she snuck around and checked the records to see just how much the Kennashaws give each year, and she wasn't surprised to find that it was the minimum specified in the bylaws." She stirs the ice in her glass and continues. "The Kennashaws couldn't care less about the cause. All they want is to attend the high-profile events and rub elbows with the big shots in Pelican Cove." She looks at me. "People who give tens of thousands of dollars to that charity."

"No one cares that she barely meets the financial qualifications?"

"Well, no one knows. My friend—her name is Jalena Flores, by the way, and I think you'll like her because she's crazy as hell. Anyway, she can't tell anyone because she'd get into big trouble because Caboose Charity is adamant about privacy"—Tia punches her straw around in her ice—"which works great for Lenore."

"What about the fact that she's a stupid bitch?" I say. "She can't hide that."

"Oh, but she does." Tia gives me a sly look. "She only shows her true colors to people she considers 'beneath' her on the socioeconomic ladder."

"I'll black that heifer's eye," I say, and Tia laughs out loud. "I can't believe she acts like that and no one notices."

"No one but me." Tia smiles a devilish smile. "And I tell everyone I work for that Kennashaw Home and Garden sells second-rate products at ridiculous markups and that they'd be better off going to Lowe's or Home Depot." She looks out at the water and raises her eyebrows. "A lot of people listen to me, but others are so hell-bent on buying local that they just go over there and give them their money, thinking they make all these big donations to charity." She looks at me. "Don't get me wrong—I'm all for buying local, especially in this economy, just not from Kennashaw Home and Garden."

"I bought something from there," I confess.

"Oh, we can't be friends, then," Tia says, laughing. "I'm so sorry."

"I took it back," I say. "Does that help?"

"No," she says. "What was it?"

"Paint."

"Oh, I knew you were going to say that! Their paint is the worst! Did you get your money back?"

"Sure didn't. And it made me mad as hell."

"What did you do?" Tia asks, looking amused.

"I thanked them and left because I'm trying to turn over a new leaf down here and be a nice person instead of a short-tempered nut job like I always was in Bugtussle." I lean forward and put my elbows on the table. "So instead of pouring that damn worthless paint all over their parking lot like I wanted to, I took it back to my studio, where I'm going to try to work it into some of my projects."

"Did you just say 'Bugtussle'?" Tia asks with an odd look on her face.

"Yes," I say, smiling. "Bugtussle, Mississippi. And before you ask, yes! That is the real name of a real town, and I used to live there."

"So what did you do in Bugtussle, Mississippi?"

"I taught art at Bugtussle High School."

"Bugtussle High School," she says, obviously still very amused by the name of my former hometown. "Wow."

"Yeah, it was a nice little job in a nice little town, and I worked with my two best friends." I feel a pinch of homesickness and try to ignore it.

"And now you've just opened your own art gallery and you're engaged to marry a guy you met how?"

"Oh Lord!" I moan. "That's a long story."

"Give me the short version today and we'll make a date for the long one later," she says with a look on her face that makes me laugh.

"Okay," I say. "Well, when I was eleven, my family moved to Bugtussle from Nashville, Tennessee, and I met him at church."

"How sweet."

"Right," I say, and snort. "And we've had this long, drawn-out on-again, off-again thing going ever since."

"Since you were eleven? Are you serious?"

"Sadly, yes," I say, realizing how ridiculous that must sound coming from someone who just turned thirty-one. "We were boyfriend and girlfriend in middle school. Dated off and on in high school. Had a few torrid affairs in college, then—" I pause because I don't want to tell her the whole truth about the past few years, when I spent so much time acting like a crazed lunatic with severe trust issues. I look up at her and decide to give her the short version like she asked for. "I actually lived down here for a month and a half last summer."

"Here?" Tia asks, surprised. "In Pelican Cove?"

"Yes," I say. "After a few 'off' years, Mason and I ran into each other at the annual Ole Miss–Mississippi State football game and he asked me to marry him and I said yes." I laugh at the memory. "We were both somewhat intoxicated at the time, but we carried on a long-distance love affair for several months. Then when I got out of school for the summer, I packed up and moved down here."

"What happened?" Tia asks, thoroughly immersed in my drama. "Wait, I'm sorry. It's none of my business—"

"Oh no," I say casually. "If we're going to hang out, then you should know that I'm a psycho."

She starts laughing and tells me she's a psycho, too.

"Well, I got mad at him for something stupid and packed up and moved back home."

"But here you are, back again, with a big, shiny rock on your finger."

"Here I am," I say, looking at my engagement ring. "A whole new life." I feel a pang of sadness when I say that, because my old life wasn't that bad. It just didn't have Mason in it.

"Trying to be a nice girl," Tia says.

"Yep," I say, nodding.

Our lunch arrives and the crab cakes are indeed the best I've ever had, and I've had some good crab cakes. Tia tells me that she has a daughter named Afton who graduated from high school this past May and moved to Gainesville, where she enrolled in the veterinary medicine program at the University of Florida. She doesn't mention a husband or a boyfriend and I decide not to ask. We get on the subject of pets and she tells me that she has a thirteen-year-old wiener dog named Mr. Chubz. I tell her about Buster Loo and we decide they should have a play date sometime in the not-too-distant future. Then we start talking about Lenore Kennashaw again.

"I still can't believe that conversation I had with her. I swear, I was telling myself to be polite, but it just wasn't happening."

"She's such a hag," Tia says. "And just so you know, hanging out with me is going to get you blacklisted from the upper echelons of Pelican Cove society, because Lenore's claws sink deep into the social scene here."

"Well, thank goodness," I say, laughing. "Maybe that'll keep me away from her so I won't be tempted to judo-chop her in the face."

Tia starts laughing and assures me it would be okay with her if I judo-chopped Lenore in the face. When we finish eating, Tia orders us each a slice of key lime pie, and those arrive a few minutes later on chilled saucers. After the first bite, I graciously thank Tia for the suggestion, because it's almost ridiculous how tasty that pie is.

We talk and carry on some more, exchange phone numbers, then agree to meet again for lunch soon. I head home and spend the remainder of the afternoon lounging around with Mason and Buster Loo. For dinner, I make shrimp kebabs, which Mason cooks on the grill while Buster Loo stands guard in case a wayward piece of anything happens to land on the ground.

After eating, we head out onto the back porch to watch the sun set. Leaning against Mason in the swing with Buster Loo curled up in my lap, I feel my worries slipping away with the daylight. I miss Chloe and Lilly; I miss hanging out at Ethan Allen's bar; and I really miss Pier Six Pizza; but there are no sunsets by the sea in Bugtussle. What's there instead is a surplus of small-town drama, and I don't miss that at all. My life is here now. With Mason and Buster Loo. And today I met my first new Florida friend.

4

◇◇◇

Monday morning, Mason has already left for work by the time I get out of bed. I throw on some junky shorts and an old T-shirt and take Buster Loo for a walk along the gloriously landscaped sidewalk, which offers magnificent views of the Gulf. He scurries and sniffs and flounces around while I take big long breaths of the salty ocean air and think about how lucky I am to live in such a beautiful place.

When we get back home, Buster Loo barrels over to his doggie bowls and I barrel upstairs to shower. I get dressed quickly, then head to the gallery, excited and anxious about the first official day of business for Mermaids of Pelican Cove.

When I get to the gallery, I go up to my studio and grab the fish-shaped OPEN sign I painted last week. I take it outside and hang it on the little hooks Mason installed on the column next to the front door. I walk back inside, thrilled out of my mind, and take a seat behind the counter. I look around, not sure what to do next.

Jittery and eager to do something constructive, I get up and walk around the gallery, straightening every piece of art whether it needs it or not. I wander into my office, but, discouraged by the stacks of junk that need to be dealt with, I head back to the front counter, where I notice a basket of brochures and business cards that must've been left by people who attended the opening on Saturday night. I don't recall putting out a basket, and after thinking about it for a second, I'm sure that was Chloe's doing, because she's all proper like that.

I dig out all the business cards, find one from Kennashaw Home and Garden that I promptly toss in the trash, then stack the rest on the counter and start flipping through the flyers and brochures. I toss the ones that have little or no relevance to me personally, like one from a Montessori school and another about window installation, and make a neat stack of the ones I might need, like the menu for Big Boy's BBQ and a pet-grooming service. At the very bottom of the basket, I find a brochure about the West Florida Festival of the Arts that's held every year in nearby Pensacola.

I heard about this festival when I was a junior at Mississippi State University, and there have been several times throughout the years that I've seriously considered submitting an application but never did because I always chickened out for one bullshit reason or another. I look over the brochure and start getting excited when I think about sending in an application.

The festival is in November, but the application deadline is the first of September, so I need to get busy if I'm really going to finally do this. I have to send three high-resolution pictures of my work, plus the submission form and a small fee.

I run into my office to get my camera and have to dig through five different cardboard boxes before I find it. I walk around and snap pictures of what I think is my best work and then decide that since I have a few weeks, I might need to paint something new and altogether different. Feeling inspired, I head upstairs to the studio. When I'm halfway up, the doorbell chimes, and excited by the prospect of my first real-live customer, I run back down and around to the main hall of the gallery, where, much to my dismay, I find Lenore Kennashaw.

She's standing smack-dab in the middle of my gallery in between two other ladies who look to be about her age and social status.

Great.

I muster up all of my self-control and decide to be pleasant, no matter what. If Lenore Kennashaw wants to push my buttons, she can damn well do it, but she'll break her fingers trying before I give her the satisfaction of seeing me lose my cool. I put on a happy face and step out to greet them, thinking that Lenore Kennashaw will pay top dollar for anything she buys today.

"Well, good morning, Mrs. Kennashaw," I say with sweetness dripping like warm molasses. "How *very* nice to see you today!" She's wearing a dark green boatneck top, superstarched plaid shorts, and ugly green sandals. A long gold chain with a small hammer pendant hangs around her neck.

Lenore Kennashaw touches the tiny hammer and appears to be surprised by my hospitable tone. I give her a good stare down, then reach out to shake her hand, thinking, *I'm from Mississippi, bitch, the Hospitality State.* She looks at my hand like I just wiped my tail with it and then glances at her sidekicks, who are staring at her like they find her hesitation offensive. She reaches out and shakes my hand.

I smile.

"My friends wanted to come by," Lenore says, not moving her gaze from mine.

"Well, I'm happy you were kind enough to accompany them," I say politely, not moving my eyes from hers. "It's *so* good to see you again!"

I turn to the taller, plump lady, who's just stepped up to my right.

"Well, hello," I say kindly, "I'm Graciela Jones."

"Nice to meet you, Miss Jones," the lady says. "I'm Ramona Bradley. I missed the opening because I was out of town, but Lenore told me all about it."

Ramona Bradley has on a hot pink polo and black capris that have tiny pink flamingos like polka dots stitched all over them. She's wearing black leather wedges and her manicured toes are the same color as her shirt.

"I'm sure she did," I say, smiling at Ramona Bradley like she's the queen of England. "Mrs. Kennashaw placed the winning bid for the prize piece at the auction," I coo, wanting to add, *Then left without writing a check for it*, but instead I say, "Such a lovely and benevolent woman." The short lady to my left gives me an odd look, but I keep smiling.

"She donated it to the charity house," the short lady says flatly.

"Oh, really?" I say and show no reaction even though that makes me furious.

"Of course," Lenore says. "I took it by there as soon as I left." She makes a face like she's referring to the removal of a dead, bloated skunk. "It certainly wasn't suited to the décor of my home."

"How very generous of you, Mrs. Kennashaw," I say with more sweetness than a truckload of cupcakes. "You'll be happy to know that I'm quite the versatile artist, so I'm confident I could paint something that would fit right in at your home." I visualize an oil painting of a gigantic corncob wedged between clenched butt cheeks.

"Oh, really?" the short lady says, and I'm afraid she's picking up on my insincerity. "Have you been to the Kennashaws' place?"

"Oh no, but I hope to be invited soon," I gush and step over to the little lady. "Graciela Jones," I say, holding out my hand. "And you are?"

"I'm Sylvie Best," she says, studying me. "I missed the opening as well." Sylvie is wearing a denim one-piece dress that looks like it was designed for someone forty years her junior, and even with her high-heeled, cork-bottomed sandals, she can't be more than five feet tall. Her skin is a leathery brown and she's either in a permanent state of being startled or she's had a face-lift. Or two.

"And you're a friend of Mrs. Kennashaw's?" I ask, looking over at Lenore.

"We're both on the board of Caboose Charity," she says evenly.

"I see," I say and wonder how her annual donations measure up to Lenore's.

"Ramona and Sylvie were anxious to see the community's new art gallery," Lenore says, looking around like one might look around a sewage-treatment plant. "And since we're here, you should know that our annual fund-raising event is coming up, if perhaps there is another *masterpiece* you might be willing to part with." She really pours on the sarcasm, and I tell myself not to take the bait because I need all my brain cells in harmony to execute my next snipe. She eyes a large portrait of potted calla lilies.

"Do you like that one?" I say, following her gaze, knowing the only reason she's looking at it is because it's the biggest piece in the gallery. The other ladies turn and look.

"That's quite lovely," Sylvie says.

"Thank you," I say, calculating my next move. "Take that one, and since it's for charity, I'll also give you this." I walk to the other side of the gallery and point to the boat picture that triggered our disagreement this past Saturday night. I look at Lenore Kennashaw and smile. "I do believe this is one of your personal favorites. Am I right, Mrs. Kennashaw?"

In your face, bitch! I think. This covert-ops manner of exchange is not as much fun as kicking her in the shin would be, but it's close. Lenore looks at me like she wants to kill me.

"Perfect! How very kind of you, Miss Jones," Ramona Bradley says, and then turns to Lenore. "Why, she's lovely, Lenore, nothing like you said."

"Ramona," Lenore says, smiling nervously, "you must've misunderstood something—"

And Ramona unknowingly scores one for the home team!

Ramona looks like she's about to launch into an explanation when Sylvie takes her by the hand. "Ramona, do you think your nephew would mind picking up these portraits for us and taking them over to the charity house?"

"Oh, I'm sure he wouldn't mind at all because he's such a fine boy!" Ramona says, clearly distracted. "Let me just give him a call." She looks at me. "He has a very big truck."

"Great!" I say. "How convenient."

Ramona steps away to call her nephew while Sylvie stands there and stares at me. I look at Lenore and smile. She smiles back. Then she winks at me and my blood pressure goes through the roof. I stand there, holding my phony smile, thinking that if Lenore Kennashaw had known me before I moved down here, she wouldn't put so much effort into rubbing me the wrong way because she would know that I might just punch her right in the nose.

"Miss Jones," Ramona says, jerking me out of my reverie, "he's out of town right now, but he can come by next Monday if that's okay with you."

"It is."

Ramona wraps up her call, then slips her smart phone back into her Louis Vuitton bag. "His name is Kevin Jacobs and he's a really nice boy. Well, I say boy; he's not a boy—he's almost forty years old and he's a bit of a redneck like his father, but he's very handsome." She places her porky hands together as if to pray. "We really appreciate you giving so generously."

"Thank you for giving me the opportunity to, uh, give," I say, thinking about how ugly Kevin Jacobs must be if his ol' auntie Ramona goes around telling people he's a handsome redneck. "I'll have the pieces packaged and ready to go."

"Thank you so much for your time today, Miss Jones," Lenore Kennashaw says as she turns to leave.

"Nice to meet you," Ramona says, turning to follow Lenore. "Good-bye, now!"

"Good-bye," I say. "Come back anytime."

After the two of them walk out the door, Sylvie steps up to me and, in a very low voice, says, "Lenore and I have known each other for over forty years, Miss Jones. Our families moved to Pelican Cove around the same time and we've been the best of friends ever since."

I'm not sure what to say and since the only thing that comes to mind is, "I don't give a shit," I just stand there and nod.

"Very few times have I seen her as upset as she was after you publicly accosted her here at your humble gallery. From what she told me, you were a most ungracious hostess, and that's regrettable because people who succeed in this town tend to be ones with a bit more respect for, shall we say, the powers that be?"

My jaw drops and then I bite my lip because I know if I open my mouth again, it's going to be bad for Sylvie Best.

"What I'm saying is that it would behoove you to knock off that phony smile and thinly veiled attitude and find a way to show some esteem for the people who can and *will* determine your success in our quaint little town. Understood?"

I take a deep breath and decide to let her know with as much profanity as possible that she will have nothing whatsoever to do with the success or failure of my art gallery, but then it dawns on me that she might not be bluffing. Tia just told me yesterday that Lenore's claws sink deep into the social scene here, and while I'm not even sure what that means, I don't know if I'm willing to run the risk of running my mouth and ruining myself on my very first day of business.

Seeing my hesitation, Sylvie smiles and nods. "That's right," she says, turning to go. "No need to say a word. Good girl." She stops at the door and turns to look at me again. "You might make it in this town after all, Miss Jones. Especially now that you know where you stand."

I watch her walk out of my gallery and get into a silver Mercedes-Benz. "Those bitches!" I say to myself, watching them pull out of the parking lot. I'm so mad I feel faint, so I go to the break room and get a Diet Mountain Dew out of the fridge. I walk up to my studio, stop in the doorway, and look out at the bay. I run the entire conversation through my head again and then, at the top of my lungs, I yell, "Those stupid bitches!"

I want to run and get in my car, ride around until I find that Mercedes, and then fist-whip Sylvie Best in her too-tight face until her eyeballs pop out, but that probably wouldn't be good for business, so I just stand there, seething. Then I think about the paintings I just *gave* to those idiots and get even madder. I reluctantly go back downstairs to pack those up, telling myself it's not for them, but for charity.

Right.

I pluck the giveaways off the wall, not believing I'm really doing this, and haul them into my office. I have to burrow through a few boxes before I finally get my hands on the packing supplies, and after thirty minutes of wrapping and taping, I'm satisfied they're ready for transport. I take the pictures out to the gallery and prop them against the wall behind the counter. I feel a small tug of sadness when I realize that I'll never know what kind of people will end up with these two pieces or the large painting Lenore won, failed to pay for, and subsequently donated to her charity.

I plop down on the stool behind the counter and think one more time about the one-sided conversation I had with Sylvie Best. Or I should say that she had with me. It makes me mad *and* it depresses me because I'd really made up my mind that I was going to come down here, make a fresh start, and be nice. And I can be nice all day long as long as people don't start any shit with me, but if someone starts some shit, especially some *stupid* shit, well, that whole being-nice thing has to go.

I look around the gallery and ask myself if it's worth it. Could Sylvie and Lenore really ruin me here in Pelican Cove? Is telling them off worth taking that chance? Or would I be better off to just let this whole thing go and turn the other cheek? I think about all the work I put into this place and start feeling nauseated when I realize what it would mean to fail.

It would mean that I was wrong. Wrong about myself when I thought I could do this. I can live with a lot of things, but I can't live with that. Not now. Not after quitting my job, renting out my house, and moving all the way down here. I go to the bathroom and splash cold water on my face. Then I sit down by the toilet and take a few deep breaths. After a few minutes, I get myself together and stand up and look in the mirror. I look like a damn wreck, so I go get my makeup bag and dump all of the contents into the sink. After touching up my face, I comb my hair and reapply a coat of hair spray.

"I can do this," I say, popping my freshly glossed lips. "I just have to be nice, and that was my plan to begin with, so what of it? Those women are nothing but dried-up nuggets of stinking idiotic horseshit, so maybe good things will come my way if I'm nice to a pack of hags who don't deserve it." I take a deep breath, put everything back into my makeup bag, and promise my reflection that I can function like this.

I walk upstairs to my studio and start thinking about what I might do for the art festival submission. It takes me only a minute to decide that I should paint the marina next to the Blue Oyster Restaurant, because it really is one of the prettiest sights I've ever seen. Plus I might score some points with the selection panel for doing something local. I carefully position a medium-sized canvas on my easel, pick up a pencil, and sketch out the buildings, the boats, and the water, but my mind isn't on it. Forcing myself to stay on task, I take out my paints and bring the marina to life.

5

◇◇◇

The following Monday, I'm putting the finishing touches on a cartoonish red crab that I painted just for fun when the doorbell chimes and scares me to death. After tossing my brushes in the sink, I wash my hands and head downstairs. I'm still wiping my hands with a towel when I round the bottom of the stairs and feast my eyes on what can be described only as a big sexy beast of a man. I stop walking and just stare.

This fellow is obviously involved in some kind of construction, because his boots and jeans are dusty, as well as that neon green SALT LIFE shirt he's wearing. His dark blond hair is curled over the back of a camouflage Alabama baseball cap, and his eyes are so brown they're almost black. I throw the towel off to who knows where, brush a hand through my hair, and do my best to look cool and nonchalant as I walk to meet him in the center of the gallery.

"Miss Jones, I presume," he says, holding out a large, chiseled hand. I'm shaking his hand, reveling in his manly, outdoorsy scent, when he says, "You just smeared paint in your hair."

"Oh," I say coolly, "that's how I like it." I smile. "Please, call me Ace."

"Well, Ace, I'm Kevin Jacobs, Ramona Bradley's nephew, and I'm here to pick up a picture or something?" He cocks his head sideways and smiles, and I almost fall on the floor from cardiac arrest because he's so damn attractive that it almost hurts to look at him. I think about Birdie Ross and how she's always telling men they're "hot to trot" and I can't help but think she would love this guy.

"Those two," I say, pointing to the pictures propped against the wall behind the counter.

"Well, I just walked right past those, didn't I?" he says, and I swoon over his deep voice.

"Lucky for you it's not too far of a walk back to where they are." I blush, ashamed of my shameless attempt to flirt.

"Nice place you got here," he says, looking around.

"Thank you," I say, wishing he'd get those pictures and get the hell out the door before I do something crazy like ask him to whip out his goober.

"I know your fiancé, Mason," he says, and my giddiness evaporates like ice on hot asphalt.

"Yeah," I say, feeling like a dirtbag.

"Yeah," he says, flashing that thousand-watt smile. "He did the closing on my house a few years back and we've been fishing buddies ever since."

"Oh, that's nice," I say, hoping against hope that Kevin Jacobs never shows up at our place for a fish fry or something, because I'd hate to get caught staring at his crotch like I've been trying *not* to do for the past five minutes.

"Over here?" he asks, pointing. I nod, and when he turns around, my cheeks start to burn as my mind becomes consumed with X-rated thoughts about Kevin Jacobs.

"Well, I guess I better get these things and head on down the road." He picks up the first picture and turns to go. I walk over and stand behind the counter, staring at his ass until he's out the door. I try to act busy when he comes back in a second later, but there's nothing on the counter except that basket of brochures, so I piddle with those like a moron.

"Saved the big one for last," he says, smiling as he picks up the painting.

"That's my policy," I say, and then snigger and snort as my cheeks continue to burn.

"Is it, now?" he says and laughs out loud.

"I do what I can," I say, then realize that I am making no sense whatsoever. I walk over to the door to put some distance between us so I don't jump on him like a fat kid on a cream cheese brownie. "Let me get this door for you."

I walk outside and hold the door open, hoping the sun might insta-bake some sense back into my head.

His arm brushes my boob as he steps out the door and, even though I know better, I tell myself it was *not* an accident. He carefully places the bigger painting in the back of his truck with the smaller one and then secures them with what looks like ski rope while I stand there and stare at his ass some more. He turns around and walks back to where I'm standing, still holding the door open.

"Lettin' your cold air out, sweetie," he says.

"It was too cold in there anyway," I say, letting the door go.

"Well, I'm all for warming things up," he says, cocking his head sideways again.

And before I even know what's going on, I blurt out, "I bet you are." Then I toss my head back and start cackling like I've just heard the greatest joke in the history of the world, and he starts laughing, too. I have a sneaking suspicion that he's not laughing with me.

"You're a feisty one, aren't you?" he asks.

"Maybe," I say and realize that he has got to leave before I start peeling off my clothes right here on the sidewalk. "Thanks for coming by and picking those up." I nod toward the pictures sticking out of the bed of his truck.

"It was my pleasure," Kevin Jacobs says, and I bite my lip so I don't blurt out something awful about pleasure. He does that two-finger salute-wave like country boys do and says, "Nice to meet you, Ace."

"Nice to meet you, too, Kevin," I say, holding his gaze for a second too long.

"See you around," he says, turning to go.

"Bye!" I holler and get myself back inside where it's cool. I run to my office, grab my phone, and call Lilly.

"Hey, Ace *McKenzie*," she says when she answers. "What's going on down in sunny Florida?"

"Don't call me that! We're not married yet," I whisper, even though there's no one in the building but me. "Lilly, I have just seen the sexiest man on the face of the Earth."

"Are you looking at a picture of my boyfriend, Dax?" she asks and starts giggling.

"No, you goofball, this guy's old enough to be Dax's daddy, but he is so damn *sexy*! He just came in to pick up some pictures I donated to charity and I swear he was the sexiest thing I've ever seen with my own two eyes."

"Ace, you are crazy as hell," Lilly says.

"I think I have a crush on him!"

"Well, that's okay," she says, laughing. "There's not a thing in the world wrong with that. What does he look like?"

"He's this big country boy built like a brick shithouse and he drives a jacked-up pickup truck."

"A brick shithouse with a jacked-up truck, huh?" Lilly muses.

"Yes, and the truck was filthy. Like he just got back from mud riding or hunting." Lilly laughs, and I continue. "Lilly, this is serious! I was drawn to him like some kind of wild animal or something. It's not right!"

Lilly laughs and makes fun of me for getting all hot and bothered over a guy built like a brick shithouse. "Try to get a picture of him next time you see him and text it to me, because I have *got* to see what this dude looks like," she says, still laughing. "I've never heard you carry on so!"

"Lilly." I hesitate for a second. "It's not funny! I'm getting married. I'm in love! I'm perfectly happy! Why was I, like, instantly attracted to him? It worries me. I mean, I was standing here picturing him naked."

Lilly laughs again. "Ace, that's how men think all the time. It just has to be a superhot guy for us to think that way."

"He wasn't superhot—" I cut in.

"It doesn't matter," she says calmly. "It's not like you're going to have a fling with him just because you think he's attractive. Don't worry. It's perfectly normal."

"Me wondering how big his penis is is not normal!" I say.

"I wonder that about everybody," she says casually.

"Well, you're a pervert!" I say, laughing and telling myself to get over it. "So, what's been going on with you?" I ask, desperate to talk about something else.

As she fills me in on all the Bugtussle gossip and drama, I get this odd feeling like I'm homesick yet happy to be gone all at the same time. I chalk the confusing emotions up to Kevin Jacobs coming in and kicking over my think-right buggy. Thirty minutes later, I hang up the phone and see that I missed a call from Mason and start freaking out wondering whether he could've possibly overheard any of the conversation I just had with Lilly. I look at my phone again to make sure I didn't accidentally merge the calls and see he sent me a text telling me he'll be late coming home. Since it's already after five, I decide to lock up and call it a day.

When I get home, I leash up Buster Loo and head down to Pelican Trails Park, which is right around the corner from where we live. The intense summer heat has started to subside, which makes early evening a very pleasant time to walk. I let Buster Loo pick a trail and we head off on a walkway lined with gigantic shade trees dripping with Spanish moss and clusters of big leafy bottle palms rustling in the evening breeze. After a few minutes, Buster Loo starts getting beside himself, and I see why when we round the bend and come upon a pair of pelicans bobbling in the creek. I reel him in to try to calm him down, and then turn around because I see more birds on up the way and I don't think his little doggie nerves can handle it.

As soon as we get back to the house, Mason calls and asks if I'd be interested in meeting him at Credo's Wild Wings and I tell him I'd love to. I hop in and out of the shower, throw on some clothes, and head out the door for the short walk down to Credo's.

During dinner, Mason seems distracted and tired. I ask him what's going on and he says that he and Connor took a case today that put him in a bad mood. He doesn't want to elaborate, so I perpetrate small talk as we sip cold beer and wait for our hot wings. I casually mention Kevin Jacobs, and Mason tells me that he caught his first shark on a fishing trip with Kevin. I tell him about my plans to submit an application for the West Florida Festival of the Arts, and he smiles and tells me he thinks that's a great idea. I can tell his mind is elsewhere, so I pipe down after our food arrives. When we get back home, we split a bottle of wine, then head upstairs and have some hot, lovely sex.

During which I think about Kevin Jacobs.

6

<><><><><><><><><><><><><><><><><><><><><><><><><><><><><><><><><><><><><><>

On Tuesday, I wake up before dawn and realize I've had what Lilly calls a "sexy dream" about Kevin Jacobs. Mason is still sleeping, and my guilty conscience drives me to the kitchen, where I set about making omelets. All I can think about while I stand there chopping onions and peppers is how immediate and intense my attraction was to Ramona Bradley's good-lookin' redneck nephew.

Thirty minutes later, I'm taking toast out of the oven when Mason bustles down the stairs. He's on his cell phone and looks ridiculously handsome in his suit and tie, but I can tell by his expression that he's already in a foul mood. He pours himself a cup of coffee, waves off the omelet sitting on the counter, and leaves without kissing me good-bye. I tell myself it's a work-related oversight and his actions have nothing to do with the magic wearing off our relationship or my mad crush on Kevin Jacobs or anything ridiculous like that.

I eat my omelet and half of his, then decide to go for a walk on the beach to try to clear my head. After kicking off my flip-flops and trudging through the powder white sand, I wade into the water, where I stop for a moment and admire the magnificence of the blue-green expanse. I step back into the firm, wet sand and start walking toward the pier. I put Kevin Jacobs out of my mind and start thinking about how much my life has changed in the past few months.

I went from being a high school art teacher in little-bitty Bugtussle, Mississippi, to owning my own art gallery in the prestigious coastal community of Pelican Cove, Florida. I moved from a comfy little two-bedroom bungalow with a big, beautiful yard into a huge three-story stucco structure with a tiny, professionally manicured lawn. I've been so busy that I haven't had much time to think about this new life of mine, but walking down this peaceful seashore alone with my thoughts, I start to feel lonesome.

I pick up a seashell and think about Mason and our impending nuptials. The one and only detail we actually have worked out is that we want to have a small ceremony on New Year's Eve followed by a big party; we just don't have any idea where that's going to happen.

Despite the fact that I agreed to narrow it down to three places and let him pick the one he liked best, it bothers me that he has no interest in making any suggestions other than the deck at Credo's Wild Wings. He's the one who's lived here for the past several years. He's the one who's been out and about on the social scene. He's the one with all the friends. Not me. I have only one.

When I reach the pier, I toss my shell out into the surf and start walking back. I allow myself to think for a moment about the sex dream I had about Kevin Jacobs and get terribly embarrassed by how graphic it was. I tell myself to let it go, that there's nothing wrong with having a silly little insta-crush on a guy who is very obviously attractive. Hell, what woman wouldn't react that way to him?

I put him and the dream out of my mind, yet again, and let the rhythmic sound of the waves wash all my worries away.

When I return home, I find Buster Loo sunning himself in the backyard and decide to join him on the small square of picture-perfect grass. We play fetch for a while before he barks two times at the sky and runs inside. I take a hot, steamy shower, get dressed, and walk out the door feeling good again.

I get to the gallery and have just walked into my office when the doorbell chimes and I turn around to see Mason.

"Hey, baby," I say, walking out to meet him. "How are you?"

"I forgot something this morning," he says, smiling. His ice blue eyes glow in the sunlight as he puts a hand behind my head and presses his lips against mine.

"Thank you," I say, my cheeks burning. "What did I do to deserve that?"

"Well, I had a lot on my mind last night, and I was running late this morning and left without kissing you good-bye." He smiles and I bask in his attentive gaze.

"Aw," I say, laughing. "I love you so much."

"I love you, too, baby. I was just on my way to the courthouse and thought I'd drop by and give you a quick smootch and apologize." He pulls me into a hug.

"Not necessary, but much appreciated."

"Well, I've got to run. I just wanted to come by and tell you that I don't care if you have to chase me down the driveway—don't let me leave the house again without kissing you good-bye."

"I don't know about chasing you down the driveway," I say. "I could fall and hurt myself."

"Well, it wouldn't be the first time, now, would it?" he quips as he turns to go.

"Hey! Would you like for me to bring you some dinner tonight?" I say, hoping he'll say that won't be necessary because he'll be home by then.

"Connor's wife is taking care of it tonight, but it would be great if you'd join us, and maybe you can bring dinner tomorrow night."

"Sure thing," I say, trying to sound enthusiastic.

"Great," he says. "I'll call you!"

Not long after he leaves, I have a few people come in and look around. Some make pleasant conversation. Some don't. After they leave, I get bored and start feeling lonely again. I decide to close up shop and go grab some lunch.

7

<><><><><><><><><><><><><><><><><><><><><><><><><><><><><><><><><><><><><><><><><><><><>

I'm sitting in the drive-through at Bueno Burrito, reading the news on my phone, when I hear a long honk from the car behind me. I look up and see that the car in front of me has moved forward, so I move up, too, but the honking doesn't stop. I look in my rearview mirror and see a hefty woman in a light blue station wagon leaning forward on her steering wheel and flipping me off with both fingers. I feel my pulse quicken but keep reading the news, careful to hold my phone up so I can see when I need to drive forward, because the woman behind me is obviously in desperate need of burritos.

The car in front of me pulls up, and before I even get my foot off the brake, the woman behind me starts honking again. I decide to sit still for a minute, just to show her that all that honking can't make me do a damn thing. When the car in front of me moves up a second time, I finally pull up, too, and when I roll the window down at the speaker, the woman behind me makes such a racket that I have to shout my order. I roll up my window and pull forward, telling myself to be calm.

I shouldn't have sat there like that, antagonizing her. A nice girl wouldn't do that. A nice girl would've ignored the entire situation. I look back and see that she's still flipping me off with both middle fingers.

When I roll down the window to get my food, she starts honking again, and I tell myself not to get involved with this maniac. The drive-through girl gives me my change, and just as I'm about to hit the gas and remove myself from the situation, I feel a thump and realize the heifer has rolled her crusty old station wagon into the back of my car. Now, I don't have a new car, but I do have a nice car that I try to take pretty good care of.

I pull forward, so mad I'm shaking, and before I can roll up my window, I hear the woman shout, "That's right. Get on out of here now before I jerk you outta that car and whup your ass!"

And to think I was just going to drive away.

I pull a car length away from her, then stop and get out. I walk around behind my car, and when I see the fresh scratch across the bumper, I completely lose what little composure I have left. I turn and walk toward the station wagon.

The woman doesn't see me because she's too busy cramming her hand down into her burrito bag as she pulls away from the drive-through window. I step to the side so she can't run over me, then pound on the hood of her car and shout, "Stop this car! Right now!"

She hits the brakes and I can tell by the look on her face that she wasn't expecting to see me. She slings her burritos into the passenger seat and starts rolling up her window, and I imagine her arms haven't moved that fast in years. She locks her door just as I reach for the handle, so I tap my finger on the window and shout, "Get out of this car!" She's frantically looking around and starts to pull forward, so I walk along beside the car, tapping on the driver's-side window with my knuckles.

"I will *kill* you if you hit my car again, do you understand? I will *kill* you!" She stops the car but doesn't look up at me. "Flip me off now!" I yell. "Honk that damn horn at me now!" She looks to her right, then starts turning the wheel of the station wagon. "Where are you going?" I shout. "You can't get out of here! Get out of that car! Get out here and whip my ass like you just said you would!" She glances up at me and I give her my best crazy-eyed look. "I'm not the one you want, lady!" I yell. "I'm not the one you want!" She guns the engine and I step back just in time to watch her bounce that big station wagon over the land-scaped curb and out into the parking lot. I look around and see people staring, some wide-eyed, some amused. I try to think up something to say, but what *do* you say after an incident like that? The truck that was behind her is about to pull away from the drive-through window, so I run back to my car and get out of there before somebody calls the law.

"Why did I do that?" I yell at myself on the way back to the gallery. "Why didn't I just ignore her? I suck at this being-nice thing! I suck at it!"

I get back to the gallery, eat lunch alone in the break room, and then spend the better part of the afternoon feeling guilty for losing my temper and making a fool of myself in the drive-through of Bueno Burrito. Not a soul graces the doorway all afternoon, and I leave at five o'clock on the dot.

When I get home, I take Buster Loo for a walk around the block. I wave to a few neighbors and they wave back, and Buster Loo sniffs mailboxes, shrubs, and random patches of grass until eventually the mailbox he's sniffing is ours. After playing some speedy-dog fetch in the backyard, I shower and get dressed, then head to the law firm of J. Mason McKenzie, where I dine with Mason, Connor, and his wife, Allison, in the conference room.

I can't decide if Allison is someone I'm going to like or not, and I think it's because she hasn't decided what kind of person she's going to be yet. She and Connor are pretty much still newlyweds, and while they appear to get along great, something seems off with them. Mason has told me that she comes from a wealthy family, goes home to Tallahassee a lot, and flits in and out of Pelican Cove society.

I think she can't make up her mind if she wants to be a snobby bitch or a nice person, because sometimes she's so nice it gets on my nerves and sometimes she's so snobby I want to slap her jaws. I've wondered if she's having an identity crisis or if she might actually be schizophrenic. Whatever the case may be, she's sporting her nice-girl persona during dinner and even cracks a few jokes. One is actually funny.

As far as looks go, Allison Dexter McCall is ridiculously beautiful. She's almost as pretty as my friend Lilly Lane, who is a former lingerie model. And like my friend Chloe, Allison radiates that all-put-together perfection that gals like me just can't seem to figure out. She notices me staring at her and gives me an odd look, so I compliment the Chinese food she had delivered to the office. She smiles and starts telling me about their weekly specials.

The dinner chatter is light as we talk about movies we've seen and movies we want to see and then what the weather is going to be like for the rest of the week. I tell a few jokes that are way funnier than Allison's so she doesn't get to thinking that, between the two of us, she's the funny one.

After dinner, I hang out in Mason's office for a few minutes before telling him good night and heading home. I snuggle up with Buster Loo and end up falling asleep on the couch watching a *Saturday Night Live* rerun. Mason wakes me when he gets in, and I look at the clock on the cable box and see that it's 10:34.

"Come to bed with me, beautiful," he says, taking my hand.

"Baby, it's so late," I whisper.

"I know," he says, leading me up the stairs. "I'm sorry."

"What's the deal?" I ask, turning back the covers and climbing into bed. "I didn't think real estate lawyers had to work like this."

"Normally I don't," he says. "But yesterday, a man my daddy's age walked into the office and told Connor that he lost his house last year in a foreclosure and now the bank has just filed a deficiency judgment against him and frozen all of his bank accounts."

"I don't know what all of that means, but that last part is terrible."

"What's terrible," he says, tossing his clothes on the floor and joining me in bed, "is that the man lost his job *three* years ago when he was fired by a company that decided to save themselves some money by getting rid of all the people who were about to retire. When he told us that, I said we could sue them as well and assured him it wouldn't cost him a dime, and he said he'd love to but the company went bankrupt six months ago." He pulls the covers up and sighs. "So anyway, the man and his wife did everything they could to keep their home and, after draining most of their savings, ended up losing it anyway. Now the bank is back and trying to collect the difference between what was owed on the house and what they sold it for. The only cash the man had was what was in his pocket when his debit card was turned down at the gas station. You want to know how much that was?"

"How much?"

"Eight dollars," Mason says. "And his truck was on empty, so he was able to buy *almost* two gallons of gas. Just enough to get home and get his emergency credit card."

"That makes me want to cry," I tell him.

"Well, you'll be crying tears of joy when we get finished with this, because banks are supposed to be sure someone has the assets to cover the deficiency before they file a judgment against them, and there's no way this man and his wife fit into that category. This was not a strategic default. The man agreed to let us take a look at his foreclosure documents because it's my guess that if that piece-of-shit bank is ignoring the rules now, they probably ignored the rules during the foreclosure. But we can't worry about any of that until we get the damn hold off his bank account." He rolls over. "Sons of bitches."

I lie beside him, trying to think up something to say that might make him feel better, but I have no idea how to respond to what he just told me. I reach over to pat him on the shoulder and tell him that I'm proud of him for helping those people, but he doesn't respond because he's already asleep.

8

<><><><><><><><><><><><><><><><><><><><><><><><><><><><><><><><><><><><><>

Another week passes during which I keep to myself in an honest effort to avoid dramatic confrontations of any kind. The next Tuesday, I wake up early and, much to my dismay, cannot go back to sleep no matter how hard I try. I throw on some clothes and go downstairs to find Buster Loo sitting at the front door. He twists his head around sideways and looks at me like, "What are you doing? I'm waiting!" so I grab the leash and take him for an early-morning stroll. I let him walk where he wants and wait patiently as he does his whole stop-and-sniff routine at each and every mailbox on the block. I notice several little signs around the neighborhood announcing the quarterly homeowners' meeting, which is apparently tomorrow night at seven p.m. in the community center. Buster Loo notices the signs as well and stops to raise his leg next to one.

"I'd rather be shot in the face than go to that," I tell Buster Loo as he kicks grass up onto the sign with his back paws. He gives me a "ruff" reply and I laugh because my little dog has no idea how funny he really is.

An hour later, I'm sitting at the kitchen table reading the morning paper when the doorbell rings, causing Buster Loo to rocket-launch himself out of his deluxe doggie bed and have a furious barking fit. I pick him up and try to sweet-talk him out of his guard-dog rage, but it's too late. He's in full-fledged beast mode. I open the door to find a petite little lady wearing what looks like athletic gear. I can't help but notice that her shirt has creases pressed into the sleeves, and the shorts look equally crisp.

"Hello," I say, and Buster Loo growls and shows off his teeth. "Hush," I whisper to him.

"Hi, I'm Margo Kiltzwich."

"I'm Ace Jones. Nice to meet you," I say, and Buster Loo continues to growl and snarl. Margo whatever-her-name-is looks at my ten-pound dog like he's an enraged lion about rip her face off.

"I'm the president of the homeowners' association, and I'm just out reminding everyone that the quarterly meeting is tomorrow night, so if you have any complaints—" She stops talking and looks at Buster Loo, who has stopped barking but continues to snarl and show his off his chiweenie choppers.

"I don't," I say, shocked at how incredibly annoying her high-pitched, nasal voice is. Buster Loo starts to bark again. "Excuse me," I say. I step into the study, put Buster Loo down, and pull the door closed. Back at the front door, Margo has a smile on her face but looks like she smells something that stinks.

"Thank you," she says, and I assume she's referring to my taking her out of harm's way by removing my ferocious man-eating chiweenie from her haughty presence. He's still barking his crazy little head off, and I smile, thinking he's an excellent judge of character. She continues. "Okay, well, it's very important that everyone attend in case anyone submits any complaints that involve you."

"Are there complaints that involve us?" I ask, shocked.

"Oh, well, not that I'm aware of, but there could be by tomorrow night."

She keeps chattering while I smile a phony smile and tell myself not to laugh out loud. I can't help but think this annoying knucklehead would get along great with Lenore Kennashaw. I wonder whether they're friends and, if so, whether they get together and have little ironing parties for their casual clothes. I'm sure if they do, they have people on hand to do the actual work. Then I start thinking about Tia and wondering if she might be the only normal person in this entire town. I wish she would call and invite me to lunch again. "I'll be sure to remind Mason," I say, and start to close the door.

"Oh, you should come, too!" she says with a bit too much enthusiasm. "We'll have snacks and drinks—nonalcoholic, of course. And since you live here now, you have a responsibility to the community, and I can't help but notice that Mason hasn't been to a meeting since you moved in." She raises her eyebrows and looks at me like I stole something from her.

"Thank you, Margo," I say. "Nice to meet you." I put my hand on the door and remind myself that I'm a nice person now.

"See you both tomorrow night. Seven p.m. on the dot!" I push the door closed as she yells, "Don't be late!"

"Oh Lord," I tell Buster Loo as I open the door to the study. He runs straight to the front door and starts growling.

On Wednesday, I get to the gallery at five minutes before ten, unlock the front door, and hang out the OPEN fish. I have a flurry of potential customers streaming in and out throughout most of the morning, and even though no one buys anything, I tell myself that it's good to have so many people looking around. At one o'clock, the gallery is empty, so I run out to grab lunch, hoping I don't run across any crazy-ass-idiot people because I've met enough of those lately to do me for a while. Luckily, I make it to the sandwich shop and back without getting into any kind of altercation. I eat lunch at the desk in my office so I don't have to sit in the break room by myself.

After walking around the gallery for a few minutes, I decide to dedicate the afternoon to creating a large painting of a glamorous mermaid to hang right in the center of the gallery. I have a few smaller mermaid portraits and several undersea paintings, and I think if I grouped them all together alongside the mermaid I have in mind, it would give the gallery a unique and mystical ambiance. Maybe then someone might actually buy something.

I run upstairs, where I get out my paints and line up my brushes, and then I sketch out a big, beautiful mermaid. I make her plump and curvy, with come-hither eyes and long, flowing hair. I mix up my paints and feel a rush of excitement as I get started. I'm almost finished with her shimmery tail when, at a quarter till four, the doorbell rings, so I step out onto the balcony. I look down and see what appears to be a gypsy standing in the middle of the gallery.

"Hello," I call out. "I'll be right down." I toss my brushes in the sink, rinse and dry my hands, then head downstairs.

"Hello," the gypsy girl says sweetly when I greet her downstairs. "I've been so excited about this gallery, and I hate so bad that I missed the grand opening."

"That's okay," I say, trying to figure out just exactly what I'm dealing with here with this strangely dressed person.

"Would you mind if I looked around a bit?" she asks, her voice barely above a whisper.

I take in the multicolored ankle-length skirt, the pink polka-dot tank top over a light blue fitted T-shirt, and what look to be real ballet slippers for shoes. She's beautiful in a very exotic way, with thick lips and perfectly white teeth. She's wearing long, feathered earrings and a passel of beaded necklaces, some of which reach almost to her waist. Her dark blue eyes are speckled with gold, and when she looks at me, I feel like I'm gazing at a much older soul than her youthful complexion conveys.

"Of course," I say, trying to be quiet the way loud people do around people who aren't. "I'm Ace Jones and this is my gallery."

"Hello," she says. "I'm Avery Cambre. I'm studying studio art specialization at the University of West Florida."

"Studio art specialization," I say, genuinely impressed. "What year?"

"I'm a junior," she says softly. "Going for a bachelor of fine arts."

"Wow," I say, consciously keeping my voice low. "Nice."

"Thank you." She smiles at me. "So you don't mind if I look around?"

"Not at all," I say, flattered by her interest. "If you have any questions, I'll be right over there."

"Great—thanks." She pitter-pats away in her ballerina shoes, and I go sit down behind the counter. I make a mental note to find something to keep up here so I can look busy when I need to instead of reshuffling these business cards and brochures over and over again. She makes a round through the gallery, then comes back to where I'm sitting and doing a horrible job of looking busy.

"How long did it take you to do all of this?" she asks in her quiet voice.

"Well, it's been a gradual accumulation," I say, trying to speak quietly. "I actually taught art for several years, and most of what you see here are things I did during that time. Some pieces are from college, and some, like those little mermaids over there, I painted last week."

"Where do you paint?"

"Upstairs," I say. "Would you like to see my studio?"

"I was hoping you'd ask," she says, smiling.

She follows me upstairs and into my studio, where she hardly notices the stunning view of the bay.

"I need a place just like this," she says, looking around at all of my supplies.

"You should get one after you graduate," I tell her.

"That's easier said than done," she says with a frown. She goes on to tell me that her parents aren't exactly thrilled with her program of study and nag at her constantly about changing her major so she can pursue what they call a *real* career.

"Oh," I say and get a tiny bit pissed off at her parents. "Sorry."

Then I get a tiny bit sad because I always wanted to have my own gallery but was too much of a chicken to go after my dreams so I went the safe route and became a teacher. But that all changed when Mason bought me this building, which was a gesture that said, "I believe in you," in a way words never could. That was a pivotal moment in my life, and now here I am, standing in my brand-new studio, with this sweet girl telling me she has the same dream and no one to support her.

I decide to go out on a limb.

"Let me show you something else." I walk out of my studio and down the balcony corridor until I reach the end of the hall. I open the door and step into a room only a bit smaller than my studio.

"Do you think this would make a nice studio?"

"Yes," she says, looking around. "Of course."

"Let's make a deal, then," I tell her, and then I start lying. "I could use some part-time help," I say, thinking instead it would be nice to have some company. "You work for me a few hours a week in the gallery and you can use this space as your studio for as long as you like."

Avery looks like she's about to pass out. "Are you kidding me?"

"No, I'm not. You might stay here a couple of weeks and decide this isn't for you, or you might stay here a couple of weeks and decide that there's nothing else that makes you happier. Either way, you'll know a lot more about what you want after you've been here for a while." Avery looks like she's about to cry. "Where do you keep your stuff?"

"At home. In the attic."

"Well, go home and start packing," I say, happy with my spur-of-the-moment decision to become a quasi employer. "When do you go to school?"

"Monday, Wednesday, and Friday from ten until noon and Tuesday and Thursday from eleven until three, so I could work in the gallery Monday, Wednesday, and Friday from one to five, maybe come in and paint some on Tuesday and Thursday, and then what about Saturday?"

"I'm just doing Monday to Friday right now, and we can discuss your hours after you get all moved in—how about that?"

"Oh, okay," she says. "So when can I move in?"

"How about next Monday?" I answer, thinking that would give me a few days to think up a job description.

"Great," she says, beaming. "I'll see you Monday at one, then?"

"Sounds good!"

I follow her down the stairs to the front door, wave good-bye, and watch as she gathers her long skirt and gets into a gorgeous little convertible Audi. As she drives away, I immediately start second-guessing myself. I mean, I don't know that girl from Adam and I just issued a standing invitation for her to hang out in my gallery as much as she likes.

"Oh well," I say aloud to my paintings. "At least I'll have someone to talk to."

I glance at the clock because I'm ready to go and see that it's thirty minutes before closing time. I ponder that for a moment, then decide to take off early because I'm in charge of taking dinner to the conference room tonight and it's not like people are lined up outside the door waiting to get in anyway.

9

⟨◇◇⟩

"**Y**ou hired who?" Connor McCall says over a basket of hot wings that I picked up at Credo's and delivered to the conference room along with baskets for Mason and me, a gallon of sweet tea, and a side salad for Allison.

"Avery Cambre," I say, looking at Mason, who shrugs and picks up a celery stalk.

"Do you know who her father is?" Connor asks.

"No, I don't," I say, getting nervous.

"Her father is Dr. Leo Cambre, a bone doctor who came up with some kind of medical gadget and made about a hundred million dollars, but he still runs a clinic here in the Cove. Seriously, he's like one of the richest people in the country." Connor picks up a saucy wing. "And you hired his daughter to work for you for free? Holy shit!" He laughs, then sticks the whole chicken wing in his mouth. Connor McCall is a typical has-been high school quarterback, and even though he hasn't completed a pass in more than seven years, he's still as cocky as a chicken house full of roosters.

"Connor, it's disgusting the way you eat those things," Allison says, picking at her salad, on which she put no dressing.

"What?" he says, gnawing on the bone. "It's chicken wings, baby-cakes. How am I supposed to eat them?"

I pick up one of my wings and try to nibble in a way that won't offend Allison, but all I do is get hot sauce all over my lips, so I end up taking a bigger bite and hope she's not looking.

"What do you think her father is going to say when he finds out?" Allison asks, staring at the wing in my hand.

"I don't know," I say, wiping my fingers on a wet nap. "She's a junior in college, so it's not like they don't know."

"You'd think they'd just buy her a place of her own with as much money as they have," Connor says. "Maybe on an island with a nice, new yacht to take her out to it." He sniggers and Mason laughs and Allison doesn't look amused.

"Honestly, I think they're hoping she'll change her mind and then her major," I say and wonder for a second if the Cambres might pay someone to kill me for encouraging their daughter to do what she wants with her life.

"Well, that is just the craziest thing I've heard all day," Connor says, dipping a French fry into his ranch dressing. "You just hired Leo Cambre's daughter. Unbelievable."

"So have you guys decided where you're going to get married?" Allison asks, and from the corner of my eye, I see Mason stiffen up.

"Wherever she wants," he says, smiling like his lack of input is actually helpful.

"I'm going to pick three places and he's going to choose one." I look at Mason. "And if he doesn't pick the right one, then he'll have two choices, and then one."

"See there, Ace!" Mason says. "That's why I don't even say anything, because I know you're just going to pick the place you want anyway." He looks at Connor. "Where did y'all get married?"

"Tallahassee," he says flatly. "At her church. Her mother was kind enough to handle every aspect of the planning, and by *kind*, I mean overbearing. We didn't do a thing."

Allison slaps him on the arm. "Connor! You got to choose the groom's cake!"

"Yeah, I picked out one shaped like a fish, so imagine my surprise at the reception when I got to the table and saw this big chocolate cake shaped like a penis with all these powdered grapes around the bottom."

"Connor, that was a sculpted fish cake! Mother paid a fortune to have that done."

"Well, it looked like a penis." He looks at Mason. "No kidding, man, it looked like a giant chocolate dick with triangular balls. I had to have my picture taken with it. I'll bring it and show you sometime."

"I'd love to see it," Mason says, laughing. I'm scared to laugh because Allison, yet again, does not look amused.

"How long had y'all been married when you started working for Mason?" I ask, not wanting to change the subject but realizing it was necessary.

"Two weeks, so I'm glad he hired me, because Allison's mother was about to fix me up real good with a job in Tallahassee." He looks at his wife, who is glaring at him. "Which was really nice of her," he says lightly, and Allison rolls her eyes again.

"You're starting to piss me off."

"Your mother pisses me off."

"Okay," Mason says, getting up. "Hate to cut things short, but I better get back to work."

"Me, too," Connor says, tossing his basket of chicken bones in the trash. "Very much enjoyed it, Ace!" He gives Allison a devilish grin, then walks out of the conference room.

"Yes, thank you so much for bringing dinner," Allison says sweetly, getting up. "And thanks for calling to see what I wanted. I appreciate it."

"Don't mention it, Allison," I say, thinking that no one in their right mind would bring hot wings to a girl like Allison Dexter McCall.

"And I'm sorry you had to witness my barbarous husband sucking chicken meat off a bone," she says and shivers at the thought. "He's so disgusting."

"Aw, that's why you love him, Allison," Mason says.

"Maybe," she says with a smile. "Maybe not!" She looks back at me. "Good night, Ace."

"Night," I say, and she disappears into the hallway.

Mason helps me clear off our side of the table, and then I follow him down to his office.

"I forgot to tell you about the unusual visitor who stopped by the house yesterday," I say, easing into one of the two fancy chairs opposite his desk. "She said her name was Margo something. Buster Loo hated her. He got really upset."

"You must be referring to Margo Kill-Switch," he says and starts laughing.

"Oh, Is that how you pronounce it?"

"Nah, that's just what everyone calls her behind her back." He looks at me. "What the hell did she want? Is our grass trimmed too tall or too short?"

"She said she was out reminding everyone about the quarterly homeowners' association meeting—"

"Shit! That's tonight, isn't it? Those damn signs are everywhere." He glances down at his watch. "I don't guess you'd want to go for me, would you? You'd have to be there in twenty minutes."

"I'd hate to, but I will if it'd help you out."

"It would *really* help me out. I don't give a shit about her, but I don't want to come off as disrespectful toward my neighbors, you know?"

"Okay," I say, thinking about how much fun that *won't* be, but happy to be doing something for Mason besides delivering food to his office.

"There'll be some normal people there," he says. "I promise that all of our neighbors aren't like her. Thank God."

"Yeah, I've met some nice folks since I've been here," I say. "Don't worry, I'll be fine. I've got you covered."

"Baby, I appreciate it so much." He looks down at his watch, so I get up, and then he walks me down the hallway to the back door. "You're the best," he says, giving me a quick hug and a kiss. I get in my car, not believing that I have to go sit through a damn HOA meeting.

"Shoulda kept my damn mouth shut about Margo," I mumble as I pull out of the parking lot.

10

◇◇◇

I pull up in the driveway and Buster Loo is waiting at the front door, no doubt wondering why he's been having so much doggie alone time lately. I go inside and pick him up, pet him for a minute, then apologize for having to leave again so soon. He looks crushed as I walk out the door, and I get even more irritated that I have to go to this stupid meeting. When I get outside, I see several neighbors going the same way, and the whole scene, taken in from a distance, reminds me of a herd of zombies walking as if they've already lost their souls.

When I get to the clubhouse, I survey the crowd and pick a seat next to Don and Becky Collins, who live across the street from us.

"First meeting?" Mr. Collins asks.

"Yes," I say, then explain that Mason won't be here because he has to work late.

"Well, this is nonsense, if you ask me. He's trying to make a living and these people think we have nothing better to do than line up and listen to their stupid shit."

"Don Collins!" Becky, says. "Watch your mouth!"

Don leans over to me and whispers, "I've been out of the navy for fifteen years and I've still got better things to do than come to these damn meetings." He smiles and then says, "Like picking up dried dog turds. It's about the same thing, only dog turds don't stink quite as bad." Becky punches him in the arm and he straightens up and apologizes to her. I laugh to myself, understanding now why Mason is so fond of Mr. Don Collins.

I hear a commotion at the front of the room and look up to see Margo bustling in, followed by a tall, thin wisp of man.

"That's her sissified husband, Liam," Don whispers, nodding toward the man, who flits around and somehow manages to drop half of his files in the floor.

Margo heaves a sigh, props her hand on her hip, and scowls at Liam as he pulls the papers up into a sloppy, disorganized pile.

"Poor Liam," I whisper back to Don Collins.

Liam stacks the papers on the rectangular table, and Margo snatches up the first one, rolls her eyes, and then picks up the second.

"I'm Margo Kiltzwich, and I officially call this meeting to order!" she barks, and the man seated to my left, who had apparently drifted off, jerks and snorts and sits up in his chair.

After thirty minutes of listening to her talk about the proper length of grass after trimming and the maximum height allowable before, the board decides to call a vote about a quarter inch of grass. Margo announces that I won't be voting because I'm living with my fiancé and we aren't legally married. I smile and nod as if I really appreciate her calling me out like that in front of the whole neighborhood and then I tell her, very nicely, that not voting is fine with me.

This riles up some of the board members, who obviously aren't as offended by the whole living-in-sin thing as Margo. They get into a bitter argument about absentee versus proxy voting and I just want to scream that I don't give a flying rat's ass about the length of the grass, just please let me go home and get on the couch with my dog. I stand up and attempt to politely excuse myself from the meeting, but I'm promptly told to sit back down. I do, and Mr. Don Collins sniggers, pats me on the back, and tells me it was a good try. One of the board members scowls at me and asks if he saw me at Bueno Burrito last week. I assure him that he did not. The argument splits on itself because half of the people become worried that Mason could file a complaint if he disagrees with the new standards for grass trimmings and the other half argue that Mason forfeits his right to a say by not being at the meeting.

Some stupid-looking woman named Cindy, whose function is apparently to assist Margo, stands up and gives a long and painfully boring lecture about how I'm considered a visitor and not a legal resident of the community because Mason has not submitted any paperwork to the HOA with my name on it. She turns her smirk on me, and I smile and tell her I don't have a problem with that at all. This pleases half the board and enrages the other half.

I try to leave again and Margo asks me where I'm going and I tell her that I'm going home because I'm not a member of the community. She tells me to sit down because after the vote they'll be moving on to the quarterly review of association rules and then start addressing complaints. I look at Don and he rolls his eyes, and the man on the other side of me is snoring again.

"Miss Jones," Margo says, waving a finger at me, "sit back down, please."

"Of course," I say, taking a seat. She looks like King Leonidas after he kicked that guy into the bottomless pit, and I spend the next fifteen minutes fantasizing about beating the creases out of Margo's starched activewear.

I sit and fume because I know Margo's type all too well. People like her will treat cash register clerks and waitresses like they're human garbage and spread animosity like it's going out of style, but they don't drink and they don't cuss, so they run around acting like they exist on some kind of elevated moral ground. As I sit in my metal folding chair, bored out of my mind with their hateful banter, I imagine them as a herd busting down the church doors every Sunday and begging the good Lord to help them abide the lowly sinners who drink beer, use the F word, and have their grass trimmed all wrong. Idiots.

Cindy starts a PowerPoint presentation featuring community rules and regulations and then brings up a picture of someone's mailbox that has a package sticking out, thus preventing the mailbox door from closing, and Margo explains how this is a violation of code. Next on their agenda is garbage cans, and they spend thirty minutes talking about how all receptacles including recycling containers must be inside by dark.

"Inside," Margo stresses. "Not rolled back from the driveway and leaning on the garage door, but *inside* the garage and therefore *out* of sight."

I wonder how long it took her to come up with that clever little wordplay and how many times she practiced it in the mirror before getting it to that perfect pitch of bitchiness.

After that, they start talking about dogs barking.

"Well, we have a new dog in the neighborhood, and I think that's causing quite a stir."

"My dog," I say, looking around. "Are you talking about me?"

"Well, yes," Margo says with a sneer and a shrug. "Who else would we be talking about?" Cindy rolls her eyes and snorts.

"There's been a complaint about *my* dog?" I say and remind myself to stay cool. Gramma Jones always used to say that I should never argue with an idiot because anyone just standing around looking might not be able to tell who the idiot is.

"Well, no," Margo says. "There hasn't been an actual complaint, but the other dogs know he's here, so obviously his presence in the neighborhood upsets the dogs that have lived here longer."

I want to scream, "Are you freakin' kidding me?" But I don't. I simply sit there with a fake smile plastered on my face and try not to laugh out loud at the sheer idiocy of this pitiful excuse for a community meeting.

"What do we plan to do about that?" Margo says, looking at her panel of assholes.

"We could require all dogs to wear shock collars," Cindy says promptly. I'm about to tell Cindy that I'll put a shock collar on her goofy ass, but I don't have to say a word because she's riled up another dog owner.

"Hey, I'm not puttin' a shock collar on my dog, I can tell you that," a big man drinking from a red plastic cup bellows. I make a mental note to bring my own drink to the next meeting. "If you want to put a collar on something, you can put a collar on that damned cat of yours, because it keeps getting in my Corvette and pissing everywhere, and I'm sick of it!"

"You don't know that's my cat, Roger," Cindy says with a smirk.

"As a matter of fact I do, because I installed a camera in my garage and I've got it on video."

Roger gets up and walks to the podium. He pops a thumb stick into the computer and cusses under his breath while he taps the keys so hard, I'm afraid he's going to pop one off and put out one of Cindy's heavily made-up eyes.

"Roger," Cindy starts, "you haven't requested authorization to speak at this meeting, so you need to step away from the computer and return to your seat, then call and make an appointment to speak, and then if the board approves, you can show your video then." I smile to myself because I can tell by the tone of her voice that she knows it's her cat.

"Is this your computer, Cindy?" Roger asks, boring a hole into her with his beady red eyes.

"No, it's the association's!" Cindy snaps back.

"That's right, and I pay the *association* over five grand a year in dues, so I think I'll go ahead and use it like the piece of community plastic that it is." Roger's really putting on a show, smirking back at her and whatnot. I decide I really like Roger.

"It's not my cat," Cindy mumbles. She looks at the board members, all of whom have just taken a keen interest in the papers in front of them. "Roger! I said that you have to have the board's permission to speak! You can't just come up here and—"

Roger stops and stares at her, then looks over at the board members. "Who has a problem with me doing this?" No one looks up at Roger.

"This is not necessary!" Cindy wails.

"Yes, it is, Cindy, because it's your cat and it's been pissing in my carport for months and it just started pissing in my car and it's going to stop before I kill the damn thing!"

"Roger, you wouldn't! I'll sue you!" she hisses, and I can feel the tension in the room thicken into a fog. The man to my left is now wide-awake and watching with great interest.

"Well, you've got me scared now, Cindy," Roger says and keeps typing. "You think I can't afford to replace a cat?"

"Roger," Margo says, grabbing for the computer. "I won't have this foolishness! I'm the president of this association, and you have to have my approval before you present anything at these meetings."

Roger pulls the computer to the side, just out of Margo's reach. "Margo, you own one house, not the entire goddamned neighborhood. So step back and shut the hell up for a minute!"

"You will not continue using language like that at this meeting!" Margo shouts. Furious, she looks down at Liam, who appears to be sniggering. His face straightens and he gets pale when he sees Margo staring at him.

"Oh, Cindy," Board Member Number Three says, "I do believe that is Pebbles."

Cindy looks at the projection screen, sees her cat prancing around on the hood of Roger's vintage Corvette, and gasps. "Turn that off, Roger! We've seen enough!"

"No, let's just watch this for a minute longer."

"Roger," a man in the back yells, "we get it. It's Margo's cat. Can we move on, please?"

"No, Mike, we can't," Roger says, glaring at him.

Mike sighs and we all sit quietly and watch Pebbles prance around on Roger's car. It's starting to get pretty dull, but then someone appears on the right side of the screen. I can see only the back of her head at first because she's skulking like a robber.

"Who is that?" Mike asks.

"You'll see," Roger answers.

The figure walks up to the car and starts laying down a line of something I can't make out, but Pebbles obviously likes it, because she's eating it up. The perpetrator starts at the front of the hood and goes all the way up the windshield, then drops a piece of cat goody into the seat of the Corvette. She turns around, and several people in the room gasp in surprise when Cindy gets so close to the camera that we can see the moles on her face. I look at Cindy and then at Margo, both of whom are staring at the screen in total horror, having no choice but to sit and watch Cindy toss cat treats all over Roger's pristine Corvette. Pebbles jumps back and forth between the seats, and the audio is sketchy, but everyone in the room can make out Cindy saying, "Pee-pee, Pebbles! Pee-pee! Good girl!" Roger is glaring at Cindy; then everyone gasps again when Pebbles hunches up and pisses in the passenger seat.

"Hey, I found some cat food in my seat the other day," another dog owner says. "Was that you, Cindy?"

"No," she says, "of course not! That's not me! I wouldn't do such a thing."

"Uh, it's pretty obvious that it is you, Cindy," Mike calls from the back of the room. "You stand up there bitching about uneven grass and open mailboxes and then here you are throwing cat food into Roger's Corvette. Really? These meetings are such a waste of time."

"Roger, you doctored this video!" Cindy yells. "You must be following me and filming me in secret and using the images to create false videos with all of that media crap you have in your house that's probably illegal!"

"Shut up, Cindy," Roger says.

"What I get from this is that we should all keep our garage doors down if we're not home," Margo says, accusation heavy in her voice.

"Well, it doesn't surprise me at all that *you* would miss the whole point, Margo," Roger quips. He looks at the board. "I make a motion to have Cindy keep her cat on a leash and that she and her leashed cat both stay at least five hundred yards from my house."

Cindy leaves crying and Margo runs out after her, but not before starting a slide show about upcoming events in the community. Included in the show are about a million guidelines, aka restrictions, on holiday decorating, rules for trick-or-treaters, and so forth and so on. Margo comes back in and, like nothing ever happened, starts talking about the monthly social. I decide not to miss the potluck this Saturday, because if it's half as entertaining as the past ten minutes of this board meeting, I'll make a casserole for that.

When the meeting is dismissed, Roger walks back down the street with Don and Becky, and I insert myself into their little crowd. Roger is telling Don about how he rigged up a motion-sensor camera, and even Becky laughs when Roger talks about the look on Cindy's face when she saw herself up there, as guilty as sin. I ask Roger what kind of dog he has, and he tells me that he has a black pug named Moses that he loves like a son.

I stand in the Collinses' yard and hem-haw with them for a minute; then Don tells us he has to go to bed. I shake Roger's hand and tell him that I'm very sorry about the cat piss in his car, but that he certainly made my first trip to the homeowners' meeting unforgettable. He chuckles and takes off toward his house. I decide to ask Mason if we can invite him over for dinner sometime, because that Roger is quite a character. Plus Buster Loo might like to meet Moses.

I head back to an empty house and talk to Buster Loo as I do a few loads of laundry.

Mason gets home late and falls asleep on the sofa while I'm relaying the finer points of the board meeting. I wake him up and drag him upstairs, and I swear he's snoring before his head hits the pillow. I run my fingers through his hair a few times, then kiss him on the cheek and lie down on the bed beside him.

I hear Buster Loo scamper up the stairs, and a second later, he's snuggled up between Mason and me. I flip off the lamp and lie awake in bed thinking about Cindy and Margo and wondering how people get to be so abnormal.

◇◇◇

11

Thursday morning starts out slow, and by slow, I mean not a soul stops by before noon. I drive to Bee Bop's Burgers & Shakes and order a cheeseburger, and while I'm waiting for it, my phone rings and it's Tia. After making sure I know who she is, she invites Buster Loo and me to accompany her and her wiener dog, Mr. Chubz, to the Peanut Festival this Saturday. She goes through the details and I quickly accept, happy to have something to do besides make a casserole for a neighborhood social that might or might not be as entertaining as last night's homeowners' meeting.

She goes on to tell me that she and a couple of her friends have what they call Girls Night In every Thursday night, and they all pile up at someone's house for drinks and gossip. She asks if I'm interested and I tell her that I most certainly am. Much to my disappointment, she tells me that tonight's get-together is a no-go because the hostess had to keep two of her four kids home from school today because they were sick.

"My house has to be spotless before I can have people over," she explains. "And Jalena can't do anything without a month's notice, but definitely plan on coming to my place next Thursday night."

"I can host Girls Night In tonight," I say, because I haven't had a Girls Night Anything in more than three months and I'm ready to have some fun. "We could meet at the gallery."

Tia is quiet for a moment, and I get nervous thinking that if she says no, then I'll feel like one of those women who tries too hard to push the friendship too fast and talks about stuff like anti-itch cooter cream before it's appropriate.

"Tell you what," she says finally. "How about we have it at the gallery next Thursday?" Oh, this is horrible. I should probably just go ahead and start a conversation about hemorrhoids right now. "Because we've already called it off for tonight." Or ask her if she wants to talk about the last time she had diarrhea.

"Okay, that sounds good," I say lightly, trying *not* to sound like the disappointed eager-beaver weirdo that I obviously am.

"That way you'll have time to invite some of your friends as well," she says, and that really stings, because I think about Lilly and Chloe and get depressed and homesick, because you don't have awkward conversations like this with people you've been friends with forever. "I can't wait for you to meet Jalena," Tia continues, and I can tell she's hedging. "I think you guys will get along great."

"I can't wait to meet her," I say, making every effort to sound sufficiently excited as opposed to overly excited, completely embarrassed, and/or totally disappointed.

"Okay, great! I'll see you on Saturday, then!" Tia says, and I tell her good-bye and toss my phone into the passenger seat like I just found out it was rotten. I finally get my damn cheeseburger, and after I eat it, I wish I had six more. I order a brownie sundae, which I eat on the way back to the gallery.

To try to get my mind off my extraordinary ability to make a fool of myself, I decide to go ahead and send in my application to the West Florida Festival of the Arts. I go to my office and look up the guidelines, carefully reading over them one last time to make sure I haven't overlooked any relevant details. I get my camera, go upstairs, and take several pictures of the painting I titled *Marina at Blue Oyster*, then go back downstairs and transfer those, along with photos of my other favorites, onto my laptop. I study each photograph carefully before choosing what I think are the three best pictures of my three best paintings. I go online and pull up the application, fill in the all the necessary blanks, and then upload the pictures. On the next screen, I'm prompted to pay the small application fee, so I grab my purse and realize that my debit card isn't in my wallet.

"Shit!" I yell, because no one is here to hear me. "I must've left it in the car after I paid for my lunch."

I walk out to my car, and I'm bent over with my ass in the air when I hear a loud truck pull into the parking lot. I grab my debit card out of the console and turn to see Kevin Jacobs leaning out the window of his big Chevrolet pickup, smiling and waving. I cram the card into my pocket and strike a pose like I think a stripper might just before she jumps on a greased-up pole. Then I wave back.

He climbs down from the cab and I walk over to the sidewalk and he smiles and says, "What's up, Ace?"

"Hello, Kevin," I say, wondering what he's doing here but not really caring.

He's wearing a royal blue T-shirt with a white number five on the front, black athletic shorts, and tennis shoes that look like they have little rubber bulldozers attached to the bottom. On his head I see what looks like a brand-new Florida Gators hat.

"Walk you inside?" he asks.

"Why, certainly," I say with a bit too much Southern drawl. I look at his cap. "Thought you were a Roll Tide man," I say, careful not to slip back into my Scarlett O'Hara tone.

"Why would you think that?" he says, reaching for the gallery door.

"Well, you were wearing an Alabama hat last time you were here," I say, walking past him and into the gallery.

"Aren't you observant?" He follows me inside.

"Which is it?" I ask, walking around behind the counter so I have a sizable obstacle between me and Mr. I Wanna Sex Him Up.

"Which is what?" he asks, leaning on the counter, getting close enough for me to smell his seductive scent. I think about those men's body-spray commercials and decide maybe they aren't so far-fetched after all.

"Are you a Florida fan or an Alabama fan?" I say, taking a step away from his aroma. "Can't be both!"

"I'm both," he says, smiling. "I went to both schools, so I'm entitled."

"Really?" I say, genuinely interested and thankful for such innocent small talk so I don't say something stupid like, "Would you like to see my boobs?"

"Yep. Went to Bama on a football scholarship, got injured, packed up and went to Florida for a year, quit, and came home and went to work for my daddy."

"Doing what?"

"Construction."

"So you build houses?"

"Not much." He shrugs. "My dad retired fifteen years ago and I ran the family business for a while, but then things got slow and me and the crew had to start going wherever we could to find work."

"Oh."

"Yeah, well, most of the crew. The guys with families had to find other jobs so they could stay around here, but the rest of us just ramble around like a pack of wolves."

I nod, wondering if the whole crew is as sexy as he is, and if they are, would they make me a pinup calendar or something. I look up at him and he smiles. "Aren't you wondering why I'm here?"

The only thing that pops up into my mind is "Are you here to make love?" so I just stand there and grin.

"No?" he says, eyebrows raised.

"What can I help you with, Mr. Jacobs?" I ask, wondering what kind of man fragrance he's wearing and if Satan bottles it himself or has the other people in hell do it for him.

"I'm looking for a painting."

"Then you came to the right place," I say. "Do you have something in particular in mind?"

"It's for my mother," he says, and I stop thinking about him naked. "She likes flowers, and I had to unwrap that big picture I picked up here last week and that looked like something she would really like."

"Oh," I say, flattered out of my mind.

"Personally, I liked the boat picture better," he says, looking at me. "But that's beside the point. Momma's birthday is tomorrow, and I'd really like to surprise her with something nice."

"Follow me," I say, walking out from behind the counter. "What size are you looking for?"

"What do you suggest?"

"Where will it go?" I ask as I walk across the floor of the gallery, thankful I wore my make-my-fat-ass-look-good jeans today because I can sense his eyes on my backside. "Like, what kind of room do you think she might she hang it in? The kitchen? The sunroom?"

"I have no idea."

"That's helpful," I say, teasing.

"Sorry."

I get to where I'm going and whirl around, and he's a lot closer to me than he needs to be. He looks down at my boobs and then takes a step back.

"Sorry," he says again. "I almost ran right over you."

"My fault," I say, praying I don't break out in hives, because I'm so hot for him that I feel light-headed. "I should have brake lights installed." There we go! Here I am: The master of squelching sexual tension, Ace Jones, is on the scene. Kevin starts laughing, and I stammer, "Not sure exactly, uh, never mind."

He looks at my boobs again, then raises his eyebrows and shakes his head.

"Ok, let's get down to business," I say and start pointing at a painting of some daisies. "Are you looking for a happy, light-hearted image like that or something more along these lines?" I point to some petite pink roses with a twilight background and, in the distance, a sliver of the moon.

"Not that one," he says, nodding toward the roses. "That looks a little too romantic to get for my mother." He looks at me. "I don't need her and Daddy sitting in the living room watching *Walker, Texas Ranger*, then looking up at that picture and getting all worked up by some affectionate notion and start making out and have somebody roll off the couch and break a hip or something. Then it'd be all my fault."

I laugh out loud and he just smiles.

"I really think she'd like something like that big one I picked up here the other day." He inspects the other pictures on what I like to call the floral wall. "What kind of flowers were in that picture?"

"Calla lilies."

"It kind of made me think of those pictures on the wall at Las Cantinas."

"That's because it's the same flower."

"Are you Mexican?" He looks at me.

"My mom's side of the family is from Spain, like way back a long time ago." My cheeks start burning, and yet again, I can hardly believe the stupid shit that comes out of my mouth.

"Well, señorita, do you have any more calla lilies?"

"No, that was the only one."

"How much was that one?"

"Five hundred dollars."

"Whoa, now!" He says, "And you just gave it away?"

"That was the asking price, not the actual cost," I tell him and then think maybe that's not the best thing to say to a potential customer.

He points back to the daisies. "How much for that one?"

"How about a hundred bucks?" I say and don't tell him that I just gave him a fifty-dollar discount for being so charming.

"I'll take it."

"If you've got a minute, I can wrap it for you."

"That would be great."

He follows me to my office and flirts with me until I'm afraid my cheeks will burn off my face. He appears to be the quintessential midlife bachelor, and it occurs to me that he goes around getting women hot and bothered for sport. The thought also crosses my mind that at his age and as many girls as he's probably gotten freak-nasty with, he can surely see that I want to sex his brains out. To soothe my guilty conscience, I tell myself that looking at Kevin Jacobs is like looking at a T. rex exhibit in a museum. I can stand there all day long and stare, but it's not like I'm going to mount it and try to ride it out the door. Satisfied with my commitment to chasteness, I get back to thinking perverted thoughts.

"So what's with the jersey?" I ask.

"Flag football," he says.

"Oh, really?" I say, thinking he could tackle my ass any day of the week, and then I remember that nobody gets tackled in flag football.

He asks about Mason and we make small talk about my fiancé while I tell myself there's nothing wrong with finding him attractive because, hell, anybody with eyeballs can see that he is.

"I hope your mom is most pleased," I say, handing him the package. I want to ask him why his aunt Ramona hangs around with mean old bitches like Lenore Kennashaw and Sylvie Best, because Ramona doesn't seem to be quite so wicked. Then I start wondering if they sent him in here to try to seduce me in an effort to completely ruin my life and decide to just keep my mouth shut about that.

"I'm sure she will be," Kevin says, and try as I may, I can't make myself believe that he's the kind of person who would be involved with something like that.

"Thanks so much for stopping by," I tell him, and I'm fairly sure my face is beet red at this point. I'm going to have to get a watercooler with a spray nozzle if he's going be a frequent visitor. Or maybe put a water hose out back.

I get up and speed-walk to the front of the gallery, step behind the counter, and silently curse my complete lack of professionalism. He picks up his package and follows me, but stops before he walks out the door.

"See ya!" he says, then does his two-finger salute-wave.

"Bye!" I say, bitterly disappointed in myself for being so disappointed that he's leaving. I watch him walk out to his truck, then notice a silver Mercedes backed into a shaded parking space on the other side of the lot. I step up to the window and see Lenore Kennashaw sitting in her car. I stand and watch her, wondering if she can see me through the glass. Finally, I get mad and walk outside, ready to address whatever issue she has with me today. When she sees me, she quickly pulls out of the parking lot into the road, where a few cars have to slam on their brakes to keep from hitting her. I walk back inside trying to convince myself that Kevin Jacobs is not a minion of Lenore Kennashaw's, and while I'm not a hundred percent sure he isn't, there is no doubt in my mind that Lenore Kennashaw is out to get me.

12

I go back to my office, dig the debit card out of my pocket, and sit down at the desk. My online session has timed out, of course, so I have to start the whole application over from page one. I do that, pay the fees, and sit back in my chair, thrilled that after ten years of thinking about it, I finally sent my application in to the West Florida Festival of the Arts. One whole day before the deadline.

I think about Mason and how proud he'll be when I tell him. Then I think about how proud he *wouldn't* be if he knew I spent the past hour lusting after Kevin Jacobs. Especially after that bad breakup I caused last year when I left Mason's house in a fit of jealous rage and refused to speak to him for months because he was nice to some Barbie-doll-looking chick from his past who showed up out of the blue at his house one night. After all the stink I caused about that, I feel foolish and guilty now that I have this psycho-crush on a cat-daddy that I wouldn't act on if my life depended on it. I hope. I force myself to stop thinking about Kevin Jacobs and get back to being excited about the art festival.

I go upstairs and tidy up the studio, then walk out on the balcony and look down at the gallery. I take a deep breath and smile because, for the first time in a long time, I feel a faint shimmer of hope about my ability to succeed. I just made my first official sale and even though I'd hoped to sell a lot more in these first few weeks, it still makes me feel like a huge success.

On the drive home, I feel hopeful and happy instead of fretful and anxious, and I think that maybe, just maybe, I can pull off this living the life of my dreams. Not many people get a chance like I've got down here in Pelican Cove, Florida, and I swear to myself that I won't blow it by being stupid.

As soon as I pull up in the driveway, I hear Buster Loo barking up a storm. I see his little brown head and floppy ears in the bottom pane of the front door, and I feel so happy I think I might cry. I unlock the door, just as glad to see my crazy little fur ball as he is to see me, if not more so. I take him out back, and after he hits a few speedy-dog crazy eights, we roll around and play fetch in the patch of grass that is our lawn.

After about fifteen minutes, I toss his toy, and instead of barrel running to fetch it, he barrel runs to the doggie door and disappears into the house. I get up, follow him inside, and find him sitting at the front door. "Buster Loo wanna go for a walk?" I ask him.

He starts running around in circles, so I grab his leash and we head out. We circle the neighborhood a few times, stopping here and there for chitchat and little-dog butt sniffing. I see Cindy outside her house with Pebbles and raise my hand to wave, but instead of waving back, she snatches up Pebbles and stares at me like I'm a registered catnapper.

"Freakin' weirdo," I tell Buster Loo as we walk back toward our house. I meet Roger, who is out walking Moses, and stop to chat with him for a second. He tells me he caught Margo and Cindy on video lurking around his house in the wee hours of the morning.

"Doing what?" I ask.

"Hell, who knows?" he says. "They woke Moses up and he got all excited, so I got up and got the gun, thinking someone was breaking in the house. I looked out the window and didn't see anybody, so I went to the computer and checked the surveillance video, and what do you know? I see Margo and Cindy out in my front yard on their hands and knees with little flashlights."

"That is the craziest thing I've ever heard," I tell him. "Do you think they were measuring your grass?"

"Oh no, they come during daylight hours to do that because they have to be able to see those millimeter marks on their little rulers," Roger says, laughing. "Those two goof-asses are surely gonna try to pull something after I played that video at their silly little meeting, but I'm not too worried about it." He looks at me and smiles.

"You're probably right," I say, laughing. "But I wouldn't worry about it too much, either."

Moses is pulling at his leash, obviously ready to continue his walk, so I tell Roger I'll keep an eye peeled for suspicious behavior and let him go on his way.

I'm back home cleaning Buster Loo's food and water dishes when my phone starts buzzing, and I look down and see that it's Mason. I think for a second about the time we spent apart and how, after he stopped calling because I wouldn't answer, I wished every single phone call and text message would be from him. I decide then and there that I will never think dirty thoughts about Kevin Jacobs again.

"Hello, sweetie," he says, and he sounds tired.

"Hey, baby," I say. "How are you?"

"Hungry. You wanna meet me at the Blue Oyster in an hour?"

"I'd love to," I say, drying off Buster Loo's bowls.

"Great, see you then."

I run upstairs to get ready, excited about our date. When I get to the Blue Oyster, he's already there, and he's already drinking. A bucket of peel-and-eat shrimp is on the table, along with two frosty mugs of beer. I sit down and tell myself again that I can live this dream with Mason McKenzie.

"How was your day?" I ask.

"Let's talk about yours first."

I tell him that I submitted my application for the West Florida Festival of the Arts, and he is indeed very proud of me for that. I casually mention that Kevin Jacobs stopped by and bought a painting, and he nods and I don't see any indication that bugs him, so I tell him what Kevin said about his parents getting it on.

"That Kevin Jacobs is one funny dude," Mason says, shaking his head. "I love to go out fishing with him, and not just because he knows the best spots, but because he's so much fun to be around." He looks at me. "One day, he got so drunk he passed out on the boat and wouldn't wake up even after me and the other guys loaded it on the trailer. So I drove that big-ass truck to his house with him asleep in the cabin of the boat." He looks at me. "So, how many paintings have you sold?"

"That makes one," I say with no small amount of pride. "And two giveaways."

He reaches out and puts his right hand over my left. "That is great," he says quietly. "I'm so proud of you."

"How are things at the office?" I ask.

"Well, we got the hold off Mr. Marks's bank account, so that was good." He glances around, I assume to see if anyone is paying attention to our conversation. He lowers his voice and continues. "Connor found out that the bank had also filed for a continuing writ of garnishment, which means that in addition to trying to get every cent Mr. and Mrs. Marks have in the bank, they were going to try to take what little he makes working part-time at Home Depot."

"How can they do that?" I ask.

"They can't," he says, peeling a shrimp. "And they won't because Connor took care of that today, and after we make sure they're not trying to screw them some other way, we're going to get started with *our* lawsuit." He dips the shrimp in cocktail sauce, then looks at me. "I don't think I've ever wanted to nail somebody as bad I want to nail this bank, because they are *literally* trying to *rob* someone who has *nothing*. And I can just imagine those pompous-ass big bank executives sitting up in their big, fancy offices on the twenty-fifth floor of some downtown building whining about not getting a million-dollar bonus check; then one of them decides to do something like this." He shakes his head in disgust. "Cocksuckers." He takes a drink of beer, then says, "Let's talk about something else. Please."

I tell him about Roger catching Margo and Cindy on video, and that cracks him up a little.

"What is *wrong* with those two?" he asks after I tell him they were on their hands and knees with flashlights in his front yard.

"I have no idea," I say, wondering whether Margo and Cindy have jobs or if they're just full-time morons.

"Tell me something else funny," he says, and I start getting stressed-out because I can't really think of anything. I tell him about seeing Cindy and her cat, and he laughs a little about that, but I get the feeling I'm not being as entertaining as he would like for me to be. But I can't help it. I'm not a stand-up comic. I can't perform on demand.

◇◇◇

13

Friday morning, I get up before Mason and go downstairs to make coffee. Buster Loo is already outside with all four paws in the air basking in the morning sun. When he hears me clanking around in the kitchen, he jumps up and runs inside, no doubt hoping I'll fry some bacon. I hear Mason rumbling around, so I pour him a cup of coffee and head upstairs with Buster Loo right behind me. Mason is lathering up a thick beard of shaving cream, so I put his cup of coffee on the sink.

"Would you like some breakfast?"

"No, thanks," he says. "I think I had a few too many last night."

"Would you like a Sprite?"

He eyeballs the coffee, then looks at me. "Not after getting a whiff of that."

"Let me know if you change your mind." I look at Buster Loo, who is sniffing a stray speck of shaving cream. "Buster Loo! No! C'mon out of here and let's let Daddy get ready."

"Hey," Mason says, "Connor and I are leaving the office at five o'clock today, so you and I will have a night at home like normal folks. Is there anything in particular you'd like to do?"

"You decide," I say. "You're the one working from sunup till sundown."

"Wanna grill some steaks?"

"I'd love to," I say. "I'll pick some up on the way home."

"Great!"

At the gallery, the morning turns out to be quite busy, but I don't sell a damn thing, and that puts me in a foul mood. When the place is empty, I go upstairs and flip through my inventory, thinking that maybe I need a different selection on the floor. I have quite a few ship paintings left over from my days of teaching school, because every year I did an extensive unit on maritime art. I spread those out across the floor and think for a minute about the six years I spent in the classroom. I never thought the day would come when I would miss teaching high school, but here I am thinking about all of my students and how much fun I always had hanging out in the lounge gossiping with and about my fellow teachers.

"Never saw that coming," I mumble as I get up off the floor. I gather the paintings and stack them by the door, determined to press onward with my dream. I decide to do some rearranging this afternoon so the gallery will look completely different next week and maybe people will stop looking and start buying.

I hear the doorbell chime, so I step out onto the balcony and see Avery in the gallery below.

"Well, hello!" I call out. "Be right down."

When I join her downstairs, she smiles and says, "I wanted to stop by and see if you needed any help with anything. I'm sorry. I couldn't wait until Monday."

"Well, I was thinking about doing some rearranging, if you'd like to help with that," I say, pleased with her enthusiasm. She's wearing hot pink Converse tennis shoes, red hose with so many runs I don't really see the point of even having them on, a Pink Floyd T-shirt that looks two sizes too small, and a supershort denim skirt with fringe where a seam should be.

"I'd love to!"

"Okay, I've got some stuff upstairs that I was going to bring down," I say, glad to have some help but more excited about the company. "I thought it would be nice for the place to have a fresh look come Monday."

"I couldn't possibly agree with you more," she says.

We haul paintings down the stairs and spend the remainder of the afternoon rearranging, hanging and rehanging dozens of portraits, leaving the main wall open for my mermaid. I ask Avery if she'd like to have an area to display her work and she tells me she'd love that but she needs a few weeks to "get a feel for the soul of the building." That makes me think she might be a little more bizarre than I already thought she was, but that's okay because I thought Chloe Stacks was bizarre at first and she turned out to be one of the best friends I've ever had.

When we finish, Avery looks around, obviously pleased.

"Can't wait to get to work on Monday," she says. I tell her I can't wait for her to get to work on Monday, either. I'm looking forward to having someone to talk to.

We walk out together and she hops in her shiny Audi, puts the top down, and drives away. I grab my OPEN fish, then step inside, pick up my purse, and head back out the door. I stop by the butcher shop, where I pick up two thick and what I know will be juicy, delicious steaks. I accept the man's offer to preseason the meat, and he wraps the steaks in thick white paper before sticking them in a brown paper bag.

"Thanks!" I say, thinking I can't wait to smell these babies on the grill.

Mason gets home at five thirty on the dot, and I whip up my special superfattening twice-baked potatoes while he fires up the coals. As Mason cooks, Buster Loo stays on full alert, circling the foot of the grill in hopeful anticipation of a stray morsel. We polish off several Coronas, and I've got a great buzz by the time we sit down to eat.

"Tell me something I don't know, baby," Mason says, picking up his knife.

I tell him about my day, omitting the part when I realized how bad I miss my old job and talking instead about rearranging the gallery. Mason looks about as interested in what I'm saying as I am in getting up from the table and jogging around the block. When I ask him about his day, he starts telling me all about strategic defaults, negative equity, and asset protection in the state of Florida, and I start thinking that sawing my own arm off might be more fun than listening to him talk about work.

"This dinner was amazing," he says, leaning back in his chair and rubbing his belly.

"Wasn't it?" I say, thankful that at least we're not in the conference room at his office. "Must've been the potatoes."

"Yeah," he says, jerking both his thumbs up to his chest, "or the man with the mad grill skills."

"Right," I say, and we both start laughing even though nothing is really that funny. He doesn't mention wedding plans, so I don't, either.

"Let's deal with this tomorrow," he says, looking around at the kitchen. "I'm ready to go upstairs." I follow him upstairs, and he's fast asleep by the time I finish taking off my makeup. I lie down beside him and start thinking about the Peanut Festival tomorrow. I've never heard of such, but I don't even care what it is because I'm just looking forward to hanging out with Tia.

14

◇◇

Mason is still sleeping the next morning when I wake up, so I tiptoe down the stairs, start a pot of coffee, and quickly tidy up the kitchen. I take Buster Loo out for a walk and stop by the Donut Shop and get a bag of goodies because I woke up feeling bad for thinking I'd rather saw off my own arm than listen to Mason talk about his job. When I get home, Mason is sitting at the kitchen table, sipping coffee and pecking away at his laptop. His face brightens up when he sees the Donut Shop bag.

"For me?" he says, like a child.

"Caramel apple fritters," I say, setting the bag on the table. "Two of them just for you." I walk over to the sink and wash my hands.

"Sounds good," he says and starts digging in the doughnut bag. "What time are you leaving?"

"Tia is coming at nine."

"That's right." He looks at the clock on the stove. "Looks like we've got about an hour to ourselves, then." He nods toward the chair across from him. "Join me?"

I pour myself a cup of coffee and take a seat at the table. Buster Loo runs in circles around the chairs until Mason finally tosses him a piece of apple, which he smacks on with great enthusiasm.

"So," Mason says, looking at me. "Let's talk about our honeymoon."

"Oh goodie!" I say, chomping on a chocolate-covered doughnut, delighted to know he's been thinking about our Happily Ever After.

"I need to know what kind of experience you're looking for."

"A very sexual one," I say and bat my lashes like a floozy.

He laughs and gets up to get himself some more coffee. "Well, baby, I can deliver that anywhere, anytime." He turns to face me. "You need to see the helicopter this morning?"

I eyeball his boxers and shake my head from side to side. "Think I'll pass on that, but thanks for asking," I say, wondering if there has ever been a woman anywhere on the face of the earth who actually *needed* to see her man shake his hips and swing his ding-dong around in circles. Jeez.

"Well, it's always ready to fly for you, baby."

"I do not doubt that at all," I say, laughing and rolling my eyes.

"So where am I taking my lovely bride on our honeymoon?" he asks, topping my cup off with steaming-hot goodness. "Somewhere like Italy or Greece, or would you prefer a good dose of winter in a secluded cabin in Breckenridge or maybe a bed-and-breakfast in Vermont?" He sits back down at the table.

"Oh wow! I don't know," I say with stars in my eyes. I haven't been out of the country since I took a year off from college to study in Europe, so I'd love to go abroad again, but on the other hand, a snowy getaway sounds terribly romantic. "Those are excellent choices."

"We can do it all eventually; I just need to know what you like best so I can get the travel arrangements set up."

I ponder the choices and then go with the snow. "Let's do winter!"

I say, so excited I'm afraid I might piss myself. I put my coffee cup down on the table.

"Winter it is!" he says, smiling. "East Coast or Rockies?"

"You pick."

"I pick Vermont," he says without hesitation. "Connor and Allison went up there last year, and he said it was great, plus the bed-and-breakfast where they stayed allowed pets."

"Yay!" I exclaim. "Vermont it is!" Buster Loo, as if sensing his sudden involvement, is back on the scene running around in circles again. I lean down and say, "Buster Loo's going to Vermont! Buster Loo's going to be a snow dog! We've got to get you a new sweater!" I look back up at Mason. "I didn't know Connor and Allison had a dog."

"Yeah, it's one of those little bitty fluffy fuzzy things that barks nonstop and bounces around like a tennis ball. Got a big bushy bunch of fur around its neck and a big bushy tail. What's it called?"

"A Pomeranian?"

"Yes, that's it, because Allison gave it a long complicated name that Connor thinks is ridiculous so he runs around calling it the PoPo and Allison gets all pissed off."

"It's hard to tell if they're happy together or not so much."

"Oh, they're perfectly happy," he says, waving off my comment. "They're just young so they still think it's cool to bicker and fight all the time. They'll be married forever."

"The PoPo," I say, giggling as I imagine Connor saying that in front of Allison.

"Ask her about her dog sometime," Mason says. "I can't believe she hasn't mentioned it to you."

"She may have," I say honestly and think that she could have told me all about it during one of those times I was taking a nap with my eyes open while she talked. "I'll be sure to ask."

"Well, just to give you a heads-up"—he raises his eyebrows—"she really, and I mean *really*, likes to talk about that dog."

"Great," I say and make a mental note to take a steak knife with me next time I go to the office. Just in case I need to start sawing on my arm.

"Well." he sighs and looks at me. "I better go upstairs and get ready. Another day at the office awaits!" He comes over and kisses me on the forehead. "Have fun at the Nut Festival."

"I'll bring you something."

"I have nuts, thank you." He flashes a wicked smile and disappears up the stairs.

Thirty minutes later, I'm standing on the porch waving good-bye to Mason when I notice a jet-black Tahoe with tinted windows sitting at the curb. I'm wondering if it might be the president of the United States or perhaps someone from the Mob, but then the passenger-side window rolls down and I see Tia. She backs up, pulls into the driveway, and hops out.

"Hey, my GPS was wigging out on me and I couldn't remember what house number you said it was." She's wearing a fuchsia Nike top that matches both her shorts and her shoes.

I invite her and Mr. Chubz into the house, and the minute her weenie dog places one paw on our front porch, Buster Loo appears at the door and loses his little chiweenie mind. He's jumping and growling and snarling and scratching, and I just stand there and stare at him for a minute wondering if he's blown some kind of fuse in between his floppy little ears. Mr. Chubz walks up to the door and sticks his snout to the pane, and Buster Loo bares his tiny teeth and starts snapping.

"My dog is in rare form today," I tell Tia. I nod toward Mr. Chubz, who is clearly unaffected by the manner in which Buster Loo is carrying on, and advise her to pick him up before we go inside. When we step in the house, Mr. Chubz looks down at Buster Loo like a king might glance down at a new court jester, and Buster Loo continues his all-out balls-to-the-wall crazy fit.

"Mr. Chubz is certainly a calm soul," I say, picking up Buster Loo and trying to settle him down.

"Well, he's old, God bless him," Tia says. She looks outside. "Maybe we should go out back."

"Good idea. Mason built kind of a dog-run thing out there, so they might like playing on that together." I look down and see that Buster Loo is still all bristled up. "Maybe."

When I step out the back door, Buster Loo starts jerking and wiggling, so I put him down and he runs over to Tia and starts barking like a maniac. We take a seat on the lounger and Tia hands Mr. Chubz over to me, then leans down to pet Buster Loo, who decides to rocket-launch himself into her lap at the exact same time. He rams his little chiweenie skull right into her forehead, and then she scoops him up and tries in vain to sit him on her lap. Tia is hee-haw laughing, and Buster Loo, showing no signs of getting off the crazy train, proceeds to jump all over her and speed-lick her between the eyes. Mr. Chubz takes notice of the fracas and starts to growl.

"Oh, it's been so long since I've had a puppy around," she says, still laughing. "C'mon, you little fireball!" Tia says, nuzzling Buster Loo. "Let's go *run*." Buster Loo soars off her lap, lands on the very edge of the concrete pad of the porch, loses his balance, and rolls out into the grass. "He's a stunt devil!" Tia calls, while Mr. Chubz watches her like a hawk and continues to growl. She makes a few circuits around the yard and they both appear to be having a great time when Mr. Chubz slinks out of my lap and makes a beeline for Buster Loo.

They line up snout to snout; then Mr. Chubz starts to bark and Buster Loo does the same, ramping up the volume with each yelp.

Neither dog moves an inch; they just stand there and bark. I stop beside Tia and we laugh till we're both crying. I run inside to pee because I drank too much coffee this morning and I don't want to embarrass myself by pissing my pants in front of my new friend.

When I get back outside, the dogs are still standing in the exact same spot, but they've stopped barking. Finally, Buster Loo breaks the standoff and runs around to sniff Mr. Chubz's butt and Mr. Chubz takes off running with Buster Loo right behind him. They make several laps around the yard like that, then reverse order and run some more. All of a sudden, Buster Loo stops and they start rolling around in the grass like old doggie friends. I get really nervous thinking about Buster Loo's proclivity to hump, but he doesn't attempt to mount Mr. Chubz and I'm relieved.

"Okay," Tia says, walking up onto the porch. "I think we're good to go, if I could just use the facilities, please."

"Sure, right inside and to the left."

The dogs play for a few more minutes, and then we call them to the porch and lead them out to Tia's Tahoe. Buster Loo has to sniff every square inch of the vehicle, while Mr. Chubz sits in Tia's lap like a high-ranking lord of canine aristocracy.

◇◇◇

15

We leave Pelican Cove, driving north, and I can't help but notice that the farther we drive, the more things start to look like north Mississippi. To pass the time, we tell stories and laugh and carry on like old pals. Mr. Chubz has relocated to the backseat, and he and Buster Loo are snuggled up snoring.

"This looks just like home," I tell her when we round a curve, and I swear we could be on Highway 78 between Bugtussle and Tupelo.

"Isn't it beautiful?" she says. "I always come up here when I need to get away from the hustle and bustle of the Cove. There's a great little country store a mile or so up the road that has a down-home buffet run by the nicest people you'll ever meet in your life. My grandparents used to live in Jay, so I drive up every chance I get because it makes me happy being here."

"I can understand that," I say, thinking about my two-bedroom bungalow that belonged to Gramma Jones. I start feeling homesick again and think I might need to plan a trip to Bugtussle pretty soon before I wind up in some kind of depressed funk.

When we get to the Peanut Festival, Tia pays to park in someone's yard and I can smell the barbecue the minute I open the truck door. We hook the dogs up to their leashes and walk through the lush green grass to the festival. Mr. Chubz carries himself like a blue blood on a Sunday stroll, while Buster Loo leans forward as he walks, straining against his leash.

"He doesn't have much experience with places like this," I say, nodding toward Buster Loo. "Plus that aroma is only adding fuel to the crazy fire."

We walk past a horse and wagon and a choo-choo train for kids on our way to the gate. Tia gets a cup of boiled peanuts first thing, and, curious, I try one and cannot get it out of my mouth fast enough.

"That's like the raw oyster of the peanut world," I say, looking around for somewhere to get a drink.

"Oh, they're great!" she says, laughing, popping another one in her mouth. "I love 'em!"

I get a Coke and we loop around to a field lined with all sizes, colors, makes, and models of tractors. Behind the tractors are some farm animals, and I get a good grip on Buster Loo's leash before we walk around there. He sees a chicken in a coop and starts flouncing around like a fish out of water and honking and carrying on like he does when he wants to be freed from the constraints of his leash. Mr. Chubz stops and looks at Buster Loo, then sits down at Tia's feet.

"Is he okay?" Tia asks, genuinely concerned, as several people stop to stare at Buster Loo, who is lying on his side doing his signature goose honk.

I lean down to pick him up, and he jumps up and dashes toward the chicken coop as fast as his little legs will take him and as far as the leash will allow. Then, when the leash stops him, he goes down on his side and starts flouncing again.

Some lady gives me a dirty look as I'm dragging Buster Loo back across the grass. I want to tell her to mind her own effin' business, but I don't because she looks pretty stout. Plus, I don't need to get involved in a fistfight that might cause me to accidentally let go of the leash, at which point Buster Loo would run a hundred and fifty miles an hour straight into that stack of chicken coops.

"You wanna move on, Ace?" Tia asks, smiling. "I don't think Buster-Skip-to-My-Loo can handle much more exposure to the farm animals."

"That would be great," I say, tugging at the leash, hoping Buster Loo might get on his paws and walk. Finally, he does.

"Hungry?" Tia asks.

"Always," I say. "That barbecue smells divine!"

"Well, let's have some," she says, then turns and starts walking toward a big gray plastic thing that looks like a some kind of fancy water fountain from outer space.

"What is this?" I ask, following her. "A souped-up hand-sanitizer station?"

"Even better," she says. "Check it out." She puts her foot on the silver pedals at the bottom, and water flows from a hidden faucet somewhere behind the gray plastic. She puts her hand under the soap dispenser and lathers up.

"Nice," I say. "The Peanut Festival has all the tricks!"

We wash and dry our hands, then get in the barbecue line, which has about fifty more people in it than it did five seconds ago.

I feel a tug on the leash and look down at Buster Loo, who is straining toward a garbage can.

"Buster Loo, c'mon," I say, reeling him in and locking the leash so he can't get more than six inches from my feet. He starts whimpering and looks at me like I just stomped his favorite bone to bits.

We get plates piled high with pulled pork, French fries, and baked beans and topped off with a gigantic ear of corn. I follow Tia as she navigates her way through the crowd to a vacant picnic table. She sets her plate down, then digs two little doggie cups and a bottle of water out of her bag and places them under the picnic table. "Here you go, fellas," she says, pouring them both some water, which they waste no time lapping up.

I run back to the food truck and get us each a cup of sweet tea, then sit down for a good, hearty lunch. I hear Buster Loo crunching on something and look down to see peanut shells flying out of his mouth.

"Oh, so you eat peanut shells now?" I ask him, but he ignores me and starts sniffing around, looking for stray bounty. I toss him a small piece of meat and hope that will discourage him from chomping on peanut shells. I look at Mr. Chubz, who is having himself an afternoon snooze.

"What a pair," Tia says, giggling.

After lunch, we wander over to the booths, and Tia looks around and chats with the vendors while Mr. Chubz obediently follows her every move. I can't look at anything because Buster Loo is still acting like a wack job and I can't take my eyes off him. He hikes his leg next to a carved wooden bear, so I reach down to get him, and when I raise back up, I'm face-to-face with the station-wagon lady from Bueno Burrito.

I recognize her before she recognizes me, but when she does, she snarls and says, "You!" She's wearing denim culottes, a yellow T-shirt with birds stitched on the front, and one of those weird foam visors.

"You what?" I hiss at her, hoping to scare her away.

"You better not let me catch you somewhere by yourself," she says in a low voice. "'Cause I owe you a good one!"

"The only thing you owe is an apology to that curb you ran over with all four wheels," I say, my voice just above a whisper. I glare at her with my crazy eyes.

"No, I owe you an ass whippin'," she says slowly and glares right back at me.

"Best I remember, you rolled up that window of opportunity back at the Bueno Burrito," I quip like a real smart-ass.

"What are you talkin' about?" she asks, narrowing her eyes.

"You figure it out," I scoff.

"I figure that smart mouth of yours needs fixin'."

"Yeah? Well, you and your crusty old station wagon are gonna need fixin' after I beat the brakes off you and it, too!" I hope she backs down soon because I really don't want to make a scene, and to be perfectly honest, I'm almost sure this woman could beat me to death.

"You wouldn't dare," she says. "I'm here with my grandkids."

"I wouldn't dare because I'm here with my dog," I say and nod toward Buster Loo, who, instead of barking and snarling like I need him to, is looking at this lady like he'd like to lick her on the cheek.

"I'll have you know that wasn't my station wagon! I drive a brand-new Buick! And I didn't mean to roll that junky land sled into the back of your car!" she snaps in a raspy, low voice.

"Well, you did!" I say, backing off the sarcasm, but only a little. "And you scratched it!"

"Well, I'm sorry. My husband owns a shop and he can fix it. He was servicing my car that day and made me go get him some damned burritos in that piece of crap he traded somebody for some work he did one time. I was mad, okay? And I thought you were just trying to piss me off on purpose, and I wasn't havin' it!" She looks at Buster Loo, who leans toward her and whimpers, so she starts petting him. "Haven't you ever had a bad day?"

"All the time," I say without a trace of sarcasm. "I'm Ace Jones. What's your name?"

"I'm Erlene Pettigo," she says, smiling. She reaches in her purse and pulls out a business card. "My husband's name is Sam and I'll tell him you'll be bringing your car by. Maybe he'll let you drive the station wagon while he fixes that scratch." She smiles at me.

"That might be fun," I say, smiling back at this feisty grandmother in her yellow bird shirt and matching visor. "Well, it was nice to meet you—I guess," I say, and she starts laughing and pats me on the back.

"Nice to meet you, too," she says. "And I'm real sorry about your bumper."

She turns to go, and I watch her walk down the aisle to where she stops next to a man in denim overalls sitting on a bench with two little boys. She picks up the smallest boy and takes the other by the hand, and the four of them start walking toward the bouncy slides.

"Friend of yours?" Tia asks, sneaking up on me from behind.

"Hard to tell," I say.

"Let me know whenever you're ready and we'll head back to the Cove," she says, stepping over to look at some beaded jewelry.

"I'm ready when you are," I say, because I'm worn-out, physically and emotionally.

"Let's get out of here, then."

We get in the Tahoe, and while she's chattering about a good deal she got on some earrings, I start thinking about Erlene Pettigo and wondering if that's how I'll act when I'm her age. Tia keeps chattering and it's all I can do not to fall asleep on the ride home. Before I get out at my house, Tia and I finalize plans for the Thursday night Girls Night In, and much to my relief, the conversation is not awkward at all. As she drives away, I remember that I forgot to ask her if she knew of any good places to get married.

I go inside, and Buster Loo and I head straight for the couch, and that's where we are when Mason gets home from work a few hours later.

"Hey," I say groggily when he wakes me up. "How are you?"

"I'm great," he says, tousling my hair. "How are you, sleeping beauty?"

I sit up on the sofa, and he goes into the kitchen and fixes us each a drink. Buster Loo hops down on the floor and stretches.

"Well, how was the Nut Fest?"

"Let me just tell you, baby, boiled peanuts are the nastiest damn thing I've ever tried to eat."

"What? I love those things!" he says.

"Seriously?" I ask. "I would've brought you some—"

"Tell you what," he says, rubbing my leg. "Go out and eat with me tonight and you're off the hook for not bringing me any squishy nuts."

"Good deal!" I say. "Where are we going?"

"Let's ride over to Gulf Shores and go to Lulu's. I could really use a fried green tomato BLT."

"Double good deal!"

We get to Lulu's well after the rush, and I have a cheeseburger while Mason enjoys his FGTBLT. After sharing a Brownie in Paradise, we head back home, talking on the way about our plans for Sunday.

"Hey, baby," he says. "Don't take this the wrong way, but do you want to start going to the gym with me now that you've got the gallery up and running?"

"Mason, sweetheart," I tease. "Don't ever start a conversation with a line like 'don't take this the wrong way' because there's not but one way to take whatever you say next, and that's the wrong way."

"Okay, let's try this again," he says, grinning. "Ace, I think you are a sexy vixen. I am going to the gym tomorrow and would like for you to go. Not because I think you need to exercise, but because I'd like to hang out with you. I never asked you to go before because you were working all the time. Now you're not working all the time." He looks at me. "Do you want to go?"

I think about the Bratz Pack ladies I used to see at the gym in Bugtussle. They were always piled up on those megamonster treadmills, speed-walking in their skintight short-shorts and flopping their long, sleek ponytails all over the place. I can only imagine what the workout women of Pelican Cove, Florida, must look like, and I imagine I'd feel less welcome at the gym here than I did back home, where I didn't feel welcome at all.

"Nah," I say finally. "But thanks for asking."

"Okay, baby," he says, then starts singing along to an old George Jones song, and I ride the rest of the way home wishing I were deaf.

16

◇◇◇

Sunday Mason and I enjoy a big breakfast at Round House Pancakes and then go home and take Buster Loo for a walk in an effort to relieve that stuffed-to-the-gills feeling that always follows eating there. Mason tells me that our honeymoon is booked and I casually mention that I've been checking out locations for the wedding even though I really haven't. I decide to get over my issues and get on the ball because I feel bad for putting that off now that he's booked us a bed-and-breakfast in freakin' Vermont.

After our family walk, Buster Loo retreats to his deluxe doggie bed, Mason takes off for the gym, and I decide to spend the remainder of the morning at the beach. I pack up my gigantic polka-dot bag and head out to the sandy white seashore. I open my umbrella, get my chair situated, then sit back and gaze out at the ocean.

After relaxing for a few hours and then taking a light nap, I pack up and walk back to the house, cursing myself for forgetting my water bottle. I have sand everywhere it doesn't need to be, which makes the walk back fairly miserable. Mason is home when I get there, and after a quick shower, I hang out with him in the living room, where I sneak another nap in while pretending to watch football. Later in the afternoon, he decides to make some gumbo, so I join him in the kitchen and fix some spicy cream cheese wraps. When we sit down to eat, I say a silent prayer that he won't start talking about work, and then he starts talking about work and I start thinking about gouging my eyes out with my soupspoon, because then he'd have to stop talking and drive me to the emergency room. Or the nuthouse.

I sit and do my best to appear interested in what he's saying, and he asks what I've got planned for the week and I just say, "Lots," and then he remembers something he didn't mention earlier about homeowners' rights during foreclosures.

He goes right to sleep as soon as we get in bed, and I lie awake and tell myself that it wasn't a mistake to move down here. I look over at Mason and wonder how it could possibly be a mistake when I have wanted to be with him for as long as I have and now here I am, right next to him. I try to convince myself that Mason is just talking about work all the time because he's so excited about helping Mr. and Mrs. Marks. I'm actually very proud of him for what he's doing. I just don't want to hear each and every detail about it, because it's the most boring thing I've ever tried to listen to. I tell myself that Mason and I are just temporarily out of sync and that things won't always be this way and that, in the meantime, I need to get some plans made for that wedding.

I remember that Avery is coming in to work tomorrow and make a mental note to ask her for some suggestions about where Mason and I could get married. Because we're getting married. I'm not backing out on this just because he's started getting on my nerves. I've wanted to marry him since I was eleven years old, so I'm going to get this done and be happy, dammit!

◇◇◇

17

Monday afternoon, Avery comes at ten minutes before one, and she's wearing khaki slacks, a cream-colored blouse, and a spectacular pair of Christian Louboutin heels, which I recognize only because of my pal Lilly Lane's obsession with the red-soled shoes. I'm standing there in my cuffed denim capris and leather Børn sandals looking up at her in total confusion.

"Avery, you look stunning!" I say. "What's with the outfit?"

"Well, it's this or what I usually wear." She shrugs. "One extreme or the other. I don't have any normal clothes."

"What you normally wear would've been fine, but I have to say that you dress up quite nicely." I look down at her shoes, dying to ask how much those cost. "Can I please take a picture of those shoes?"

She looks at me like I'm crazy. "Why?"

"Because my friend Lilly Lane is a label whore, and she is going to die when she sees these."

Avery kicks off the shoes and comes down four inches closer to me.

"You should put them on and let me take a picture of you wearing them and send that to her!"

"Oh no," I say, waving that suggestion off. "I'm pretty sure my fat little feet wouldn't fit in those. Plus, I don't need to fall over and break something." I look down. "Like the floor."

Avery starts laughing and slips the shoes back on. "You are so crazy!" she says, then strikes a pose. "Where's your phone?"

"I'll be right back." I run into the office and get my phone out of my purse. I go back out into the gallery and snap a few shots of Avery's fabulous shoes and text the pictures to Lilly, who immediately responds with a flurry of text messages laced with "OMGs" and several other acronyms, most of which I understand. Then she demands to know whose feet are in those shoes and if the shoes are the "real" thing. I realize that I haven't talked to Lilly since hiring Avery, and it takes me nine text messages to explain what's going on and confirm that the shoes are indeed designer and not impostor, and she finally responds with, "Must meet Avery!"

"My friend Lilly is a power texter," I tell Avery. "She can't talk because she's in class right now, but she wants you to know that she can't wait to meet you."

"That's nice," Avery says, and I get the feeling she knows way more people who wear expensive shoes than Lilly and I do. I watch her glide around the gallery in her designer heels. "This place looks great, Ace. It really does."

"Thanks," I say. "And thanks for stopping by on Friday to help." I look at her, thinking that she looks like she owns the place and I look like the hired help, and wonder if I should start dressing nicer.

"I swear that I would live here if I could," she says.

"Well, there's plenty of room upstairs for a bed," I say with a chuckle.

"Speaking of upstairs, why don't you run on up and get to work? I mean, that's why I'm here, right?"

"Technically, yes," I say. "But, you see, I have this wedding that I need to plan."

"Oh wow!" she says. "Can I help?"

"But of course," I say and make a grand gesture toward the sitting area. "Would you mind sitting for a second, Miss Cambre?"

"Why, no, ma'am, Miss Jones," she replies with equal flourish.

We sit down and discuss possible wedding locations, and then I ask if she knows anyone who caters, does flowers, and/or bakes wedding cakes. I have to grab a notebook because, as it turns out, Avery is quite the authority on party planning. I realize that I'm having a blast chatting with her, and even though I had a few second thoughts about our arrangement at first, I'm thrilled with it now and so thankful that she will be hanging around.

Forty-five minutes later, we have to put the conversation on hold when a passel of customers arrives at the gallery. One couple quizzes Avery about one of the paintings, and when she directs them to me, it's clear that they think she's the gallery owner and I'm there to sweep the floors or dust the walls or something. I decide then and there to stop thinking about it and start dressing better.

Avery volunteers to go pick up some afternoon snacks, and when she asks me what I want, I tell her to surprise me. Boy, does she ever when she comes back up with a flat piece of bread covered with bean sprouts and some kind of nasty-looking dressing from what I learn is her favorite restaurant, Eden's Treats. I squeeze my eyes shut when I take a bite, and I'm so surprised to find that it's not the worst thing I've ever tasted. I like it way better than I did those boiled peanuts.

"You didn't think you'd like it, did you?"

"Honestly? No, I didn't. I don't guess I need to tell you that I don't have a lot of experience with the—I don't know what you call it—organic and whole foods movement."

"Oh, I can tell you all about it!" she says enthusiastically, and I don't have much trouble containing my enthusiasm about that conversation. I watch her nibble on something that looks like a dark gray banana and I don't even ask. Because I don't want to know.

I finish my sandwich or whatever it's called, thank Avery for both the advice and the snack, then head upstairs to paint. I finish the voluptuous mermaid that I started last week, then sketch out some new things I've had on my mind for a while. A little after five, Avery appears with the OPEN fish and I stop working and take my paint and brushes to the sink.

I adamantly refuse her offer to help because she's dressed to the nines and I don't want to get in a situation where I have to sell a kidney to pay for a piece of her clothing or sell my soul to the devil to replace those shoes should I accidentally splatter some paint her way.

I ask her about school and she tells me about her classes, her professors, and a few projects she's working on. I ask if she has a boyfriend and she says no. Then she launches into a tale about the last guy she dated, who broke up with her when he found out her family was wealthy. I dry my hands, flip off the light, and follow her out the door.

"What was his name?"

"Well." She looks back at me and then rolls her eyes. "His real name is Jason Smith, but he had it legally changed to Jacques Le Sumay."

"Is he French?" I ask, trying not to laugh.

"No, he's from DeFuniak Springs. That's like a hundred miles from here."

"Oh."

"He accused me of not being a real artist because I'm not poor," she says as we walk down the steps together.

"Well, you're better off without someone that idiotic and narrow-minded," I say, then wish I hadn't. "Wait, I don't mean—"

"No, it's okay, he's definitely a narrow-minded idiot, but he's also a genius in his own special way." That Luther Vandross song starts playing in my head while I watch her get her purse and keys from behind the counter. "I see him all the time on campus, and he's dating this horrible-looking girl with bad teeth, and I want to pull her aside and tell her to make sure she doesn't stumble into any money, because if she does then he'll put her ass on the road." She starts laughing and so do I. "But I don't. I don't say a word. I don't think she even knows who I am, and that's fine. Better for everybody."

"That's a pretty tragic love story," I tell her as we walk out the door.

"Tell me about it. And to make it all worse, my parents were thrilled when he dumped me because they were so appalled by him that one and only time they met."

"That's terrible, Avery!"

"I know, but it's like—" She shrugs and looks at me. "Whatever. I'll live."

We bid each other adieu and I drive home wondering what Jacques Le Sumay, artistic champion of poverty, looks like. I'd be willing to bet good money that Avery was more attracted to his soul than his looks. Maybe I'll ask to see a picture of him one day.

I get home, hop up the steps to the front porch, and see Buster Loo peeking at me through the bottom pane of glass. He yelps a few times when I open the door, so I pick him up and give him lots of good chi-weenie love, after which I take him for a walk around the block. I see Margo out in her yard and I wave at her, and she pretends not to see me. I wonder what she would do if I flipped her the bird. Or mooned her right here next to her mailbox. No way she could pretend not to see that.

"Goofy bitch," I mumble, and Buster Loo starts to growl.

18

◇◇◇

Allison calls dinner in at the Blue Oyster so I go pick it up and head over to the law office of J. Mason McKenzie. She's on a roll with her nice-girl persona and we exchange polite but dull chatter as we spread the food out on the conference room table.

I ask her about her dog, whose name turns out to be Princess Parisa Persephone, and after she pronounces if for me the second time, I can see why Connor runs around calling it PoPo. I wonder if he chose that moniker because it's short for "Pomeranian" or if that's something he started after Allison came up with that tongue twister of a dog name or if he just does it to make her mad. I have a feeling Connor McCall doesn't miss an opportunity to get his lovely wife all riled up.

She talks about the precious pup that she calls Princess to the point I think my eyes are going cross and I'm going to fall face-first into the shrimp scampi. Don't get me wrong—I love hearing dog stories as much as the next dog lover, but Allison has embarked upon the dog story that refuses to end. I'm grateful when Mason and Connor finally join us in the conference room, and I sit quietly while the three of them discuss the day's business. It's almost as bad as listening to Allison ramble on about PoPo, but not quite.

"I heard you went to the Peanut Festival this weekend," Connor says to me, and I jump like I've been startled out of a bad dream.

"Oh, yes, I did," I tell him. "I hated the peanuts, but the barbecue was fantastic."

He laughs and asks me whom I went with.

"Tia Wescott," I say. "We took our dogs, Buster Loo and Mr. Chubz."

"Buster Loo and Mr. Chubz?" Connor sniggers.

"Mr. Chubz?" Allison says. "Is he overweight?"

"Her daughter named the dog when she was five." I didn't feel like watering that one down for her.

"Oh," Allison says and starts drumming her nails on the table like she's bored. She looks at Connor. "What was the name of that dreadful hillbilly fest that you took me to last year and we had to sit in traffic for three hours trying to get home?"

"That was the Redneck Christmas Parade," Connor says. "We're talking about the Peanut Festival. Two different things."

"Oh," she says again.

"So is Tia a lesbian?" Connor asks and Mason looks up in surprise.

"I don't know," I say, somewhat shocked by that comment as well. "Would it matter if she was?"

"Not at all," Connor says. "I was just wondering because she hasn't dated anyone since she got rid of that shitbag husband she had, and that's been, what? Ten or twelve years now?"

Allison is looking closely at him now.

"What? My brother graduated with Tia," he says. "I've known her all my life. She was a Buckman before she married Bernie Wescott. She played softball and she's always had short hair and she hasn't dated anyone in a long time, so I just thought—"

"You just thought you'd do a little sexual profiling?" Mason asks. "Connor, you're crazy as hell."

"I think she's been more concerned about raising her daughter than anything else, but I'll be sure to ask her for you."

"Ace! No!" Allison exclaims.

"I'm kidding," I say. "I don't care if she is or if she isn't, but if I find out either way, I'll let you know, Connor."

"Thanks," Connor says, standing up. He looks at Allison. "What? I'm just curious. What's wrong with being curious?"

"Nothing," she says, getting up. "Nothing at all. Except that it's rude."

"It's rude to be curious?" he says, walking out of the conference room.

"It's rude to be so disrespectful about a woman's sexual preference," Allison calls out after him.

"I'm not being disrespectful! Damn!" Connor yells from the hallway.

Allison collects our take-out plates and tosses them in the trash. She thanks me for picking up dinner again and I can tell she likes me a lot better now that we've bonded over her dog. I kiss Mason goodbye and go home and snuggle up with Buster Loo, whose full name is actually Señor Buster Loo Bluefeather, but I didn't tell Allison that because she didn't bother to ask.

19

◇◇

Tuesday passes with no excitement whatsoever, and the highlight of my day on Wednesday is hauling my big mermaid picture downstairs and hanging it front and center on the main wall of the gallery. I gather up all of my other under-the-sea-themed paintings and arrange them around my new mermaid.

"Lovely," I say to myself and decide that I need to paint more mermaids, because mermaids make me happy.

Avery comes in dressed in her usual outlandish garb, and I stay downstairs and chat with her the entire afternoon, because the last thing I want to do is sit by myself in a quiet room. Avery tries to coax me upstairs a few times, but I refuse. I think about using one of Gramma Jones's old lines, "You ain't the boss of me!" on her but decide she might take it the wrong way, so I just keep that to myself.

Before she leaves, I invite her to Girls Night In the following night and she quickly accepts.

"Tia says everyone brings a snack, like an appetizer or a dessert or something," I say and want to tell her not to bring any of that shit from Eden's Treats but remember that first of all, it's not my place to tell her what kind of snacks she can or can't bring to a party and second of all, that wad of grass she brought me Monday was actually pretty tasty, so perhaps I should be a bit more open-minded.

Wednesday night is another tiresome meal in the conference room, and the only thing that gets me through it is looking forward to Thursday, which, lo and behold, finally arrives.

I get up early, take Buster Loo for a walk, and get to the gallery fifteen minutes early. No one comes in all morning, but I don't care because I'm so excited about Girls Night In. I've just finished a tasty lunch from Bee Bop's Burgers & Shakes when the doorbell chimes and I walk out into the gallery to find Lenore Kennashaw. She's standing beside the counter wearing a lime green blouse and starched khaki shorts. She has on the same ugly green sandals she wore in here last time and that same necklace with the stupid hammer pendant.

"Hello, Mrs. Kennashaw," I say, thinking I'm going to need another cheeseburger to calm my nerves after this heifer leaves. "What brings you in today?" I make up my mind that I don't care what she says; I'm not giving her a damn thing. And I decide to be nice in the least pleasant way possible.

"Oh, just out looking around," she says with a tepid smile.

I want to ask her if she ever plans on paying for that calla lily painting she took out of here on opening night, but that would be tacky since I know she donated it to charity. What's even tackier than that, however, is that she'll take full credit for the donation and never mention that she stiffed me on the payment. It's so obvious to me now that she operates just like Tia said she does. I watch as she prowls around my studio, turning up her nose at my work. She stops in front of my big mermaid and grimaces like she's in physical pain.

"Who would want a painting of an enormous imaginary sea crea-
ture?" she asks, glancing down at my thighs.

I look at her and sigh. Then I remember what Sylvie Best said about
the people who can and will determine my success in this quaint little
town.

"Someone who likes mermaids," I say flatly.

She shakes her head like that's the most ridiculous thing she's ever
heard and moves on to my wall of flowers.

"This looks like something you'd find at a cheap whorehouse," she
says, pointing to the picture of roses at twilight that Kevin Jacobs said
was too romantic to get for his mom. I remember what he said about
his parents getting it on and that amuses me to the point I'm able to
smile.

"Mrs. Kennashaw," I say, "if you need anything, I'll be in my office.
Otherwise, have a nice day and thank you for stopping by."

I walk straight to my office, plop down at my desk, and text Lilly
until Lenore Kennashaw finally leaves fifteen minutes later. It just so
happens to be Lilly's planning period, so I give her a call and whine
and complain about Lenore Kennashaw being so intolerable.

"Is she gone?" Lilly asks.

"Yes, she left without saying good-bye and I'm so upset," I say sarcastically.

"Don't worry about her, Ace," Lilly says. "She just one of those
people who mistakenly thinks her opinion matters to those of us with
good sense."

"You're saying I have good sense?" I ask. "Thank you."

She starts laughing and I ask her if she thinks Lenore is trying to
frame me by sending Ramona's nephew in here to get me all hot and
bothered so she can tell Mason.

"The only framing you need to worry about is the kind that involves art," she says matter-of-factly.

"I just don't know if I can stand it, Lilly," I say. "I mean, she comes in here showing her ass and I'm supposed to stand around and act like I appreciate it?"

"I'm sure they don't have *that* much control over what goes on in Pelican Cove," Lilly says with a noticeable lack of conviction. "Do you know what you need?"

"What's that?"

"You need Gloria Peacock down there."

"Oh, my goodness," I say, laughing. "And Birdie Ross."

"Birdie Ross would set those bitches straight," Lilly says.

We talk for a minute about how great it would be to have Gloria Peacock and her friends at the gallery one day when Lenore and her pals show up.

"It would be like a senior citizen smack down!" Lilly says.

We laugh and start scheming up ways to make that happen.

"You need to host another event there," Lilly says.

"Yeah, but it would be my luck they wouldn't even show up after Gloria and Birdie drive all the way down here."

"Gloria and Birdie drive down to Seaside to see Daisy all the time," Lilly says. "They wouldn't mind at all."

"Yeah, but *why* would I host an event?" I ask. "We missed Labor Day, it's a month and a half until Halloween, and I'd look like an idiot trying to plan a last-minute Columbus Day celebration."

"Just wait and host a Christmas party," Lilly suggests. "You could paint up some holiday cheer to sell."

"I don't know if I can put up with it until Christmas."

"Have an early one. Like the week after Thanksgiving. That means you would only have to keep your mouth shut for the next, uh—" She pauses. "Okay, that's not going to work, is it?"

"Exactly!" I tell her. "I need some relief *now*!"

"Well, the bell just rang to start sixth period, so I've got to go," she says in a hushed tone. "Let's think about this and talk later."

I tell her good-bye and then start fantasizing about how funny it would be for Gloria Peacock and Birdie Ross to be here one day when Lenore Kennashaw showed up with her pit-bull pal, Sylvie Best. I wouldn't have to say a word. I could just sit back and watch the showdown.

I piddle around for the rest of the afternoon, then decide to lock up thirty minutes early and head home. When I turn in to my subdivision, I see some weirdos walking down the street, so I slow down to check them out. I'm not surprised when I see it's Margo and Cindy, but I am surprised to see they're wearing safety goggles and yellow kitchen gloves.

"What the hell?" I mumble as I drive past them. Margo has a handful of green plastic bags and Cindy is holding a scoop, so I can only assume that they are out on voluntary shit patrol. I wave but they don't wave back. They only stare at me through their safety goggles. I start laughing and can't stop.

When I get to the house, I run to the garage and rummage through Mason's sporting goods cabinet until I find a pair of binoculars. I take them to the kitchen to clean them up, and with Buster Loo hot on my heels, I run upstairs to the guest bedroom. He jumps on the bed and barks like a mad dog while I scan the neighborhood with the binoculars. I spot Margo and Cindy and watch with great amusement as Cindy bends over and scoops something into one of Margo's green bags, which Margo promptly ties up. Then Cindy stands up and Margo steps behind her, places the bag against her back, and starts writing on it.

Buster Loo is going nuts, so I cease and desist with the undercover surveillance. I close the blind and go downstairs, and after whipping up some ham dip and sticking it in the oven, I go outside and play fetch with Buster Loo. When the kitchen timer goes off forty-five minutes later, I get the dip out, set it down to cool, and start getting really excited about Girls Night In.

◇◇◇

20

I get back to the gallery at ten minutes before seven, go inside, and piddle with the lighting until I get it like I think it needs to be. Tia arrives a few minutes later, followed by Avery. At five minutes after seven, the door opens and Tia shouts, "Olivia! You made it!"

"Help me, Lord, yes, I did," the woman named Olivia says, walking back to the break room. "It's like my kids knew instinctively that Mama was trying to have a little fun so they all went nuts when I picked up my purse. Their daddy got 'em settled back down with some *Toy Story*, so I was able to slip out the door." She looks at me. "Well, hello there. You must be Ace Jones."

I smile, and Tia goes through the introduction process with Olivia, Avery, and me.

"Oh, I know you. You're Dr. Leo's youngest," Olivia says to Avery. "The artist, of course."

"Of course." Avery smiles a painful little smile and looks like she's embarrassed.

"My family knows Dr. Leo very well," Olivia explains. "Every year, one of my kids breaks something and we have to go see Dr. Leo." She looks at me. "He's a wonderful doctor. Great with kids."

"Oh, okay," I say and try to think up something to add to that, but don't have to because the door flies open with the arrival of another guest. I turn to see a woman who looks just like Olivia, only instead of being long and lean like her, she's pleasantly plump like me. She's wearing a pink T-shirt that I've looked at a dozen times on Old Navy's "exclusively online" plus section and a pair of knee-length jogging pants that fit her like a glove. In a good way. I make a mental note to ask her where she found those pants before she leaves tonight.

"Hey, y'all!" this big, beautiful woman calls as she crosses the gallery floor. "Y'all know I don't cook, so I went to Walmart and got some frosted cookies and cheesecake!"

"That's why you don't have a man, 'cause you don't cook," Olivia calls out.

"Well, I ain't ever gonna start cookin', then," she says, and that cracks us all up.

"Ace Jones, meet Jalena Flores, Olivia's younger sister."

"Oh, you a chubbily-bubbly like me, girl!" Jalena crows, then gives me a big bear hug.

"Nice to meet you," I say and tell myself not to start squalling because I'm so happy to have a fellow chubster on the scene. I haven't had a fatty gal pal in nearly three years.

I had a bunch of pudgy friends in college, but when I moved back to Bugtussle, I had only one, and that was Nelda Graves. She was from Olive Branch, Mississippi, but took a job in Bugtussle because she didn't want to move back home after graduating from college. She'd been teaching there for two years when I got hired and we became fast friends. She made fun of me when I had a fling with the new baseball coach and I made fun of her when she had a fling with the new football coach, and it was fun and games until he got a job in Senatobia and they got married and moved.

Tia introduces Jalena to Avery while I spread the food out on the counter. Tia mixes up what she calls her World Famous Magic Punch, and Avery creeps up and whispers that she left her dish in the car.

"Why?" I whisper back.

"It's tofu pot stickers from Eden's Treats," she says, eyeballing the meat-filled tater-tot casserole that Olivia brought.

"So what?" I whisper back. "Go get it!"

She does but insists on telling everyone beforehand that it's a vegetarian dish. No one seems to mind, and everybody has a pot sticker and no one makes any gagging noises, so I chalk that up as a win. The only awkward moment comes when Tia, who obviously missed the cue, offers Avery a sausage ball and Avery politely declines. Only after Tia looks down at her plate and sees that she had three pot stickers and a frosted cookie does it register that Avery doesn't eat meat.

"Avery, I'm so sorry for trying to force this pork on you."

While Avery tries to explain that she isn't bothered by what others eat, Jalena effectively vanquishes all traces of uneasiness by loudly declaring that it would make her day if someone tried to force some pork on her.

After we finish the first round of snacking, Tia insists we all top off our cups with her World Famous Magic Punch and relocate to the couches in the gallery. Avery tells the others that I'm planning a wedding, so they have a lively discussion about the various places someone could get married in Pelican Cove. After almost an hour, they all agree that I need to start my search at the Beach House Bed and Breakfast. I pick up my phone and punch that info into my notes app while they carry on about which of the two bakeries is the best, and then they start on florists. I go get my notebook and cross off some of the places on my list after Jalena tells a few horror stories about Flora-zillas ruining a couple of weddings in which she was a bridesmaid.

"This is some great information," I say, making more notes. "I appreciate it!" Then, not wanting to hog up all the party time with my personal issues, I close the notebook and put it on the coffee table.

"Who needs some more World Famous Magic Punch?" Avery asks, getting up. Everyone does, so she ends up hauling the whole punch bowl out to where we're sitting.

We talk about music and books and movies, and after discussing the latest celebrity mishaps, we start talking about men. Jalena, as it turns out, has several memberships to online dating Web sites and, despite her sister's concern for her safety, goes on all kinds of blind dates. This intrigues Avery, who starts quizzing her about the men she's met online.

"Tell us about the worst guy you ever met," Avery says, and Jalena throws her head back and laughs.

"Girl, they've all been awful!" she says, and that cracks us all up again. "That's why I'm still single!"

"Yeah, but there had to be one," I say. "One that was so bad you won't ever forget him."

"Tell them about Travis!" Olivia says, taking a swig of her drink. "Travis is my favorite one to hate!"

"Olivia, I just met these two girls and you want me to start off with a naughty story like that?"

"I like naughty stories myself," I say.

"As do I," Avery chimes in.

"Let's hear it!" Tia says, with a twinkle in her eye. "We're all grown-ups!"

"So y'all want to hear my story about a dirty dog named Travis?"

she says with a cunning smile, and we all whoop and holler and carry on until she says, "Well, just remember that you asked for it!"

And so she begins. "Travis was shorter than me, which, you know, is going to happen sometimes, and that was okay with me at the time, because Travis was a stud. A short little stud." We giggle about that while Jalena stirs her drink and shakes her head. "But you couldn't tell by looking that Travis was a stud. He had these small hands and these little-bitty fingers, and on our first date I thought, 'Yeah, Travis is rocking a two-inch dong, but I'm going to go ahead and let him buy me dinner and then I won't ever speak to him again." We all squeal with laughter, and Jalena continues. "Girls, I was wrong about Travis. Travis wined me and dined me and we went back to my place, and, y'all, he talked the panties right off this big, round rump." She points to her backside, and I think that's so funny that I almost spit my drink everywhere. In trying not to, I end up spewing most of it out my nose. I hold up my hand and she pauses while I run to the restroom get myself back together.

"Okay, I'm okay now, please continue," I say, sitting back down.

"I'll just get right to the point. Travis had a wiener that looked like something they sell by the pound at the butcher shop. It was this big, long, fat monster of a penis. I swear, girls, I've never seen anything like in my *life*!"

We start squealing again, and I glace at Avery to see her reaction to all of this. She has her eyes squeezed shut and her face is flushed red because she's laughing so hard, so I stop worrying about her getting offended.

"Travis was a *stud*!" Olivia hollers and raises her drink. "And Jalena couldn't get enough of that little man with the big snake in his britches."

"No, I couldn't," Jalena says, looking starry-eyed. "I know y'all have heard about men being pussy whipped; well, I'm here to tell you that short dude had this big girl *dick whipped*!"

"Dick whipped, I tell ya!" Olivia yells.

I'm laughing so hard I'm afraid I might faint, Tia has tears rolling down her cheeks, and Avery appears to be on the verge of hyperventilating. I look at Jalena and say, "Please, don't stop!"

"That's what she said." Olivia snorts and we all squeal with laughter again.

"Well, Travis was a shady bastard from the start. He only wanted to date on Tuesdays and Thursdays and claimed he was going to surprise me with a weekend date. Well, I was surprised all right when Travis and I had hot, lovely relations every Tuesday and Thursday for a month and I had yet to get my weekend date. Now, normally I don't get all up in a man's business and start asking questions, because I know better. They lie like dogs about shit that don't matter, so of course they're gonna lie about important stuff, *especially* when they're getting some good poon-tang pie. But I was starting to think something was amiss, so I asked him, I said, 'Travis, I'm waiting on my surprise weekend date.' He was slick as an onion, y'all, and he told me to just hold on because he was planning us something really special. And so I waited."

"Because you were dick whipped?" Avery asks, and then falls backward against the cushions, laughing. "I'm sorry! I'm sorry! I just had to say it!"

"Exactly! And two weeks and four booty calls later, Travis shows up at my door with two tickets to a four-day cruise to Mexico."

We all clap and whoop and Jalena gets up and does a little victory dance around the sofa. "So little Travis and I drive over to N'awlins, where he buys me dinner at Emeril Lagasse's fine eating establishment; then we go get on our cruise ship, and, ladies, I'm here to tell you that I had the time of my life! When we went to the beach in Mexico, he insisted I go topless, so I did, and I swear on Tia's sausage balls that I have never felt more beautiful than I did that day. I thought I was fallin' in love, girls. We had pictures made and he bought me all kinds of liquor and jewelry and gave me money to gamble with and it was the best four days of my life." She stops and takes a long sip of her drink. "So I guess y'all wanna know what happened when we got home? I mean, why I'm not married to the man, right?"

We carry on and beg her to tell us and she takes a deep breath and continues. "Well, we were the last couple off the ship because we snuck off behind the stage and had sex while everyone else was standing around waiting to disembark. He said he didn't want our time together to end." She looks around and sees that we're a captive audience, so she leans in and lowers her voice. "Well, I soon found out why he didn't want our time together to end." She nods and looks at her sister, who shakes her head and rolls her eyes. "Because when we got out to the parking garage, his *other* girlfriend was parked right beside his convertible Mustang, and, let me just go on and tell y'all, that bitch was crazy! When we got out of the elevator, there she was—cussing and yelling and carrying on like a fool."

"How did she know?" I ask, rapt with suspense.

"Well, from what I gathered from her screaming fit, she hacked into his e-mail and found out where he was, who he was with, and when our boat was coming in." Jalena shakes her head.

"What did you do?" Avery asks, like she might die soon if she doesn't find out.

"I jerked my liquor out of his hand and told him I had to go. Then she starts in on me, calling me whore and all that, and I just turned around and walked away. Well, she came runnin' up behind me and pushed me, and I turned around to face her, put my finger in her face, and said, 'Listen up, girl. This can go one of two ways. You can get yourself back over there and act a fool or you can act a fool right here and I'll stomp your ass in the pavement.' Well, she took off back toward Travis, and then that little rat bastard looked at me, shook his head, and yelled, 'I'm sorry, Jalena. I don't know why she's here. I broke up with her three months ago.'"

"You are kidding!" I exclaim.

"Wish I was," she says. "He was caught red-handed in the act and was still trying to hold on to his other piece of ass."

"Right in front of his ex-girlfriend that was really his girlfriend?" Tia says. "Wow. Sounds like my ex-husband."

"Had they really broken up?" Avery asks, wide-eyed.

"Hell no!" Jalena says. "When he said that, she lost her shit for real and started crying and squalling and yelling about an engagement ring. I went downstairs, caught a cab to the French Quarter, and got myself a room. I had a good cry and then ripped up all those pictures we took together and went out on Bourbon Street and had myself a blast. Next day, I rented a car and drove home."

"That's terrible," Avery says.

"What's terrible is that I let myself get into a situation like that for a little—okay, a whole lot of man-sausage." That gets us all tickled again. All except Avery, who looks like she's about to cry.

"So he broke your heart?" Avery asks.

"I wasn't really in love with that ugly little chipmunk; I just let my emotions get the best of me because he was like Macho Man Randy Savage in the sack!"

"Then there was the married man—I'm sorry, men," Olivia says.

"I ain't even gettin' into all that," Jalena says, waving off her sister's comment.

"Just please tell us how you knew the men were married," Avery begs.

"Stalking," Jalena says simply, and my ears perk up. So not only have I found a fellow fat girl; I've found a fellow stalker!

"Isn't that against the law?" Avery asks, and I want to tell her to stop being so serious because she's killing my buzz.

"Only if you get caught," I say.

Jalena's eyes light up when she looks at me. "You stalk, too, girl?"

"Every chance I get!" I say.

"Oh good Lordy, help us all," Olivia says. "Y'all two are going to get into some trouble. I can see it right now. Arrested for trespassing. Mug shots in the paper."

We move the party into the break room and start munching on snacks again. When Olivia announces that she has to go home, Tia tells her she'll call her designated driver, and ten minutes later, Kevin Jacobs walks in the door.

"Holy guacamole," I say when I see him. "Hello, Travis!" I call out, and everyone dies out laughing and I stand there wondering what's so funny, and then I realize the error of my ways. He's looking at me like I'm crazy and I stumble over and pat him on the shoulder. "I'm so sorry. Hello, Kevin. I just heard a fabulous story about Travis and I got confused."

"Y'all know each other?" Tia asks.

"For a minute," I say, despite the fact that the conversation had moved on.

"We've met," Kevin says, smiling. "How are you, Ace?"

"Drunk as a bicycle," I say, smiling and putting my arm around Tia.

"I didn't know bicycles drank," Kevin says, and Tia dies out laughing.

"They don't," I say, still smiling through the foggy haze. "That's why it's so bad." I laugh at myself because I have such a way with words. A way to make a fool of myself, that is.

"C'mon, ladies, you know the drill!" Kevin calls. "Everybody in the Tahoe!"

Kevin Jacobs hops in the driver's seat of Tia's Tahoe and we all pile in the backseat. We continue to have ourselves a fine ol' time as he drives all over town, dropping us off one by one. When he pulls up at my house, I invite Tia to stay with me, but she looks at me and says, "Oh, I'll just stay with him. He lives right around the corner."

My jaw drops while I process the fact that, first of all, Kevin Jacobs the sexpot lives right around the corner from me and, second, Tia just said she was staying with him. I poke her in the arm and whisper, very loudly, "You and him are doin' it?"

She starts laughing, raises her eyebrows, and nods. I stare at her for a moment in total disbelief, not wanting to accept this as fact. They both turn to look at me, so I reach for the door handle and mumble something stupid about the weather as I crawl out of the Tahoe.

"You need me to walk you to the door?" Kevin asks.

"No, thanks," I yell, looking back and waving. "I'll be—" I don't finish my sentence because I step off the driveway and fall down in the yard. I roll around, cussing like a sailor because the wet grass feels so nasty. I finally get up and see Tia is standing outside her Tahoe bent over laughing. I look at Kevin, who's just stepped out of the vehicle, and even in my drunken stupor, I can see he really wants to laugh.

"Go ahead," I holler at him. "I'm a professional."

"A professional what?" Tia squeals.

"Damn rodeo clown. Hell, I don't know." I look back at Kevin. "But I'm sexy, ain't I, yo?"

"Yo, baby, that you are," he says when he finishes laughing.

"Are you sure you're okay?" Tia asks, walking around to help me brush the grass off my arms and back.

"I don't remember the last time I was any better!" I say, crawling up the steps on all fours. She goes back to the Tahoe and they wait for me to open the door and get in the house before they leave.

Mason still isn't home, so I go inside and lie on the floor with Buster Loo for a while. When he wanders into the sunroom, I roll around and somehow manage to get on my feet, and then stumble up the stairs to the bathroom. I step in the shower, still not believing all that time I spent lusting over Tia's designated driver.

21

<><><><><><><><><><><><><><><><><><><><><><><><><><><><><><><><><>

Friday morning, Mason brings me some aspirin, ice water, and a cold rag. I get up, take one look at my hair, and head straight to the shower because no amount of heat could tame the mess on my head after going to bed with wet hair the night before. After a nice, warm shower, I put on some comfy clothes and ease down the steps.

Mason hands me a plastic cup of Sprite with six cherries, which has long been my go-to hangover remedy. He sips coffee and waits for me to get ready so he can take me to work. He drives me to the gallery, making fun of me the whole way for getting so drunk at Girls Night In. He tells me that when he got in bed last night, I flipped over and started talking about going on a cruise with a rabbit.

"Travis," I say, laughing despite my aching head. "It was a story Jalena told us about the worst experience she's ever had with one of her online suitors."

"Jalena Flores?" he asks. "I think Connor used to date her. I know I've heard him mention that name."

I roll my head over on the headrest so I can see him. "Honestly, I can see those two getting along great." I hold up two fingers. "Peas in a pod."

"I'll ask him about her sometime when Allison isn't around."

I look back at the windshield and tell myself not to read anything into that comment. I'm glad I have a headache because that's the kind of offhand remark that would normally get me fired up.

"Nice," I whisper. "Be nice. Keep that new leaf turned over the right way."

"What?" Mason asks.

"I'm sorry," I mumble. "I was just thinking that Jalena has to be several years older than Connor."

"Yeah, I think so." He glances at me. "She has a sister, right? Olivia Kennashaw."

That got my attention. "What did you say?"

"Doesn't Jalena have a sister named Olivia Kennashaw?"

"I didn't catch Olivia's last name," I say, thinking back to when she came in. Despite my hellish hangover, I'm certain Tia used only her first name when she introduced Olivia to Avery and me. I would've remembered had she mentioned the last name of my archenemy.

"Her in-laws own that chain of home and garden stores." He looks at me. "What's wrong?"

"Nothing," I say. "Are you sure that's who she is?"

"Yeah, I'm pretty sure. Her husband's name is Josh and his mother was at the grand opening." He looks at me. "What is her name?"

"Lenore?" I ask, praying he'll say that's not her.

"That's her! Lenore Kennashaw. She does a lot of charity work, and, hey! Didn't she take home the last item at the auction?"

"Yes, she did, and she didn't pay for it, and then she went and donated it to charity."

"Well, that was nice of her."

I look at him to see if he's serious, and he is. I just stare out the window and don't say a word.

"Ace?" He's looking at me now.

"Yeah, sweetie, I'm sorry. My head just really started thumping." And that's the honest truth. Mason turns into the parking lot, where Kevin Jacobs's truck is parked two spaces down from my car. All the other vehicles are gone.

"Well, I guess everyone but Tia got an early start this morning," I mumble.

"Is that Kevin's truck?" Mason asks, pulling in beside it.

"Yes, he drove us all home last night," I tell him. "I think he and Tia have a little thing going." I imagine him and Tia having buck-wild sex all night, and that makes me so mad and jealous that I want to get out and kick the fenders off his truck, only I'm pretty sure I couldn't get my foot up that high right now. I look back at Mason, who looks ridiculously handsome this morning, and wonder what in the hell is wrong with my brain.

"Ah." He looks over at me. "Well, I guess that answers the lesbian question."

"I guess it does."

"I'll be sure to pass that along to Connor," he says, and we both laugh.

"Thank you so much for taking such good care of me this morning," I say, and I mean it with all my heart. I lean over and he gives me a hug and a kiss and we tell each other that we love each other and I hop out of his shiny Escalade.

I unlock my car and move it to the back corner of the parking lot, where it's nice and shady. Walking back toward the gallery door, I drop my keys in the shrubbery and have to get down on all fours to try to scratch them out of the bushes.

"I am about to marry my dream man," I tell myself as I poke around the leafy gardenias. "What the hell is wrong with me?"

"Well, you're on your hands and knees on a sidewalk, for starters," I hear someone say. "Did you crawl to work today?"

When I raise my head, I see a pair of tennis shoes with bulldozer grips on the bottom. I look up a pair of muscular legs and past black athletic shorts, a belly button, and a bare chest. My eyes finally come to a stop on the smiling face of Kevin Jacobs.

"Well F me in the A!" I mumble, finally getting my fingers around my keys.

"What?"

"Nothing," I say, getting up on my feet and brushing off my knees. I look at my reflection in the plate-glass window. My hair is pulled back in a bushy ponytail and I'm wearing my oldest khaki Bermudas with a Margaritaville T-shirt. So much for dressing for success.

"Good morning, Ace Jones," he says and shows no signs of getting in his truck to leave.

"Good morning, Kevin Jacobs," I say. I look from his dark brown eyes down to his chest, and then up again. "Out for a morning run?"

"Yeah, had to come pick up my pickup truck."

"I see." He doesn't mention Tia, so I don't, either. The sun is beating down on my face and giving me a worse headache than I already have, so I ask him if wants to come inside and I'm secretly pleased that he does. He follows me into the gallery and I point him toward the water-cooler in the break room.

"Looks like y'all had a big time in here last night," he calls out.

"Yeah, we had a blast," I answer, wishing he would leave but at the same time fantasizing about him coming into my office and throwing me up on top of the desk.

Then the questions start flying around in my head: Why couldn't he come by earlier? Why did he have to come inside? Why couldn't he just get in his damn redneck fuck-a-billy pickup truck and go to the store and get himself some water? Why does he show up when I'm outside on my hands and knees scrambling around in the bushes? And why is he not in here letting me look at him without his shirt on?

I lay my head down on my desk and curse myself for having a raging crush on a guy who most certainly boned my new BFF last night and probably hasn't had a shower since. With that image to clear my head, I walk into the break room and find him looking in the fridge.

"What's all this stuff from Eden's Treats?" He looks at me. "Are you a vegetarian?"

"Do I look like a vegetarian to you?" I ask. I want to scream for him to get the hell out of my refrigerator and get out of here, but when he turns back around and leans over again, I feast my eyes on his backside and then decide to let him keep looking so I can, too.

"No," I say, taking a seat at the table. "That's some of Avery's left-overs."

"Ah, yeah, the young girl?"

The young girl, I think. *Nice. So what am I?* "Yes."

"She looks like the type that would eat stuff from there."

"It's her favorite restaurant."

Thankfully my cell phone starts ringing and gives me an excuse to get out of there and back into my office.

"Just help yourself to whatever you want."

"Oh no, I was just leaving," he says and closes the fridge.

I don't get to the phone before it goes to voice mail. I check it and hear Chloe's sweet voice telling me it's nothing urgent; she just wants to chat. I make a mental note to call her later and go back out in the gallery, where Kevin is perusing my new display of mermaids.

"That is one sexy mermaid," he says, moving his eyes from the picture to my boobs.

I look at him in his running shorts with the band of his underwear showing, and there's nothing I can say or do to deny the fact that I want him so bad I can hardly stand it.

"Thank you," I reply and just stand there, looking.

"You're welcome," he says and finally looks me in the eye. I just can't help myself. I start thinking about him naked again. I mean, he's already halfway there.

"So how'd your mom like her picture of the daisies?"

"Oh, she loved it!" he says enthusiastically, and my ego inflates to heights previously unknown.

We make small talk and I'm thankful for my killer headache so I don't suggest that we go upstairs and bang on the balcony. He finally leaves and I go splash water on my face and stretch out on the sofa, and that's where I am two hours later when Avery bounces in at lunchtime, a full hour before her usual time of arrival.

22

<><><><><><><><><><><><><><><><><><><><><><><><><><><><><><><><><>

"Hey, I got out of class early and wanted to see if you needed some lunch." Avery stops to look at me. "Are you okay?"

"I think I might live, but I'm not sure yet," I say, rubbing my eyes. I look up at her. "Oh, it must feel good to be so young and drink like a fish and not hurt all over the next morning."

"Here," she says, walking over to the couch. "Come sit on the floor and lean back on the sofa."

"Why?"

"Just trust me," she says. "I promise I'm not going to hurt you. Lying down is one of the worst things you can do when you have a bad hangover."

"Please don't try to pop my neck."

"Oh goodness!" Avery says as she slides onto the sofa behind me. "Who in their right mind would try to pop someone's neck?"

"I had a great-uncle who fancied himself an amateur chiropractor."

"Did he paralyze anyone?"

"Not that I'm aware of," I say.

"Popping bones is dangerous," Avery says with authority. "Massage, however"—she places her hands on my shoulders and starts to rub—"is a different story. I bet you've been taking aspirin all morning, haven't you?"

"Yes," I say, "and drinking lots of water."

"Water is good," she says in a motherly tone as she takes down my ponytail and combs through my hair with her fingers. "But this is better."

I moan and groan as Avery massages my head, neck, back, and shoulders. Then she starts massaging my scalp and I feel sure I'm going to overdose on pure pleasure. She moves her fingers to my temples, then back down on my neck, and I don't ever want her to stop, but she finally does.

"Avery!" I say, getting up off the floor. "You should think about setting up one of those funny-looking chairs at the mall."

"Yeah, right," she says, laughing. "So have you had lunch?"

"No."

"I figured as much, so I picked you up something," she says and pats me on the back. I pray a thousand little prayers she's about to hand me a greasy brown bag from Bee Bop's. "I picked it up at Eden's Treats and I think you'll really like it."

No! I think. *I need an effin' cheeseburger!*

"Thanks, Avery, that was very thoughtful."

"Don't worry," she says, getting up, "it's not a vegetarian dish. Eden's does serve meat, well, chicken, and it's cage-free, no hormones."

"Okay," I say and wonder what the hell difference it makes if a chicken lives in a cage or roams the prairies before being shipped off to the slaughterhouse. I guess happy chickens taste better.

Avery grabs two white bags off the counter and invites me to join her in the break room. I walk across the gallery like the bride of Frankenstein.

I fix us both some water, and she grabs two paper plates and unloads the bag. One rolled-up little thing for her and one rolled-up little thing for me.

Great.

I look down and don't want to touch it, let alone eat it.

"It's buffalo chicken," she says.

"What's buffalo chicken?" I ask, eyeballing the mysterious little thing on my plate.

"It's a shredded buffalo chicken wrap," she says enthusiastically, and I know that I'm going to have to eat this thing or it's going to hurt her feelings. I pick it up and sniff it and Avery starts to laugh.

"There's no ranch dressing," I whine.

"No, but there is a celery stalk," she says cheerfully.

"Hey, did you catch Olivia's last name last night?" I ask, thinking if maybe I talk nonstop until she finishes her lunch, then she'll leave and I can toss this giant rat pellet into the trash.

"Uh, no." She thinks for a minute. "Tia didn't say, did she?"

"Don't think so."

She looks at my alleged buffalo chicken wrap. "Just try it. You won't die."

Shit.

"I might, you never know," I say, wondering if I could convince her that I was allergic to chicken that wasn't still on the bone. She bores a hole into me with her exotic blue eyes, so finally I pick the damn thing up and take a bite, and much to my surprise, it's good.

"Dang! This is tasty!" I exclaim.

"Told you," she says and gets back to nibbling on what she claims is a veggie wrap.

After lunch, it doesn't take much coaxing to get Avery to go upstairs and spend some time in her new studio. When it sounds like she's good and settled in, I go lie back down on the sofa like she told me not to. I think about Tia and wonder why she wouldn't mention that Olivia is Lenore Kennashaw's daughter-in-law. Olivia doesn't strike me as the type who would go for Lenore's bull, but you never know about people when it comes to their families. Tia can't stand Lenore any more than I can, so I can only assume that Olivia feels the same way or they wouldn't be such good friends.

My cell phone rings and it's Chloe again, so I pick it up and apologize for not calling her back. After a few minutes of polite chitchat, she tells me she's thinking about buying a house.

"Okay," I say. Just before I moved to Pelican Cove, Chloe divorced a horribly wicked man that I hated with a passion, and she's been renting my grandmother's house in Bugtussle ever since. "Are you about to get married?" I ask, thinking how great it would be if she married J. J. Jackson, the handsome and genteel sheriff of Bugtussle, Mississippi.

"No!" she says adamantly. "It's a little too soon for that!" She goes on to explain how she's never had a place of her own and that's really what she wants right now.

"What will you do with the house if I move out?" she asks cautiously.

"I don't know and it doesn't matter, Chloe," I tell her. "You've got to do what's right for you. That's all you need to be concerned with."

"I don't want to leave you in a tight spot."

"You won't leave me in a tight spot at all. Gramma Jones's house was empty for two years back when we were in college, remember? Besides, that'll be a great place to stay when I come back to Bugtussle for a visit, which I think is going to have to be sooner rather than later."

"I'd be happy to show it for you if you decide to sell," Chloe says, and although I haven't even thought about what I'd do if she moved out, I immediately balk at that suggestion.

"I don't want to sell it," I say quickly.

"Okay, well, you don't have to worry about it right now, because even if I wrote a check tomorrow, it would probably be the first of the year before I actually move out."

"Have you found a place?" I ask, not even wanting to discuss putting my house on the market.

"Well, I've been looking around for a while, but nothing really caught my interest until this past weekend. Do you know John and Ginger Moon?"

"Yeah, I went to school with him and she's from Corinth, right?"

"Yes, them. Well, he got transferred to Texas with his job, so they just put their house up for sale."

"Don't they live in that big white house on the lake?"

"That's the place," she squeaks, and I can tell she's really excited.

"Wow, you would be crazy not to buy that place! It's gorgeous!"

"I know! I want it so bad!"

"Well, go get it, my friend!" I say, genuinely excited for her. "I can't wait to plan the housewarming party."

"Oh, Ace, I was so afraid you would be mad at me for moving out of your house."

"Chloe, you're crazy. You've got to live *your* life, sweetheart. And you should probably get off the phone with me now and call your Realtor before someone else snatches that place up."

"I think I'll do that," she says.

"Keep me posted," I say.

We say our good-byes, and I hang up the phone knowing there is no way in hell that I'm selling my grandmother's house in Bugtussle. It's all I have left of my family, and I'm not getting rid of it. Not now. Not ever.

At five o'clock, Avery goes outside and fetches the OPEN sign. She can tell something is bothering me, but I chalk it up to the prolonged hangover. I don't know if she buys that or if she's just being polite, but she doesn't say anything else. All I can think about is getting home and snuggling up on the sofa with Buster Loo.

I call Mason and ask him what time he'll be home, and he tells me that it's going to be after dinner. I wonder if he would've been able to come home on time had he not gone in late this morning because of me. I ask him if he needs some supper and he tells me that he and Connor are having pizza delivered. I ask about Allison and he tells me that she and Connor got into it at lunchtime and she left and went to Tallahassee for the weekend.

"So she'll be back?" I ask, worried and thinking I should try harder to listen to her boring stories.

"Oh yeah," he says, like it's no big deal. "They do this every couple of months. She'll be back at work on Monday."

For some odd reason, I'm relieved to hear that. "Mason, is there anything I can do?" I ask him. "Make some copies, file some papers, anything?"

"Oh no, sweetie, it's okay," he says. "I just finished going over Mr. Marks's foreclosure documents and, like I suspected, mistakes were made, so now we're just doing research and getting ready to go to battle with these bastards."

"Okay," I say, praying he won't elaborate any more than that. "Well, I guess I'll go get a cheeseburger and head home, then."

"All right, babe, see you later."

"Hey!" I say. "Do you have to work tomorrow?"

"Yeah," he says, slowly. "When we reopen this case, things are going to get nasty and we've got to be prepared." He pauses. "I'm sorry."

"Oh, it's okay," I say and tell myself that it has to be.

I drive to Bee Bop's and get myself a double cheeseburger with bacon, an order of loaded tots, and a gigantic cherry limeade. I put the food in the backseat so I won't touch it on the way home and then eat in the kitchen with Buster Loo perched next to my foot. He's sitting up like a Coke bottle, waving his front paws, begging. When I'm finished, I offer him a dog treat, but he won't go near it. Instead, he goes and sits by the garbage can where I just threw the Bee Bop's bag and gives me that "I can't believe you treat me this way" look.

I open the fridge and get him a piece of cheese, and that makes him happy, so he follows me into the living room and we snuggle up and watch TV until we both doze off.

23

◇◇

Saturday morning, I take Buster Loo for an extralong walk at Pelican Trails to make up for not walking him the day before. The weather is nice and warm, so after I get back home, I decide to spend a few hours at the beach.

I'm sitting on my beach towel, spraying myself down with sunscreen, when I notice I'm the only female in sight sporting the prototypical skirted swimsuit favored by chubby girls. I don't know if some kind of sorority of skinny girls has invaded the area or if the gym was closed and all the hot-bodied ladies took to the beach, but there are tanned and toned bikini-clad chicks as far the eye can see in either direction.

I tell myself not to worry about it. I mean, I wasn't worried about it last night when I scarfed down that bacon cheeseburger and tater tots smothered in chili and cheese, so there's no sense in worrying about it now.

I call Tia to see what she's doing, and she's working, so I call Jalena.

She tells me all about a new guy she went out with last night and I listen with great interest as she rambles on about him. She's at the Tanger Outlets mall in Foley and apologizes for not inviting me to join her.

"I thought you would be hanging out with your man-honey today, and I didn't want to impose," she says.

"The man-honey has been working a lot lately," I tell her.

She asks me if I've been to the outlet mall yet, and when I tell her that I haven't, she gets excited and starts telling me all about the "big girl" shops they have there.

"You can actually find something to wear that doesn't look like it was made for a circus clown," she says with great enthusiasm. "And the best part is that you won't have to rob a liquor store to buy an outfit!"

"What a novel concept," I say wryly. "Cool clothes for fat girls at affordable prices. I'm tempted not to believe you."

"Girl, I know, but I swear on my stack of low-fat cookbooks that I'm tellin' you the truth," Jalena says, laughing. "You've got to come shopping with me sometime."

"I would love that," I say, thinking again how great it is to have a fellow fatty for a friend.

We talk for a few more minutes; then I tell her to have a good day shopping and she tells me to have a good day at the beach. I push the button to end that call and then dial up Lilly Lane and talk to her for an hour.

She tells me there's a rumor going around about two teachers at the middle school having an extramarital affair, so we gossip about that for a while. I tell her I wish I was there so we could do some undercover investigating, and she laughs and says she thought the same thing when she heard about it.

"You need to come home," she says. "I know we were just down there a few weeks ago, but we didn't have time to really visit."

"I know," I say. "I'm ready."

She asks how things are going with the gallery, and I tell her I sold one painting to Kevin Jacobs, the guy I called her raving about the first day I was open for business. She has a good, hearty laugh about that. We talk about Chloe and the house she's looking at, and how happy we are for her that she's finally getting her life all ironed out. She asks about wedding plans and I tell her I'm working on it but a long way from having it done. We have another "wish you were here" conversation, and I hang up the phone feeling worse instead of better.

I look out at the ocean, ignoring all the swimsuit supermodels, and hope this homesick thing is just a phase. I tell myself again that it was not a mistake to move down here.

"So what if I'm a miserable failure and have sold only one painting in a month," I say out loud because the sound of the waves drowns out everything. "I came down here and I tried. That's more than most people get to do."

I pack up and head home, wondering how in the world anyone could feel worse after a few hours on the beach. Before going up the steps to our neighborhood, I turn to look at the ocean, hoping it hasn't stopped working its magic on my soul.

Saturday night, Mason comes home and I don't know if it's because we start drinking or because he's gearing up for a big legal battle, but he takes it upon himself to share what seems like each and every individual detail about the lawsuit. I never thought I would have absolutely zero interest in listening to Mason McKenzie, but as it turns out, I was wrong. The more he talks, the more I drink, and I wish we could go back to when he didn't want to talk about work.

I think for a second about giving him a thirty-minute lecture on the pros and cons of the eight main brushes I use for acrylic paint just to get him off the subject, but I don't because that wouldn't be fair to him.

It's not his fault I'm in a bad mood. It's mine. So I sit patiently and listen, nodding and doing my best to feign interest.

He finally wraps up his lengthy discourse with, "I don't know why I'm telling you all of this, because I know you have no idea what I'm talking about," and that just rubs me the wrong way.

"Well, maybe if I was smart like Allison I could better understand your lofty and intellectual conversation," I say, not even checking the sarcasm in my voice.

"What?" he says. "Why would you say something like that? That's not what I meant at all."

"I'm sorry," I say, reminding myself again that he is not the bad guy here. "That was uncalled for."

"Is there a problem?" he asks. "Something you want to talk about?"

"I'm just homesick," I tell him. "And I'm disappointed because I didn't sell a single painting this week and I really thought I would be doing a lot better at this point. Especially after so many people turned out for the opening." I sigh and think maybe after that horrendous speech I gave, everyone collectively decided that I was a dipshit unworthy of their patronage no matter how good my artwork was. "I'm never going to make any money if things don't pick up." I think about what Sylvie Best said to me and wonder if they went ahead and sabotaged me just for the hell of it.

"Ace," he says, coming to sit next to me on the love seat. "You have to give it time. Remember when I first opened the office down here? I had to work part-time at the Blue Oyster for almost a year to make ends meet."

"I didn't know that," I tell him.

"Well, I didn't tell many people, because I wanted everyone back home to think I was a hotshot lawyer making big bucks down in Pelican Cove. As a matter of fact, I think the only person I told was Ethan

Allen." He smiles at me. "But you don't have to worry about that because you have me to take care of you. It doesn't matter if you ever make a dime at that gallery; just go in there and do your thing and be happy."

"I can't be happy if I'm not making enough money to at least cover the damn utility bill," I say. "I barely made enough at the auction to cover my set-up cost, and I've brought in a whopping one hundred dollars since. I can't just be a bum."

"You aren't being a bum," he says. "It's a man's job to take care of his wife."

I look at him and say nothing because all I can think about is his mother, who, in my opinion, is a worthless, snobby bitch. She grew up rich and went off to Ole Miss, where she wasted no time finding and marrying Mason's dad, who, to this very day, caters to her every need. Rachel McKenzie's entire existence depends on the success and benevolence of her husband, and I cringe at the thought of being like her. I look at Mason and hope against hope that he doesn't expect me to live off him like that for the rest of my life. Because I won't do it.

He puts his arms around me and I put my head on his shoulder and Buster Loo barrels in from the sunroom, jumps into my lap, and then wedges his little chiweenie head in between ours.

"Look at us," Mason says. "Family hug!"

Sunday my mood is somewhat better. Mason decides to rent a catamaran and we spend the day on the water and I forget all about my problems. We pick up dinner on the way home and get in bed just before eight o'clock, both of us exhausted from a full day of salt water and sun.

24

◇◇

Monday, Mason is gone before I get up, and I take Buster Loo out for a seaside stroll before getting ready and heading to work. Avery and I didn't do any rearranging on Friday, and since it didn't seem to make any difference anyway, I elect to leave everything where it is for now.

I go straight to my office, flip open my wedding notebook, and get to work. I look up the Web site for Beach House Bed and Breakfast and decide to drive out there this afternoon. I piddle around the rest of the morning, making to-do lists and such. I have a few customers but no buyers. Avery comes in at one and she's all excited about something she wants to paint, so she runs straight upstairs and gets to work.

I go back to my desk and look at the online pictures of Beach House Bed and Breakfast again and get excited because it looks pretty fabulous.

When I leave the gallery at five o'clock, I call to see if Mason could possibly meet me over there, and I'm not surprised and only mildly disappointed when he tells me that he can't. I call Tia and she doesn't answer and I call Jalena and she's working late, so I take off by myself. I really wish Lilly and Chloe could be here, because this is the kind of things a girl is supposed to do with her friends. I turn up the radio and try not to think about how lonely I am.

When I pull up in front of the Beach House Bed and Breakfast, I forget about all of that as I gaze in awe at the Greek Revival–style home surrounded by large oak trees filled with Spanish moss. Behind the house, I see the Gulf of Mexico.

"This is it," I whisper to myself. "This is the place."

As I follow the cobbled sidewalk leading to the guest entrance on the left side of the house, I imagine being here in my wedding gown. I glance around the edge of the house at the splendidly landscaped yard, beyond which I see waves lapping onto a narrow strip of snow-white sand. I think about how Lilly reacted the first time she saw Gloria Peacock's estate.

"Oh, Lilly," I whisper, knocking on the door, "it's magical."

I laugh at the memory and then realize that I miss her so bad I could cry. She should be here with me now. I shouldn't be doing this alone. I get upset and think about running back to my car and going home, but I know I need to get this done, so I just stand there and tell myself that I can do this because I wear my Big Girl Panties every day.

After the passing of three eternities, I finally hear the click of the lock, and a very elegant-looking lady opens the door and frowns at me.

"Hello," I say nervously. "I'm Ace Jones and I was wondering if I might have a look around."

"Do you want to make a reservation?" she asks, without even a hint of a smile.

"I'd like to get married here," I say and start to get a bad feeling about this.

"It's five thousand dollars to rent the place for one event, and I require half of that up front to hold the date." She looks down at my flip-flops. "Are you still interested?"

"Yes, ma'am," I say, trying to be as polite as possible. "I am."

She motions for me to come in, but it's painfully obvious that she would prefer dealing with someone in pressed slacks and a silk blouse. In other words, someone dressed just like her. I tell myself not to let her attitude bother me, but it does.

She shows me around the house, including the honeymoon suite upstairs, which she pointedly explains is not included in the price she quoted earlier. She takes me down a secret set of stairs to the kitchen and then out the door, where even her snidest comments cannot detract from the beauty of the lavishly landscaped backyard.

She leads me back inside to her office, where she sits behind a desk that has no chairs on the opposite side. I ask her if the place is available for December 31, and she reluctantly admits that it is. I ask about the honeymoon suite and, after studying her date book for what seems like six hours, no doubt hoping against hope to find a reservation, she smirks and tells me it's available as well.

I tell her I'll take it and she looks about as excited as a woman who just realized that she unleashed a loaded fart in a white dress. After I hand her the check, drawn on Mason's account, she eyeballs my wide-leg yoga pants and asks me what the dress code will be. I want to tell her that no one will be allowed on the premises unless they're wearing cut-off jeans, mesh trucker hats, and rubber boots. But I don't. Because I'm nice.

I politely inform her that I'll get back with her on the details after I speak with my fiancé. Like she's entitled to know, she asks who that might be. I want to say Larry the Cable Guy just to see her reaction, but I realize the reference would be lost on this snobby old coot, so I just tell her the truth.

"Oh," she says, and I can tell I just moved up a few rungs on her ladder of judgment. "The real estate lawyer? Why, what a handsome and charming young man he is." She pauses and looks at me, and I can read her expression like a book. "That's who this is for? For you and him?" She doesn't even try to hide the fact that she's aghast. "You're engaged to marry J. Mason McKenzie?"

"Yes, I am," I say, and instead of jerking that check out of her hand and ripping it to pieces, I decide to leave it where it is and stand my ground. Mason's money is good enough for her and I'm good enough to get married at her precious little bed-and-breakfast.

"Do tell him that Mrs. Adday sends her"—she looks me up and down—"I guess I should say, kindest regards."

I decide to clear the air in the nicest way I can at this point.

"Why don't you just say what's on your mind?" I say casually, like we're talking about the weather.

"Whatever do you mean, dear?" Mrs. Adday snaps.

"Say that you can't believe he's marrying a girl who wears yoga pants and flip-flops during daylight hours?" I say with all the pleasantness I can muster, which isn't much. "Because it's written all over your face."

Mrs. Adday smiles as she says, "Why, no! I would never want J. Mason to think that! No! How dare you say such a thing?"

"You've made it fairly obvious since you opened the door that you'd rather I take my business elsewhere."

"Absolutely not!" She starts fanning herself with the check. "Why, I never!"

"You never what? Never thought anybody would pick up on your not-so-subtle hints?" I look at her like one might look at a naughty child. "Or did you think no one would ever bring it to your attention that they noticed?"

Mrs. Adday puts the phony kindness on full blast and showers me with compliments and apologies, all of which make me want to vomit right in her face. She wraps up her monologue with what an idiot might think was a heartfelt, "Oh, Miss Jones, I think you will make a lovely bride." She smiles and folds her hands in front of her, as if to pray, but she is *still* looking at me like I'm a maggot.

I pluck the check out of her hand and give her a good stare down. "I most certainly will be, but not here."

"What?" she says, looking frazzled. "Give me back that check."

"I don't think so," I say. I rip the check in two and turn to go.

"But I do think the world of J. Mason," she says in a really pathetic voice as she follows me out of her office.

"His name is Mason," I say flatly, just before walking out the door. "Jeez."

25

◇◇◇

Jalena calls me when I'm on my way home and asks if I want to meet up at Credo's for a beer, and I tell her that I would love to but I have to stop by and check on Buster Loo first. I call Mason just to check in, but he doesn't answer. When I get home, Buster Loo is ready for a walk, so I take him for a quick loop around the neighborhood, and when we get back to the house, it's clear he wants to keep walking. I decide then and there to start taking him to work with me so he doesn't have so much little-dog alone time. I put him in the house and apologize for leaving again so quickly. Buster Loo stands at the door and watches me leave, no doubt feeling extremely betrayed.

Mason finally calls me back just as I get to Credo's, and after we talk a minute, he tells me that he was going to invite me to eat Chinese with him and Connor and Allison, but he'd rather I have some girl time with Jalena. I don't even attempt to argue and slip my phone back in to my purse, relieved to escape dinner in the conference room.

I walk into Credo's, stopping short when I see Kevin Jacobs

propped up in the middle of the bar with a giant mug of beer in his hand.

"Ace Jones!" he calls. "Get over here and let me buy you a beer, pretty lady!" I look around and don't see Jalena, so I go over and join him. Three beers and thirty minutes later, Jalena shows up and finds me sitting in between Kevin and his friend Reed, having more fun than I probably should be. When Kevin sees her, he insists we all move to a table. He and Reed argue about whether to sit inside or outside, and Jalena says they can sit wherever they want, but she's staying inside under the air conditioner.

Jalena and I slide into opposite sides of a booth, and Kevin, after exchanging a look with Reed, sits down next to me. We talk and carry on, and I learn in the course of the conversation that Reed works with Kevin and they know Jalena because their favorite place to grab lunch is Frog's Bayou, the marina on the north side of town that Jalena's family owns.

They tease her about spending her whole life at Frog's Bayou and she tells them there's nowhere else she'd rather be. We joke around some more, and then someone cranks up the jukebox and the four of us hit the dance floor and get with it.

We dance and laugh and drink, and then the guys order a round of appetizers and insist Jalena and I eat with them. She's flirting shamelessly with both of them, so I give up trying not to flirt with Kevin and lay it on thick. I make sure to flirt with Reed some, too. When we finish eating, I can't finish my beer and tell them that I've got to go home or else I might pass out. Jalena, however, is still ready to party, and when she tells me she's going to hang around a bit longer, Reed declares he can stay as long as she can. I pay my part of the tab and Kevin walks me outside.

"Did you drive?" he asks.

"I'm on foot because I'd planned on doing some heavy drinking," I tell him as we walk down the steps to the dimly lit parking lot.

"Yeah, well, you can check that off as done," he says. He glances down at me and I feel like our minds are on the same thing. He puts his arm around me and says, "What time do you have to be home?"

I stop walking and turn to face him. With his arm still on my shoulder, I look up, and it's obvious that he's had the same kinds of thoughts about me that I've had about him. He runs a hand through my hair, and at that very moment, there is nothing I want more than to go home with him and boink his brains out.

"I really don't know Tia that well—" I say, then stop. I've got to get this crazy train stopped before it runs off a cliff and ruins everything.

"Well, I know Mason well enough to know I shouldn't be standing out here with you like this." He looks away and then lets his arm drop to his side. "I'm sorry," he says. "Let me walk you home. It's on the way to my house." I look up at him in a panic and swear that I haven't been this sexually frustrated since I was thirteen years old. "I didn't mean anything by that," he says quickly.

"I'm sorry," I say, taking a step away from him. "I don't want you to think—"

"I don't," he says. "Don't worry. C'mon, let's get out of here."

He buries his hands in his pockets as we move toward the sidewalk. We walk in silence to the entrance of my neighborhood.

"I go this way," he says, pointing left.

"Thank you for walking me home," I say, not looking up.

"Hey," he says, lifting my chin so I have to look at him. "We just had a good time tonight. That's all we did."

I smile and nod, wondering if that's how he really feels or if that's just what he's going to tell Tia.

I walk home and find Buster Loo still sitting at the front door, and it's all I can do not to start squalling before I get up the steps. I pick him up, go out back and light the tiki torches so the mosquitoes won't eat me alive, and then slump down into a lounger. I cry until my eyes are almost swollen shut because I'm so ashamed of myself for being so disappointed that Kevin Jacobs didn't kiss me. Buster Loo sits with me the entire time, periodically licking the tears off my face. My phone beeps and it's a text from Mason telling me he's on his way home. He asks if I'm home yet and I send him a text telling him I am. I run upstairs and get in the shower because I don't want to look like a wreck when he gets here.

"You went out to Mrs. Adday's place?" Mason says later that night when we're in bed. "I love her. Isn't she the sweetest?"

"She's lovely," I lie. I turn my head and roll my eyes.

"Her place is beautiful," he says, cuddling Buster Loo. "I would love to get married there. Ace, you're the best!"

"Wonderful!" I say, and then I lie some more. "I'll call back tomorrow and see if we can book it."

"Great," he says. I tell him I had too much to drink at Credo's, then roll over and pretend to go to sleep.

"Good night, sweetheart," he whispers.

"Good night," I whisper back, and then squeeze my eyes shut and try not to start crying again.

26

$\diamond$

Tuesday, I take Buster Loo to work with me, and he has himself a fine time exploring the gallery. When he's finished prancing around, he comes into the office and snuggles up in the brand-new dog bed I picked up at the pet store on the way over. I sit at my desk, staring at my wedding planner, wondering what to do next.

I push the wedding planner aside, check my e-mail, and then read a little celebrity gossip, but nothing can take my mind off the moment I had last night with Kevin. I send Jalena a text message and ask her to call me when she can. When she calls thirty minutes later, I try to gauge her response to the good time we had without being too obvious. I tell her that I had more fun with her last night than I've had in a long time.

"Don't get me wrong," I say. "Girls Night In last week was the most fun I'd had in ages, but last night topped that."

"I had a good time, too," she says. "Kevin and Reed are some pretty fun guys to hang out with. I see them in there all the time."

"Yeah, they were a blast," I agree. She doesn't mention them again, so I don't either. We talk about Girls Night In and she mentions my brilliant idea to have it at the gallery every Thursday night, and even though I have no recollection whatsoever of saying that, it sure doesn't mean that I didn't. She tells me how much she appreciates that suggestion, because now she won't have to worry about her house being clean on the fourth Thursday of every month.

"I just don't like to do housework during the week," she says. "I'm too tired after working all day to fool with some mops and scrub brushes."

We get off the phone and I sit there and think about Kevin Jacobs until I feel like I'm going to lose my mind. I wish I had someone to talk to about this, but I don't. Lilly and Chloe would die if I told them, I don't want Jalena to think I'm a home wrecker, and I can't discuss it with Tia for obvious reasons. I think about Avery, but that's just not a conversation I'd feel comfortable having with her, so I sit and try to work it out on my own.

I've been in love with Mason McKenzie for almost twenty years. He's everything a girl could want in a guy. He's good-looking and has a wonderful personality and a great career. He loves dogs, likes hanging out at home, and, most important, wants me to be his wife. He has plenty of money, a three-story house a block away from the ocean, and he loves to take great vacations. What fool would be distracted from a man like Mason by a big redneck country boy who is so obviously a ladies' man?

Me. That's who. I am officially obsessed with Kevin Jacobs and I can't help it.

I can't help that he had to come pick up those pictures for his aunt Ramona. I can't help that he chose to buy his mother some painted daisies for her birthday. I can't help that he showed up at the gallery the same time I did the morning after I found out he was Tia's booty call. And I can't help that he was in that bar when I walked in last night. I didn't ask for any of that to happen. And I can't help that I had the best time ever hanging out with him. I didn't ask for that, either, but it happened and I almost wished that it hadn't, because my life would be lot less complicated right now.

What I'm really doing by entertaining this fantasy of Kevin Jacobs is creating a way to sabotage the best chance I've ever had of being happy. So what if Mason talks about work all the time? So what if it's a whole lot on the dull side? It's not a crime for a man to love his job. I just need to adjust my attitude and try to be a better listener, and while I'm at it, I need to stop being so negative about having to sit through those unbearable dinners in the conference room.

I tell myself that Mason will not expect me to live off him like his mom lives off his dad, but how in the world am I going to address that if he does? By saying something glib like "Thanks for buying me this nice building, but I'm not making any money, so even though it doesn't matter to you if I make money or not, I'm closing this down and going back to teaching school so I can have reliable income and people to talk to on a daily basis?" I think not.

I wish I didn't have this notion that at some point in my life, every-thing is going to turn out perfect. Because that's not the nature of real-ity. All I've wanted since the first time I laid eyes on Mason McKenzie was for him to be mine, and now he is and all I do is sit around and find problems with what should be an ideal life. What the hell is wrong with me?

I think really hard for a minute about whether I might be finding fault with Mason because I met Kevin or if maybe Kevin is getting more appealing because I'm getting bored with Mason or if maybe I'm just crazy as a shithouse rat. I'm sitting here thinking about throwing my entire life away for a big sexy country boy who looks like he might be a blast in the sack? Am I really having this conversation in my head? A dream life with the love of my life or a roll in the hay with a midlife bachelor who acts like he's seventeen? Really? Am I entertaining this as a viable option?

Disgusted with myself, I push back from the desk and get up. This startles Buster Loo, who goes into a full state of guard-dog rage and runs barking into the gallery. I walk up to my studio, but my frustration has squashed my creativity, so I go back downstairs and play fetch with Buster Loo. I look up at my mermaid and ask her why she can't bring me better luck.

Mason calls just after I lock up and tells me they won't be leaving as early as they'd planned, so I get to join him, Connor, and Allison for another dinner in the conference room. I try to muster up a positive attitude, but I can't, because Allison has taken to assaulting my nerves with constant and never-ending tales of PoPo, yet she never thinks to ask about Buster Loo, whom I drop off at home before reluctantly driving to the law office of J. Mason McKenzie.

I try to convince myself that all the one-sided conversation might be a good thing, because if Allison doesn't remember that I have a dog, then maybe she has forgotten about that doggie play date she mentioned last week. I can honestly say that I'd rather be shot in the face with a twelve-gauge than hang out at the park with her and her dog.

I think about how that scenario would play out, and despite the funk I'm in, it makes me smile when I think about her showing up in some six-hundred-dollar riding boots, denim leggings, and a flowing white blouse, and there I'd be in some cutoff sweat pants and flip-flops. Then Buster Loo would probably try to hump PoPo and Allison would get all offended, and then she might try to start a fight with me and she'd be scratching and clawing and I'd have to punch her in the face and then she wouldn't want to work for Mason anymore and she'd surely tell her damned mother about what happened, and then her mother would make Connor quit his job and they would have to move to Tallahassee and Mason would be left all by himself in that godforsaken conference room with nobody to help him work.

This is what I'm thinking about during dinner when Allison asks me what I'm thinking about. I ask her some dumb-ass question about Princess, and she launches into another tale and I just sit there and wonder if there's a steak knife lying around anywhere or if I could just saw off my arm with this plastic knife from the sandwich shop.

After a while, I start worrying she might invite me to the park to watch her play with PoPo. Luckily, she doesn't and I'm able to escape thirty minutes later and go home. Once I'm out of there and in the comfort of my car, I decide that maybe she's not as bad as I make her out to be. Maybe having to spend so much time with her in such a confined space just gets my imagination all wound up.

27

◇◇

Wednesday, I wake up in a bad mood and take Buster Loo for a walk down by the beach, hoping the fresh ocean air will lift my spirits, and I'm sorely disappointed when it doesn't. I reluctantly get ready for work, then decide to leave Buster Loo at home today because, come hell or high water, I'm leaving that gallery at five and coming straight back to the house. I grab a Sprite out of the fridge and the whole bottle of Midol from the cabinet and head out the door.

I haven't been in the gallery five minutes when the doorbell buzzes and I turn around to see Lenore Kennashaw and Sylvie Best.

"Where's Ramona?" I ask.

"She had better things to do," Lenore snaps.

"Too bad you didn't," I mutter, because I've got cramps and PMS and I'm not in the mood. Forget the covert ops and veiled insults. Today I might just kick that bitch in the face and be done with it.

"What was that?" she asks with a snip in her voice, and Sylvie stiffens up like we're about to have a fistfight.

"What was what?" I say, walking around behind the counter, making her turn to face me. *Be nice, be nice, be nice. Or at least keep your smart mouth shut.*

"I just stopped by to let you know that your application was reviewed, but you were not selected to be a featured artist for the West Florida Festival of the Arts." She looks around the gallery with disdain, and even though that makes me furious, I just stand, stunned by what she just said. "Your work was found to be uninspiring, unoriginal, and lacking in talent compared to the other submissions." She smiles at me and winks, and the black dog is tearing my brain out of my skull. With all my might, I summon the white dog.

"Well, I'm sorry to hear that," I say, and then massive disappointment overpowers the rage, and before I even think about it, I blurt out, "I've been wanting be in that festival since I was in college." The look of victory on her face makes me sick at my stomach, but I just stand there, defeated. "Is there anything else I can do for you?"

"Of course not," she says with a sneer and turns to leave.

Sylvie follows her to the door, then stops and looks back at me. "By the way," she says, "how's business?"

"Pretty slow," I say, resisting the urge to walk over there and literally kick them out the door.

"Pity," Sylvie says with a smirk, and she and Lenore walk out the door and get in Lenore's silver Mercedes.

I go back to my office, slump down at the desk, and play solitaire until I'm bored out of my mind. Then I get my wedding notebook off the shelf next to my desk and carefully place it in front of me.

"So fucking what?" I say to myself. "I'm happy. I'm planning a New Year's Eve wedding to the man of my dreams. So fucking what if I don't get to be in that fucking art festival?"

I dig the Crown Royal out of my bottom desk drawer and look up the number for a pizza delivery. I go sit in the break room and drink Crown and Coke until the pizza arrives, then eat half of a mediocre-tasting large, after which I put my head down and squall for an hour. I go to the restroom, wash my face, give myself a pep talk, and walk back to my desk. I look down at the wedding notebook and sigh. Then I flip it open and start surfing the Web.

Wedding checklists, cake ideas, decorating projects—I print off everything I can find. I get a file box, fill it with hanging folders, and write WEDDING on the side. I make a to-do list and write out a schedule of when to get the to-do list done and then rewrite it all so I can read it. Then I organize and reorganize all of my wedding-planning para-phernalia, and that keeps me busy until Avery comes in at one. She's got vegetarian pizza from some bagel shop, and while I'm trying to choke down a piece of that, I can't help but think that the people who own Pier Six back in Bugtussle could make a million dollars if they opened a store down here in Pelican Cove.

"What happened?" Avery asks. "And don't say nothing, because I can sense that something is very wrong."

"Nothing," I lie. "Having a bad Wednesday."

She gives me a skeptical look. "Let me know if you want to talk about *nothing*," she says and leaves the office.

"Thanks for the pizza," I call after her.

"Anytime!"

I continue with my flurry of wedding planning. A few people come in late in the afternoon and don't buy anything, but I'm already so depressed that I don't even care. I go back into my office and look through my collection of wedding material again, pleased with the progress I've made, but all the happy thoughts in the world can't shake the sadness and disappointment I feel about not being selected to par-ticipate in that art festival. The fact that Lenore Kennashaw took the time to drive over and tell me in person makes it that much worse. And why did this have to happen today, when I already felt like shit before she even walked in the door?

I wander out into the gallery and plop down behind the counter. I gaze at each individual painting and tell myself that I'm a great artist regardless of what any selection board thinks about my work. I try to rationalize the situation in order to drag my confidence up out of the dirt, but I can't. I sit and think for a long time, then realize there's something gnawing at my soul besides the fact that my rejection was delivered in such a shocking manner by such a dreadful person.

It takes me a while, but I finally figure it out. Deep down, I'm disappointed in myself for not unleashing the fury on Lenore Kennashaw and Sylvie Best, because they had no right to come into my art gallery today and treat me like a patsy idiot. Come to think of it, Lenore Kennashaw had no business waltzing up to me at *my* grand opening and creating an opportunity to insult me *and* one of my favorite paintings. And Sylvie Best certainly had no right to talk to me like she did the first time she came in here, *especially* after I had *just* donated two of my prized paintings for their stupid fund-raiser. And then Lenore came back in here last week just to terrorize me about my fat-ass mermaid and whorehouse picture? That's ridiculous.

What really bothers me is the realization that I've been keeping my mouth shut, not because of my commitment to being a nicer person, but because of their threats. Lenore Kennashaw and Sylvie Best are nothing but bullies who expect people to step back and be nice while they run over everyone like a freight train.

When I moved down here, I really did want to start over and be a nicer person, but nowhere in that plan was a tolerance for bullies. *Be nice.* Some asshole probably came up with that concept to keep the dignified people out of their way. But I'm not dignified. And, try as I may, I'm not nice. I'm a fat girl with a bad temper, and no amount of wedding planning, painting, or pretending is going to change that.

So I'm throwing in the towel on the *be nice* campaign because the only people it's hard to be nice to are the ones who are assholes anyway, and they don't deserve the courtesy. From here on out, if Lenore Kennashaw and Sylvie Best want to pick a fight with me, they damn well better have their gloves laced up. Consequences be damned, I'm done with tolerating the two of them. I know that's not what Jesus would do and I hope he can forgive me for this, but I can't be nice anymore, because it's driving me crazier than I already am.

"Ace," I hear. "Are you okay?"

Avery is waving a hand in front of my face.

"Avery!" I say, snapping out of it. "I'm sorry. I went into some kind of rage coma there for a minute." Avery starts laughing. She hands me her phone and I watch myself, staring off into space, mumbling and gritting my teeth, my face getting red.

"I thought I'd better stop you before you turned green and ripped off your shirt," she says, laughing. "Don't worry." She taps the screen of her phone. "It's deleted."

"You keep that phone handy, because the next time Lenore Kennashaw and Sylvie Best come in here, you might have to call 911."

"Okay, what's going on?" Avery asks, taking a seat in one of the chairs opposite my desk.

I fill her in on Mrs. Kennashaw dropping by, and Avery—sweet, tree-hugging, yoga-practicing Avery—completely loses her cool.

"Avery, really, I think you need to calm down," I tell her, but she's not listening. "Why don't you do, I don't know, a downward-facing dog or something?"

She continues her tirade, and I realize this is the first time I've ever seen Avery angry. And I don't know if she's really getting *that* loud or if it just seems that way because up until today, I've only heard her speak just above a whisper. Finally, I say, "I'm okay, Avery. I'm not three years old and this certainly isn't the first big disappointment that life has handed me. It's fine. I'll be fine. Let's just move on."

"Oh no, we're not moving on! You can sit there all day long and tell me everything is okay, but we both know it's not. We both know this is not right." She starts drumming her aqua blue nails on the arm of her chair. "This is what was bothering you when I came in today, wasn't it?"

"Yes, Avery, and I appreciate your concern—"

"You should call them," she says.

"Call who?"

"I don't know." She picks up her phone. "Whoever is in charge of submissions. You should call and tell them something like, I don't know, you just found out you weren't selected, but wanted to thank them for the chance to apply."

"I'm not going to do that."

"If you don't, then I will."

"Go ahead," I tell her. "It's not going to make any difference."

And so she does.

After fiddling with her phone for a few minutes, she puts it up to her ear.

"Yes, ma'am, this is Graciela Jones," Avery says, speaking very slowly in a mock Southern accent that cracks me up. "And I jus' wanted to thank y'all for allowin' me the opportunity to apply to y'all's art festival. I'm real sorry I didn't get picked, but I just wanted to tell y'all how much I appreciate gettin' a shot at it." I cover my mouth to keep from laughing, and Avery puts the phone down on her shoulder and hisses, "Stop it!" She picks up phone and says, "Why, yes, ma'am, I can hold," she looks at me and smiles.

"I do *not* sound like that!" I tell her.

"Yes, you do," she whispers. I shake my head, and then she gets back to being me. "What? Yes, I did apply for this year's festival." Her eyes light up and she says. "Oh, really? So what you're sayin' is that whoever told me I wasn't picked for the festival was tellin' me a lie?"

I stop sniggering and sit and stare at Avery.

"Who told me that? Well it was Lenore Kennashaw, that's who it was, and she wasn't very nice about it, either."

"And Sylvie Best," I whisper.

"And Sylvie Best." She pauses. "Okay, my application number, well let me look that up here right fast."

I shake my head at her atrocious Southern dialect while I look up the application number online. I scribble it on a notepad and slide it across the desk.

"Five-five-four-three-three-six-seven." Another pause. "Why, no, ma'am, I did not withdraw and/or cancel my application. Can you please look and see who did? You can't tell me? Well, why not?" A pause. "Privacy protection?" Avery scowls at me. "But, ma'am, you ain't runnin' no doctor's office, and this is *my* application we're talking about here."

Avery carries on for a few minutes and says, "Well, can I reinstate it?" She looks at me and rolls her eyes. "Well, why not? I didn't want it canceled to begin with!" She loses her grip on that faux country twang but quickly recovers and gets back to rolling her vowels out long and flat. "Did my fee get refunded?" I shrug my shoulder because I don't know. "I don't know." She pauses a beat and says, "Did you refund it to me?" Another pause. "Well, if you didn't then I guess I didn't get a refund, now, did I?"

I shake my head, thinking that if I wasn't already out of the running, they would certainly disqualify me now for being so redneckish and rude. She wraps up her hillbilly dialect and then places her phone in her lap. I can see she's upset, so I try to make light of the situation.

"Avery," I say, "you think I sound like that. Really?"

"What? I watched *The Beverly Hillbillies* when I was a kid."

I start laughing and tell her she deserves an Oscar for that performance, insulting though it was. She finally cracks a smile and we discuss what was said, and she tells me that my application was marked as a cancellation, but they wouldn't tell her who did it.

"Well, we know who did it or had it done or whatever, so that's fine."

"I'm so sorry, Ace. The judging is over, but they haven't started the official notification process yet." She looks at me. "Lenore knew exactly when to come in here and tell you this. She had to know it would be too late for you to do anything about it." She sighs. "That lame-ass lady on the phone said that Lenore and Sylvie's misconduct would be 'duly noted.'"

"I'm sure it won't be, but who cares?" I say, even though I really do. "Avery, it does make me feel a lot better to know that my submission wasn't even judged. I mean, that's way better than sitting here thinking they didn't think it was good enough."

"I guess," Avery says, shaking her head.

"Does Caboose Charity have anything to do with the art festival?" I ask. "Or do you know?"

"I know that there is one little group of women that gets involved with everything that goes on around here, and it might not surprise you to know that Lenore Kennashaw and Sylvie Best are the ringleaders of that little group." She looks at me. "Don't you get the paper? They're in there almost every week for something."

"Hmm," I say. "I think I'm going to do a little investigating."

"Investigating or stalking?" Avery asks, giving me a wary look.

"I'll start with an investigation"—I smile—"and only resort to stalking if it's absolutely necessary."

"You are a bad influence on me," she says, getting up.

"Avery," I say, and she turns around at the door. "Thank you. For doing that."

"No problem," she says.

"I mean, your impersonation was extremely abusive to my self-esteem, but I appreciate it nonetheless."

She laughs and goes upstairs after making sure that I don't need her to man the front counter.

28

◇◇

I call Jalena when I leave the gallery to see what she's doing, and she says she was about to call to ask me the same thing. She mentions Credo's, and as much as I'd love to meet her there and get as drunk as a barber's pole, I know I have to pass. I don't need to be anywhere Kevin Jacobs might even think about showing up, because I'm almost sure I'd do something stupid.

I invite her to my house and she offers to bring a pizza, and even though I've already had pizza two times today, I tell her to bring it on. Because today is a good day to eat pizza all day long. When she arrives thirty minutes later, Buster Loo falls head-over-heels in love as soon as she walks in the door, and even after the pizza boxes are long gone, he stays as close to her as he can possibly get.

I bring up Lenore Kennashaw and she acts like she doesn't really want to talk about her, but when I tell her how she's been terrorizing me for the past several weeks, she softens up a bit.

"That's Olivia's mother-in-law, and I think the world of Josh." She looks at me. "Josh is Olivia's husband, and he's a great guy, so I try to keep my mouth shut because I don't want to cause them any more problems than what they've already got being kin to her, you know?"

"So Josh is nice?" I ask, not even trying to hide my surprise.

"Josh is an amazing man," Jalena says. "He is *so* good to Olivia and the kids, and he even remembers *my* birthday every year."

"How did he turn out like that?" I ask. "Did he take after his father?"

"Oh no." Jalena shakes her head. "Frank Kennashaw is just as bad as Lenore, if not worse, and Olivia says they embarrassed and humiliated Josh pretty much nonstop when he was growing up. Olivia and I figure he turned out so good because he must have a powerful desire *not* to be like his parents."

"Why doesn't he move away?" I ask.

"Well, he wanted to. After he went to college, he didn't want to move home, but he was dating Olivia hot and heavy by the time he graduated, so he came back and he's still here." She looks at me. "That's actually one of the few ways Olivia and I *are* alike. Neither one of us will ever leave Pelican Cove, because, you know, this is home."

"So what does Josh do?" I ask, ignoring all the emotions stirred up by that last comment.

"He owns a big landscaping business and just tries to get along with his parents as best he can. They make it hard on him, but he sticks to his boundaries. For example, the Kennashaws like to have these big knock-down, drag out brawls during the holidays and stuff, but Josh won't have any part of it. And that works out great for Olivia, because they're always at my parents' house for Thanksgiving and Christmas. They go the 'Kennashaw Brawl,' as Olivia calls it, either before or after the actual holiday. Never on it."

"That's terrible."

"Naw, it's really not," she says. "Josh makes it all work. When he sees the trouble brewing, he gathers up his brood and makes a hasty exit. All smiles all the time. That's Josh Kennashaw."

I start laughing and ask if Josh has any brothers or sisters. She tells me that he has a brother who plans on taking over the family business.

"He'll run Kennashaw Home and Garden straight into the ground," Jalena says. "He's dumb as a box of rocks. When Mr. Frank dies, that business is gonna go with him. It's just barely limpin' along as it is, but you sure can't tell that by how Lenore acts." She shakes her head in disgust. "Ridin' around in that big fancy Mercedes like she can afford it. I can't stand that woman."

"So can we talk about her for a second?" I ask. "And I assure you that whatever you tell me will not leave this house."

Jalena gives in and tells me all kinds of awful stories about how Lenore has ruined birthday parties, baby showers, and Sunday dinners but doesn't mention anything about Charity Caboose.

"I think she's a fraud and I want to expose her," I say. "Show her socialite friends who she really is." I look at Jalena. "But I know you can't be a part of anything like that."

"She is a fraud and actually I can," Jalena says. "It's just that no one can know."

"Too easy," I say and act like I'm zipping my lips.

"I already know a way to knock her down a notch or two," Jalena says in a conspiratorial tone that I like. "Lenore runs Caboose—you know that, right?" I nod to indicate that I do. "Well, that's just one more reason she makes me sick, because that organization does a lot of good things for underprivileged kids, and it deserves to have better leadership than what it's got." I point at her. "No! That ain't me! That's not what I'm saying at all. I just like to volunteer and help out and stuff. What I'm saying is that there are a lot of respectable people in that organization, and dang near any of 'em would make a better chairman than her."

"So what do you have in mind?" I ask.

"Well, she's never going to step down, so what we need to do is take her down."

"Can we do that?" I ask, getting excited.

"I think so," Jalena says with a devilish grin. "And if you're serious about this, we need to get a move on, because our annual fund-raiser, the Caboose Charity Ball, is weekend after next, and I can't think of a better time to jerk her off that high horse."

"I am so serious about this," I tell her as my brain goes into overdrive. "Who can go to that fund-raiser thing?"

"Anyone who buys a ticket," Jalena says. "Why? Do you have someone in mind? I mean, besides you?"

"I have a few people in mind. Some friends of mine from Bugtussle," I say and tell her all about Gloria Peacock and Birdie Ross. "They're some feisty little old ladies and they love me like family, so when I tell them what's going on, I'm almost sure they'll come down."

"They sound really cool, but what would they do?"

"Just rub Lenore and Sylvie the wrong way like they've been doing to me for the past month." I look at her. "Gloria Peacock has the money and Birdie Ross has the mouth."

"Got it," Jalena says. "All right, so let me tell you what I've got on my mind, and then we can come up with a way to use it."

"Okay," I say, and I'm so excited to be up to no good with Jalena.

"The people who fund Charity Caboose are seated at the annual fund-raising gala according their contribution category, which doesn't make the most sense when you think about how secretive they are about who gives what. I mean, they don't want anyone to know *exactly* how much a person or an organization gives, but it's okay to publicize *about* how much. Whatever. Anyway, they do it by stars. Like, the five-star people donate the really big money: over ten thousand a year. Four-stars give five to ten thousand, three-stars give one to five, and two-stars give less than a thousand."

"Wow! Those are some high-dollar categories!"

"Well, there are some high-dollar people around here, if you haven't noticed," she says. "Like Avery's dad, Dr. Cambre. He's a five-star and so are most of his friends."

"Wow."

"Tia is a four-star."

"Seriously?"

"Tia makes a *lot* of money," Jalena says.

"Well, she works hard enough, so I'm glad to hear it," I say. "So is there a one-star?" I ask, thinking that would be the category I'd fit into with all the money I haven't been making at my fancy new art gallery.

"One-stars just donate their time," she says. "Like me, because I don't have a lot of money."

"That's so sweet," I tell her and decide that I'm going to start donating some of my time and maybe some of Mason's money to Caboose Charity. Right after we get rid of Lenore Kennashaw.

"Yeah, well, like I said, it's a great cause," she says, waving off my praise. "Anyway, since Lenore got herself elected chairwoman a few years back, she's been seating herself at the five-star tables, and I know for a fact that she only gives five hundred dollars a year, which is the minimum required to be eligible for election to the board."

"How do you know that?" I ask.

"Tia didn't tell you about me sneaking into the office and having a look at the financial records?"

"No."

"She said she did," Jalena says, giving me a funny look.

"Okay, yeah, she did," I say. "She told me about that the first time we had lunch, which was the day after my grand opening, when I had the displeasure of meeting Lenore for the first time." My cheeks are burning from embarrassment. "I just didn't want to rat her out."

"She told me she felt like she could trust you," Jalena says, smiling. "I guess she was right."

"I'm a vault," I say, thinking Tia can trust me all day long with a secret but better not give me thirty seconds unattended with her boyfriend or whatever he is.

Jalena says, "I can get in there and get those copies she told you about. Caboose has to keep meticulous records, but they don't have any kind of security system because no money is ever left in the office and all you have to do is slip a credit card in the crack of the door and it's open." I raise my eyebrows and look at her. "Don't even ask, okay? Let's just say I was on a date with a guy and was feeling a little adventurous and there's a nice view from the roof." Her phone beeps and she looks down. "Speaking of, it looks like I might get to see Luke tonight."

"Who is Luke again?" I ask because I can't keep her men straight.

"He's the one I went out with last Friday night."

"Gotcha," I say. "You get on about your business, and we'll finish planning this tomorrow night."

"Girl, Luke can wait a minute," she says, moving her thumbs across her phone at the speed of light. "Don't need him thinking I'm too excited about seeing him, even though I really am." She giggles and then looks up at me. "Plus we've got to get this plan together ASAP!"

"Hold on," I say. I jump up and go to the study, where I dig a notebook out of the desk cabinet. I grab a pencil, a pen, and a highlighter and go back to the living room.

"You are too prepared," Jalena says as I flip open the notebook.

"Teacher habits," I tell her. "They stay with you. Now, tell me all about this fund-raising event."

"Let's see, it's a black-tie affair with a catered buffet table and a full bar that serves drinks weak as well water. I told you about the stars and how that determines who sits where, and that's a big-time status thing because the charity ball is pretty much the social event of the year— here in the Cove, anyway—and then there's an auction of things people donated—"

"Uh, I'd like to say that I'll have three paintings in that auction."

"Oh, so you won't have to buy a ticket then, because they gave you one when you made the donation, right?" She looks at me. "Wrong?"

"Wrong," I tell her. "They didn't give me a ticket."

"What about when they picked the stuff up?"

"Kevin Jacobs picked it up," I say and blush despite my best effort not to. Jalena notices but doesn't say a word. "That was the first time I met him," I say, looking at the floor.

She looks at me for what seems like ten hours.

"What?" I say, finally.

"Nothing," she says, smiling.

"Moving on," I say. "Was I supposed to get a ticket?"

She's still looking at me funny. "I'll make sure you get your ticket and one for Mason, too," she says, finally. "We have a meeting sched-uled for Monday night, so I'll pick those up then." She starts talking about the fund-raiser again, and my ears perk up when she mentions a program brochure. I ask her to elaborate on the program, and she says that the first half is all pictures and articles about what Caboose has accomplished since the previous charity ball. "There are a few pages of advertisements, and then, in the very back, all of the benefac-tors are listed according to their 'star' ranking." She looks at me. "Again, that's a major status thing because only the biggest of the big shots can afford that five-star ranking. At first Frank and Lenore just *sat* with the big shots, which was plenty pathetic enough, but last year when Kennashaw Home and Garden was actually *listed* in the program as a five-star patron, that's when I decided to do some investigating."

"With your man friend?"

"No, I did that by myself after I found out how easy it was to get in." She looks at me. "What I would love to do is get Lenore in the right category."

"Have the programs already been printed?"

"I'm sure," she says. "Why?"

"Do you know if the programs are in the same building with the records?"

"I'm sure they are." She narrows her eyes. "What's on your mind?"

"Maybe we should add a little announcement to the program," I say. "Something small, stuck in the middle, that would fall out when someone flipped through it. Like those magazine subscription cards."

"Saying what?"

"You said Kennashaw Home and Garden gets the five-star treatment, but it's only a two-star contributor, right?" She nods. "Well, then, I think we should add a correction. Along with the amount that they actually donate."

"It would take forever to do that," Jalena protests. "There'll be like five hundred programs and then the first person who saw one would take it straight to Lenore and then nobody would get another program until they checked each and every individual program."

"How about this? When you go to that meeting next week, check and see if the programs are still in the building. If they are, let's make fifty postcard-sized leaflets proclaiming the truth about Lenore Kennashaw, and while you're in the office making copies of the evidence you already found proving her puny donations, I'll pick a random box and get to work stuffing programs. The ones containing our little cards might be the first ones handed out at the charity ball or they might be the last, but either way, everyone doesn't need to see the actual announcement." I give Jalena a knowing look.

"We just need a few people to see it," she says, understanding.

"Then it'll spread like a wildfire. It's like a warped use of supply and demand. Maybe a few of the people who find our little addendum will realize they've got something scandalous and then hang on to it so they can show it off."

"I kind of hate to do this at the fund-raiser because, you know, it's raising money for the kids," Jalena says.

"Will any of the kids be there that night?"

"No."

"Well, then, I don't see a problem, because what we're doing really is in the best interest of the organization, right? And the money will still be raked in, right?"

"Well, yeah," she says slowly.

"Girl, we're just gonna put some extra 'fun' in the annual fund-raiser."

"You know what would be even better?" Jalena says. "If we could get her name card moved to a different table." She starts giggling. "Then she would be over there looking for her seat with the big shots and wouldn't be able to find it." She gets up and mimics what Lenore would look like as she tried to find her seat. I laugh until my side hurts, and Buster Loo runs circles around Jalena's feet, barking and wagging his tail. "If we could get those place cards swapped around, that would be great, because the committee that sets up the seating chart strictly forbids seat swapping." She looks at me. "But that's going to be hard to do because they guard that place like a tomb after they set everything up."

"Even at night?" I ask.

"The gala is held in the conference center at the Downtown Inn, and I'm pretty sure they keep it locked up day and night even when nothing is going on."

"We'll think about that, and I'm sure we can figure something out."

"Oh, I just thought of one more thing," Jalena says. "They have valet parking for this event even though the parking lot is just across the street, so wouldn't it be hilarious if when she left, we could have some kind of crappy car waiting on her instead of her Mercedes?"

"That would be so freakin' hilarious!" I think about the station wagon. "And I might actually have a way to arrange that." I tell her all about Erlene Pettigo rolling into the back of my car at Bueno Burrito, then how I met her at the Peanut Festival and she said her husband might let me drive the station wagon while he fixed my car.

"Oh, that would be too much," Jalena says, laughing, then starts shaking her head. "But there ain't no way all of this is gonna work, because it would be too perfect."

"We have to try," I tell her. "We can try it all and hope *some* of it works, and if it all falls flat, then we'll just have to come up with a new plan."

"I like the way you think," Jalena says, laughing. "Check into that paddy wagon."

"Okay, but if I do get it, how are we going to get it to the curb instead of the Mercedes?"

"A fifty-dollar bill and some cleavage will go a long way with a valet," she says with a smile. Her phone beeps again, and after she looks at it, she tells me that Luke can hardly wait any longer.

"You take off," I tell her. "I'll see you tomorrow night."

"Girls Night In!" she says, walking toward the door. "Hey, don't say anything about this in front of Olivia," she tells me. "We need to get

Tia in on it if we can, but not Olivia, because when her husband asks her if she knows anything about how it all happened, I don't want her to have to lie."

"Let's just hope something will happen that she won't have to lie about," I say, getting up.

"Right. But who knows, Ace, we might get lucky!" she says on her way to the door. Buster Loo follows her, watches her leave, and then starts his most pitiful whimpering.

"C'mon, little man," I tell him, walking into the kitchen, because that gets him every time. "I bet I can find you an olive."

29

◇◇

I call Tia on the way to work on Thursday, and we discuss drinks and snacks for Girls Night In. I suggest more appetizers and she suggests BYOB, and I tell her that's a great idea because her World Famous Magic Punch nearly killed me last week. She gets a kick out of that and then thanks me for volunteering the gallery as the permanent Girls Night In venue.

"Yeah," I say, wondering if I'll ever remember saying that. "Well, it's the perfect place."

"It is," she says. "Hey, you want to have lunch today?"

"Sure," I say.

"Blue Oyster at noon?"

"I'll see you then." I hang up feeling apprehensive because my feelings about Kevin have yet to subside, despite my best efforts not to think about him. I really like Tia and want us to be good friends, so maybe the more I hang around her, the less I'll be crushing on Kevin, because being a shitball friend is not really my thing.

I get to the gallery at fifteen minutes past ten and don't even care that I'm late. Buster Loo hops out of the car and runs into the bushes like a rabbit on crack, and it takes me fifteen minutes to get him out of there. I hook his leash to his collar right about the time two squirrels launch themselves out of the shrubbery and scamper across the parking lot. He takes off and almost chokes himself trying to give chase. When we finally get to the door, Buster Loo notices a lizard on the sidewalk and pounces on it. A brutal battle ensues in which the lizard loses its tail, but I manage to get Buster Loo pulled inside before he eats the poor thing whole.

Once in the gallery, he starts wagging his tail and looking at me like he's been a really, really good dog. I unhook him and he prances around, reinvestigating the place, and I'm happy with my decision to make every day a bring-a-chiweenie-to-work day.

Despite the good company of my dog, the morning still creeps by at a snail's pace. A nice couple from Michigan drops by and they think Buster Loo is the greatest little dog they've ever seen, so I don't even care that they leave without even pretending they might buy something. A few more people breeze in and out, and one lady does more than breeze out when Buster Loo sneaks up on her and scares her. She jumps and shrieks, which scares him, so he starts to growl and bark, and she looks at me like I threw a rattlesnake at her and hustles out the door in a huff. Again, Buster Loo looks at me and wags his tail like he's being the best dog ever.

I take him out for a short walk, then fluff his bed and fill up his water bowl before leaving to meet Tia for lunch. I'm dying to ask her about her relationship with Kevin, but I don't because I'm not a good liar and would hate to blow my cover by blurting out something about how bad I want to see his penis. So we make small talk and have a very nice lunch, and I leave there even more jealous of her than I was before. When I get back to the gallery, I find Avery sitting in the parking lot, waiting. I apologize as I unlock the door and go immediately into my office and get her a key.

"I don't know why I haven't given you this already," I tell her.

"Maybe you don't really trust me," she jokes. "Maybe you secretly think I'd loot the place."

"Right," I say. "You got me. I have you pegged as a thief." I roll my eyes at her, and she smiles. "I just had lunch with Tia, and she was asking if you were coming to the Girls Night In. Are you?" I ask her.

"I wouldn't miss it for the world," Avery says. I tell her it's BYOB and she tells me that since last week's snack from Eden's Treats went so well, she's going to bring another one of her favorite dishes from there. I tell her I think that's great and secretly hope she doesn't bring something awful and get her feelings hurt if no one eats it.

I don't talk to Mason all afternoon, because he's apparently having a busy day, so I remind him via text message that I won't be joining him for dinner in the conference room because it's Girls Night In again. He texts back and says he'll pick up some extra aspirin on the way home. I smile, thinking how happy we could be if we could just spend some time together. I remind myself that I was the one working around the clock before I opened the gallery, so the least I can do is afford him the same amount of patience. I assure myself that we'll get out of this relationship funk when he finishes up the case for Mr. Marks. Because things have to get better.

Avery wants to take Buster Loo out for a walk, and after she leaves with him, I spend a few minutes cleaning up the place. When they get back, it's almost closing time, so we go our separate ways in search of drinks and snacks.

I stop by the grocery store because I know we don't have anything in the fridge and end up spending six times what I'd planned, but that's okay, because I like to have things like milk and cheese and Oreo cookies in the house. I go home, and I'm in the middle of making my signature seven-layer bean dip when I realize I forgot to buy chips. I glance at the clock on the stove and see that I'm going to be late if I don't get going. I look around for Buster Loo because I want to tell him good-bye, and find him curled up in his deluxe doggie bed. I smile because he's all tuckered out from a big day.

Since I'm already running late, I forgo a trip to Discount Liquors and pick up a slightly more expensive six-pack at the grocery store. Beer in hand, I'm speed-walking down the chip aisle when I hear someone call my name. I look around and see that damn Lenore Kennashaw coming up behind me. She smiles and waves and I turn back around and keep walking. A minute later, I'm scanning the chip bags looking for that one particular brand I like to have with my bean dip when she pushes her buggy in front of me and starts talking like we're old friends. I keep scanning the chips, completely ignoring her.

Then she snaps her fingers in front of my face and says, "Talking! Talking to you!" I look at her and she stops snapping her fingers. She smiles at me and says, "Good, now that I have your attention—"

"Lenore," I say, cutting her off by putting my hand up in her face. "If you *ever* snap your fingers at me again, I swear to you that I will break them off your hand and shove them up your ass sideways. Got it?" Not the best line I've ever come up with, but it'll do for today.

While she's gasping with her hand on her chest, I finally locate the chips I want, so I push her buggy out of my way and grab two bags. Before I walk away, I look at her and wink. Then I laugh out loud like a crazy person all the way down the chip aisle while the black dog in my mind howls triumphantly.

30

◇◇

When I pull up at the gallery, everyone is already inside.

"I hope it's okay that I used my key," Avery says in a quiet voice.

"Well, it is this time, but if you do it again, I'll probably have you arrested," I say and then have to tell her six times that I'm joking. "This is exactly why I gave you a key, Avery," I say finally, and she tells me not to joke like that because she's already nervous about the Bianca pizza she brought to the party. I tell her to stop worrying about that, too, because if no one eats it, then she'll have more leftovers for herself. That seems to make her feel better and she starts acting normal again. Well, normal for her.

We eat and chat and have a good time, and when we retire to the couches, I get a kick out of the beverage variety. I have a Corona, Avery has a four-pack of mini wine bottles, Olivia's sipping on some kind of watermelon mojito, and Jalena is drinking Mad Dog 20/20. Tia, however, is drinking water, so I guess she won't be calling her designated driver tonight.

"I just want y'all to know that while I *am* drinking, I have no plans to get drunk," Olivia announces as she sets her bottle down on the end table beside her. "I was so ill last Friday that I almost killed my damn mother-in-law."

"You know, I just saw your mother-in-law at the grocery store," I say.

"I'm sorry," Olivia says and starts sniggering.

"At first she tried to be nice, which was really weird," I say. "Then she snapped her fingers in my face."

"Who does that?" Avery asks, and Tia just shakes her head.

"Oh lordy," Olivia moans. "You shoulda slapped her right in the mouth."

"I thought that would be too harsh, so instead I told her if she ever did it again, I'd break her fingers off and stick them up her ass sideways."

"Oh no, you didn't," Jalena says and starts hee-haw laughing. Olivia leans over and gives me a high five, and then when I tell her that I winked at Lenore before I walked off, she gives me a double high five. Tia laughs a little but not much. Jalena picks up on her lack of enthusiasm and asks her if something is wrong.

"No," Tia says with a sigh.

"You don't feel like drinking?" Avery asks, and I'm glad she did so I didn't have to.

"No, I don't have a designated driver," she says, and everyone gets quiet.

"What's up with that?" Jalena asks cautiously.

"Oh, who knows?" Tia shrugs. "He's already called and said he wouldn't be available tonight. Wait, I'm sorry, did I say 'called'? I meant to say 'texted' because he's stopped calling." She stops talking and I take a big swig of beer because that statement just ripped my nerves to shreds.

"Is it some kind of hunting season?" Olivia asks.

"I don't know and I wish I didn't care," Tia says. "I don't want to talk about it."

I want to scream that I want to talk about it, but of course I can't so I look at Jalena and ask how it went with Luke last night.

"It went very well," Jalena says, grinning from ear to ear.

"Obviously," Olivia says. "Because you're here and not hacked up dead in a ditch somewhere, right?"

"Right," Jalena says, making a face at her sister. "But really, I'm afraid he's going to be another one that turns out to be a little too good, if you know what I mean."

"How could he be *too* good?" Avery asks.

"Well," Jalena says, "it's been my experience that when a man seems too good to be true, he's usually on the hunt for some, shall we say, supplemental sexual favors? In addition to, you know, what he gets from the wife or steady girlfriend he's never gonna break up with."

"Or he could just be a really nice guy who's also a mass murderer in search of his next victim," Olivia says.

"Shut up, Olivia," Jalena says in the nicest way I've ever heard anyone say that. "I think I'll drive by his house later and see what's up."

"How do you know where he lives?" Avery asks.

"I've seen his driver's license," Jalena says. "Anytime I go out with someone I've met online, I always start up a conversation about my driver's license photo, and then whatever he says about his, well, I don't believe a word of it until he hands it over. That way I can do two things. One, see if he's using his real name, and two, see where he lives."

"Slick," I say with genuine admiration.

"Have you ever caught someone using a different name?" Avery wants to know.

"There was this one guy who wouldn't let me see his license," Jalena says. "So I pretended I was silencing my phone and snapped a picture of him; then I went straight to the ladies' room and texted it to Olivia. I told her exactly where I was and instructed her to call the police if she didn't hear from me by a certain time."

"I love getting messages like that from my baby sister." Olivia looks at Jalena. "Call the police in two hours because I'm probably getting raped by this ax murderer I just sent you a fuzzy picture of." Olivia shakes her head and laughs. "Man, I wish you would stop finding men online."

"I will when I find the right one," Jalena says.

"I don't believe you're looking in the right place to find the right one," Olivia says.

"Thank you, Olivia." Jalena snorts.

"So where does this guy live?" I ask.

"Eighty-nine fifty-six Briar Bay Circle in Pelican Cove, Florida."

"Well, let's go drive by and see what's up!" I say, but I get a mixed response.

"I'm game," Tia says. "I haven't had a drop to drink and my truck has tinted windows, so y'all grab one for the road and let's go see what we can find out about this guy."

After Olivia and Avery reluctantly agree to go along, Jalena says she has to run out to her car before we leave. A few minutes later, we're all loaded up in Tia's Tahoe, and the fact that I'm so excited about doing something so crazy makes me wonder if my life has gotten a bit too dull.

Jalena, who is in the front passenger seat, starts digging around in her bag and a moment later pulls out something that looks like a small satellite dish.

"Are we going to watch some cable on your iPhone?" Tia asks, eyeing the apparatus.

"Oh no," Jalena says, putting on a set of headphones that looks like something an air traffic controller would have worn in 1987. "Y'all be quiet a minute and let me do a test run on this thing."

We all pipe down and I'm leaning up watching Jalena mess with some buttons on the handheld part of the device when Olivia hollers, "Hey, what are you doing up there? Did you bring that silly little spy machine of yours?"

Jalena jerks the headset off her head and sticks her fingers in her ears and shakes her head. "Dammit!" she exclaims. "Yes, Olivia, I brought my silly little spy machine and now I'll be tone-deaf for the rest of my life."

"What is it really?" I ask.

"It's called a directional sound device."

"Where did you get it?" I ask, marveling.

"Got if off eBay for seventy-five bucks," she replies.

"What a bargain!" Olivia says, and Avery starts giggling.

"Okay, it's the next road to the right," Jalena tells Tia.

"Why am I doing this?" Olivia cries from the backseat.

"Because it's fun," I tell her. "You know you're having a blast."

"Right down there," Jalena says, pointing. "Olivia, please, I beg you, don't say anything when I put these back on."

"Okay, I won't. I promise," Olivia whispers.

"Just drive by real slow—" Jalena says.

"I wish there was a way you could hook your spy machine up to the speakers so we could all hear what's going on!" Olivia bellows, and Jalena rips off the headphones and turns and scowls at her sister.

"Oops, sorry," Olivia says, grinning. "Won't happen again." Jalena puts her headset back on and turns around.

I lean back and whisper to Olivia that I think that's a really awesome idea. Without turning around, Jalena calls, "I can hear you!"

Tia rolls up beside a mailbox with 8956 painted on the side, and Jalena turns her baby satellite toward the house. Tia and I lean toward Jalena, and I can hear noise coming through the earphones. As we creep slowly past the house, Jalena turns the listening device, holding it steady.

Tia taps her on the arm and points to the rearview mirror. "Someone's coming," she whispers.

"Go, then," Jalena whispers back, and Tia accelerates.

"Well," Olivia shouts from the backseat after Jalena takes off the headset, "what did you hear?"

"Nothing really," Jalena says. "There was a lot of background noise. Probably the TV."

"Well, there were two bikes and a tricycle in the front yard, if that helps any," Olivia offers.

"What do you think he drives?" Avery asks. "The Ford truck or the Nissan minivan?"

"There was a minivan?" Jalena says, whirling around.

"Parked in the carport, yes."

"Well, looks like I didn't need my high-tech spying device to figure this one out."

"No, but it did make the entire experience that much cooler," I say.

"Oh well." Jalena sighs. "Another one bites the dust."

On the drive back, Olivia tells us some hilarious stories about what her kids have been doing, I tell them about seeing my neighbors sporting goggles and kitchen gloves while out on poop patrol, and then

Avery shocks us all by quietly mentioning that she has a new romantic interest.

"What?" I say. "Why didn't you say something earlier?"

"It's not official," Avery says, blushing. "We're just talking."

"What does that *mean*?" Olivia asks her. "Just talking."

"I don't know. It means we're, like, just talking," Avery says.

"Olivia, you've been out of the game too long," Jalena says. "You're just talking when you're interested in each other but haven't decided yet if you want to date or just bone."

Even Tia starts laughing at that explanation.

"So do you have a picture of him?" I ask, thinking of Jacques Le Sumay formerly known as Jason Smith, who I had imagined looked like a cross between Andy Dick and a long-haired Nicolas Cage.

"Yes," she says, giggling. Avery pokes around in her hobo bag until she comes up with her phone. She hands it to Olivia first.

"Oh, he's handsome," Olivia says with a genuine smile, so I start thinking that maybe he is, because he needs to be if he's interested in Avery.

Olivia hands the phone to me and I turn it around to see the ugliest dude I've ever laid eyes on in my whole entire life. He looks like Donatella Versace with a blue mohawk. I glance up at Avery, who is looking at me expectantly. Then I look at Olivia, whose eyes are round like saucers, and she kind of shakes her head back and forth as if to say *not really handsome!* I look back down at Avery's phone and say, "He's adorable!" then pass it to Jalena.

Jalena looks at the picture, dies out laughing, and says, "Good one, Avery, now show us what he really looks like." She holds the phone up for Tia to see, and Tia doesn't say a word. I look back at Avery and she looks like she's about to cry.

"That *is* what he really looks like," she says, and Jalena looks like she wants to die.

Tia jerks the phone out of Jalena's hand and says, "Don't listen to her, Avery. She doesn't know anything about men. Remember that story she told us last week about Travis?" Tia looks down at the phone. "He has really nice, uh, lips."

I almost bite through my own lip trying not to laugh. Tia hands the phone back to me and I give it back to Avery without looking at it or her.

"He can't help it he's ugly," Avery whines, and the rest of us start lying like dogs and telling her how ugly he isn't. Then Olivia gives her a speech about how the only thing that really matters is the way he treats her, to which Avery replies, "He said his last girlfriend broke up with him because he was too nice."

"Well, good," Olivia says in her most motherly tone. "You're a beautiful young lady inside and out, and you deserve a very nice guy."

When we get back to the gallery, everyone starts gathering up their stuff and I'm sad the night has already come to an end.

"What are we eating next week?" Jalena says.

"How do y'all feel about Mexican?" I say.

"Sounds good to me," Avery says.

Tia, Olivia, and I call off a few dishes we might fix, and Avery volunteers to furnish tortilla chips and fresh guacamole.

"I'll bring the tequila," Jalena says. "My cooking skills leave much to be desired, especially when I venture off into international dishes."

"She's telling y'all the God's honest truth," Olivia says. "I promise."

"Thank you, Olivia."

We cackle about that, then say our good-byes and good nights, and after everyone walks outside, I make a round through the gallery turning off lights. When I walk out into the parking lot a few minutes later,

Jalena is just leaving and Tia is standing on the sidewalk. She walks over to me with a sly look in her eye.

"Hey," she says quietly. "I've got a little project I need you and Jalena to help me with."

"Great! What is it?"

"We'll get to that," she says. "Can you meet us at Credo's tomorrow night at seven?"

"Of course I can, because, as you know, that's only, like, three blocks from my house." I smile because I'll get to skip another conference room dinner. "Don't leave me hanging here, Tia. What's up?"

"I'll tell you tomorrow." She smiles. "And we're going to discuss all of that other business that you and Jalena talked about last night, too."

"Okay, then," I say, waving.

31

<><><><><><><><><><><><><><><><><><><><><><><><><><><><><><><><><><><><>

Mason isn't home when I go to bed, and he's gone by the time I get up, so I kind of hate to text and tell him I can't make it to dinner in the conference room, but I do. Tia has my curiosity stirred up way past what would normally be considered appropriate, but I can't help that I'm obsessed with her shady designated driver.

I take Buster Loo to work, and not a soul graces the doorway until Avery comes in at one. We have a few afternoon visitors, and after they leave, I start wondering if I'll ever get used to my gallery being treated like a museum rather than a place where things are actually available for purchase. I tell myself that I should welcome the interest in and appreciation for my work, but at the end of the day, it just seems like one more thing I have to add to the list of things that *have* to be okay with me these days.

Before we leave at five o'clock, Avery tells me about some kind of bohemian party she's going to at Seville Square with the Mohawk guy, whose name is actually Rob.

"Just Rob?" I ask. "That's it?"

"Yep," she says. "Just Rob. Rob Evans."

"Well, I think it's a good sign that he hasn't changed it to El Roberto Leon Evawashu or something."

"Right," she says, rolling her eyes.

I drive home and, when I turn in to the subdivision, can't help but notice a new sign has been put up at the entrance. I slow down to get a closer look at the plywood fixture and see that four little green bags have been tacked up in each of the corners. Underneath each bag is an address.

"Oh, you have got to be kidding me," I say to myself. I stop the car and roll down the window so I can read the large-print notice posted in the center of the board.

It says WARNING TO RESIDENTS WHO REFUSE TO PICK UP AFTER THEIR PETS! START USING THE GREEN BAGS OR DNA TESTING WILL BEGIN SOON! Then there is a little smiley face followed by the letters "MK."

Buster Loo, who has wormed his way up to the open window, is having a field day sniffing the air. I grab his hind legs so he doesn't try to jump out, because he's carrying on like he really needs a better sniff of that sign. I roll up the window, drive a few blocks, and see Roger outside with Moses. I decide to stop and talk about the new sign.

"Hey, Ace," he calls as I get out of the car. I don't let Buster Loo out because I'm certain he would make a break for the dooky board and I don't feel like chasing him all the way back up there. "How are you today, young lady?"

"I'm good, Roger. Thank you." Moses runs up and starts sniffing my feet. I lean down to pet him, and Buster Loo starts barking like crazy in the car. "How are you?"

"Couldn't be better if I tried," Roger says, leaning on his rake. "Did you happen to notice our new neighborhood sign?"

"Yeah, that looks nice," I tell him. "Smells good, too. You know, I saw Margo and Cindy walking down the street wearing safety goggles and kitchen gloves, picking up dog crap and putting it in those little green bags." I stop and think for a second. "But that was like a week ago."

He looks at me and shakes his head. "You think they froze it while Margo had poor Liam make the sign?"

I shudder with disgust and ask Roger how long he thinks it will be before someone makes Margo make Liam take it down.

"I've already called Phillip Wheatley," Roger says gruffly. "He's one of the few board members with a grain of sense." He looks at me. "What's going to be funny is if they send all of that in for DNA testing and find they've got four bags of shit from deer and stray dogs because everyone around here picks up after their pets and they always have. It's never been a problem until Margo took over the neighborhood."

"I bet that's what they were doing in your yard that night," I tell him. "Looking for a little Moses turd for their collection." Moses looks up at me and I tell him again how adorable he is.

"I bet that's exactly what they were doing," Roger says, snapping his fingers and laughing. "Well, they must not have found anything since my address didn't make the display."

"Mine, either." We talk some more and he asks about Mason, and then we talk about the weather for a minute and I say good-bye. I drive the short distance down to my house and carry Buster Loo inside, and he runs straight out the back door. I go outside and play fetch for a while with him, then go upstairs and freshen up a bit. At fifteen minutes before seven, I walk into the kitchen and open the cabinet to get Buster Loo a good-bye treat. When I open the cabinet, I notice Mason's binoculars on the shelf above the dog biscuits. I don't know what kind of adventure Tia has planned, but I like to be prepared, so I grab those to stick in my purse. I toss Buster Loo his snack and then head out the door for the short walk down to Credo's.

I walk past Tia's Tahoe, which is parked right next to Jalena's Jeep Cherokee, and as I climb the steps to the door, I become a nervous freakin' wreck, because if Kevin Jacobs is in here I might have a heart attack and die on the spot. I don't see his truck, but that doesn't mean that he didn't come on foot like I did. I start thinking again about how I need to get over this ridiculous crush. I take a deep breath and open the door.

I look around and don't see him or them inside. I walk to the door that leads out onto the deck and see Jalena and Tia at a table off to the side, but there is no sign of Kevin. Relieved, I go out and join them.

Jalena is sipping on a draft beer, and Tia is drinking Diet Pepsi, and I order a beer, then spend a few minutes hoping against hope that Kevin Jacobs doesn't show up tonight, because I just don't think I can handle it. We order appetizers and hot wings, then make small talk until I've had all I can stand and tell Tia that I have to know what's going on.

She looks at Jalena, then back at me.

"She wants to stalk her boyfriend," Jalena says quietly, looking down at her beer. "I told her we could do that."

"Kevin?" I ask, and my heart starts thumping. I drain my beer and raise my glass to the waitress, who promptly brings me another one. I get the feeling Jalena is watching me very carefully.

"He's not really my boyfriend," Tia whispers and looks around to make sure no one is paying attention, and even though we're the only good-looking chicks in a mostly dudes joint, we are, for the moment, flying under the radar. "We've just been having this"—she pauses and shrugs—"thing for a long time, and—"

"What kind of a thing?" I ask, because I simply have to know.

"Well, let me just tell you the whole story," she says, and I get that sick feeling like you do when you know someone is about to tell you something that you don't want to hear. "I was renovating a house a few years ago and I had hired him to do some major repair work because I'd moved some walls around and stuff. Well, he flirted with me like crazy, but I didn't think much of it because everybody in town knows he's a player, plus I'm older than him so I didn't think he would really be interested." Jalena and I both roll our eyes at this. "Anyway, I went to the house one night to see how things were coming along, and he was there finishing up some stuff, but his crew was gone. He had a cooler of beer in his truck like he always does, and we started drinking. Then he turned on a radio that one of his guys had left at the house, and, corny as this sounds, we started dancing—"

"Like slow dancing?" I ask, glad to feel a good buzz coming on before my nerves go completely haywire.

"Oh no, like club dancing. It was some hard-core bump and grind."

She starts giggling but stops when the waitress shows up at the table with our appetizers.

"Well, we ended up having sex in the bathroom upstairs, because that was the only room in the house that didn't have a huge window in it, because, of course, the house had no curtains." Tia's face turns bright red. "And we've been doing it ever since. That was almost five years ago."

"Y'all have been having sex in that same bathroom for five years?" I whisper, and Jalena cracks up.

"Of course not," Tia snaps.

"I was kidding," I say, wishing I would've just *not* said that.

"We always went to his house, because I decided way before he came along that I would never drag a man in and out of the house I shared with my daughter. We never actually discussed it; we just always kind of kept it on the down low."

"Right," I say, overcome with jealousy despite my increasing level of intoxication. I want to ask her how he is in the sack, but I feel like I already know. Men like Kevin Jacobs tend to be heaven in the bed and hell in a relationship. "So now since your daughter is off at college—" I look at Tia.

"Now that Afton is off at college, I'm having all of these feelings, and I'm not sure if it's because she's gone and I'm trying to fill that void or if I might possibly be in love with him."

"Oh my," I say, wondering how in the hell I wound up in the middle of a mess like this. I look up at Jalena, and she's looking at me funny again.

"So," Tia says with a sigh, and I'm on the verge of begging her to stop talking, but I know I *need* to keep listening. "I've been dropping little hints here and there, and he's kind of backed off these past few weeks, so I want to know what's going on but I don't want to make a fool of myself."

"So that's why you want to do some stalking?" I ask, and despite myself, I can't stop wondering if Kevin backed off because of the hints or because of me.

"Can we call it spying?" Tia asks.

"Sure," I say. "Why not?"

"You know, you could just ask him if he's seeing anybody else," Jalena says, and Tia assures her that she cannot and will not be the one to start that conversation.

"I'd talk about it if he brought it up," Tia says. "But I'm not putting myself in a position to get shot down like a sitting duck."

"Well, can't say I blame you for that," Jalena says, and I nod in agreement.

Tia clams up and looks like she's about to cry, and Jalena looks out at the bay. I don't say a word because I don't know what would be appropriate, and since I'm always erring on the side of inappropriate, I just sit there.

"I miss Afton," Tia says finally.

"Oh, Tia," Jalena says quietly. "I know you do."

"You know, it was just me and her for so long, and now she's at college and she's so busy and doesn't call me very often and—" She stops talking and tears up. "Sorry," she says, dabbing her cheeks with a napkin. "I've just been a basket case these past few days, and I don't know what to do, and to make matters worse, I'm too old to be having stupid problems like this."

"Girl, those women at the old-folks home are probably still having problems like this," Jalena says, smiling at Tia. "Some lady named Ethel is over there and she's got the hots for old man Jack, who doesn't like her because he's got a crush on Mabel, but Mabel only has eyes for Cecil, who just so happens to be madly in love with Ethel. Relationship problems are timeless."

We have a good laugh at that and Tia peps up a little, but not much.

"Go on," Jalena says, looking at her. "Get it all out. Whatever is on your mind. It'll make you feel better."

I just sit there like a knot on a log, nursing my beer and looking at Tia, who looks so pitiful it makes my heart ache. To make matter worse, my crush on Kevin Jacobs rages on, unaffected and unchecked, heaping mountains of guilt onto the mountains of guilt already piled up in my tormented conscience.

"After the divorce," Tia says, "I vowed not to date until Afton was out of the house. I didn't tell anyone I'd decided to do that because I knew everyone would get all upset and start nagging at me and people would be going out of their way to fix me up on blind dates and such, so I just kind of quietly went about staying single." I think about what Connor said when he got on that kick about her being a lesbian. "The only thing that mattered to me was spending quality time with Afton and doing everything I could to make her feel safe and loved. I was determined not to put her through anything else that might cause her the slightest bit of anxiety or pain." She takes a deep breath. "Well, that was easy enough when she was young, because she took up all of my time with her hobbies and stuff, but when she got to high school and started hanging out with her friends, well, I got lonely. I got bored. I got—" She stops talking.

"Horny?" Jalena says, once again hitting a comic relief home run.

"Yes!" Tia says, looking around to make sure no one is eavesdropping. "That, too! I have known Kevin Jacobs all my life, and he's always has been a womanizer. But"—she shakes her head—"I don't know what I was thinking getting involved with him."

"Well, let's see—he's sexy, charming, and persuasive," Jalena says. "That's a killer combination. Women don't stand a chance against all that."

"No kidding," Tia says. "I just need to know if he's interested in taking it to the next level and, like, going out to dinner and stuff," Tia says. "But I don't want to make things awkward."

"Hey! Aren't you going to the charity ball next weekend?" Jalena asks.

"Yes, why?"

"You know, it's kind of like the prom, where your date can just be your friend." She smiles at Tia. "That would be an easy way to make a first 'public' appearance. Why don't you ask him to go with you?"

"I did," she says flatly. "And I invited him over to my house one night and he politely declined."

"Oh," Jalena says. "Oh no."

I glance up at Jalena, and she's making an awful face.

"It's fine," Tia says. "I had no reason to think that just because my daughter moved out and I lifted my secret ban on dating that he would want the world to know about our little—"

"Tête-à-tête," Jalena says with great flourish, trying to recover.

"Or whatever," Tia says. "And I'm not going to sit here and make excuses for him, because I learned from Bernie Wescott that thinking up nice ways to explain away a man's behavior is a complete waste of my time." She looks at me. "I'm sorry, Ace. I'm probably boring you to death with all of my depressing drama."

"No," I tell her. "Not at all."

"You're so lucky. You've known since you were eleven that Mason was the love of your life. Now you've got things all worked out and your life is great and I'm over here being Debbie Downer."

"Nobody's life *or* love life is perfect," I say. "Mine is certainly no exception."

"Eleven?" Jalena asks. "You've been in love with Mason McKenzie since you were eleven?"

"Sadly, yes," I tell her.

"Did you ever date anyone else?" Tia asks.

"Oh yeah, I dated a few other people, slept with some other people. I actually burned a few years with a ladies' man, too," I tell her, thinking about my old flame Logan Hatter. "He loved to party and was *so* much fun to hang out with."

"What happened to him?" Jalena asks.

"It fizzled out after a while," I say. "I've just never met anyone that could take my mind off Mason." *Until I met Kevin Jacobs, that is.*

"That's what I need," Tia says. "I need to find my Mason and settle down, because I don't like it when things are complicated."

I look down at my beer and start feeling uncomfortable again.

"Personally, Tia," Jalena says in a very grown-up tone, "I think it's very impressive that you made it five years with Kevin before things got complicated. Usually that only takes a week or two, so pat yourself on the back for that." She pats Tia on the back and then says, "Are you ready to do this?"

"Yes," Tia says, taking a deep breath. "Let's do this. I'm ready to get it over with."

The waitress brings our check, and after settling our tab, we quietly hash out our spying plans. Tia wants to go in Jalena's Jeep, and she wants me to ride in the front and hold the listening device while she crouches in the backseat with the headset on. Jalena and I agree that sounds like a good plan, so we load up in the Jeep and head around the corner to stake out the residence of Kevin Jacobs.

32

◇◇◇

I was hoping Kevin Jacobs might not be home, but of course he is. His work truck is parked in the driveway right next to his big ol' pickup truck, and the front door of the house is wide-open. Jalena puts the headset on and gets everything ready, and then hands the headset to Tia and the handheld part to me. The connecting cord isn't very long, and Tia has to lean forward with her head between the seats.

"I'm probably going to regret this," she whispers as she slides on the headset.

"Naw," Jalena says. "It's all in fun."

I point the receiver at the house, and in a matter of seconds, I hear noise coming from the headphones and Tia gives us a thumbs-up. After we sit there for fifteen minutes, Tia slides the headphones off and tells us that Kevin is going to take a shower.

"How do you know?" I ask.

"I could hear him talking," she says. "I think he was playing *Call of Duty* online."

"You mean, like, on his computer?" I ask.

"No, on his Xbox. He has a headset kind of like this." She holds up the one she just took off her head. "Sometimes when I sleep over, I wake up and he's in the living room playing that stupid game at three o'clock in the morning talking about calling in air strikes and knifing people."

"Weird," I say.

"Men are *so* weird," Jalena says. "Well, what do you want to do now, Foxy Cleopatra?"

"Could we go to the store and then come back?" Tia asks sweetly. "I'm not sure what I'm accomplishing by doing this other than wasting time, but—"

"What you're accomplishing is seeing if it's worth getting your panties in a wad over him!" Jalena says.

"That's right," I say, desperately wishing I could get my panties *out* of a wad over him.

We drive down to the gas station on the corner, stock up on re-freshments, and head back to Kevin Jacobs's house. His front door is still open, so we discuss for a moment what kind of man showers with his front door wide-open and decide that's probably a bachelor thing.

We get everything set up again and I've just gotten the receiver turned toward the house when blue lights illuminate the night sky.

"Oh, holy shit!" Jalena says, and Tia jerks the headphones off her head.

"What the—" She turns around and sees the cop car, then wiggles her way onto the floorboard. "Oh God, y'all please handle this and don't let anyone see me, please! Oh my God, I knew this was a bad idea."

"Shush, Tia!" Jalena says. "Let me see if I can talk to him." Jalena opens the door of her Jeep and has one foot on the ground when we hear the loudspeaker.

"Get back in the vehicle!" the voice booms. "Ma'am, get back in the vehicle immediately."

"You have got to be fucking kidding me," Jalena says indignantly and jerks her leg back inside the Jeep.

"Close the door, ma'am!" the voice booms again, and I see the neighbors peeking out of windows and doors.

I hear another siren, and then a second patrol car swoops by and hastily backs in right in front of the Jeep.

"Ma'am, close the door!" the voice says again.

"Motherfuckers!" Jalena says under her breath.

The second patrol car is parked directly behind Kevin Jacobs's work truck. I bury my face in my hands, and when I look up again, I see him standing in his doorway wearing only a towel. Jalena is slinging stuff out of her purse and cussing like a sailor, and Tia is rolled up in a ball on the tiny back floorboard of the Jeep. I stare at him for a second, then grab the binoculars out of my purse and have a closer look.

"What in the hell are you doing?" Jalena asks me. "Where did you get binoculars?"

"From my house," I tell her, not taking my eyes off Kevin Jacobs and his towel. Then I realize how I must look sitting here having a peep show when we're surrounded by law enforcement and shove the binoculars back down in my purse. "What?" I say, like it's perfectly normal to tote things like that around.

Jalena gets back to digging in her purse and finally fishes out a tin of Altoids and promptly tosses a handful in her mouth.

"Can you move your seat up, Ace?" Tia whispers.

"Tia," I say quietly, "you might want to get up off that floorboard, because if the officer sees you back there, he's probably going to ask you to get out of the car."

"No!" she barks. "I'm not moving. Kevin cannot see me here like this. I would die!"

"Tia, just get up and sit behind Jalena. Sit up in the seat and don't put your head down when the officer looks back there, okay? Just get up and act normal."

"I know every cop in this town! I am not moving. Just stop talking to me!"

I look up and Kevin has disappeared. No doubt getting dressed to come outside and investigate the ruckus.

"Tia, I've got a blanket back there somewhere," Jalena tells her. "Get as far under the backseat as you can, and then cover yourself up with that." Jalena looks at me. "Drop that receiver between your feet and kick it under the seat; then put your purse back there on top of her. Keep it low and don't turn around. Just slide it back there nice and easy."

"Ew!" Tia squeals. "There's a dildo back here!"

"Shut up and leave it alone!"

"That thing had better not be used," Tia whispers. She knocks my purse over as I'm trying to slide it back there, so now the binoculars are lying in plain view. In addition to a dildo.

"Shut up, Tia, and be still. The officer just got out of his car." Jalena looks at me and smiles. "I've been looking for that thing everywhere." I start laughing and can't stop, even when the cop starts tapping on the window and motioning for Jalena to roll it down.

"Is it okay if I roll down the window?" she yells, and I start laughing even harder. "Are you sure it's okay for me to roll it down?"

"Hey! Don't be a smart-ass!" Tia whispers. "Are you crazy?"

Jalena finally rolls down the window.

"License, insurance, and registration," the officer says flatly. Jalena hands him the paperwork with a smile. He looks over her information, then leans down and shines the light in my face. "What are you ladies doing tonight?" he asks. He shines the light in the backseat, and I start to feel nauseous.

"Just girl stuff," Jalena says, acting totally cool. "Riding around, you know."

"Humph," he grunts and moves to the back windows. The officer from the other car joins him, and they circle the Jeep, shining their ten-thousand-watt flashlights all over the interior of the vehicle.

Without saying a word, Jalena presses a button and rolls down all the windows so we can hear what the officers are saying.

"Oh me," she whispers. "We are so busted." I follow her gaze and see Kevin Jacobs coming down the steps from his front porch.

"Oh no," I mumble.

"What the hell is that?" I hear one of the officers exclaim.

I turn around just enough to see the officers standing shoulder to shoulder. Both of them are shining their lights inside the back of Jalena's Jeep.

"Oh shit," she says and starts giggling. "I bet they're looking at that dildo."

"What's going on out here?" Kevin Jacobs calls, walking toward the front of the Jeep. "Brady, is that you?"

"Yeah," one of the officers answers. "We got a call about a suspicious vehicle stalking the neighborhood."

"It sounds so bad when they say it," Jalena whispers.

"Yeah," I say and take a drink of my Coke. My nerves are shot and my tummy is rumbling and the fact that I downed twenty hot wings and four beers isn't helping my situation at all.

Kevin is walking toward the police officers when he sees Jalena and stops. He leans over and looks at me, then looks back at her.

"Hey, what are y'all doing?" he says like he just ran into us at the grocery store instead of catching us outside his house in a vehicle framed by patrol cars with two police officers standing back there shining their flashlights on a dildo.

"Oh, you know, just getting pulled over," Jalena says. "That's about it, really."

He looks at me, so I add, "Yeah, pretty much a normal night for us."

He laughs and I hear the officers having a lively conversation but can't make out exactly what they're saying. Kevin walks back to where they are.

"Hey, Munson!" I hear him say. "What's up, man?"

"Hey, Jacobs. How's it going?" and they proceed to chat it up with one another while we sit in the Jeep like idiots.

"I wish they would turn those damned lights off," Jalena whispers.

"No kidding," I whisper back.

Kevin walks up to the front of the Jeep and leans against the fender. "Munson, why are y'all giving these two pretty ladies a hard time?" he says, smiling at Jalena and then me.

"Hell, somebody around here called 'em in for creeping, so we had to check 'em out," Officer Munson says. The two police officers are now standing outside the driver's-side window, facing Kevin. "So you know 'em?" He leans down to look at us and he's grinning from ear to ear.

"Yeah, I know 'em. That's Jalena Flores—her daddy owns the marina out on Frog Bayou—and the other one is Mason McKenzie's fiancée. You know, the lawyer? He lives right around the corner. Why don't y'all just let 'em go?"

The other officer, Brady, leans down and looks at Jalena. "Tell me one more time what y'all are out doing tonight?"

"Girl stuff," Jalena says, but all the conviction is gone from her voice and her cheeks are flushed red.

Officer Brady gives us a smug look, hands Jalena back her paper-work, and raps on the window seal with his big-ass fist.

"Well, have a good night, ladies, and find somewhere else to do your girl stuff, if you don't mind."

"Oh my God," I say.

"Don't!" Jalena whispers as he turns around. "Just don't say a word." She pulls back, then forward. Kevin waves and yells good-bye and we pull out onto the road.

"Tia?" I say. "The coast is clear. Are you okay?"

She doesn't say anything, but I can hear her crying.

"Tia, sweetheart, it's over!" Jalena says. "C'mon, now, you threw that dildo out to distract them and it worked."

Tia says nothing but keeps crying, and I decide the dildo rolling out into view might have been an accident. I reach back and pull the blan-ket off her. She gets up off the floorboard and her hair is soaking wet and stuck to her head and her cheeks are streaked with mascara.

"Tia, it's okay," I tell her. "It's over."

Tia takes a deep breath, wipes her nose on her shirt, and says, "I am forty-three years old! What the hell was I thinking trying to pull a stunt like that? What if we'd been arrested? How would I ever explain that to Afton? She would never have any respect for me again as long as she lived."

"Tia," Jalena says. "We didn't get arrested. Everything is fine. Listen, we won't do anything like that ever again."

"You're damn right *I* won't," she says and starts squalling again. "What would I have told my daughter?" she sobs. "I am so ashamed of myself!"

Jalena pulls in at Credo's Wild Wings and rolls to a stop next to Tia's Tahoe.

"I don't ever want to talk about this again," Tia says, in between sniffles. "I don't ever want to talk about *this*, and I don't ever want to talk about Kevin Jacobs. Not ever again."

"Okay, Tia," Jalena says. "Done."

"No problem," I tell her. "I already forgot about it."

"I am so humiliated!" she says.

"Don't be, Tia——" I begin, but she cuts me off by holding up a hand.

"Please, don't. I just want to go home."

"Well, be careful." I get out and open the back door for her. She walks to her Tahoe and gets in without saying another word. I shake my head and look back at Jalena. "Well, that went well."

"You ain't right, Ace Jones!" she says, laughing. "You ain't right, girl!"

I hop back in the Jeep and ask Jalena if she can drive me home.

"Okay, seriously," she says, pulling out of the parking lot. "We can't ever talk about what happened tonight in front of her. She won't ever think it's funny. Ever."

"I won't say a word," I assure her.

"She probably won't ever mention Kevin again, either."

"Really?"

"Yeah, she's real touchy like that, so just don't think anything of it if she don't, okay? That's just how she is." She looks at me and I nod. "And she really won't ever do anything like this again, which means we'll have to pull off that charity ball stunt by ourselves."

"That's okay," I say. "I think we can handle it."

"That's what I was thinking," she says and then starts talking about the meeting that's coming up on Monday night. "I'll go in there and do some reconnaissance," she says, laughing. "And we'll reconvene next week."

"Okay, double-oh-crazy, that sounds like a plan," I say as she pulls up in the driveway behind my car.

"Hey! Is your man-honey working tomorrow?" she asks.

"Of course," I say.

"Well, I'm going over to Foley to try to find something to wear next weekend. You wanna ride with me?"

"Sure!" I say. "I'd love to. What time are you leaving?"

"How about I pick you up around nine?"

"Sounds great," I say, getting out of her Jeep. "Drive safe, now. You don't want to get pulled over."

33

◇◇◇

I get up early Saturday morning and take Buster Loo for a walk around the neighborhood, during which I notice that the dooky sign and bags have been removed. I speak to several neighbors who are out working in their yards, but no one mentions the sign, so I don't either. After another big loop around the neighborhood, Buster Loo and I wind back around to our house. Mason is drinking coffee on the back porch when I walk in, so I toss Buster Loo a treat, wash my hands, then pour myself a cup and join him.

"Correct me if I'm wrong," he says when I sit down, "but when I turned in here last night, did I see a sign with a bunch of little dog-do bags nailed to it?"

"Indeed you did," I say and start laughing. I tell him that I stopped to inspect it and then discussed it with Roger, who had called someone on the board to complain.

"Margo could be the stupidest person alive," he says, and I agree.

"The sign isn't there anymore," I tell him. "Buster Loo and I walked up that way earlier."

He shakes his head and asks me what my plans are for the day. I tell him that I'm going shopping with Jalena, and he tells me that's great and then starts talking about that case they're working on while I sip coffee and do my best to look interested. During a break in the discourse, I ask him if he'd like to get dressed and go have breakfast at Round House Pancakes. Lucky for me, he does, and forty-five minutes later, I'm still listening to him talk about work, but at least I've got a short stack to help me see the conversation through to the end.

We exchange hugs in the parking lot, and he goes off to work and I head home, telling myself on the drive back that I have got to fix this communication issue with my future husband. Changing the subject doesn't work; bragging about how handsome he is doesn't work; asking nosy questions about Connor and Allison works for a minute, but not much longer. I sit at a red light and wonder if things will always be this way, if he'll always talk incessantly about his job. I think about the women I know who are married to coaches and how they eat, sleep, and breathe athletics. Looks like I'll be eating, sleeping, and breathing legal monologues until death do us part.

"Oh my," I say when I walk into the house. "What to do?" I go in the kitchen and load up the dishwasher with what is essentially two racks of cups and glasses and a few pieces of silverware. "It looks like I'm going to have to redefine normal," I say out loud.

Buster Loo comes in the kitchen and gives me a sweet little-dog look like he really understands what I'm saying. He disappears and returns a minute later with his squeaky ball. He drops it at my feet as if to say "Playing fetch will solve all of your problems." I go outside and play with him until the doorbell rings, and I do have to admit that I feel better.

"Come on in," I tell Jalena after I open the door.

"Good morning! Good morning!" she says, sliding her shades up on top of her head.

Buster Loo is so happy to see her that he drags a cushion off the couch and starts humping it right in the middle of the living room floor.

"Buster Loo!" I say, grabbing the pillow. "Stop that!"

I step in the kitchen to get my purse, and when I come back out, he's on the couch humping the same pillow and Jalena is bent over laughing.

"Buster Loo is getting his freak on!" she says, still laughing.

"He's really showing off for you," I say, collecting all of the pillows from the couch and tossing them into the study. I close the door behind me and say, "He only does that for the ladies he really wants to impress."

On the way to Foley, Jalena and I have a hearty chortle over the dildo incident and agree that we were probably the hot topic of conversation at the police station last night. I ask her if she's heard from Tia, and she hasn't.

"It'll be a few days," she says. "Poor thing. She's so embarrassed." Jalena looks at me. "I honestly don't know what she expects from Kevin. He's just a wild-ass man and he's always been a wild-ass man and he's always going to be a wild-ass man." She looks at me. "What do you think about him?"

"He's a damn sexy wild-ass man," I say.

"He likes you," she says, and my heart skips about sixteen beats.

"What?" I say. "What are you talking about?"

"Don't worry," Jalena says. "I won't say anything to anybody."

"How do you know he likes me?"

"He told me."

"When?" I say, reaching down to flip the air on my side of the Jeep to high.

"Yesterday when he came in the store to get some lunch."

"Why didn't you tell me?" I ask her, and my pulse is beating like a jungle drum.

"When could I have told you?" she says. "Oh wait! I know! I guess I should've mentioned that while you were checking him out with your handy-dandy binoculars."

"Leave my binoculars out of this," I say with a snigger. "You could've mentioned it on the way home."

"I forgot," she says. "All that excitement got my brain off track."

"I have the *worst* crush on him, Jalena!" I say. "It's terrible and I feel horrible about it because Tia is my friend and I would *never, ever* cheat on Mason."

"Yeah, he knows, and that's why he made me swear not to say anything to you." She puts her hand up to her mouth. "Oops." She giggles.

"What did he say?" I ask, feeling like I'm right back in the seventh grade.

"Well, he kind of let it slip, and after he did, I badgered him until he came clean."

"And?"

"Are you sure you want to know?" she asks. "It's kind of crude."

"I'm a crude girl, if you haven't noticed."

"Well, we were talking about when we all hung out at Credo's together the other night and he was saying what a cool and funny girl you are, and then he said something about you being sexy as hell, and I was all over it after that." She looks at me. "I sat down beside him and told him I wasn't blind and could dang well see how y'all flirted with each other, but he didn't want to talk about it. I kept on until he finally gave in and told me that since the very first time he saw you—" She looks at me. "He said you had paint in your hair or something?"

"I did," I say. "That was the first day the gallery was open and he came to pick up those pictures for his aunt Ramona, and when I saw him, I freaked out and started trying to primp and smeared paint in my hair." I look at her. "'Cause that's how I roll."

"Right. Well, according to him, all he's been able to think about since that day is effin' your brains out." She looks at me. "Only he didn't say effin'."

"Oh no!" I wail. "I've been thinking the same thing since the same time. I want to have sex with him so bad I can hardly stand it, and it's driving me crazy. There—I said it! I've been holding that in for over a month now."

"I suspected as much that night we hung out." She glances at me. "Y'all were just having a little too much fun together."

I start laughing and tell her how horribly guilty I feel all the time.

"And not just because of the crush I have on him," I say. "I get bored to death in that art gallery, and I just don't think this whole full-time-artist thing is for me. I mean, I always had this idea that it would be so cool to have my own studio and paint all day every day, but it's nothing like I thought it would be. I really don't enjoy it that much at all, and I'm not making any money, and I miss teaching school."

"Oh my," Jalena says, laughing. "If you miss teaching school, it must be rotten!"

I start laughing, too, and tell her that teaching school isn't *that* bad, but she doesn't look convinced. Even after I tell her it's not boring at all and comes with a very reliable income and lots of time off.

"Well, your life sure looks good from the outside," she says. "You're about to marry a big-shot lawyer, you own your own business, and you have an adorable little dog that humps pillows like a champ, not to mention that big, beautiful home with a view of the ocean." She looks at me. "I just don't see how it can be that bad."

"It's not that bad," I tell her. "I'm so lucky to have what I've got, and that's why I don't understand why I'm so damn attracted to Kevin Jacobs."

"Are you happy with Mason?" Jalena asks, and the directness of her question catches me off guard.

"I love him so much," I say.

"That's not what I asked."

I hold up my left hand and point to my engagement ring. "I've dreamed about this my entire life. All I've ever wanted was to be with him."

"Still didn't answer my question."

"Yes," I say. "I'm happy with him. I just thought it would be different. I mean, I love him so much, I really do, but he talks my damn head off. And don't get me wrong, I think he's a great guy, and I have *so* much respect and admiration for him, but when he's not boring me to death talking about work, he's *at* work, because he's got this big, important case that is unbelievably time-consuming—"

"So it's just this one case?" She looks at me.

"I don't know, but I think so," I say. "Honestly, I thought he worked whenever he wanted to and I didn't think that was ever very much. I certainly didn't know it would be like this with him working sixteen hours a day six days a week."

"So what will life be like once he's finished?"

"It's got to get better." I sigh. "We've somehow managed to get really out of tune with each other, and living with him has just turned out to be so—I don't even know how to explain what I'm trying to say—"

"Disappointing?" she says.

I look at her and sigh again. "Exactly," I say. "I know I must sound like a spoiled child when I say this, but the entire experience has not turned out anything like I thought it would, and, yes, I'm a little disappointed that it hasn't."

"Nothing taints a big dream like a good dose of reality."

"That's depressing as hell," I say, and she starts laughing.

"Being a grown-up sucks," she says. "Too much of the *real* world, you know?"

"I couldn't possibly agree with you more."

"So what are you going to do, Ace Jones, now that your dream life let you down?"

"I don't know. I can't bring myself to tell Mason how I feel about the gallery because he bought me that building. Just *bought* it for me, and, hell, even if I did want to tell him, I'd never have a chance because he's always talking nonstop about this case. And then I have to go eat dinner in that damn conference room all the time with him and Allison and Connor." I look at Jalena. "You can start billing me by the hour for this if you need to." She laughs and tells me to keep talking. I ask her if I can call her Dr. J and she says no. Then I remember something Mason mentioned that I've been meaning to ask her about. "Hey!" I say, narrowing my eyes. "Mason said you used to date Connor."

"Uh, that was a while back, and I don't think 'dating' would be the right word, if you know what I mean."

"Do tell," I say, thoroughly distracted from my pathetic personal problems.

"It started way back when he was in the tenth grade and I was a senior and we hooked up at a party one night, and then we just kept on hooking up for a long time after that," she says. "It was never anything serious, but I won't lie and say I wasn't crazy about him."

"So when *was* the last time y'all hooked up?"

"It was after he moved to Tallahassee, and, yes, before you ask, he was dating Allison at the time. I knew he'd started seeing someone, and that was fine because I had, too." She looks at me. "I used to be kind of a *bad* girl."

"Used to be?" I snort.

"You're a funny girl," she says lightly. "Anyway, the first two years he was at Florida State, we hooked up pretty much every time he came home. Then one weekend, he brought Allison home to meet Mama, and the minute I saw her, I knew our affair was over because she's just the type of girl that a guy like him is 'supposed' to end up with. You know what I mean? One of those nice, polite girls who look like they model for Ann Taylor Loft, and they're calm and quiet and lovely *all* the time." She bats her eyelashes and looks at me.

"I know exactly what you mean, because that's exactly what Rachel McKenzie is looking for in a daughter-in-law. She would very much prefer for Mason to have a clone of Allison."

I ask Jalena if she ever thought Connor was marriage material, and when she stops laughing she says that she most certainly did not.

"We're too much alike," she says. "Which makes for a great affair, but we would've killed each other in a real relationship. Men like him have to have a woman who can put up with a lot of shit, and that ain't me."

I tell her what Mason said about Connor and Allison getting into it all the time and how she goes home to Tallahassee after a lot of these fights. We discuss whether their problems stem more from Allison being spoiled or from Connor being a jerk. I tell her I think it's about even. She asks me what I think about Allison, so I take that as an opportunity to share snippets of stories about PoPo, to which I add a considerable amount of personal flair. She laughs so hard she starts snorting.

"But she's nice," I say. "It's just that we're *so* different and we won't ever bond over anything other than her dog. But I think she's a good person. I really do. Just not very exciting."

"Well, that's okay, too."

"Yeah." I look at her. "So you didn't consider Connor the marrying kind and you've dated an assortment of other fellows but you've never found that one that you just couldn't get off your mind?"

"Nope," she says without even having to think about it. "Not even close."

"That's terrible," I say, holding on to the door handle as she wheels into the parking lot of the outlet mall.

"Is it?" she asks, and I just sit there because I don't know what to say. "C'mon," she says, getting out of the Jeep. "Let's go get our fat-girl retail therapy on."

◇◇◇

34

Jalena shows me around to all the stores that cater to those of us above a size sixteen, and I end up spending a truckload of money and making three trips back to the car to drop off bags. Out of the fifty-something clothing stores at the Foley outlet mall, only six are what Jalena calls "fat-girl friendly," but that's okay because most malls have only one fat-girl-friendly store, two at the most, and unless they're having one hell of a sale, I can't afford to shop at either one.

We have lunch at the pizzeria and talk about how we wouldn't be confined to the fat-girl-friendly stores if we didn't love food so much.

"But I do," Jalena says. "And that's just how I am and that's okay. Skinny people ain't perfect; they just have a different set of snags."

"And a better selection of places to shop," I say.

"Well, we've got a better selection at restaurants and grocery stores, so I guess everything has a trade-off," Jalena says, and we both start laughing. "Like those iced cookies at Walmart that I'm addicted to. Skinny girls can't eat those every day like I do."

"Freedom," I say, picking up a piece of pizza. "It's a sliding scale."

"Nobody needs a scale, girl!" Jalena says. "We just need to be happy with who we are. All of us. Fat ones, skinny ones, short ones, tall ones, ugly ones, pretty ones, smart ones, dumb ones."

"Well, it's a lot easier to be happy when you have decent clothes to wear, so thanks for bringing me over here."

"Amen and no problem," she says.

On the ride back to Pelican Cove, she asks me what it's like to be in love with someone for as long as I've been with Mason.

"It's miserable!" I say, then tell her the whole story from the first time I saw him.

"I think y'all will be okay," she says. "You said you were under a lot of stress when you first moved down here, working all the time and stuff, and now he's under a lot of stress because he's working all the time, so I think if you just give it some more time and let y'all's work schedules even out, it'll all work out just fine." She looks at me. "Hopefully."

"Hopefully," I say. "And I know I need to give us a fair chance by doing my part to make it work." I look at her. "Why did you tell me that about Kevin this morning?"

"That's need-to-know information that you needed to know," she says, not taking her eyes off the road. "Even Reed noticed that y'all had chemistry, and he was drunk as Cooter Brown."

"Really?" I say. "It was that obvious?"

"Well, he didn't use the word 'chemistry,' but he did say that y'all looked like a pair of horny coon dogs." She looks at me. "And after I talked to Kevin yesterday, I knew I had to let you know."

"Got it," I say. "Thank you for that."

And then we start reviewing our plans to orchestrate the fall of Lenore Kennashaw.

*   *   *

Later that night, I'm trying on all my new outfits in the bedroom when I hear Mason pull up in the driveway. I slip on the sexy red dress I bought to wear to the charity ball and wiggle and squirm while I zip it up. I walk down the stairs as fast as the dress will allow, then strike a pose on the staircase just as Mason opens the front door.

He's got a sack full of crab legs in one hand and a box of Corona in the other. When he sees me, he promptly puts the beer on the floor and sets the bag on the table by the door. He whistles as he walks toward me, then takes my hand and turns me around.

"Oh, baby, is it my birthday?" he says, running a hand over the silky fabric.

"I was wondering if you would be my date for the annual Caboose Charity Ball next Saturday night."

"I'll be your date for anything," he says, sliding his hand behind my back. "I really like your new dress." He pulls me up close to him and I can feel how much he likes it.

I hear paper rustling and look over to see Buster Loo up on the couch, straining toward the crab legs on the end table.

Mason turns to look, too, then looks back at me. "Don't move. I'll be right back."

"Now, Buster Loo," he tells the dog when he reaches for the bag. "You know we have to cook these first." He grabs the sack of seafood and the beer, which he takes into the kitchen, and I hear him cramming it all into the fridge. When he steps back around the corner, he's loosening his tie with one hand and unbuttoning his shirt with the other. He puts his arms around my waist and we have the hottest make-out session we've had since the night I showed up on his doorstep and told him I was back.

He stops kissing me, takes off his shirt, and nods toward our bedroom. When we get upstairs, he unzips my dress, and when it falls to the floor, he admires my brand-new camisole.

"You need to go shopping every day," he tells me, running a hand over the lace. "Baby, you are so *hot*."

"I'll understand if you need to get downstairs and boil those crab legs," I tease.

"Fuck those crab legs," he says, taking off his pants.

We fall into bed and have some earthshaking sex, during which I don't think about anyone but him. After he falls asleep, I lie awake in bed thinking that talk I had with Jalena must've done me a lot of good.

Sunday morning, Mason wakes me up early because he's ready for breakfast.

"You seduced me last night and I forgot all about eating supper," he says as we walk downstairs. He starts the coffee and I start frying bacon and Buster Loo parks himself next to the stove and gets in his Coke-bottle stance. A minute later, Mason pours us both a cup of coffee and gives me a hug.

"I was starting to think you didn't like me anymore," he says.

"You know better than that," I tell him.

"I do after last night," he says and slaps me on the butt. He goes outside to get the paper, then comes back in and spreads it out on the bar. He flips through it section by section, reading me the parts he finds interesting or funny and asking me what I think about this or that news story. He sets the table and refills our coffee cups while I butter the biscuits and we sit down to eat. I smile to myself because *this* is more like the life I'd always imagined having with him.

After breakfast, Mason takes Buster Loo for a walk and I go out on the porch and plop down on a lounge chair. I think about the fact that I haven't been to church since I moved down here almost four months ago and decide that today might be a good day to start back. Especially since I've got a brand-new dress and some cool new heels to wear. Plus I need all the help I can get staying on the right track and steering clear of temptation.

When Mason gets home, I ask him if he'd like to go with me and he tells me that he's already told his workout buddies he would be at the gym today. He promises he'll go next week, then asks what church I plan to go to.

"I don't know," I say. "I guess I'll go to that big round one just up the road. You know the one with all the flags outside? Have you ever been there?"

"No, but if you like it, that's where we can start going if you want."

"Okay, great."

An hour later, I pull into the parking lot of the Greater Praises Worship Center. I walk to the front, where I stop and stare for a minute at the stunning display of cut beveled glass. A nice-looking teenage boy opens the door for me, and I walk into a meticulously decorated lobby where people are milling around all over the place. Some guy gives me a very elaborate church bulletin and three mints with a picture of the church printed on the wrapper. Another fellow holds open the door as I walk into a gigantic sanctuary that's shaped like a stop sign. I look up and see flags from a bunch of different countries hanging from the ceiling. A few people come up and shake my hand; then after a few minutes, the doors to the lobby simultaneously close and the lights go dim. I decide to have a mint.

Next thing I know, the lights go completely off and I'm standing in the pitch-black darkness. Music begins to play, softly at first, then louder and louder to the point where I start to get nervous. All of a sudden, beams of light start flashing across the auditorium in blue, yellow, and red, and then a light show commences that makes me wonder if that mint I just had might have been laced with hallucinogenic drugs. A spotlight comes on and whirls all around the room before finally coming to a stop on the choir, which somehow magically appeared on the large circular stage in the center of the sanctuary. Spotlights beam down on a band that starts jamming out to the music that's already playing, and then the light show starts again. The choir is dancing and clapping and singing, but I can't understand a word of their song. The recorded music stops and the band takes over and spends a few minutes playing some hard-core rock and roll, during which everyone in the sanctuary starts jumping around like monkeys, including the choir.

I'm thinking it's about time for me to go when another spotlight comes on and beams down on the choir leader, who is doing what looks like a tribal dance as she makes her way down the middle aisle toward the stage. Something about that person looks very familiar, but it might just be that my mind has gone squirrely from all the special effects. The choir leader hops up onto the stage, holds up both hands, and points toward the ceiling. I watch as three movie screens descend simultaneously from the flag collection. The choir starts to sing and the band rocks even harder and the lights start flashing, and then it goes completely dark.

I look around in a panic, but all the doors are still closed and the only thing I can see is the faint glow of the movie screens. The place is so quiet I could hear a pin drop. The screens light up and I see the choir leader, eyes closed and hands stretched toward heaven. The music starts again, the choir harmonizes, and Lenore Kennashaw opens her eyes as the camera zooms in on her face.

She orders the band to start playing, and then the choir starts singing and everyone starts jumping around like monkeys again. Lenore starts chanting praises and I start making my way to the back of the sanctuary. I see a man posted up next to what looks like it might be a door, and when I get up there, he grills me on why I'm leaving. I look at him and he looks possessed, so I decide to take the easy way out and tell him I've got a raging case of the squirts.

I stumble out into the hallway, disoriented by the sudden exposure to daylight. I start walking toward the lobby, and the doorman follows me. I head for the beautiful cut-glass façade, picking up my pace with each step. I put my hand on the door and the man behind me starts shouting that I missed the ladies' room. I run out into the parking lot past rows and rows of cars until I finally get to mine. I get in and drive home, extremely unsettled by the entire experience.

Mason is in the living room when I walk in. He's back from his workout and fresh out of the shower. "Hey, baby," he says. "You look beautiful. How was church?"

"I think I need something a little more low-key," I tell him.

"Hey, you wanna watch some football?" he asks.

"Sure," I say. "Just let me change clothes first."

I put on some old cutoff sweatpants and a T-shirt and go join him and Buster Loo on the couch. We watch football all afternoon, cook shrimp and crab legs for dinner, then a have bottle of wine on the back porch at sunset. The only time Kevin Jacobs crosses my mind is when I realize that I haven't thought about him at all. I lean my head on Mason's shoulder and smile because today was a good day. Except for that fifteen minutes I spent at that weird church.

◇◇◇

35

M onday morning, it's back to reality, because Mason is gone when I wake up and I know I've got another full week of conference-room dinners to look forward to. I tell myself to think positive as I roll out of bed and get dressed. I take Buster Loo for a walk on the sidewalk that runs next to the beach and I'm happy when the sight and sound of the ocean lift my spirits once again. After a steaming-hot shower, I put on some new clothes and head to the gallery feeling good.

Buster Loo really loves his new gig as Gallery Dog, and it makes me happy to have him there with me. I give Gloria Peacock a call to see if she and Birdie Ross might be able to come down for the charity ball, and she tells me that she's got some doctors' appointments lined up that would take months to reschedule.

"I'm so sorry, Graciela," she says. "It sounds like my kind of adventure, and I do hate that I'm going to miss out. Birdie's going to hate she missed it, too, because that kind of thing is right up her alley." I tell her it's okay and she asks when I'm coming to see her. I promise her it will be soon. I hang up the phone sorely disappointed that part of my plan didn't pan out.

When Avery comes in at one, she carries on about how nice I look to the point where I start wondering how bad it was before I went shopping with Jalena. I ask about her date and she tells me about Rob and all the creepy-sweet things he did over the weekend that ushered them from the "just talking" to the "hanging out" phase.

Turns out Rob comes from a wealthy family also, and Avery thinks that, should they graduate to the "seeing each other" phase, at least she won't have to worry about him dumping her because she has money. She shows me a picture of him, one with her in it, and he doesn't look as bad as he did in the one she showed us at Girls Night In. She shows me another one of him with his hair laid down instead of spiked up into a Mohawk and painted blue, and he actually looks really handsome.

"Bring him in here sometime so I can meet him," I tell her.

"You wouldn't mind?" she says. "I told him all about this place, and he thinks we have a very cool arrangement."

"As do I," I tell her. "Bring him in anytime." Then I start worrying that they might start sneaking in here and having sex on the couches. "Where is he from?"

"Biloxi, originally, but he's been living in Pensacola for the past few years." She looks at me. "He rents a room in one of those awesome historic homes downtown. I think I mentioned that I would *love* to live in that area."

"Oh yeah," I say. "I remember you saying something about that."

"Yeah, his place is awesome. The common area has really cool red leather furniture and the kitchen has all updated appliances. It's fabulous."

And so I stop worrying about my couches.

Just before closing time, Jalena texts me and tells me she's on her way to the meeting at Caboose Charity and asks if I want to meet her at Credo's later for a drink. I think about that for a second and, confident I'm over my crush, tell her I probably will. I call Mason and ask if he needs anything, and he tells me that Allison is taking care of dinner tonight. He asks me if I'll come eat with them and I tell him Jalena invited me to Credo's. He tells me that he doesn't blame me for not wanting to have dinner in the conference room all the time and encourages me to go ahead and meet up with her. The guilt monster really gets after me, but I text Jalena and tell her I'll meet her there at seven thirty.

I take Buster Loo home, and he retires to his doggie bed as I lie on the couch and watch the most recent *Saturday Night Live*. At twenty after seven, I flip off the television and head out to Credo's. When I get there, I see Jalena's Jeep in the parking lot and go inside to find her sitting at an indoor table off to the side. I sit down and take a quick look around, and she says, "He's not here."

"Good," I say. "Not that I wouldn't want to see him, but you know, the less temptation the better." I smile and she laughs and tells me I'm not right.

She talks about the charity ball meeting and then pulls a folder out of her purse. She opens it up and pulls out a stapled stack of papers and a very fancy program brochure.

"These," she says quietly, pointing to the program, "are all stacked up in the hallway outside the main office, so I think the 'leaflet' idea is going to be easy to pull off."

"Great," I say. I have a moment's hesitation when I realize that we could really go through with this, and then I think about Lenore getting my application tossed from the art festival submissions and get mad at her all over again. I get my notebook out of my bag, put it on the table, and open it up to a clean sheet. I write the words "Special Addendum" at the top.

Jalena opens the program, then turns it around to where I can see Kennashaw Home and Garden listed in the five-star category.

"How does she do that?"

"She has one hundred percent control over the production of this program."

"How did she manage that?"

"It's something she volunteers to do and it's a toilsome task that no one else wants."

"Right," I say and think about Margo the HOA president. "It's funny how much control people can accumulate by volunteering for things the rest of us are too lazy or busy to do or are just plain not interested in."

Jalena looks at me and says, "Why did I start thinking about politicians when you said that?"

"Why indeed?" I say. "And speaking of elected officials, does that organization not have a secretary?"

"Yeah, that's Sylvie Best," Jalena says, giving me a wry look.

"Of course," I say, looking down at the program. "Well, there's Sylvie in the five-star as well. Is that legit?"

"I don't know, but I can see when we get those records," Jalena says. "Her husband owns a couple of car dealerships here in town, so it could very well be."

"Maybe it won't be and I can add her name to this little notice," I say, tapping my notebook.

Jalena laughs and we start discussing what exactly the memo should say.

"It needs to be professional and polite," Jalena says. "Like someone is trying to make a serious clarification. It shouldn't sound mean or hateful or judgmental."

"Bummer," I say and start doodling in the margin.

After a lengthy discussion and two pages of drafts, we finally decide the notice should read:

Caboose Charity greatly appreciates each and every dollar donated to our organization, and we strive to protect the privacy of our benefactors while adhering to the specific guidelines stated in our bylaws. In a recent audit of our records, it was discovered that a mistake has been made in one particular area of categorization. Correction is as follows:

Frank & Lenore Kennashaw (Kennashaw Home and Garden)—One Star

Thank you, and we apologize for any confusion this may have caused.

"Are you sure we should list her as a one-star, even though she's really a two?" Jalena asks, eyeing my chicken-scratch writing.

"Absolutely," I say. "Think about how much more that'll get people stirred up. That's what we need. We need people to start asking questions."

"We cannot ever let anyone know we had any part in this," she says warily.

"Covert ops," I tell her. "We just can't react at all if people start talking about it."

She puts the program back in the folder, then slides the other papers to my side of the table. "Seating arrangement," she says. "Lenore and Frank are at table twenty-two on page three."

"Do you know what the place cards are going to look like?" I ask, looking over the names.

"No, they change that up every year," she says. "But I have a plan." She smiles at me. "Set-up starts on Wednesday, and they asked everyone to pick one night to come in and help, so I picked Friday."

"Okay."

"Each table is a ten-top, and most have two or three open seats in case people show up at the last minute or someone brings a date they didn't RSVP or someone important or high-profile comes in or something like that. So my plan is to try to swap Lenore and Frank's place cards out with a pair of blank cards at a lesser table." She looks at me. "I'm going to look it all over Friday night and try to pick up two extra place cards, because blank ones are usually lying around everywhere. I'm going to wait until Saturday to actually attempt the switch, because everyone will be running around like crazy, so I think that'll be my best bet in terms of getting away with it."

"That sounds like an excellent plan," I say.

"It'll be an excellent plan if it works," Jalena says. "Now let's talk about that station wagon."

"I'm going to call Mr. Pettigo on Wednesday and ask if I can bring my car in on Friday or Saturday," I say. "If he offers to let me drive it, we're good. If not, we're shit out of luck, because that's the only clunker I have access to. Let's just say he does, though. Are you sure we'll be able to get that old jalopy to the curb instead of her Mercedes?"

"The hotel doesn't have valet parking unless there's an event at the conference center," she says. "They just hire temps and it's all pretty lax because this is one of those deals where everybody knows everybody and they're more worried about people feeling special than about someone stealing a car. So *if* we get the station wagon, then we need to take it over there and park it at the very back of the conference center parking lot. It's just a big open lot across the street. The parking places are numbered, so I'll have to know what spot the paddy wagon is in, in order to execute my switcheroo plan." I nod and she continues. "Since I'm on the set-up committee, I'll be one of the first ones there, so I'll just keep an eye out for Lenore, and when I see her, I'll slip out the door and walk out to the parking lot and see what her parking space number is. Then I'll wait until the valets are really busy, pull one of them to the side, and explain that I left my purse in my car and my husband has the valet ticket and I can't find him anywhere, and I just need to borrow the keys for one quick second to unlock the door. I'm just going to talk until he gives me the keys, and I'll be all dressed up, so it's not like I'll look like a common criminal. When I get the keys, I'll step aside and pretend to press the unlock button, but I'll really be snapping the valet clip off. At that point, I'll piddle around for a few minutes and let a few more people drive up, and then when I return the station wagon keys with Lenore's valet tag attached, I'll casually mention the parking space number of the station wagon." She looks at me. "And I'll make sure to be flashing plenty of boob during all of this."

"You sure know a lot about valet parking," I tell her. "Let me guess—you used to date a valet."

"No," Jalena says with a chuckle. "Me and another girl had to work the valet stand one year because a few of the temps got caught smoking weed behind the hotel."

"You're kidding!"

"Naw, but we only had to do it for like an hour. Just until they got two more guys to come in. It's a process you pick up on fast because it's so repetitive." She looks at me. "What else?"

"Well, the station wagon probably won't have keyless entry," I tell her. "That thing is a real piece of crap."

"I'll be sure to hand the keys back to a different guy, then."

"Good idea."

"And if that doesn't work, I'll figure out something."

"You mentioned boobs," I say.

"There's always plenty of that."

"Okay," I say, laughing. "So, let's review. Phase one: Switch around the place cards. Phase two: Put inserts in *some* of the programs. Phase three: Valet service with a station-wagon smile. Wait—what are you going to do with Lenore's keys if you're able to get the tags switched around?"

"I don't know," she says with a shrug. "I didn't think about that."

"They need to find their way to the hotel lost and found, and then maybe it'll all look like an accident," I say. "Or something."

"I can make that happen," she says. "What about your little-old-lady friends?"

"I called Gloria Peacock today and she said they wouldn't be able to make it," I tell her. "Bunch of doctors' appointments and stuff."

"Okay, then," she says and starts digging around in her purse. "Well, here are your tickets to the ball, my friend." She hands me a small white envelope. "And the night of the charity ball, I don't think we should be seen around each other."

"Excellent point," I tell her. "So, when are we going to break into the office?"

"I was going to say Thursday, but they might move the boxes to the conference center before then, so . . ."

"So?"

"So how about I type up our little announcement tomorrow at work? I'll put four to a page, print 'em out, and cut 'em up, and then we go tomorrow night and put 'em in the programs? No one will move anything until Wednesday, and, honestly, I think the leaflets could be the only part of our plan that might really work, so I want to make sure we get this done."

"Great," I say, thinking that'll get me out of another conference room dinner.

36

◇◇

Tuesday turns out to be fairly boring and I end up taking a short nap on the sofa in the gallery with Buster Loo after lunch. My phone starts buzzing, and it's a text from Jalena that contains a picture of our big announcement.

"Looks great," I send back. Buster Loo stretches, and I go get his leash and take him for a walk around the parking lot. It's unseasonably warm and the sun is out full force, so it doesn't take him long to set his sights back on the gallery door.

I go upstairs and think about painting but ask myself what the point of that would be since all I'm doing is basically running a museum anyway. I have plenty of paintings to swap out with the ones on display, but I really don't see the sense in doing that when hardly anyone even comes in to see the ones I do have hanging up. I sit down in my studio and stare out at the bay, wondering how I ever thought this was what I wanted to do with my life.

I go back downstairs and surf the Net until Mason calls an hour before closing time to tell me all about his busy day. He says they're working through dinner and asks me if I want to come eat with him in his office or if he should just have Allison pick him up something. I tell him I'm hanging out with Jalena again tonight, but I promise him I'll bring dinner tomorrow night.

"You know what?" I say to quell my guilty conscience. "I'll take off a little early tomorrow and go home and cook. How about that?"

"Oh, man, that would be great!" Mason says. "I would appreciate it so much. What are you going to fix?"

"I was thinking lasagna," I say, knowing that's his favorite.

"It makes my day today knowing I'm going to have your lasagna tomorrow," he says, and I smile because at least I've got my love life back on track.

I hang up with him and look up the Florida Department of Education Web site. I read over the guidelines for applying for a teaching certificate, and apparently all I have to do is send in my Mississippi teaching license and a couple of hundred dollars. When I think about being back in the classroom, part of me recoils with dread, but another part of me gets very excited.

"Slow down, Bessie," I say to myself. "I was one hundred percent excited about this art gallery before it opened up, and now look where I am." Instead of downloading the application, I click the button that takes me back to Google. I look down at Buster Loo, who is snoring away in his dog bed. "Oh, to be so happy and content," I say, and Buster Loo perks up and looks at me. "I have got to get my mind right, Buster Loo."

I waste a few more minutes online; then Buster Loo and I check out thirty minutes early. Since I have his leash, we get out at the house and head straight for Pelican Trails Park.

I see Margo out in her yard, and when I wave, she just stares back at me, and that really pisses me off. I mean, if someone waves at you and you don't want to wave back, that's fine. But don't stand there like a dipshit and stare. Turn your head or something. Jeez. I can't help myself; I yell out, "Hey, Margo, what happened to the shitbag sign? I kind of liked it." She scowls at me and I just keep walking.

When we get back, Jalena is parked on the curb, and I scare her to death when I walk up and tap on the window of her Jeep.

"Where have you been?" she asks when she rolls down the window. She looks down at Buster Loo. "Oh, walking, I see. Hey, Buster Loo!" she calls out, and he starts bouncing up and down like a basketball with too much air.

"Uh, yes, ma'am, would you mind telling me what you've been doing in this neighborhood?" I say in my best mock-policeman voice.

"Hardy-har-har," she says sarcastically as she picks up a file folder from the passenger seat.

When she gets out of the Jeep, she picks up Buster Loo and hauls him into the house. I get him a treat and myself some water and ask her if she'd like anything.

"Let's order pizza!" she says, and I tell her that's the best idea I've heard all day. Because it is. She calls it in and I get out some paper plates and napkins. The pizza arrives thirty minutes later and we hash out our plan for breaking and entering over dinner and Diet Mountain Dew.

"What if we get caught?" I say.

"If we get caught by the police, I can just tell them I'm looking for my cell phone, which I'm going to say I left inside the night before, and explain how much I volunteer for Caboose and so forth and so on."

"And if he asks how we got in?"

"I'm going to tell him I used a dildo," she says with a straight face, "because that tends to be a good distraction." I almost choke on my pizza I start laughing so hard, and eventually she starts cracking up, too.

"I got it! I got it!" I say, getting hysterical. "We can say we shoved that thing right in the hole even though it was a really tight fit."

"Yeah, and then we can tell him that we had to work it from side to side for a minute, but the door *finally* came open," she says and starts laughing so hard she snorts.

After we calm down, we get back to business. We discuss going in her vehicle since she's affiliated with the organization, then decide to go in mine and park around the block.

"We'll be incognito with those Mississippi tags," she says.

"Yeah, either that or everyone will know it's me because I'm one of the few out-of-state tags in town and probably the only one from Bug-tussle County," I tell her.

"Does your tag really say that?"

"Yeah, go look."

"I'll take your word for it," she says. "We better go in mine."

She drives to the town square, where the office for Caboose Charity is a block off the main road. She parks in front of the courthouse, then takes a credit card out of her wallet and sticks it in between the rings of her key chain.

"It'll look like I'm unlocking as opposed to jacking if anyone surprises us," she says, getting out. I grab the file folder and follow her down the shallow hill to the front door. I look around, hoping this town doesn't have any eye-in-the-sky cameras.

She slips the card through the space between the door and the frame, then slips it through again, and the door eases open.

"You have a lot in common with my friend Lilly Lane," I tell her.

"Really," Jalena says, stepping inside.

"She also has a proclivity for small-time criminal activity."

"Sounds like I'd like her."

"You would," I say, following her inside.

"There they are," she whispers, pointing to a wall lined with white cardboard boxes. She looks at me. "Are we really gonna do this?"

"We've come too far to stop now," I say and slide a few boxes off the top and set them to the side. "Let's take this one in the middle," I say, pulling it out of the stack. "That way maybe if they get stacked and restacked, it will just stay in the middle."

"Excellent reasoning," she says. "Look," she says, nodding toward a room on down the hallway. "That's the office. They didn't even close the door after the meeting last night."

"Good," I say. "I like it when things are easy."

She goes back to the office to make copies of the contribution records, and I pull out a stack of programs and start adding the inserts. A few minutes later, she comes back with a neat stack of papers and tells me the bookkeeping file hasn't been moved since the last time she snuck in here and took a gander at it. I still have several programs to stuff, so I hand her half of the leaflets and a stack of booklets.

"Nice card stock, by the way," I tell her.

"I'm crafty like that," she replies with a smile.

Soon we're done and I carefully stack the programs back in the box and replace the lid.

"Number twenty-one," she says, pointing to the label. "Box number twenty-one."

"Should we do another one?" I ask.

"We've only got about ten cards left."

"Let's get out of here, then."

We put all the boxes back in place; then Jalena goes to the door and peeps out.

"Wait a minute, someone is coming," she says, and I break out in a sweat and start feeling like I'm going to vomit.

"Do we need to hide?" I ask and start fanning myself with the file folder.

"No, it's just some teenagers," she whispers back. I walk over and stand next to her. "Don't skulk out of here like you've just robbed the place, okay?" she whispers, and I nod to indicate that I understand. Then I follow her out the door skulking like I just robbed the place. "C'mon!" she says when we're back outside.

She starts talking normal, and I try to act normal, but my nerves are shot and I just can't. Once we're back in her Jeep, however, I start to breathe again.

"Oh man," I say, looking at her. "We have just pulled one more stunt."

She holds up the copies she made of Caboose Charity's financial records. "Yes, we did," she says.

"We need to check Sylvie Best's contributions, too," I tell her.

"Honestly, Ace, I think her husband's car dealerships do pretty good. Best Automotive Group isn't rumored to be a sinking ship like Kennashaw Home and Garden.

"Well," I say, slightly disappointed, "I want to check her out anyway."

"We can certainly do that."

"Good," I say. "Now, let's go get a milk shake."

◇◇◇

37

On Wednesday, I take Buster Loo for a walk, then decide to leave him home for the day because I plan on taking off early and making Mason a good, home-cooked meal. On the way to the gallery, I remember that I need to call Erlene's husband about that station wagon, so I grab my purse and dig through it until I find the card for Sam Pettigo's garage.

The person who answers doesn't say hello, but barks out a "Yep" instead.

"I was looking for Mr. Sam Pettigo."

"This is Sam," comes the gruff reply. I explain who I am and why I'm calling, and he says, "You can bring that thing in today if you want and I can have it done by Friday. Erlene told me about you. Said she wanted me to get your car fixed quick as I could."

"Could I bring it in Friday afternoon or Saturday morning?"

"Can you do without till Tuesday?"

"Sure can," I say, inadvertently mimicking his clipped tone.

"Bring it Saturday morning, then. I got a couple of cars sitting around if you need one."

"Okay, thank you," I say, but he's already hung up.

I get out at the gallery and look up the beautiful mermaid on my sign.

"Bring me good luck today," I tell her as I walk to the door.

For a minute I think that she will because I have several people come in throughout the morning. One couple sits down on the couches and strikes up a friendly conversation. They're from Sarasota and the wife has family in Pensacola and they tell me they always drive out to Pelican Cove to eat at the Blue Oyster.

"Well, it's worth the drive, if you ask me," I say.

"It's worth the drive just for the shrimp and grits," the woman says.

They sit and talk for about an hour, and I'm kind of sad when they leave because they were such good company. I try to call Tia just to see what she's been up to, but she doesn't answer and the call doesn't go to voice mail. I think about sending her a text but don't want to bug her, plus she'll see my number on her missed calls list. When Avery comes in at one, I ask her if she'd be okay hanging out by herself for the afternoon.

"Are you serious, Ace?" she asks in her quiet way.

"Yes, everything is tagged, and in the unlikely event that someone actually buys something, don't worry about tax," I tell her. "Tell you what," I say, patting her on the back. "Let's make a deal. If you sell a painting today, I'll give you a raise." She looks at me like I'm crazy, then starts laughing.

"You should be a motivational speaker," she says, rolling her eyes.

"Thank you," I say, picking up my purse. "Call me if you need anything."

*　　*　　*

I drive to the grocery store, excited to be cooking dinner for Mason, even though we'll be sharing it with Connor and Allison in that god-forsaken conference room.

"Oh well," I say to myself as I get out of my car. "I'll think of it as a double date." *The double date that never ends.* "This positive-attitude stuff is going to take some practice," I say to myself as I walk into the grocery store next to a man with overtrimmed hair and a golf shirt. He shoots me a funny look.

"I have a bad attitude," I tell him, and he quickly walks in the opposite direction. I get a buggy and load up everything I need for my lasagna. I stop in the last aisle and go through the checklist in my head, touching each individual item in the buggy in the order I will use it when I start cooking. Satisfied that I have everything, I go by the frozen foods aisle and grab the longest piece of garlic bread in the freezer. I check out, drive home, and happily set about making Mason's favorite pasta dish.

When I put it in the oven forty-five minutes later, I decide to go upstairs and get ready like I'm really going on a date. Buster Loo follows me and hops up on our bed, where he stays until I get out of the shower and turn on the hair dryer.

"Is this what you were waiting for?" I ask him as he jumps around and paws the hair dryer. "Buster Loo need some heat in his life?"

He runs in and out of the bathroom going a hundred chiweenie miles an hour while I finish drying my hair. Then he disappears under the bed, no doubt exhausted and probably very warm.

I get dressed and do my makeup, then go downstairs and dig around in the utility room until I find a nice wicker basket that I think will hold the lasagna pan. I line the basket with kitchen towels and place the steaming-hot dish inside. I take the bread out of the oven, partially slice it, and wrap it in foil. I find a bag to put the bread in, then load it all up in the car. I drive to the office, feeling good about how I look and even better about how my dinner smells.

I slip in the back door and have everything ready by the time Mason realizes that I'm in the building. His eyes light up when he walks into the conference room, and Connor comes in a minute later and demands to know what that smell is all about. Allison comes a few minutes after him, and she doesn't look happy.

"Hi, Allison," I say.

"Hi," she says and doesn't say anything else.

Mason and Connor sit down and I realize I don't have a spoon to dip the lasagna out with.

"That's okay," Connor says, jumping up. "I've got that covered." He rummages through all the drawers until he finds a spatula in one with a bunch of pens and other random office supplies.

Allison snarls her nose, points at the spatula, and says, "Wash that."

"No, I thought we'd just eat off it dirty," Connor says sarcastically, giving her the evil eye on his way out the door.

"So how was your day?" Mason asks, and I tell him about the couple from Sarasota who came in for a visit. Connor comes back in with a clean spatula and serves everyone a slab of lasagna.

"That's nice," Mason says with his eyes on his plate. "Thank you so much for cooking this and bringing it here." He looks at me. "That was so sweet."

"Yeah," Connor says with a mouthful of steaming pasta. "You are *so* sweet for cooking a meal at home and bringing it here."

Allison doesn't say a word. She picks up her plate and leaves the room.

"Should I go talk to her?" I whisper to Connor. He just shakes his head and continues eating.

"I try to get her to go home," Mason whispers. "Take a break, not from the office, but from him." He nods toward Connor.

"Ha. Ha. Mason." Connor snorts. He looks at me, "This stuff is really good, Ace."

"Thank you, Connor."

"Y'all spend too much time together," Mason whispers to him.

"Why don't you do me a favor and fire her then?" Connor practically shouts.

"I heard that, asshole!" Allison calls from the office down the hallway.

"Good!"

I try not to laugh and then remind myself that everyone in a relationship, regardless of the details, is dealing with some kind of crap, and nobody needs anyone sitting around sniggering about it.

Connor and Mason start discussing the nitty-gritty details of foreclosure reversal and I tell myself to just stay with it and smile. Then Connor starts telling this great story about a couple in Collier County, Florida, who paid cash for a bank-owned home, and then a certain bank tried to foreclose on their house even though they didn't even have a mortgage, and the couple ended up with a judgment against the bank.

"Which the bank wouldn't pay," Connor says. "So the couple got a moving van and some law enforcement and went to the bank and started loading up stuff. The bank officer locked himself in his office 'cause he couldn't figure out what to do, but he finally figured something out."

"What was that?" Mason asks.

"He figured he would just write the couple a check like the judge had ordered him to six months before that," Connor says, helping himself to more lasagna.

"Did you just make all of that up?" I ask him.

"Absolutely not! I saw the news clip online."

"Unfortunately, my job has never been quite that exciting," Mason says.

"Well, it might be after this case is over," I tell him.

"Yeah, especially after Mr. Marks brought in two of his friends who have the same problem he's got."

"Really?" I say, as my heart sinks.

"Hell yeah," Connor says. "That's a little thing I like to call job security."

I look at Mason and he's looking at his lasagna.

"Why didn't you tell me?" I ask him.

"Oh shit," Connor says.

"Oh no, it's fine," I say, putting my hand on Mason's arm. "I'm not mad." I try to smile.

"If I may be excused." Connor picks up his plate. "Sorry, man," he says to Mason on his way out.

A minute later, I hear Allison say, "What are you doing? I moved in here to get away from you."

I look back at Mason.

"They came in here and talked to us. Two couples. We haven't signed a representation agreement yet," he says quietly. "Because I wanted to talk to you first."

"So what does that mean for us if you agree to represent them?" I ask, and he looks down at his lasagna. "More of the same, I assume."

"I won't do it," he says. "I'll tell them no and they can find someone else to help them." I can tell from the tone of his voice that is not what he wants to do.

"But you want to help them, don't you?" I ask.

"Of *course* I want to," he says. "We may even be able to get their homes back, Ace." He rolls his office chair up next to mine. "The whole reason I became a lawyer was to help people, but I won't do it if you don't want me to." He puts his hand on mine. "I know it's hard, having to come in here and eat all the time, and I'm never home and we don't have any semblance of a normal life—"

"How long?" I ask.

"A year. Maybe two," he says. "With breaks in between, during which I'll take you anywhere you want to go. And just this morning, Connor and I discussed maybe bringing someone on board to help."

"Like another lawyer?"

"Yes." Then he grins and says in a lower voice, "And a full-time secretary."

"You love your job, don't you?" I ask. I start thinking about Gramma Jones and how she always used to tell me that selfishness would ruin the best of relationships.

"Yes," he says, his eyes pleading. "You know I do."

"If those people have to find another lawyer," I say slowly, "whoever they get wouldn't be as good as you and Connor."

"Plus we have a tremendous advantage by having three similar cases." Mason smiles and puts his arm around me. "Baby, I knew you would understand."

I smile and hope the small part of my soul that just died is worth the trade-off in the long run. He gives me a look of genuine appreciation, then picks up his fork and starts eating.

And I start wondering if Kevin Jacobs is at Credo's tonight.

38

◇◇◇

Thursday morning I'm sitting in my office with Buster Loo on my lap when Jalena calls and tells me that Tia and Olivia have both canceled on Girls Night In tonight. Then she tells me that she's going to work late and get all of tomorrow's paperwork done tonight so she can leave early Friday and get to the Downtown Inn and fulfill her obligation to help set up for the charity ball.

"Gotta get my work done and get some beauty rest," she says. "'Cause Friday is our busiest lunch day and I'll have to leave here and go straight home and take a shower so I don't go over there smelling like a chicken leg. And then I'll be there all night, I'm sure."

"Okay, then," I tell her, and I'm so down in the dumps that even the thought of getting back at Lenore Kennashaw can't lift my spirits.

"What's wrong, Ace?"

"Do you really want to know?" I say. She says she does, so I tell her that Mason just took not one, but two more people to represent in faulty foreclosure cases.

"Good for him," she says cheerfully. "Maybe he can help them get their homes back."

"Maybe," I say. "I just need to keep that in mind."

"Girl, don't be sad," she says. "Not only could he possibly get those people their houses back; he'll probably make enough money suing those banks to buy you not one but two Ferraris." She pauses a beat. "Then you can give me one."

I manage a laugh and she tells me to stop worrying and think positive.

"Yeah, I'm working on that," I tell her. I put down the phone and sit there petting Buster Loo, wondering if my misery stems from my inability to acclimate to my new life or if I really am just as crazy as a shithouse rat.

I call Avery and tell her that everyone's canceled on us, and that doesn't bother her at all because spike-haired Rob wants to take her to some kind of art exhibit that just opened up in downtown Pensacola. So that works out great for everyone. Except me.

I decide to try harder. I call Mason and ask him if he could have any home-cooked meal he wanted, what it would be. He thinks for a minute and then rolls off a classic Southern-granny-Sunday-lunch menu: roast with brown gravy, peas and corn bread, lima beans, potatoes smothered in roast gravy, fried okra, stuffed eggs, homemade biscuits covered in some more roast gravy, cream-style corn, and banana puddin'.

"Wow," I say. I scribble all this down on a memo pad, and when he stops talking, I realize I'm going to need a bigger basket with which to transport food.

"Why do you ask? Are you going to cook all of that for supper tonight?"

"As much as I can," I tell him. "But you may still end up eating takeout."

"Really?" he says, and then he has to get off the phone, but not before wishing me the best of luck with my culinary adventure.

I hang up, look at the clock, and sigh because it's not even lunchtime yet. I take a few minutes to write the most elaborate and extensive grocery list I've ever made in my life; then I start Googling banana pudding recipes.

"Thank goodness he didn't ask for chicken and dressing," I say as I hit the print button. I look down at Buster Loo. "Little buddy, we're shutting this place down early today." I pick up the three-page recipe from the printer, then clip my ridiculously long grocery list to the top of it.

I get out a sheet of paper and write, "Please call for appointment" and list my phone number with its big, bad Mississippi area code. Then I wad that up and throw it in the trash and type up a much neater sign. I print that out, grab some tape, and walk around turning off lights. I get my purse, my recipe, and my dog; then I tape that sign to the door and leave.

Two hours and two hundred dollars later, I leave the grocery store with my very first chunk of fatback and a much better understanding of why Gramma Jones always had a garden.

I go home and put the roast in the Crock-Pot first thing. On top of the roast, I put a packet of brown gravy mix and a box of French onion soup mix, and then I fill the Crock-Pot halfway up with water just like Gramma Jones used to do. I turn that on, hit the button to preheat the oven, and turn to the vegetables. I fill up pots of water for the peas and lima beans, then start chopping potatoes and put on another pot of water for those. I cover the last available stove eye with a little pan of water into which I drop four family-size tea bags.

After the tea starts to boil, I take it off the eye, cover it, and set it to the side. In its place, I put a pot filled with cold water into which I carefully place six eggs. The peas start boiling over, and while they have my full attention, I realize I forgot to add the fatback. I slice off a piece of that mushy stuff and drop it into the boiling water. Then I put butter in the limas and salt those down again. I turn those eyes down to low and put a lid on both pans. Then I grab the bag of frozen biscuits out of the freezer and pop them in the oven. Twenty minutes later, I've just finished chopping onion and pickles for the stuffed eggs when the kitchen timer goes off. I try the limas and they taste great so I take them off the stove. I try the peas and they taste like pure-D crap so I put the lid back on and let them simmer a bit longer. I take the eggs off the stove, pour the water off, then let them sit and cool.

I mash the potatoes, throw in some seasoning, try a bite, season them some more, try another bite, add some butter and a tad bit more milk, and then finally pour them into a glass bowl. I start on the fried-okra project, and it takes me about five seconds to abandon that. I think okra needs to be fresh, not frozen, and I get homesick thinking about Gramma Jones's house, because she had some of the best okra stalks in the state of Mississippi, or so she used to say. I heat up the frozen cream-style corn, which takes only a minute, try the peas again, then get busy with the egg stuffing. The cooked ball of yellow yolk smells like stinky feet, but I just keep stirring in the mayonnaise.

With everything off the stove except for the peas, I decide to tackle the banana pudding. I have to get down on my hands and knees to dig out a double boiler, and when I finally get the dang thing out, it hasn't been used in so long that it's coated with a thick film of dust.

I wash and dry those two pans, read my recipe for the tenth time, and start on the pudding. It's not nearly as hard as I thought it would be. It just requires a lot of stirring. I chop up the bananas, toss a bunch of vanilla wafers on top of them, and then pour the pudding on top. As I watch steam roll out of the bowl, I'm pretty sure I should've let that pudding cool first.

I try the peas again and they still don't taste right. I think about pouring them down the drain but decide to let them simmer some more before I do that. I go lie down on the couch and think about all the big Sunday dinners I used to have as a kid. I don't know how my grandmother cooked a meal like that and then still made it to church.

I make three trips to the car, and I've almost got dinner loaded up when I decide to take real plates and silverware. I carefully stack four plates in a small cardboard box and take that to the car along with a bag of forks and serving utensils. Buster Loo is following me every step of the way, showing great interest in every box that goes out the door. I finally get the tea jug, tell Buster Loo good-bye, and head out the door for the last time.

I call Mason and tell him I'm going to need help bringing in dinner, and when I pull up in the parking lot, he and Connor are standing out back waiting. Connor makes a big fuss about how good everything smells as he taxis food to the conference room.

"We're going to have to build a kitchen and a dining room in here if you keep this up," he says, picking up the box of plates.

"Yeah," I say and hope he's joking.

Mason comes back outside to get another box, and we finally get it all moved inside. They help me get everything uncovered and make sure every dish has a spoon, and when we're done, it's quite an impressive spread, of which I am very proud.

"Man, I haven't had a dinner like this since my papaw's birthday last month," Connor says.

"I haven't had a dinner like this since I was home six months ago," Mason says.

"I don't remember the last time I had a dinner like this," I say, because I don't.

"Well, I don't eat dinners like this because I don't want to get fat," Allison says from the doorway.

Mason stops dipping potatoes and stares at her. I just look down at my plate and try to remember all the reasons I don't need to get up and slap the hell out of her.

"You are such a relentless bitch!" Connor says to her.

Then she realizes what she said and how it sounded and starts apologizing.

"Allison," I say, not believing I'm having this conversation, "it's okay. I know you didn't mean anything by it." She keeps on, so finally I say, "Look, it's not like it's some big secret that I'm fat. I know I'm fat. I like to eat. I'm not offended by you using that word around me; now, can we please just move on?"

"I'm sorry," she says again and looks like she's about to start crying.

"It's really okay," I tell her. Again. And instead of getting up and punching her right in the face because I'm so sick of listening to her mouth, I say, "I should've picked you up a salad or something."

"No, really, you shouldn't have," Connor says quickly. He looks up at her. "Why don't you run and get yourself a salad? And while you're out why don't you run on home, pack your bags, and go to Tallahassee like you've been threatening to do all week." He gets a scoop of lima beans and she turns around and leaves. "I am so sorry about that," he says to me. A minute later, I hear her walk out the door.

"There's nothing to be sorry for," I tell him. "I can't imagine how stressed-out y'all must be."

"She wants to be stressed-out," Connor says. "She likes the drama it creates, so she can run home to her mama and whine about it."

Mason doesn't say a word; he just sits there with the potato spoon in his hand. His expression is unreadable.

"Ace, thank you so much for bringing all of this up here," Connor says. "I know it was a lot of work and I really appreciate it."

"Well, I didn't make corn bread because something went dreadfully wrong with the peas."

Connor grins and nods because his mouth is full and Mason finally starts scooping potatoes again.

"This is an amazing meal, Ace," Mason says. "Thank you."

39

<><><><><><><><><><><><><><><><><><><><><><><><><><><><><><><><><><><><><>

Buster Loo and I are snoozing on the sofa at the gallery on Friday when Avery comes in with Rob.

"Someone could come in here and murder you!" she exclaims.

"Nah, I've got my trusty guard dog," I say, pointing to Buster Loo, who is on his back doing the worm squirm.

Rob starts laughing and I stick out my hand. "Ace Jones. Nice to meet you." His hair is all laid down and he looks even better in person than he did in that picture where I thought he looked rather handsome. He's actually beautiful, in an exotic way, much like Avery. I think they make a unique and attractive couple.

She shows him around, then takes him upstairs and shows him both of our studios, and when they come back downstairs, he's very gracious with his compliments. He wants to talk shop for a while, so we settle into the couches and do just that. It's easy for me to see why Avery is attracted to him, because in addition to his dark eyes and luscious lips, he's quite the conversationalist. When our discussion winds down, I tell Avery that I've decided to take the rest of the day off and I think she should, too.

"What about the gallery?" she asks.

I go in the office and get my CALL ME sign, which still has tape stuck to it.

"Really?" she says.

"Really," I say. "I used it yesterday and it worked like a charm."

We say our polite good-byes, and Rob tells me one more time how much he enjoyed visiting the gallery. I get my purse and leash up Buster Loo while Rob carefully sticks the sign on the door for me.

"I'm going to start using that sign a little more often," I tell Avery on the way out. In the parking lot, Rob opens the passenger-side door of his Range Rover and Avery hops inside. She smiles and waves, as does he, and I walk out and get in my dirty ol' Maxima.

I get home around two o'clock and decide to take a nap. I sleep till almost seven, when Mason calls and asks if I'd like to join him and Connor for some pizza. I politely decline and watch television until he gets home at nine.

He stretches out on the couch and we discuss Allison's behavior from the night before, and he tells me that when she gets back on Monday, he's going to tell her that she can work from nine to five, and if she protests, he's going to point out that he's not asking. I ask him what Connor said about that, and he says that Connor stood by his suggestion to fire her.

"She's ridiculous," he says. "I'm not putting up with shit like that. She'd been acting like a total bitch to *both* of us for two days, and I'd already had all I could stand of her. Then when she said that to you, I just had to sit real still and not move because I wanted to tell her to get her annoying ass out of my office and never come back."

I start laughing and go over and give him a hug.

"Thank you," I say, snuggling up beside him.

"Thank you for these superb dinners you've been fixing lately."

"You're quite welcome," I say.

He asks me if I'd like to watch a movie and I tell him that I'd love to. I fix popcorn and drinks while he surfs through the movie channels; then when I curl up on the couch with him, I'm feeling good about us again.

40

<><><><><><><><><><><><><><><><><><><><><><><><><><><><><><><><><><><><><>

On Saturday, I get up early and take Buster Loo for a walk, stopping on the way home to pick up some doughnuts, which I later share with Mason on the back porch. He leaves for work and I take off to run errands, not the least of which is picking up his tux for the charity ball tonight. I'm excited, not just because of the mayhem that Jalena and I have planned, but also because I haven't been on a formal date with Mason since our junior prom in high school.

After taking his tux home and carefully hanging it in his closet, I call Jalena to see if she's ready to make the station wagon transaction. She is, so I get in my car and drive ten minutes to Sam Pettigo's garage. He's outside when I pull up and motions to where I need to park. He tells me that he has a newer-model Chevrolet truck that I could drive instead of the station wagon, but I politely decline. He hands me the keys and tells me to give myself plenty of room to stop.

"As you know," he says, glancing over at my car, "accidents happen. I adjusted the brakes, but you still have to mash 'em."

"I'll mash 'em, then," I say, and he laughs and tells me to be careful. I get into the sky blue wagon and crank it up.

I almost run through two red lights and nearly hit a pedestrian before I shake, rattle, and roll that thing into the parking lot across from the Downtown Inn. Jalena is there when I pull up, and she's standing in front of her Jeep holding up her phone.

"What are you doing?" I ask when I get out of the station wagon.

"Making a documentary," she says, sticking her phone into her pocket. "I'll do the interview later."

"Ha-ha," I say.

"Nice car," she says when we're both in her Jeep. "You should see what kind of a deal he might give you on a trade."

"Right," I say, handing her the keys to the old blue wagon. "That thing is a tank."

We have an early lunch at Las Cantinas Mexican restaurant, during which we discuss our dresses and jewelry for the night. On the drive to my house, we go over our plans one last time. We say good-bye when she drops me off, and I go upstairs and get started with the primping, which takes up most of the afternoon. When Mason comes home at five thirty, I'm sitting on the bed with hot rollers in my hair, and Buster Loo is snoozing next to my feet.

"Hey, sexy lady," he says on his way to the shower, "ready for our big night?"

I get a little nauseous when I think about how upset he would be if he knew I'd been scamming so hard on Lenore Kennashaw. "Can't wait," I say and lean back to look at him in the bathroom. "Are you going to dance with me tonight?"

"Well," he calls, "that depends on if you plan on putting out later or not."

I take the hot rollers out of my hair and start to work on my makeup. When Mason finishes his man-primp routine, he steps out of the bathroom looking and smelling like heaven. He puts on his tux, then helps me into my dress. After a lot of elaborate bragging about how great the other one looks, we go downstairs and find Buster Loo sitting beside the front door.

"Aw, don't worry, little guy," Mason says. "We won't be too late."

We pull into the circle drive of the Downtown Inn, and after a valet opens my door I step out onto a red strip of carpet.

"Look at us," Mason says, taking my arm. "Just like Hollywood."

When we walk into the hotel, we are met by a ticket taker who hands us a program, and then an usher takes us to our seats. I look around for Jalena but don't see her. Mason knows one of the two couples at our table, and as he makes introductions, I see Lenore Kennashaw up on the stage in a dress that looks like it was designed for a seventeen-year-old hootchie mama.

I look around for Jalena again and notice that the place is filling up fast. Everyone has a program, but no one appears to be going haywire about anything, so I assume our special box hasn't made it to the table yet. My phone starts buzzing inside my sparkly clutch, so I discreetly slip it out of my purse and onto my lap. It's a message from Jalena telling me that she saw me come in and I look too foxy for my own good. She sends me another text telling me that she wasn't able to swap the place cards because they had women posted around the room watching the tables like hawks, but she did get the valet tags swapped after doing some first-class flirting with the guy who parked her Jeep.

"Gold hammer key chain," she texts. "How corny is that?"

She sends me another text five minutes later and says that our box just got rolled to the main entrance. I get butterflies again and start second-guessing our plan, not because I'm worried about Lenore, but because I'm worried about Mason finding out I was involved. I send Jalena a message asking if we're doing the right thing. She sends back an immediate "Hellz yes"; then Mason asks who I'm texting, so I put my phone back in my purse. A minute later, a third couple joins us, apologizing for their "almost late" arrival. We all make introductions and small talk, and the evening begins a few minutes later.

A very pretty lady in a beautiful yellow gown steps up to the podium and announces that dinner is about to be served. She also tells us that she will start a slide show about Caboose Charity's biggest project to date, which is the construction of a new activities facility. She stops talking while everyone claps. When the applause stops, she talks about how many children have signed up for the after-school program, which began this past August, and goes on to say they were able to fully fund staffing for the entire academic year. Everyone claps again, and she starts the slide show. I almost start crying when I see pictures of such pitiful-looking kids enjoying brand-new slides, swings, and really cool project tables.

"This is great," Mason whispers, and I nod. "We should get involved with this."

"That exactly what I was thinking," I tell him. *Unless Jalena and I get caught trying to pull this stunt tonight and get banned from this organization forever.*

After dinner, the speeches start and I excuse myself and go to the restroom so I can check my phone. Chatty-Cathy-come-lately gets up to go with me, so I have to actually go into a stall and pretend to pee.

I see where I received a text from Jalena forty minutes ago that says our box of programs has been handed out. She said they went fast with the rush of people trying to get in before the ceremony started. I text her back and say I got in trouble for texting at the table and she tells me not to worry because all we have to do now is wait. I flush the toilet even though I didn't use it and step out to where my bathroom buddy is applying a fresh coat of powder to her heavily made-up face. I wash my hands, then get out my lip gloss, and she starts asking nosy questions, which I answer with very polite, but vague responses, because I'm just not one of those people who feels compelled to bond deeply with women who follow me to the ladies' room.

She tells me all about her husband and her kids and her cats and her best friend's romantic problems, and I smile and nod all the way back to the table. She sits down and picks up her program, and I get excited wondering if it might contain one of our inserts, but instead of opening it, she simply looks at the cover and lays it to the side.

"The auction is about to start," Mason says, leaning over. "Are you excited?"

"Very much so!" I can't wait to see what my paintings go for, but I don't get to see that because the auction begins and ends with no sign of a single one of them.

"I thought you said you donated something," Mason says when the auctioneer steps down. "That would've been great publicity."

"I did," I say and lower my voice to a whisper. "Remember Lenore won that big painting on opening night at the gallery?" He nods. "That was one, which she never paid for and later claimed to have donated, and then I gave them two more when they came by *soliciting* the first day I was open."

"I'm sure there's a logical explanation," Mason says, and his dismissive attitude makes me madder than I already am. I get even madder than that when I look around and see no indication that any of our notices are being noticed. I think about taking my dessertspoon and pushing Chatty-Cathy's program off the table, just to see if something flies out. But I don't because the lights go dim again and another beautiful woman in another beautiful dress starts making a speech thanking everyone for their attendance and continued support of Caboose Charity. She starts a slide show highlighting some other things Caboose Charity is involved in, and I'm once again impressed by the reach of this organization. The only thing I don't understand is how people who do such good things can't sniff out a rat like Lenore Kennashaw. I see the band setting up, and then yet another lovely lady takes the podium and announces, to avid applause, that the band is almost ready and the bar is about to open.

"I'll go get us a drink," Mason says. "Then we'll dance."

I check my phone and don't have a message from Jalena. Mason comes back with the drinks and we sip on those for a while, and then a waiter starts circling the tables with trays of champagne, so I have few glasses while we sit and chat with the other couples at our table. My purse starts buzzing, and while Mason is talking to the man to his left, I quickly check it and see a message from Jalena that says, "Notices noticed! The scramble is on!" I look around but see no sign of a scramble.

"Are you okay?" Mason asks quietly. "You seem distracted."

"I was just hoping to see Jalena, but I guess she's busy," I tell him, making one more swooping look around.

I slip my phone back into my purse, and then our entire table decides to join the party on the dance floor and I forget all about Lenore Kennashaw because I'm having such a good time with Mason.

41

<>◇◇<>

An hour later, Mason drifts into one of the man-circles forming on the fringe of the dance floor, so I go back to the table, sit down with the other ladies, and check my phone. I'm sorely disappointed to see that I don't have an update from Jalena. I've just decided that part of our plan isn't going to pan out after all, and I'm certain the station wagon stunt will flop too, when Chatty-Cathy opens her program and a little white card flutters onto her lap.

"Well, what is this?" she says. She reads it, says, "How tacky," and slips it back into her program. I get sick all over wondering if that's how everyone reacted. The lady to her right, whose name is Amanda, wants to know what was tacky, so Cathy flips open the program and hands her the card.

"Wait a minute," Amanda says. "Frank and Lenore Kennashaw are sitting over there with the rich people, and according to what I read in the program earlier . . . hold on—" She opens her program and starts running a finger down the columns of each page. "Yeah, this is grouped according to how much people give, and a one-star is someone who only donates their time." Amanda leans over and points. "So what is her name doing in the five-star column and why is she seated over there with those folks?"

Cathy is looking at her program now. "Five stars means a donation of ten *thousand* dollars or more?"

"Every year," Amanda says, studying her program.

"And this woman who gives nothing but her time is over there trying to act like she's one of them?" Cathy says.

"That is tacky," I say, hoping this isn't the only table in the building having a conversation like this.

"I can't stand that Lenore Kennashaw," Amanda says, and my heart jumps with joy.

"Now, who is she again?" Cathy asks.

"Her husband owns Kennashaw Home and Garden," the other woman at the table says. "They sell very cheap things for very high prices and refuse returns." She looks at Amanda. "I don't think much of them, either."

I listen with great interest as Amanda and the other lady, whose name I can't remember, talk about run-ins they've had with Lenore Kennashaw. I throw a little fuel into the fire every chance I get, and when they get it all figured out, Cathy is ready to talk to some other people about Lenore being an impostor. She takes her program and goes to find one of her friends. I sip champagne and listen with great interest and amusement as Amanda and the other lady, whose name I find out is Melody, talk about how ridiculous it is that Frank and Lenore are seated with the big shots of Pelican Cove. I'm about to launch into my story about the worthless paint I bought from their store when Jalena comes up to the table.

"Hello, ladies," she says politely. "It seems as if a few people have found unapproved notices in their programs, and we're out trying to collect those."

Melody flips through her program, then puts it back on the table with a visible look of disappointment. "Only one at this table," she says, pointing to Cathy's chair, "and she's gone with it."

"How'd those get in there?" Amanda asks. "And how did Lenore Kennashaw get listed as a five-star patron if she's supposed to be in the one-star category?"

It's all I can do not to laugh when Jalena says somberly, "We've been asked not to discuss it." She finally looks at me. "Thank you ladies for being here tonight, and I'm sorry to interrupt. Please enjoy the rest of your evening."

She walks off and I can't help myself. I start to smile and I can't stop.

"All they're doing by telling people they aren't going to discuss it is making people want to talk about it that much more," Melody says.

"Well, I think it's pretty funny," Amanda replies.

"Me, too," I say to my two new pals. "Let's go dance."

When we get out on the dance floor, I see Tia and she waves but doesn't make any effort to speak. She disappears a minute later, and I wonder if she somehow found out about the crush I have on her boyfriend or if she's still really *that* embarrassed.

A few minutes later, the music stops and I turn to see Lenore Kennashaw at the podium.

"If I could have a moment of your time," she says coolly. "I'm sorry for the bother, but there is an issue I need to address." She looks out across the crowd. "Let me offer my sincerest apologies for the ridiculous assertions that some of you have found on program inserts that I assure you were not authorized by me or anyone at Caboose Charity. Everyone knows that Frank and I have been giving generously to this charity for years, and I do plan to file charges of slander against who-ever is responsible for this. Thank you."

A rumble goes through the crowd, and a small group of people gather around the steps coming off the stage. I see Chatty-Cathy in that crowd, so I start working my way over there to eavesdrop. The people gathered are not fans of Lenore, as it turns out, and they badger her until she blurts out, "What do you people want from me? Get back! Get away from me! Frank!" She bustles through the crowd to her table, where Frank, who is leaning back with an unlit cigar in his mouth, looks at her and barks, "What?"

"We're leaving," she says. "I won't stand to be disgraced in this manner. Not after all I do for this organization."

Frank doesn't say a word, just gets up and follows her out, and all eyes are on them as they strut into the lobby. People gather here and there and try to look like they're not looking, but everyone is watching their every move. I go with the flow of the crowd, then post up in a corner of the lobby that has a great view of the circle drive out front. I see Jalena come out another door, and she sees me and smiles. She goes to the other side of the lobby and gets out her phone.

A few seconds later, my phone beeps. "Could this get any better?"

I text back, "Only if a station wagon pulls up." And a few minutes later, it does.

Frank and Lenore Kennashaw are standing on the sidewalk looking supremely self-righteous and proud when Erlene Pettigo's sky blue sta-tion wagon rumbles up to the curb. The two boys at the valet stand exchange a look; then the one closest to the car steps over and opens the door. He looks at Lenore like she's got cooties flying out from un-der her too-short skirt, and she looks at him like he must've misunder-stood something. When the poor guy who fetched the car walks around and hands Frank Kennashaw the keys, Lenore tears into those boys so bad that hotel security shows up and makes her stop. Lenore walks over to the valet stand and rifles through the keys. Not finding what she was looking for, she stalks back into the hotel lobby, and I try to blend in with the tree I'm standing next to as she storms to the desk. She demands that they call the police because her keys have been stolen. The clerk looks at her like she's crazy, then produces a set of keys with a gold hammer, and I hear the clerk say something about "lost and found" followed by the words "hotel security."

Lenore marches out the door and hands the keys to Frank, and they walk across the street to the parking lot. I walk outside and listen to the valets openly discuss what a hateful wench she was and then get worried when they talk about what to do with the station wagon. I think for a second that I'm going to have to go over there and fess up, but then one of the guys says that he's just going to park it back where he found it and then put the keys back where he found those, too.

I turn to go back inside and run right into Sylvie Best.

"What are you out here sniggering about?" she hisses. "You better hope you weren't involved with any of this, or we will *end* you in this town."

"Fuck off, Sylvie," I say and walk past her.

"Don't say you weren't warned," she calls out.

I don't even respond. I just stick my middle finger in the air and keep walking. The valet guys get a good kick out of that, and I make a mental note to slip each one of them a twenty before I leave.

I enter the lobby and see Ramona Bradley.

"Hi, Mrs. Bradley," I say walking up to her.

"Well, hello," she says pleasantly. "How are you doing tonight?"

"I'm great," I say. "Can I ask you a quick question?"

"But of course."

"The paintings I donated weren't in the auction. Do you have any idea why, or where they might be?"

"Sweetheart, can you tell me your name again? We've been seeing so many people, I can't keep them all straight."

"Graciela," I say. "Ace Jones. I have the art gallery."

"Oh right, yes, well, I don't know what in the world might have happened to those."

"Okay," I say, realizing this conversation is a waste of time.

I walk back into the auditorium, where I meet Mason at our table. He asks me where I've been.

"Just out getting some fresh air," I say. "I think I had a little too much champagne."

"Are you ready to go, or do you want to stay a while longer?"

"I'm having a blast!"

"Well, come on," he says. "Let's get out on that dance floor!"

We end up shutting the charity ball down, and we're in the group still on the dance floor when the band stops playing and the lights come on.

"Party's over!" someone yells as the pretty lady in the yellow dress takes the podium.

"Thank you all so much for coming tonight," she says with unflappable poise. "I hope each and every one of you had a wonderful time. Good night!" Our bunch starts clapping, and then people come in with trash cans, and we all go back to our tables, gather our things, and file out the door.

The sidewalk chatter is all about Lenore Kennashaw, and I relish every detail I hear. One man wonders aloud how much she really gives, and several others agree they'd like to know that, too. Some people think what happened to Lenore was a disgrace; others think Lenore herself is disgraceful. Someone brings up the rumor that Kennashaw

Home and Garden is going under, and that gets everyone's attention. Someone else brings up the station wagon incident, and everyone stops chattering about the hardware store and starts listening to one man's account of how the curbside drama went down.

"There it is," Amanda says, pointing across the street to the station wagon in the distance. "Way out there in the corner."

"How did the valet have the key for it?" another man asks, and that gives way to talk of a conspiracy, and then someone points out that there's usually a little truth in even the most bald-faced lie, to which someone says, "Looks to me like she finally pissed off the wrong person." Everyone is in complete agreement that Lenore Kennashaw was deliberately targeted.

I look at Mason, who has said nothing since we came outside, and he has this look on his face that tells me I'm going to have some explaining to do when we get in the truck. A little explaining and a lot of lying.

Mason doesn't say anything for the first few minutes on the ride home. Then he looks at me and says, "What do you think about what happened tonight?"

"I agree that someone was targeting her."

"Now, who would do something like that?" he says. "Who would pull a stunt like that at an event like this?"

"I have no idea," I lie.

I can sense that he's looking at me, but I keep my eyes straight ahead.

"Ace, did you have anything to do with this?" he asks, point-blank. "Because you were acting like a teenager checking your phone all night, and you went to the bathroom about fifteen times."

"I drank a lot of champagne," I say evenly. "And Jalena was there, and I was trying to figure out where she was because I wanted to see her, but she kept moving around all over the place because she was helping out with the event."

"You and Tia didn't talk much."

"Tia's got some weird stuff going on right now," I say. "She's kind of been avoiding everybody."

"I just hope that you didn't have anything to do with any of what happened," he says as we pull up in the driveway. "Where is your car?" He eyes me suspiciously.

"I dropped it off at the shop," I say. "Remember, I told you that man was going to fix it this weekend." I can't remember whether I told Mason that Erlene Pettigo was driving a station wagon the day she rolled into the back of my car at Bueno Burrito. I hold my breath in a full-fledged state of panic and wait for him to respond.

"Oh yeah," he says, and I don't know if I didn't tell him or if he doesn't remember, or maybe he just doesn't want to continue a conversation that begins with "remember, I told you."

We go inside and find Buster Loo asleep on the sofa.

"See, little man," Mason says, scooping him up. "Told you we'd be back."

42

<><><><><><><><><><><><><><><><><><><><><><><><><><><><><><><><><><><><><>

Sunday morning when I go downstairs, Mason is sitting at the kitchen table with a stern look on his face. In front of him is the notebook I used to map out the attack on Lenore.

"Before you say anything, let me read you this one part," he says and proceeds to read the final draft of the memo. "Now, I didn't actually see one of those little cards, but I heard enough about it to recognize a common theme." He looks at me and I want to die. "What do you have to say for yourself?"

"Nothing," I say and sit down across from him.

"Nothing?" he practically shouts. "You lied to my face last night about your involvement with this, and now you have nothing to say!" He pushes the notebook across the table to me. "Really?"

"I know what that says," I say. "I wrote it."

"You are unbelievable," he says.

"I'm sorry!" I say and try harder to be mean so I won't start crying, but it doesn't work so I'm sitting there glaring at him with tears rolling down my cheeks.

"What is going on?" he asks. "Why in the *world* would you do this?" He looks at me. "You're going to have to apologize to Lenore. You know that, right?"

"I'm not apologizing to *anybody* for *anything*," I say, getting angry again.

"Why would you do this? You humiliated that woman and her husband at the damn charity ball! That's one of the biggest events of the year around here. And for what?" He lowers his voice. "I am so ashamed of you."

"I'm sorry," I say in a tone that's more sarcastic than apologetic. "Maybe I've just had too much time on my hands lately." And I get up and walk back upstairs and get back in bed. Buster Loo creeps in a second later and burrows under the covers with me. I hear Mason's truck leave and I cry until I fall asleep.

When I wake up again, Mason is sitting on the end of the bed.

"I'm sorry I said I was ashamed of you," he tells me. "But I think you owe me an explanation."

"I do," I say and sound like I've got cotton balls shoved up my nose. He goes downstairs and brings back a Sprite with cherries and some aspirin. "Do I look hungover?" I ask, but he's not in the mood to joke.

I go in the bathroom, where I slick my hair back into a ponytail, wash my face in freezing water, and then brush my teeth. I wet a washcloth and press it down against my eyes. I go back into the bedroom, where he's still sitting with a cup in one hand and an aspirin bottle in the other. He hands me the drink and two tablets, and I lie back against the headboard and tell him all about the evil, wicked Lenore Kennashaw.

Then I tell him what Sylvie Best said to me, and then I tell him how

Mrs. Adday treated me at the Beach House Bed and Breakfast, and he hangs his head and looks at the floor.

He looks back up at me and says, "Do you think you create a lot of your own problems because of your attitude?"

"Are you serious right now?" I ask.

"I'm dead serious," he says. "Ace, when your career requires constant interaction with the general public, you have to bury your attitude and present yourself as an unbiased professional. It's not always easy."

"Let me ask you something," I say. "How hard is it for you to be nice to Mrs. Collins across the street?"

"It's not hard at all. What kind of question is that?"

"How hard is it for you to be nice to Margo?"

"I'm not nice to Margo because she's a fucking idiot," he says.

"My point exactly."

"You don't have to get all wrapped up in their idiocy," he says. "Did you see me out there trying to jump on Margo about that ridiculous sign she put up at the entrance to our neighborhood? No, you didn't."

"Nor did you see me do that."

"Ace, sometimes you have to let stuff go. Just let people be who they are and don't worry about it."

"Maybe you need to let me be who I am, then, and *you* don't need to worry about it."

"I can't *not* worry about it when you were involved in something like what happened last night. I have an excellent reputation in this town, which I have worked very hard for and intend to maintain!" He looks at me and I take a drink of Sprite because I'm starting to feel very sick. "And that station wagon? Don't I remember that from a little incident at Bueno Burrito?"

"Yes, you do," I say. "Her husband is fixing my bumper. I told you the truth about that."

"I cannot believe you!"

"You want to know what I can't believe?" I say and decide that if he's not going to give me a break, then I'm not giving him one. "I can't believe how well it all worked out. I'm actually quite pleased with myself."

"Well, I guess we'll have to agree to disagree on that."

"I guess we will," I say. "Thank you for the Sprite."

Jalena calls me at two o'clock and reminds me that we need to get that station wagon out of the parking lot, so I roll out of bed and get into the shower. She arrives at my house thirty minutes later, and I put on my shades and walk out the door. I don't acknowledge Mason sitting on the couch, and he doesn't say a word to me.

On the drive over to the Downtown Inn, Jalena expresses some concern about being seen because she heard that Lenore is on the warpath trying to find out who was responsible for last night's shenanigans.

"Several people from the charity have called me this morning," she says. "Some are pretty upset because of what happened; others are relieved." She looks at me. "I think most people are relieved."

"How could they not be?" I say.

"Anna Simmons called me a few minutes before I left the house," she says. "She thought the whole thing was really funny and she told me that the board is sending all of the paperwork to an accountant for an official review of the donation records, so that'll finish her off with that organization."

"Good."

"And *nobody* has *any* idea who might've done it. Anna said that people are speculating it was a disgruntled employee or maybe a *really* dissatisfied customer. So it looks like we could make out like some bandits on this if we can just get that station wagon out of there without getting caught."

"Lenore Kennashaw knows who did it," I say. "She has to. And you can drop me off around the corner from the parking lot. I'll get the car and then take the long way back to the garage and meet you there."

"Are you not worried she may be watching the car?"

"I hope she is."

"Are you not worried about Mason finding out?"

"He already knows."

"Oh no," she says. "How'd that happen?"

"Well, I left my notebook on the table yesterday and he found it this morning."

"So you haven't had the best morning?"

"Not by a long shot, and I was *just* getting to the point where I thought we were going to be okay."

"You might still be," Jalena says. "He'll get over it."

"I don't think so." I look at her. "He told me I was going to have to apologize to Lenore."

"Aw, hell no," she says.

"Yeah, I'm not doing that."

"Just hang in there," she says. "I still think y'all are gonna make it."

"I'm glad somebody does," I tell her. She gives me the keys and I make her drop me off three blocks away from the parking lot, and then I double back and walk two blocks out of the way to make sure no one sees me and her in the same vicinity. I stop on the edge on the parking lot and look around, but I don't see anyone. I walk out and get in the car, nervous because I'm not in the mood for a confrontation.

I put the key in the ignition and it won't turn. I look around and see a few cars driving by, so I lie down in the seat. I pump the brake a few times, then the gas. I have no idea why I'm doing that, but it seems better to stomp on the pedals as opposed to doing nothing. I put my hand on the key and try to wiggle it, but it won't budge. I sit up and, in a state of full panic, start shaking the steering wheel and trying to turn the key and stomping on the pedal, and finally, after I pitch the cussing fit of the millennium, the key turns and the car cranks right up.

I see traffic on the road, so I lie back down in the seat after turning the air conditioner on full blast. When the coast is clear, I pull out on the road and think for a minute that I might get away without being seen. Then a red convertible Thunderbird pulls up behind me and I know I'm in trouble. I glance in my rearview mirror and see two women wearing large shades and scarves tied around their heads.

"F me in the A," I say to myself. "Why did I think she wasn't going to be up here waiting to see who got this car?"

I pretend not to see them and proceed to drive around town, slowing down to fifteen miles an hour from time to time, but they stay on my bumper. I call Jalena and tell her what's going on, and she tells me that she's parked in a deserted parking lot behind the garage and she's out of sight. I think about going to Walmart or somewhere like that, but then I'd either have to engage in a bitter cuss fight or whip her ass, and I'm not in the mood to do either. Not today. Not after she tried to ruin my life to the point where I just took over and did it myself because she was driving me crazy. No, she'll not get the pleasure of cussing me out today. And I'll not get the pleasure of blacking both her eyes.

After another fifteen minutes of riding around side streets with the Thunderbird on my bumper, I come up with a plan. At the next red light, I do a Google search for the number to the Pelican Cove Police Department and give them a call. I glance up at the street sign, then tell the police dispatcher that I'd like to report an aggressive driver on the 1300 block of East Zaragoza.

"She's about two inches from my bumper, and I can't help that my old beat-up car doesn't go very fast and I really don't want to get run over by some woman in a shiny red convertible Thunderbird," I say, trying to sound as pitiful and country as I can.

"We'll have someone check it out, ma'am," the lady says politely. "Thank you for the call. Drive safely."

When the light turns green, I ease forward and they stay right behind me. I go a few more blocks, and I'm starting to think the police might have better things to do today when I see a patrol car, which does a U-turn in the street; then the Thunderbird has to pull over. I roll down my window, flip them the bird, and mash that accelerator all the way to the floor. Which eventually gets me up to forty-five miles an hour.

A few minutes later, I turn into Sam Pettigo's garage on two wheels. I lock the doors and stick the keys in my pocket and then speed-walk around behind the garage. I have to crawl through some creepy-looking brush with lots of briars, but I finally make it to the deserted parking lot where Jalena is parked.

"You better take me home, and then you better head home quick," I tell her. "I called the law on them."

"For what?" Jalena asks, very amused.

"Aggressive driving," I say, and she laughs and says that was brilliant.

When we get close to my subdivision, I tell Jalena to drive on up the road a bit and let me out.

"Do you want to drive on up the road a little bit more and see if Kevin Jacobs is home?" Jalena teases.

"No, thank you."

She laughs and pulls into a cul-de-sac that backs up to my neighborhood.

"Here is good," I tell her. "Call me tomorrow."

"Hey, Ace," she says before I get out of her Jeep. "High five?"

I slap her hand. "High five, sister."

43

Monday morning Mason wakes me up before daylight and asks me if I want to take him to work and keep his Escalade. I tell him I don't and go right back to sleep. When I wake up again, it's almost eleven o'clock. I look at my phone, and no one has called needing to see anything in the gallery, so I roll back over and go to sleep.

Avery calls me at one o'clock, wondering where I am, and I tell her I'm taking a few days off. I ask her if the CALL ME sign is still on the door and she says that it is. I tell her she can spend as much or as little time as she wants there. She sounds concerned and a little sad, but she doesn't pry and I appreciate it.

Monday afternoon, Jalena calls and asks if I need a ride anywhere, and I tell her that I'll need a ride to the garage in the morning. I don't go to work on Tuesday, either, and I'm not surprised at all that no one calls about the gallery for a second day. Jalena picks me up Tuesday afternoon and takes me to my car. She invites me out for a drink, but I tell her I'd rather go home and sleep, and that's exactly what I do.

I don't go to any dinners at the office all week long, and if I'm not asleep when Mason comes home, I pretend to be, and I do the same thing every morning. I cancel Girls Night In, and when Jalena calls me Friday morning to check on me, I lie and tell her I'm fine. Mason and I are civil to each other over the weekend but don't do anything as a couple. I expect an apology that I don't get, and I suspect he feels the same way.

The next week, I meet Jalena at Credo's Monday night, and when Kevin Jacobs shows up, I flirt with him like there's no tomorrow. We go back on Tuesday night, and I get so drunk that Jalena has to help me into her Jeep, out of her Jeep, and then into my house.

It takes me all day Wednesday to recover from that, and on Thursday I load up Buster Loo and go to the gallery just to get out of the house. I've been there about five minutes when I see a silver Mercedes pull up in the parking lot. I scurry over and lock the door, then hide behind the counter and watch Lenore Kennashaw walk up to the door. She raps on the glass with her fist, then cups her hands around her eyes and peers in. I'm seriously entertaining the idea of filing a restraining order against her when she finally walks back to her car. I watch her pull out her phone, and a second later, mine starts ringing. When I don't answer, she drives away.

She calls back six more times, and I call the phone company and have a block put on her number. Then I decide that what I need to do is go home. To my real home. I call Jalena and ask her if she wants to go to Bugtussle with me, and she says that she has to work.

"Take off!" I tell her. "Can't you take off whenever you like when you work for your dad?"

"Uh, you obviously don't know my dad," she says. "When do you want to leave?"

"This afternoon," I say. "If we leave by two, we can be there by seven thirty or eight and you'd only have to miss a day and a half of work. C'mon—being spontaneous is fun!"

"Let me talk to Daddy and I'll call you right back," she says, and when she calls me back ten minutes later, she tells me she's on her way home to start packing.

I call Avery to let her know I'm going out of town for the weekend. She doesn't answer so I leave her a voice mail telling her she's welcome to hang out at the gallery as much as she likes.

I make another sign that says the gallery will be closed until Monday, tape it to the door, and leave before I start getting sentimental. I go home and pack up all of my nice, new clothes and a good supply of old ones. Then I pack up Buster Loo's dishes and bed and a few of his favorite toys. When I walk out the door with all of my bags, Lenore Kennashaw is standing on the sidewalk in front of the house.

"Going somewhere?" she asks, like I should be afraid of her. She walks through the yard and stops at the foot of the steps. "You're very clever, Miss Jones. I'll give you that," she says. "However—"

"Hold on," I say. I drop my bags and get my phone out of my back pocket. I walk to the top of the steps and look down at her. Then I turn my phone around so she can see the number pad. I punch a nine and then a one.

"What are you doing?" she snaps. "There's no emergency here."

I hold my finger over the one. "No, but there's going to be if you don't get the hell out of my yard and away from my house." I look at her and she doesn't move. "Do you want to try me?" I ask her. "Do you *really* want to try me? Think about what I did to you at the charity ball."

"What's going to happen if you press that one?" she asks in her usual condescending tone. "Besides you getting arrested for misuse of the emergency system?"

"What's going to happen after I press this one is that I'm going to lay this phone down on the porch, and then I'm going to walk down these steps and beat the shit out of you until the paramedics and/or police arrive and make me stop."

"And then I'll file assault charges and sue you," she says like a real smart-ass.

"No, *and then* you will be lying on the ground with the shit kicked out of you," I say. "You didn't ask what would happen *after* I stomped your ass, *after* the ambulance takes you to the hospital, or *after* you get released from the emergency room. You asked what would happen *after* I press this one. Let's not get the cart before horse here, Lenore." She looks around and I can see that she's getting nervous. "I've been to jail," I tell her. "And it didn't scare me at all."

"Who do you think you are?"

"Somebody you can't push around," I say.

Lenore Kennashaw gives me one of her finest smirks and then turns and walks away without a word. I pick up my bags and continue packing up my car. Then I go back inside, leave Mason a note, and walk out the door with Buster Loo trotting along behind me.

44

◇◇

I pick Jalena up at her house, which is an adorable cottage about a hundred yards from her daddy's marina on Frog Bayou. She has twice as much luggage as I do, and I packed enough for two weeks. We get it all situated and she gets in the car and Buster Loo promptly nestles himself into her lap.

"Hey, thanks for inviting me," she says. "It's not every day someone invites you to Bugtussle, Mississippi."

"Don't get too excited," I caution. "So have you talked to Tia?" I ask. "I've called her two or three times, but she hasn't called me back. It kind of hurts my feelings because I thought we were friends."

"She's fickle like that," Jalena says. "I've only talked to her once, and that was after I left her a message about Girls Night In last week. She told me she was working all the time and that she went to see Afton last weekend." She looks at me. "I think it's over between her and Kevin."

"Did she say that?"

"Nope, he did when he came in for lunch today." I glance at her and she's shaking her head. "He hasn't heard from her in weeks, so he's concerned, you know, that he made her mad," she says, and I start feeling like a dirtbag again. "He was asking me all these questions, because you know how a guy will push you away until you start walking, and then they get worried that you won't come back."

"Right," I mumble, thankful to be driving in the opposite direction from my drama.

"I told him that I couldn't help him. All I know is she's working a lot."

"I miss talking to her," I say.

"She'll come back around," Jalena assures me. "She's always been like this. She's gone weeks without calling me before when nothing at all happened. I'm sure she'll be at the Halloween party weekend after next. No matter what's going on, she won't miss that because she rustles up a lot of business at these big get-togethers in town." She looks at me. "Are y'all going to that?"

"I don't know anything about it," I say.

"Oh, you have to go," she says. "After this little trip, you and Mason will kiss and make up, and then you can start planning the costumes."

"Costumes?"

"Yeah, girl! Everyone dresses up! It's like Mardi Gras in October. The city closes down three blocks of Dock Street, and the Blue Oyster has a band. It's a great party. You can't miss it."

"Sounds like fun," I say and my heart breaks as I think about the mess I'm in with Mason.

"Oh, it is," she assures me. "So where are we staying when we get to Bugtussle?"

"It's a surprise," I tell her. "Especially for the person we're staying with." Then I tell her I'm kidding and pick up the phone to call Lilly.

"What's up, sister?" I ask when she answers. "I was just going to leave you a message." We chat for a few minutes, and then I tell her that Jalena and I are on the way to Bugtussle and she squeals with delight and insists we stay with her. We talk a few more minutes, and when I put the phone down, I tell Jalena I'm taking her on a weekend getaway in a grown-up Barbie dollhouse.

"It's pink with all of this decorative white trim," I tell her as I pull out on I-10. "It's like a dolled-up mini Victorian mansion. It's really over the top, but it's also very cute."

"I can't wait," she says, scratching Buster Loo behind his ears.

Three hours later, we stop for gas in Meridian, and she takes Buster Loo for a short walk while I fill up the car. Then we drive through a fast-food joint and get some cheap and greasy supper. Three hours after that, we arrive in Tupelo.

"Tupelo, Mississippi," Jalena says. "Birthplace of the King!"

I exit off Highway 45 and take Highway 78 toward Memphis.

"How far is Bugtussle from Memphis?" she asks.

"A little less than an hour," I tell her, "depending on the traffic."

"I would love to go to Memphis."

"You've never been?" I ask.

"Nope."

"We'll go, then! You would love Beale Street."

"Let's do it," she says. "Hey, am I going to meet your parents while I'm up here? Do they still live in Bugtussle?"

I don't answer immediately because I have to think about the best way to tell her about my parents.

"Not on good terms?" she says, guessing.

I take a deep breath and tell her that my parents passed away when I was eleven after they were in an automobile accident and that I moved in with my dad's mom and lived with her until I moved off to college.

"Ace, I'm so sorry," she says. "I had no idea."

"There's no way you could have known unless I told you." I look at her. "Don't worry about it."

"And your grandmother?" She looks at me warily.

"Passed away when I was a junior at Mississippi State. I took a break from school after she died and spent a year in Europe with a study-abroad program. Then I went back to school, finished my degree, and moved into her house, which my friend Chloe has been renting for the past few months but is about to move out of because she's buying a house of her own."

Jalena shakes her head, then looks back at me. "Brothers and sisters? Cousins?"

I shake my head, and the truth about how alone I am in the world bears down on me like a ton of bricks. "My parents were both only children and Gramma Jones was the last grandparent I had." I bite my lip and try not to cry. Jalena reaches over and pats me on the back.

"I can't even imagine, Ace," she says. "I wouldn't know what to do without—" She stops. "I'm sorry. It's just my heart is breaking for you right now."

"It's okay," I say, swallowing the lump in my throat. "That's the hand I was dealt, and I deal with it."

I put on my signal for the Bugtussle exit.

"I got a feeling I'm gonna meet some good people here in Bugtussle, Mississippi," she says as we get off the highway.

"You are," I tell her, and a few minutes later, I turn onto Cotton Drive.

"Dang!" Jalena says as I turn into Lilly's driveway. "Either a whole lot of people live with your friend or she's throwing you one hell of a welcome home party."

◇◇◇

45

We get out of the car and Buster Loo makes a run for the back-yard. Lilly comes around the corner of the house and hugs me and then Jalena. I introduce them, and then Ethan Allen walks up and tells us not to even think about touching those bags. He hugs me, and when I introduce him to Jalena, he hugs her, too. She glances over at me in surprise and I just smile at her. Ethan Allen grabs two handfuls of luggage and starts toward the house.

Jalena turns to Lilly and says, "Your boyfriend is such a gentleman."

"Oh, that is so *not* my boyfriend," she says. "My boyfriend is out in the backyard drinking beer."

Jalena looks at me. "Well, whose boyfriend is he, because there's no way that guy is single."

"Actually, he is," Lilly says, smiling at me.

Jalena cuts her eyes over to me and says, "Ace Jones, why didn't you warn me about him?"

"I didn't know he would be here," I whisper, because Ethan Allen is coming back to the car.

"C'mon in the house," Lilly says. "I guess y'all want to freshen up."

"I definitely do," Jalena says, glancing back at Ethan Allen.

Lilly takes us upstairs and shows us to our rooms while Jalena continuously compliments Lilly's whimsical home.

"Lilly, will you check on Buster Loo, please?" I ask her. "He made a beeline for the crowd as soon as he got here."

"Oh, you know he's fine, but I'll go check on him anyway," she says.

When Lilly goes back downstairs, Jalena comes into my room and whispers, "Why didn't you tell me about *him*?"

"Never thought about it," I say. "He's a homeboy who won't ever leave Mississippi and you're a homegirl who won't ever leave Florida, so it never occurred to me to mention him to you."

"Who said I wouldn't ever leave Florida?" Jalena whispers.

"You did," I say, poking her on the arm.

"Well, I was lyin'," she says.

We hear Ethan Allen coming up the steps and we step out onto the landing, where he has just put down some more luggage.

"You ladies must be plannin' on stayin' a while," he says with a smile.

"Jalena said she might stay forever," I say teasingly, and Jalena punches me in the arm.

"I didn't say that," she snaps. She looks at Ethan Allen. "Thank you so much for getting my bags. That's really sweet of you."

"Ladies don't tote bags when I'm around," he says, turning to go back down the stairs. "One more trip should get it."

"I am going to kill you!" she says, picking up her makeup bag. "I've got to go get foxy."

Ten minutes later, I'm leaning on the door of Jalena's bedroom waiting for her to finish her makeup.

"C'mon," I tell her. "You're among friends. Nobody cares if you're wearing eyeliner."

"Just give me a minute," she says.

"Okay." I go downstairs and set Buster Loo's food and water bowls up in the kitchen. Then I get his bed out and stick it in the corner next to those. I hear Jalena come down the steps and I call out that I'm in the kitchen. Lilly comes in with an empty ice cream freezer and starts rinsing it out in the sink.

"When did you start making homemade ice cream?" I ask.

"Ever since you moved," she says. She looks at Jalena and nods at me. "She gets my man hooked on that damned homemade banana ice cream that nobody knows how to make but her and then she moves out of the state."

I start laughing and tell Jalena the story about the time Lilly was trying to hit on Dax and claimed to love homemade banana ice cream when she really hates it.

"Then she had to eat a cup," I say. "And they've been a happy couple ever since."

When we walk out onto Lilly's back porch, I look over and see Buster Loo sitting on the swing with Chloe.

"Well, hello!" she says, getting up to hug me. She nods toward Buster Loo. "Look who's keeping me company." I introduce her to Jalena, and then Lilly shows up and insists on introducing Jalena to everyone else. I sit down on the porch swing with Chloe and talk to her for a few minutes while Buster Loo pretends he doesn't know me. She doesn't mention Gramma Jones's house, so I don't either.

Chloe finally runs me off because she doesn't want to keep me from seeing everyone, so I walk around and talk to a lot of my old pals and thank everyone for coming by to see me.

"They're not here to see you," I hear someone say and turn to see

Dax Dorsett. "They're here for the homemade ice cream, because Lilly has become quite a celebrity with your secret recipe."

"Dax!" I say to Lilly's handsome young boyfriend. "How are you?" He gives me a hug and we chat for a minute, and then he leans down and whispers that Lilly's ice cream isn't *quite* as good as mine.

"She probably uses skim milk instead of whole," I whisper to him. "Next time you want some, pick up a quart of that and stick it in the fridge."

"Ah," he says, smiling. "I'll do that."

Someone hollers at him and he walks off and I turn around to see Coach Logan Hatter.

"Hatt!" I say and give him a big hug. "It's so good to see you. How's school going?"

"Well, it's pretty boring without you across the hall, but that mean ol' girl they hired to replace you is pretty hot, so I manage," he says and starts laughing.

"And here I was thinking I was irreplaceable," I say.

He drapes his arm around me and says, "All my old girlfriends are irreplaceable." He smiles at me. "That's why I go to such great lengths to stay in their good graces."

I shove his arm off my shoulder. "You are so full of it!" I tell him.

"How's the art gallery going?" he asks. "You're just down there in Florida living the dream, huh?"

"It's going," I say, not wanting to talk about it, so I ask him who he thinks will win the national championship in college football this year, and he forgets all about me living the dream and gives me a full breakdown of the top five teams he thinks have the best chance. Listening to him talk, I start to think I made a terrible mistake quitting my job. Because I had it made teaching art at Bugtussle High School across the hallway from Logan Hatter.

After carrying on with him for a few more minutes, I go inside to get some water. Ethan Allen follows me into the kitchen, where he props up on the bar.

"Heard you and my man Mason are in a bit of a skirmish," he says.

"You've talked to him?"

"Yeah, he called me about an hour ago when he got home and found your note." Ethan Allen looks at me. "Said you pulled quite a stunt at some ball or something?"

"I did, but it needed to be done," I say. "I want an apology from him and I'm sure he wants an apology from me, and I don't think either of us will get what we want."

"That's what he said."

My heart drops at this confirmation that Mason has no intention of apologizing, either.

"I'm tired, Ethan Allen," I tell him. "I don't like it down there. I'm not happy and I'm tired of trying to pretend that I am."

"Well, what happened, Ace? I thought things were going good for y'all."

"I don't know," I say. "I did all that work to get that gallery ready, and then after it opened, it was nothing like I expected, and even if I'd sold a hundred paintings instead of just one, I don't think I'd like it any better, so there's that, plus Mason working all the time." I look at him. "*All* the time. Then he took on two more cases just like the one he's working on now, so it'll be at least another year before life gets back to what *I* want *my* normal to be." I look down at my glass of water. "So then I went on this crazy cooking spree, and then I pulled that stunt at the charity ball, and now here I am."

"Well, you know what I think," Ethan Allen says. "I think y'all both need to move back home."

"I'm ready," I say, "but you know he's not going to do that, and he shouldn't have to, because he's perfectly happy down there."

"I know, but I still wish he would."

"Me, too," I tell him. "I just don't know what I'm going to do."

"About what?" Lilly asks, bouncing into the kitchen.

"Things aren't going so great with Mason and me," I tell her. "I'll tell you all about it later."

"Aw, man," Lilly says. "And here I was thinking you made this trip because you miss me so bad."

"You know I do," I say, giving her a hug. "And thank you so much for doing all of this. It's so nice to be around so many people that I know."

Lilly grabs some more plastic spoons out of her cabinet. "I've got to get back outside," she says, then looks at me. "You should, too."

Later that night, I'm sitting on the back porch with Lilly, Chloe, Jalena, and Ethan Allen. Buster Loo is snoozing in Jalena's lap.

"So, what do you think of all these country folks up here in Mississippi?" Ethan Allen asks Jalena.

"Love 'em," she says. "I'm a country girl myself."

"Really?" Ethan Allen asks, looking at me.

"She lives outside Pelican Cove in a nice little place called Frog's Bayou," I tell him.

"Really?" he says again, looking back at Jalena.

"You're looking at the Frog Giggin' Queen of Escambia County," Jalena tells him, and we all start laughing.

"I did not know that about you, Jalena," I say.

"True story," she says.

"You've got tidewater rivers down there," Ethan Allen says. "That ain't even fair to the frogs."

"It's not fair to the frogs because I gig like a champ," she says.

"Are there not alligators in those rivers?" Chloe asks.

"Oh yeah, but they dive when you shine a spotlight on 'em," Jalena says. "Frogs just freeze up, which makes them a lot easier to gig."

"Spotlight!" Chloe says. "You do this in the dark?"

"Oh yeah," Jalena says. "Only amateurs gig in the daytime."

"So how do you know if you're giggin' on a frog or a gator if it's dark?" Lilly asks, and I get a big kick out of how wrapped up Lilly and Chloe are in Jalena's story.

"Gator eyes reflect red," Jalena says with unwavering certainty. "Frog eyes reflect white or maybe yellow."

I've never actually seen someone fall in love, but watching Ethan Allen listen to Jalena talk about frog gigging makes me think I'm doing just that.

"Oh, that would scare me to death," Chloe says. "Looking at all of those eyes in the dark."

"No, it's so much fun. I'll take y'all next time you come down," Jalena says, and Lilly laughs and tells her she should have her own show on the fishing channel.

"I'd watch it," Ethan Allen says, leaning back in his chair but keeping his eyes on Jalena.

Chloe announces she's got to leave because she has to be at work in the morning, so she gets up to go. Ethan Allen leaves a few minutes later, and Lilly, Jalena, and I go inside and stand around Lilly's kitchen and talk. Buster Loo comes in and helps himself to some dog food, laps up a little water, and then curls up in his bed.

"What do y'all want to do tomorrow?" Lilly asks.

"You're not going to work?" I say.

"Girl, I pulled an Ace Jones and called in sick!" she says, laughing.

"You are too funny, Lilly," Jalena tells her. "Thank you so much for introducing me to everyone tonight. I really had a great time."

"Well, the fun is only beginning," Lilly says.

"Hey, why don't we get up early and go to Memphis?" I say.

Lilly looks at Jalena. "You want to?"

"I'd love to," Jalena says.

"Well, let's all get in bed so we can get up and get gone," Lilly says. We say our good nights and Jalena thanks Lilly again for her hospitality. Lilly goes off to her room and Jalena and I go upstairs, where I pick on her a little bit about Ethan Allen, but not too much. She asks if we'll see him again before we go home, and I assure her that we will. We say good night and I go in my room, close the door, and pick up my phone. No missed calls. I lie down and my heart aches when I think about Mason down there working himself to death and coming home to an empty house. I close my eyes and wish a thousand times that things could be different for us. I wish I could be different.

46

<><><><><><><><><><><><><><><><><><><><><><><><><><><><><><><><><><><><><>

I get up early Friday morning and take Buster Loo for a long walk. Then I call Chloe and ask her if it would be okay if I left Buster Loo at her place because I think he might enjoy spending the day there. Of course that's okay with her, so I load up Buster Loo and all his accessories, then tell him I'm taking him home.

When I pull up in the driveway, I'm swamped with a wave of emotions ranging from happiness to utter relief. I reach into the backseat to get Buster Loo's bag and then get out of the car. When I open the gate behind the house, Buster Loo runs into that backyard like his ass is on fire and proceeds to run around all over the place, making big circles, then smaller ones, and then he breaks out into the speedy-dog crazy eights. I use the key I still have on my ring to unlock the back door. Buster Loo jumps through the doggie door, then goes back and jumps in and out two more times. I set his food and water where they always used to be, then put his bed in the corner. Buster Loo runs around all over the house, then disappears behind the love seat. He barrels out from behind there a minute later with an old chew toy, so I toss that for him a few times; then he goes back behind the love seat and stays.

"You be good, Buster Loo," I tell him. "Aunt Chloe will be home in a few hours, so just sit tight."

I go back outside, get in my car, and sit in the driveway. As I look at the house, a feeling of pure misery grips my heart when I realize I don't want to go back to Pelican Cove. I'm not in the mood to mull over all of that depressing crap right now so I try to put it all out of my mind as I drive back to Lilly's. Lilly and Jalena are both awake and almost ready when I get back, so I run upstairs and get in the shower.

I forget about my problems on the drive to Memphis because I have such a good time hanging out with Lilly and Jalena. I exit off 240 onto Riverside, drive to Beale Street, and take a right. We park in a parking garage and the subject of lunch comes up and we end up at Rendezvous, where Jalena is most impressed with the ribs. After lunch, we walk through the lobby of the Peabody, past the Red Birds stadium, then over to Beale Street, where we poke around for an hour or so. We walk down to the river, where Jalena has to have her picture taken in front of the *Memphis Queen*, before we cross the Skybridge to Mud Island. While we're wandering around there, Lilly mentions something about Tunica, and when Jalena finds out we're only forty miles from there, we go back to the car and head that way. I call Chloe to check on Buster Loo, and she tells me they're out walking at the park. She also volunteers to dog-sit for me tonight so I can stay out and have a good time. I laugh and tell her that I appreciate it.

We visit a few different casinos, then end up at Harrah's, where, after gambling for an hour, I suggest we have dinner at Paula Deen's Buffett. Jalena has to have another picture taken, this time with the cardboard cutout of Paula Deen that stands just outside the restaurant.

When we finish eating, we collectively decide to head back to Bug-tussle because we're all stuffed to the gills and exhausted. Ethan Allen calls me on the way home and asks why we aren't at his bar, and I tell him we'll be there as fast as we can but that's not going to be soon. When we get back to Lilly's house, it's almost nine o'clock, and even though we're all worn-out, we get ready and head over to Ethan Allen's.

When we get to the bar, I chill out on a barstool with a beer, while Lilly and Jalena grab their drinks and hit the dance floor. A little later, when the crowd dies down, Ethan Allen pulls up a stool next to me.

"Does she have a boyfriend?" he asks.

"Lilly?" I ask, teasing. "Yeah, she's been dating that twenty-three-year-old cop for several months now."

"I see that you haven't lost that stellar sense of humor," he says.

"No, she doesn't, Ethan Allen. She's dated a string of losers and she told me just a few weeks ago that she's never found one she couldn't forget." I smile at him.

"Really?" he says, watching her dance.

"Really," I say, slapping him on the back. "You can thank me any-time for bringing the Frog Giggin' Queen of Escambia County to your front doorstep."

"I'll thank you right now," he says. He gets up, walks back behind the bar, and pours me another beer. "Thank you," he says, and he places the mug on a beverage napkin.

He walks over to the other bartender and has a little chat; then the guy looks at me and I smile and raise my beer. Ethan Allen walks out on the dance floor and two-steps his way up to Lilly and Jalena. A few minutes later, Lilly joins me at the bar.

"Look at those two," she says. "They're having the best time ever."

The bartender comes over and asks Lilly what she would like to drink, and she orders a shot of tequila.

"Oh no! Don't do that!" I tell her. "I don't wanna go to jail tonight."

"Girl, you're back in Bugtussle, remember?" she says, downing the tequila. "Where your two best friends sleep with the local law enforcement on a regular basis."

"Oh yeah," I say. "Well, in that case, go ahead and get crazy. Just promise me you won't start any fistfights."

"Promise."

While Lilly and I get tore down at the bar, Jalena and Ethan Allen continue to break it down on the dance floor. At closing time, I tell Jalena that she's going to have to drive us home, and Lilly and I sit in her car and jam out to an old Poison CD while Jalena wraps things up with Ethan Allen.

"Did you get some sugar?" Lilly yells when Jalena finally gets in the car.

"Uh, yes, I did," she says, giggling. "And I have a date tomorrow night."

"Woo-hoo," I say. "Let's stop by the beer store before it closes and go home and celebrate."

"The beer stores closed thirty minutes ago, you moron!" Lilly shouts at me.

"Great, then let's go home and go to bed!" I say.

Saturday we all sleep in, and I call and ask Chloe if she would mind bringing Buster Loo and all of his business back to Lilly's house. She does, and the four of us have a lazy day in the comfort of Lilly's living room. Saturday night, Jalena gets all dolled up for her date with Ethan Allen, and Lilly, Chloe, and I head over to Pier Six Pizza.

"Oh my gosh," I say when the pizza gets to the table. "They don't have anything like this in Pelican Cove."

"Do you want to talk about that?" Lilly asks.

"No, I want to enjoy this pizza," I say. On the way home, we stop by the liquor store and pick up three bottles of wine. When we're almost finished with the second one, Chloe pesters me about what's going on until I finally give in and unload all of my problems. I even tell them about Kevin Jacobs, which Lilly reminds me she already knew about.

Chloe starts crying and comes over and gives me a hug, and then we talk about what I'm going to do.

"Well, you can't leave him," Chloe says.

"Why not?" Lilly protests. "I love Mason like a brother, but if you're not happy and it's not what you want to do with your life, then move home. I understand that, remember? I had the time of my life the first few years I was on the modeling circuit, but then it got old and I got sick of it and I came home. There's no shame in that."

"You can't give up," Chloe says. "You have to fight for it."

"Or you could realize that you've been fighting this same to-be-or-not-to-be battle with him for half your life and maybe the fact that it never seems to work out with you two is some sort of indication that you might need to throw in the towel once and for all."

"I think if you just gave it some time, Ace . . ." Chloe says.

"I think you need to come home and get your old job back, because that hussy they hired to replace you is a bitch!" Lilly says.

"Yeah, Hatter mentioned her," I say. "He said she's hot."

"She's gorgeous," Chloe says, "just not very nice at all."

"She is *super*hot," Lilly says, refilling our glasses. "And she is a *super*-bitch." She looks at me. "She's one of those women who only have male friends."

"Ah," I say. "Who is she?"

"You probably don't know her," Chloe says. "She's fresh out of college, and I think she's from somewhere down south of Jackson."

"Miss Becker." Lilly smirks. "Miss Cameron Becker who loves pecker," Lilly says emphatically, and even Chloe starts laughing hysterically.

We finish the second bottle of wine and start on the third, and Lilly's suggestions get more and more outrageously philosophical and Chloe's get more and more depressing. I wake up at four o'clock in the morning and realize that we've all dozed off in the living room. I wake Lilly up and tell her to get in bed, but she refuses and Chloe never even stops snoring when I try to wake her, so I cover each of them up with some of Lilly's hot pink throws and go upstairs. I look at my phone, and yet again, not a single call or text.

◇◇

47

Sunday morning, Chloe is gone when I get up and Lilly is still asleep on the sofa. I dig around in Lilly's cabinet for some aspirin, take a double dose, and drink a glass of water. I go sit on the love seat with my shades on until my head stops thumping. Then I go in the kitchen, dig the leash out of Buster Loo's bag, and take him outside for a walk. The air is crisp and cool and it puts some much-needed pep in my step.

"Football weather," I say to Buster Loo as he prances along the sidewalk. "My favorite time of year."

On my way back to Lilly's, I see Ethan Allen's truck pull in the driveway. When I get closer, I notice he and Jalena are still in the cab, so I stop walking and hide in the bushes. She's sitting right next to him and he has his arm around her, and then he leans down and starts kissing her and I just stand there and stare like a pervert. Finally, I turn away and tell Buster Loo that his outing just got extended.

I walk back down to the end of the street, and when I turn back around, Ethan Allen is leaving. I speed-walk back to Lilly's, meeting an elderly couple on the way who stare at me with obvious apprehension. I think about speaking to them, but then I realize that I haven't combed my hair and I'm not wearing a bra, so I decide it would only stress them out more if I did.

When I get in the house, Jalena is in the shower and Lilly is still asleep on the couch.

"Dammit!" I say, and Buster Loo starts barking like something is really the matter. That startles Lilly out of her slumber, and she jumps up in a five-alarm panic and tells me to get ready because we're all supposed to be at Gloria Peacock's house at two o'clock.

"Calm down," I tell her. "It's not even noon yet."

"Oh thank goodness," she says and sits back down. She puts her hands on her head. "Oh my word, why did we drink so much wine?"

I go in the kitchen and fix her a glass of water and take her some aspirin, and we talk about how excited we are to be going to the Waverly Estate.

"Well, I called Mrs. Peacock on Thursday and invited her and her pals over, but they couldn't make it and she insisted we come for a visit today."

"That's fantastic!" I say. "Will Birdie, Daisy, and Temple be there, too?"

"I don't think Daisy is in town, but she mentioned that Birdie and Temple come over most Sundays anyway."

"Hanging around with them makes me less worried about getting old," I tell Lilly.

"Tell me about it," she says. "That bunch has got life all figured out."

"No doubt," I say, getting up. I go upstairs and get in the shower, and when I come out of the bathroom in my robe, Jalena is sitting on my bed grinning from ear to ear.

"Once upon a time, you asked me if I'd ever met a man I couldn't forget," she says with great flourish.

"Yes," I say, expectantly.

"My good lady, the answer is no longer *no*." Jalena smiles and I go pile into the bed with her.

"Lilly!" I yell. "Get up here!" A minute later she and Buster Loo come bounding up the stairs.

"Jalena! How'd it go?" Lilly asks in her singsong voice.

"Y'all, it was the best date of my life," she says. "Ethan Allen is a first-class old-school gentleman, and I really dig a man like that. I mean, now that I've actually found one."

"So you ended up at his house, I presume," I say.

"Well, you know, nothing was on at the movies worth seeing," she says. "Just a bunch of weird stuff. I remember now why I don't go to the movies much anymore. Anyway, we went by the 'movie vending machine' as he called it and didn't really find anything there, either. He said he had a bunch of movies at home, so we went back to his place and watched all three of those Jason Bourne movies. I'd never seen any of them. They were great."

"They are great," I agree.

"I didn't love them," Lilly says.

"Anyway," I say and roll my hand like *tell me more*.

"What? Y'all want to know what happened after that?"

"Uh, yeah," Lilly says.

"We made out like teenagers, and it was *great*, and then I didn't get home until this morning, so I guess y'all can figure out the rest."

"I love it," I say.

"Rock on, Jalena," Lilly says. "High five." She looks at the clock on the nightstand. "Okay, we need to leave in about forty-five minutes."

"Where are we going?" Jalena asks.

"We are going to the Waverly Estate, home of Gloria Peacock," I tell her. "She's one of the little old ladies that I had hoped could come down to the charity ball."

She nods, and then Lilly rolls off a list of everyone who'll be in attendance, and Jalena's eyes light up when Lilly says, "And Mr. Ethan Allen Harwood will be there as well."

"Nice," she says. "I better go start getting foxy."

Sunday afternoon, we pull up at the Waverly Estate, and from the time we drive through the majestic iron gates until we hop out of the royal blue chauffeured golf cart next to the clover pool, Jalena is dazed by the grandeur of the place.

"I'm sorry to gawk, y'all," she says quietly, "but I've never seen anything like this. I mean, I just saw a pair of real-live peacocks."

"We were like this the first time we came here," I tell her. "Lilly acted like a real dope. It was embarrassing."

"Shut up, Ace!" Lilly says, and Jalena and I crack up.

We are shown to the Pottery Barn deluxe sunroom, where Chloe and J.J. are chatting with Ethan Allen and Birdie Ross. Gloria Peacock and Temple Williams are seated in a pair of rockers close by. I introduce Jalena, who gets a round of hugs from the older ladies, a hug from Chloe, a handshake from the sheriff, and a hug from Ethan Allen. When she takes a seat on the wicker sofa, he works his way over and sits next to her, which tickles me almost as much as it does Jalena. Sheriff Jackson tells Lilly that Dax should be arriving any minute.

When Dax gets there fifteen minutes later, we are shown to the large round table under the thatched-roof patio, where we are served a delightful array of appetizers and finger sandwiches. Then we move out to the lake, where a dessert table is set up on yet another shaded patio, along with a wet bar.

Lilly starts telling Gloria Peacock all of my love-life problems, and

I have basically the same conversation with the older ladies that I did with Chloe and Lilly the night before, only nobody's speech is slurred today. Birdie agrees with Lilly, Temple agrees with Chloe, and Gloria says I have to go where my heart takes me. Ethan Allen, J.J., and Dax work their way away from that conversation rather quickly and relocate to the dock.

"I think her heart might have a faulty navigational device," Lilly says, cracking everyone up. "It can't figure out where she needs to be."

"Yes, it can," Gloria says, smiling at me. "And it will."

Before we leave the Waverly Estate, I promise Gloria that I will take Jalena to Seaside to meet Daisy McClellan. When we all get back to our cars, Lilly and Dax say good-bye because he has to go back to work, and I tell him good-bye, too. Chloe and J.J. wish us a safe trip home, and Ethan Allen invites Jalena to ride back to town with him. She happily accepts.

48

◇◇◇

Lilly and I make bets about whether Ethan Allen and Jalena will make a detour by his house for a quickie. I say they will and she says they won't because Ethan Allen is too modest.

"I don't think he has sex in the daylight," Lilly says, and I look at her like she's crazy.

I tell Lilly that I want to get a Pier Six pizza to-go so I can eat it for supper on the way home, and she laughs and tells me I must really be deprived of pizza down in Pelican Cove. I tell her about all the weird stuff Avery has picked up for me to eat, and she laughs until she cries about that.

"She's the one with the heels, right?"

"Yes."

"I cannot wait to meet her."

"She's really something," I say.

I call in the pizza and get a text from Jalena while I'm still on the phone, and she wants to know what time we have to leave. When I hang up with Pier Six, I show Lilly the text and tell her that I should've bet her a hundred dollars on that.

"I wasn't a hundred dollars' worth of sure," she says. "I was only about two dollars sure."

"Right," I say. I text Jalena back and tell her that if we leave by six, we can be there by midnight. She sends back a very informative, "Okay."

"Man, it's terrible they live so far apart," Lilly says. "Poor Ethan Allen. He just has the worst luck."

"Maybe he'll ask her to marry him today and then we can both move up here."

"Is that what you've got on your mind?" Lilly asks.

"Kind of. But I'm going back down there to give it my best shot first." I look at her. "He expects me to apologize to him *and* to that stupid Lenore Kennashaw, and I'm not doing it. I'm *not* sorry and I won't say I am."

"Y'all are both so damn stubborn," she says.

"He also told me that he didn't care if I ever made a dime in the gallery, that I could just live off him."

"Most women would love a proposition like that."

"I don't give a shit about *most* women."

"Exactly," Lilly says. "And that's why he loves you. I'm starting to believe that old saying about whatever attracts you most to a person will be what drives you away from them in the end."

"That's depressing."

"I know, because that means Dax's penis is going to be what drives me away from him in the end."

I start laughing and tell her I don't see that happening.

"Me, either," she says with a devilish smile.

I pull into the parking lot of Pier Six Pizza and think for a moment about what a wuss I am because all I want to do is move back home. I get out of the car, go in and get my pizza, and then drive back to Lilly's house. I stick the pizza in the fridge and then start putting my bags in the car. Jalena is all packed up and ready, so I load her stuff up, too.

I sit in Lilly's living room with Buster Loo in my lap while she fills me in on all the local gossip. At five o'clock, we hear a truck pull up and walk out on the porch to see Jalena and Ethan Allen, and they don't look happy.

"Hey, guys," I say cautiously. I glance at Lilly, wondering what might have happened, but then they both start talking to us like everything is normal and I stop worrying. I remember the pizza, so I run inside and get it out of the fridge.

"I guess we need to get on the road," I say finally, not excited at all about the drive back to Pelican Cove. Jalena and Ethan Allen exchange a look; then she hugs Lilly and tells her again what a great weekend she had. I hug Lilly and Ethan Allen; then Lilly goes inside and I go get in the car and crank it up so the lovebirds can enjoy their last few minutes together somewhat privately. A few seconds later, Ethan Allen opens the door for Jalena, leans down and tells Buster Loo good-bye, then tells me to drive safely before closing the door.

Jalena doesn't say anything until we're on the highway.

"I know you think we went and had sex today, but we didn't."

"Don't put that in my buggy, sister, 'cause I am not buying it."

She starts laughing. "Ace Jones, you are too much, girl."

"I do what I can," I tell her. "So what *did* you do if you weren't off bumpin' uglies?"

"He took me to his farm and we rode the Gator down to his lake." She looks at me. "Does everyone up here have a lake at their house?"

"Nope," I tell her. "Just the people with money. There was no lake anywhere around my house."

She shakes her head. "I'm going to be honest with you for a minute," she says.

"Go ahead."

"You were crazy as hell to leave this place."

"Well, I'm not head over heels in love with a certain farm boy that lives here," I tell her. "Plus, there's another side to life in that little town, trust me."

"Who cares?" she says. "I love it."

"Better than Frog Bayou?"

"I love Frog Bayou with all my heart, and I always will. That's home for me, but I could see myself living in Bugtussle."

"Are you serious?" I snort.

"Ace, I've been out with so many guys, so many worthless, self-centered pricks. I *know* men, and Ethan Allen is unlike any man I've dated or even met." She glances over at me. "It's going to be so hard staying down there in Frog Bayou until he asks me to marry him." She laughs out loud, and so do I. "You're going to think I've lost my mind when I say this, but when I was on that Gator with him and he was carrying on and cracking me up, I looked around and got the funniest feeling, like God put me on this Earth to find this man and live on this farm. I felt like I was right where I was supposed to be. I've never experienced anything like that in my life, and it was freaky." She looks at me. "Do you think I'm crazy?"

"Not at all," I tell her. "I think you are very, very lucky."

"Well, we'll just take it one day at a time and see how it goes."

"I've got a feeling it's gonna go well," I tell her, and I only wish I could feel that way about my life. Not wanting to discuss my "is my situation shitty or am I just crazy" dilemma, I ask Jalena what she thought about Gloria Peacock, Birdie Ross, and Temple Williams.

"Wow!" she says. "That's all I can say about that entire experience.

Wow! They make getting older look so glamorous. Mrs. Williams is beautiful, that Birdie Ross is a damn hoot, and Mrs. Peacock is the sweetest, spunkiest little lady I've ever seen. It felt like I was surrounded by family." She looks at me. "Ace, this whole weekend—the party Thursday night, going to Memphis and Tunica on Friday—it was all so much *fun*. And Friday night, I had the time of my life with Ethan Allen, and you know I had a fine ol' time last night." She giggles. "And today, it was just unreal. This whole weekend has been a game changer for me."

"Game changer?" I say.

"As soon as I get home, I'm canceling all of my online dating accounts." She looks at her phone. "I'd do it right now if I could figure out how."

"Olivia is going to be so proud of you," I tell her.

She starts laughing. "She will, won't she? Hey, would you care if I call her?"

"Of course not," I say.

She calls her sister and tells her all about the weekend, and when she gets off the phone, I suggest we have a snack. She reaches around and gets the pizza box off the top of her suitcase, which is where I had to put it so Buster Loo wouldn't have himself a little dog pizza party in the backseat. When Jalena takes a bite, she can't even believe how good it is.

"And it's *cold*," she says. "I wouldn't be able to stand it fresh out of the oven."

We chitchat some more; then she gets quiet and I pop a CD in and we listen to Adele all the way to Meridian. When we get there, we stop at the same gas station we did on the trip up.

She falls asleep shortly after we get back on the road, so I go through my whole collection of Kid Rock CDs. She's snoring when I pull up at her house and I wake her up; she can't believe she's already home.

"I'll call you tomorrow," she says, and we haul the last of her bags in the front door. "Thanks again for everything!"

I pull out of her driveway and head home. Mason didn't call or text all weekend, and I didn't call or text him, either. It's almost midnight when I turn into our neighborhood, and my stomach drops when I pull up in the drive. I leave my bags in the car and tote Buster Loo inside the house. When I put him down, he promptly disappears out the doggie door, and I stand in the living room and listen to see if Mason gets up. He doesn't make any noise, so I decide to just sleep on the couch.

49

<hr>

Monday morning, Mason wakes me up bright and early. He's dressed for work and looks and smells dapper to the max. He hands me a cup of coffee and sits down across from me on the love seat.

"How was your trip?"

"Good," I say. "It was nice to see everyone."

"I understand Ethan Allen and Jalena hit it off."

"I believe they did."

"Do you want to move back up there?"

"Yes."

"Are you going to move back?"

"Do you want me to?"

"No," he says. "I missed you."

"I missed you, too."

"So are you going to leave?"

"Would you come with me?" I look at him and he looks at the floor.

"You know I can't do that," he says.

"I know," I say. "I just thought I'd ask."

"Will you please just give me some time? I promise you that I can make you happy."

"What if I wanted to start teaching school again?"

He looks surprised by that but says, "You can do whatever you want."

"I love you, Mason. There is no one else in this world I want to be with."

"I feel the same way," he says, moving over to sit next to me. "Let's make it work."

Why does it have to sound like such a chore? "Okay."

He kisses me on the cheek and gets up. "Well, you know what I've got to do."

"Go to work." I smile at him because I really do love him with all of my heart. "Have a good day."

I go upstairs, get in the bed, and sleep for two more hours. I wake up at eight, take Buster Loo for a quick walk, then come home and make another pot of coffee. I'm exhausted from the trip and sore from sleeping on the couch, but I take a shower, get ready, and head to the gallery. I leave Buster Loo at home because I feel like he needs some rest after all that traveling.

I take the sign off the front door and go upstairs to my studio. I sit down in front of my easel and feel about as creative as a tax accountant on the sixteenth of April. I walk down to Avery's studio and open the door, only to find that everything is gone. The room looks just like it did the first day I showed it to her. I go downstairs and call her, but it goes straight to voice mail. I don't leave a message.

I sit behind the counter and stare out into the parking lot for a while. No one comes in all morning. At lunchtime, I lock up and go get a sandwich, then sit down at my desk and look up the Florida Department of Education's Web site again. I print out the application, read over it, and then set it on the corner of my desk.

Avery calls at twelve fifteen, and when I ask her if everything is okay, she seems confused.

"Of course, why wouldn't it be?" she says. "Are you home?"

"Yes, I'm at the gallery and I just went upstairs and saw all of your stuff was gone."

She starts laughing and tells me that she and Rob and several other local artists have decided to rent a storefront downtown and form a community gallery.

"Yeah, I was going to tell you before I moved everything out, but you've seemed so troubled lately that I didn't want to stress you out more. I can still work anytime you need me."

"Avery, I don't need you to work, but I would love to have the company if you ever just want to stop by."

"Great! I will, because I've missed you." She tells me their big plans for the community gallery and I tell her it all sounds great. Because it does. I wish her the best of luck and tell her to call me if there's anything I can do to help with the project.

Later that afternoon, the phone rings and it's Tia. "Well, hello!" I say when I answer.

"Hi, Ace Jones," she says sweetly. "So, I heard you took Jalena on a little road trip and she found herself a Mississippi man."

"We did and she did."

"So are we having Girls Night In this week or what? I want to hear all about it."

"Yes!" I exclaim. "As a matter of fact, we should have a special celebration in honor of Jalena deleting all of her online-dating profiles."

She laughs about that and we chat for a minute and she carries on like everything is perfectly normal, so I do the same. When we get off the phone, I text Jalena and tell her I heard from Tia and Girls Night In is on this week. She texts back a few minutes later and says that she will be there and so will Olivia. I text Avery and she says that she'll definitely be coming but that she might be a little late. After about a hundred more text messages, we decide that everyone should just pick up whatever they want for dinner on Thursday and we'll eat together in the break room.

I decide to leave an hour early, and on my way home, Mason texts me and tells me that Allison is bringing a home-cooked meal to the conference room tonight. After inviting me to join them, he sends me another text immediately and says he will completely understand if I don't want to come. I decide to go, not because I want to, but because I want to make it work between us. I go home, take Buster Loo for another short walk, then drive to the law office of J. Mason McKenzie.

Allison acts supremely nice to me when I get there, and she and Connor seem to be getting along a lot better. After a dinner that tastes almost as good as warmed-over cafeteria food, Mason walks me out to my car.

When he gets home later, I hug him as soon as he walks in the door, and we sit in the living room and chat for a while. He tells me Allison leaving at five o'clock has made the work environment much less toxic, and I tell him that there seemed to be a lot less tension. I tell him all about my trip to Bugtussle, and then we start discussing ways to make things better between us.

"I don't want you to feel that you have to eat dinner in that conference room five nights a week," he says. "You need some time to hang out with your friends."

"Maybe if I come up there on Mondays and Wednesdays," I say. "And then we'll have the weekend to be together. Or at least Saturday night and Sunday."

"Then you could hang out with the girls on Tuesday and Thursday," he says. "Do you think you could live with that for a while? I promise it won't be this way forever."

"Yes," I say and honestly feel that I can.

We go upstairs and have some makeup sex, after which he starts snoring so loudly that I have trouble falling asleep.

On Tuesday, I sleep late and don't get to the gallery until eleven. I walk into my office, get a pen, and start filling out the application for a Florida teaching license. When I finish, I put it right back on the corner of my desk. Tuesday night, I have a nice dinner with Jalena and Tia at the Blue Oyster. Wednesday, I make a casserole to take to the conference room, and Thursday, I stop by Bee Bop's Burgers and Shakes on my way to Girls Night In.

When I get to the gallery, I go inside and turn on all the lights. At just after seven, Jalena comes in with a bag from Bee Bop's as well. We're laughing about that when Tia comes in, and she's carrying a Bee Bop's bag, too.

"We should've just met at one of the picnic tables at the drive-in," Jalena says as Olivia comes through the door with a bag from Bueno Burrito. "Oddball!" Jalena calls out.

"What are you talking about?" Olivia says, looking at our bags. "What can I say? I think outside the bun."

I text Avery to see if we need to wait on her, and she says she's on her way, but she's already had dinner, so we dig into our fast-food bags and we're almost finished by the time she arrives. At this point, Jalena points out that we don't have any alcohol, and then we collectively decide that staying sober will be just fine. We leave the break room and settle into the couches, where Jalena wastes no time cranking out tales about Bugtussle.

"I'm so happy for you!" Tia exclaims.

"I'm happy, too, but I'm afraid she's gonna move up there if she gets the chance," Olivia says.

"I can tell you right now that I will," Jalena says, smiling.

"It's all so bittersweet!" Avery says.

"Well, how's your love life going?" I ask Avery.

"It's great," she says with a smile. "Rob actually met my parents last weekend and, wow, did they ever love him."

"Even though he's an artist?" I ask.

"Oh, they love that he's an artist," she says, shaking her head. "I don't know what got into them!"

"Seein' their baby girl happy, that's what," Olivia says, and Tia agrees.

"Well, that is great!" Jalena proclaims. "So who's going to the Halloween Festival next weekend?"

Everyone, apparently, so we start discussing costumes, festivities, and the best and worst Halloween decorations we've seen so far this year. At nine o'clock the conversation winds down, and fifteen minutes later, I'm on my way home.

50

<><><><><><><><><><><><><><><><><><><><><><><><><><><><><><><><><><><>

Friday, I take Buster Loo out for a long walk on the sidewalk by the sea. When I get home, I shower, fix my hair, and put on some nice clothes. Buster Loo shows no interest in leaving the house, so I take off and get to the gallery thirty minutes early.

I go upstairs to my studio, get out my brushes, and paint a large portrait of Buster Loo sitting on a sand dune with the ocean in the background. When I finish, I go downstairs and stare at the Florida teaching-license application.

"I have got to make a decision," I say aloud.

Just after lunch, a few people come in and look around, but no one buys anything. I leave the gallery a few minutes after three and find Buster Loo snoozing in his doggie bed. I change clothes and decide to take a walk on the beach.

The white sand is warm, but the water is cloudy and way colder than I expected. It takes a minute for me to get used to it, but when I do, I wade out knee-deep. I stand there and think about what Jalena said about feeling like she belonged on that farm with Ethan Allen. I wish I could feel that way about Mason, but I guess when you hang on to the same person for almost twenty years, that fanciful newness becomes a permanent fixture in a distant past. I tell myself that there has to be an upside to that somehow. There has to be some reward for "hanging in there" and "making it work."

I wade out of the water, sit down on the sand, and wish that life could be a little less complicated. After a while, I get up and walk slowly back to the house. When I open the gate to the backyard, Buster Loo leaps out the doggie door and starts going nuts. A second later, the patio door opens and Mason steps out onto the back porch.

"You're home early," I say, genuinely glad to see him.

"I got you something," he says, smiling. He holds up a white envelope.

"What is that?"

"Two tickets to Key West," he says. "Are you interested?"

"Hellz yes!" I say.

"Well, go get packed. We leave in two hours," he says.

"What about Buster Loo?"

"I've got that taken care of," he says. "Allison agreed to dog-sit."

"Do you think that's a good idea?" I say. "You know how he likes to hump soft things, and from what Allison says, she keeps PoPo all primped up and fuzzy."

"I warned Connor about that," he says, laughing. "They'll be here in thirty minutes to get him."

"Oh, Buster Loo," I say, picking him up. "I'm going to miss you so much. Please don't make PoPo your girlfriend while we're gone." He starts wiggling and squirming, so I put him down and he takes off and starts running around in circles in the yard.

"See?" Mason says. "He's excited." He hands me a ticket and I see that we're flying back on Monday. I look up at him.

"I'm all yours until Tuesday, baby," he says, giving me a hug, and I am literally so happy I could cry.

Three hours later, Mason and I are sitting on a tiny plane bound for the Florida Keys. It's almost midnight when we check into our cottage on Sunset Key, and I'm too excited to sleep, so we take a late-night stroll on the beach. When the sun comes up the next morning, I walk outside and can hardly believe my eyes.

"Mason!" I say when he joins me on the patio. "This place is so beautiful it doesn't even look real."

"I know. Isn't it great?" he says, smiling. "Let's go grab some coffee and track down breakfast."

I have the time of my life hanging out with him all day on Saturday. Then at breakfast on Sunday, he puts down the newspaper and tells me that there's something he wants to talk about. I start smiling because I think he's going ask me what I think about something he just read, but he doesn't.

He tells me that he wants me to think about apologizing to Lenore Kennashaw.

This leads to an argument, which leads to us spending the remainder of the day on different sides of the resort, which leads me to think that if two people can't enjoy being together in Key West, Florida, then hell, what's the point? We hardly speak during dinner, and the trip home on Monday is more of the same. After unloading the Escalade, Mason leaves without saying a word and comes back an hour later with Buster Loo, who is the only one in the house displaying any remote semblance of happiness.

51

◇◇◇

On Tuesday, Mason is gone when I get up, and I go to the gallery and paint the view from our room in Key West. When I'm halfway finished with that, my phone beeps and I glance over and see it's a text from Jalena. She wants to know if I can meet her at Credo's at seven. I wipe off my hands, then text to tell her that I'll see her there.

I leave the gallery at three o'clock, thinking that maybe I could get used to being a full-time artist after all. I mean, you can't beat the flexibility.

I take Buster Loo for a walk around the neighborhood, during which I have the displeasure of running into Margo and Cindy, who are out spot-checking everyone's Halloween decorations.

"I hope all of your fall décor is up to code," Margo says with a snip in her voice when I meet them on the sidewalk.

"If not, it has to be taken down immediately upon inspection," Cindy chirps as I walk past them.

"Suck a dick," I quip and just keep walking.

"What did she just say?" Margo hisses, and I hear her and Cindy having a heated discussion as I turn the corner and start toward my house. Ten minutes later, the doorbell rings, but I ignore it and walk upstairs and get in the shower.

I get to Credo's five minutes late and find Jalena at what has become "our" table. When I sit down, she looks to her left. I follow her gaze and see Kevin Jacobs sitting at the bar with his pal Reed.

"Hey, Ace," he calls out. "Can we buy you pretty ladies a beer?" I wave him over and Jalena gives me a wary look.

"Do you know what you're doing?" she whispers.

"Why can't we all just be friends?" I whisper back.

"It's not the 'we all' part that concerns me."

"Jalena, I just want to have a good time; that's all."

"What are y'all over here whispering about?" Reed says, taking a seat next to Jalena.

"Girl stuff," she says. "How are you, Reed?" Reed says he's good. She looks at Kevin as he slides into the booth next to me. "And how are you, Kevin?"

"Fine, thank you, ma'am," he says.

"Heard you two took a little vacation last week," Kevin says.

"I went to Bugtussle, Mississippi, and met my future husband," Jalena says, and they both get a big kick out of that. "He took me for a ride on a Gator," she says proudly.

"Well, I guess he'll do for now," Kevin says, then puts his arm on the booth behind my head. "Nothing wrong with a country boy."

We sit and talk and have a few beers, and I finally decide that my crush on Kevin Jacobs is never going to go away and I'm just going to have to learn to live with it. When it's time to go, Kevin offers to walk me home.

"Do you need me to drive you?" Jalena cuts in. "I've only had two beers and I'm about to get out of here myself."

"Don't worry, Jalena," Reed says, getting up. "Kevin will take good care of her."

"Yeah, I bet," Jalena mumbles. She looks at Reed. "Do you need a ride?"

"I think I'm going to stay a minute longer," Reed says, surveying the crew around the bar.

"Okay." She goes to the bar to pay her bill, then pulls me to the side. "Are you sure you don't want to ride home with me?"

"Jalena, it's fine. We're just walking."

"Okay," she says, following us outside.

"Good night, Jalena," Kevin calls to her as she gets in her vehicle. "Try not to get pulled over on the way home."

"Oh, that's so funny, Kevin. Bye, Ace. Y'all better behave!"

"Don't worry," I say, waving at her. "Call me!"

She honks as she pulls out of the parking lot and drives away in the opposite direction.

Kevin Jacobs drapes his arm around me and pulls me up close to him. We step onto the sidewalk and he asks a string of harmless questions as we walk along side by side. My heart feels like it's going to beat its way out of my chest, and I know I need to get away from him. I know I should've caught a ride home with Jalena, and I know he doesn't need to have his arm around me, but I just keep walking. When we get to the part of the walkway that's totally dark, he stops and steps in front of me.

"Come home with me," he whispers. "You know you want to."

"I do want to," I tell him. "But I can't do that."

"No one has to know," he says. "Just come home with me tonight. One night and we'll never do it again."

"Does anyone ever fall for that?" I ask him, smiling.

"All the time," he says with a big grin.

I step around him and start walking. "Well, not this girl. I'm sorry."

"No need to be sorry," he says, catching up with me. "But you know this is going to happen between us. It's just a matter of time."

"It's not going to happen while I'm engaged," I tell him. He doesn't say anything and I start to feel bad for flirting with him so much and then shutting him down. "I'm sorry, Kevin. I don't mean to be rude. I just like hanging out with you more than I should."

"It's okay," he says. "I'm good enough to party with, but you need to go home to your real man at the end of the night." He looks at me. "This happens to me all the time. I'm just a regular good-time Freddy. Very disposable."

"What about Tia?" I ask.

"What about her?" he says. "I didn't want to be her full-time boyfriend, so she dumped me. What part of that is unclear?"

"Well, you're standing here feeling sorry for yourself because you're just a good-time Freddy, but she wanted to take it to the next level with you."

"She wanted someone to fill the gap after her kid went off to college," he says, looking at me. "Tell me I'm wrong." I don't know if he is or if he isn't, so I don't say anything. "I like her just fine and we had a lot of fun but, honestly, she's not my type."

"Y'all had sex for five years and she's not your type?"

"No, she's not," he says. "Don't stand over there and act like you've never had a fling with someone just for the hell of it."

"Okay," I say. "I won't. But I hope you understand why I can't have a fling with you."

"I do," he says and stops walking again. I stop and look up at him. "But you need to know that what I want from you is more than just a fling. I just thought I'd start with that and go from there." I stand there, paralyzed by what he just said. "I *like* you, Ace. You're so much fun to hang out with. You don't bitch and moan and gripe like most women do all the time." I start laughing and he tells me that he's serious. "And I've never seen you wear any kind of shoes except flip-flops, and I like that!" he exclaims. "And while I'm being honest, I'll go on and tell you that I don't think you match up with Mason McKenzie any better than I match up with Tia Wescott." I stop laughing. "Don't get me wrong, here. I like Mason. I think he's cool as hell, but he's too . . . I don't know. You just don't seem like the type to spend your life with a man who wears a tie to work every day."

"That's kind of an insult when you think about it," I say.

"No, it's not," he says and starts walking again. "It's the truth and you know it."

We get to the intersection where he goes left and I go straight.

"Thank you for walking me home, Kevin."

"Thank you for walking with me, Ace."

I walk home thinking about our conversation and congratulating myself for not doing something I so desperately wanted to do. Then I get a little depressed because maybe I shouldn't congratulate myself until I stop craving badness.

◇◇◇

52

Wednesday passes without much excitement, and Thursday, a woman comes into the gallery and actually buys one of my small mermaid paintings. I feel a bit pathetic by how excited I get, but that doesn't stop me from calling half the people on my contacts list and sharing the news.

Thursday night, at Girls Night In, we order pizza and talk about the upcoming Halloween Festival. Rob and Avery are going as Adam and Eve. Tia and Jalena are going as female pirates, and Olivia is going as Elvira.

"Won't be long before I can't wear a cleavage-baring costume without embarrassing my kids, so I have to take full advantage," she says with a chuckle. Tia asks what I'm going as and I tell them I don't know if I'm going or not.

"You *have* to go," Jalena says. "You don't have to dress up. Everyone won't be wearing a costume, but you *have* to go."

"Okay," I say.

"You and your fiancé should dress up," Avery says.

"Yeah, I'll talk to him about that," I lie.

"Okay, ladies, I have an announcement to make," Tia says, and we all get quiet and give her our full attention. "I'm going to get all tanked up and tell Kevin Jacobs that I'm in love with him."

"What?" Jalena says while the rest of us sit in stunned silence.

"Yep, I'm going to do it," she says. "And let the candy-coated apples fall where they may."

I force myself to start breathing again and put down the slice of pizza I have in my hand.

"When?" I say, trying very hard to act normal. "When are you going to do this?"

"Halloween night," she says with a definitive nod.

"Was Kevin Jacobs our designated driver that night when we all got so drunk?" Avery asks.

"Yes," Jalena says, not taking her eyes off Tia.

Tia proceeds to give Avery the full backstory while my stomach knots up and flips over. I look at Jalena, who is still staring at Tia.

"Well, good luck with that, Tia," Olivia says.

"Yeah, he would be a fool not to trick your treat, Tia," Avery says, and I force myself to laugh even though I don't even really know what that comment actually means.

Jalena gently redirects the conversation toward which Dock Street bars host the best parties, and I sit and nod along, saying nothing. When everyone starts leaving, Jalena sticks around.

"Why would she do that?" Jalena exclaims when the two of us are alone in the gallery. "She thinks hiding in the floor of the Jeep under that blanket was a tough pill to swallow, yet she wants to just walk up to him in a public place on freakin' Halloween and declare her undying love? That is so damn crazy!"

"You have to talk to her," I say.

"And say what?"

"I don't know, but you have to talk her out of it," I say and then tell Jalena about the conversation I had with Kevin the night before.

She just shakes her head. "Could this possibly get any more fucked-up?"

"I don't see how," I tell her.

Jalena gets up. "I'll call her tomorrow and try to talk some sense into that thick skull of hers." She looks at me. "What are you going to do?"

"About what?"

"About Mason and about Kevin!"

"I'm not going to get involved with Kevin any more than I already am, and at some point hopefully get things back on track with Mason." We gather our things and head for the door. "Have you talked to Ethan Allen lately?" I ask when we get outside.

"Yeah," she says. "We text and talk all the time."

"That's great," I say. "That makes me so happy."

"I really like him, Ace," she says. "I'm so glad you talked me into taking off work and going up there, or I never would've met him."

"The Lord works in mysterious ways," I say, and she gives me a funny look. "Or so I hear."

"Well, I guess I'll see you Saturday night." She looks at me. "You are coming, aren't you?"

"With or without Mason, yes, I'll be there, just so I can see everybody all dressed up."

"You oughta get yourself a costume," she says, walking around to the driver's side of her Jeep. "It's so much fun and I'm sure I've got an extra one lying around somewhere."

"Maybe next year," I say, waving good-bye. *If I'm here.*

*   *   *

Mason is home when I get there, and our attempt at conversation doesn't turn out well at all, and I end up sleeping on the couch again. We manage to have a pleasant conversation Friday morning, then have another disagreement over dinner. Saturday morning, we make peace with each other again and have coffee together on the patio. I mention the Halloween Festival and he asks me if I want to go and I say yes, so he tells me he'll come home at five and go with me. We talk for a few minutes about what kind of funny last-minute costumes we could put together, but the conversation feels more forced than humorous.

I take Buster Loo for a walk, then spend a few hours at the beach. I call Lilly and talk to her for a while, then call Jalena and ask her if she's talked to Tia. She says that she has, but Tia is not to be deterred.

"Tia is a strong-minded, strong-willed woman," Jalena says finally. "I can't talk a bit of sense to her."

"What are we going to do?"

"Do you have Kevin's phone number?"

"Of course not!" I say. "Do you?"

"Well, no," she says. "But we need to let him know what's going on." She pauses. "You need to let him know."

"How am I supposed to do that? I'm going with Mason."

"Well, I guess there's not much we can do, then."

"What good would it do to let him know anyway?" I ask.

"I don't know," Jalena sighs. "Maybe give him time to think about it before she blindsides him. Hey! My phone is beeping and it's Olivia. Holler at me when you get there tonight."

I pack up and walk home, where I take a long shower followed by a short nap, and I wake up feeling lazy and useless. I decide that first thing Monday morning, I'm going to send in that application and get my teaching license, because apparently I'm one of those people who feels eternally worthless without a reliable job and can't stay motivated with all of this flexibility.

I take my time fixing my hair and doing my makeup and pick out my sexiest top to wear. By the time Mason gets home, I'm dressed and ready and smelling good.

"You look and smell wonderful," he says when he comes in.

"Thank you," I say.

"Give me thirty minutes and I'll be ready."

An hour later, we're walking the streets of downtown with a host of goblins and ghouls. We decide to have dinner at a little Mexican joint and enjoy several beers with our meal. When we walk back outside, its dark and the streets are brimming with people young and old who are out and about in full Halloween garb.

"This is crazy," I tell him.

"You should see this place during Mardi Gras," he says. He buys us a beer from a sidewalk vendor and we make our way down the crowded street. He talks to everyone he sees and introduces me to what seems like a thousand people, and then he gets hung up with a man who peppers him with questions about faulty foreclosures. I excuse myself from the conversation and call Jalena, and she tells me she's at the Crooked House Pub at the north end of Dock Street, which I can see from where I'm standing. I look back at Mason, who has just taken a seat on a bench with the man of many questions, and the two of them are thoroughly engrossed in conversation. I slide the phone into my pocket and step over beside Mason.

"Yes?" he says, looking up at me.

"I'm going to run over to the Crooked House and holler at Jalena for a minute, okay?"

"Sure," he says, and the man he's speaking with looks up at me like he doesn't appreciate the interruption. I want to tell him that I don't appreciate his interrupting my date for free legal advice, but I know Mason wouldn't approve, so I settle for answering his annoyed glare with a smirk and the evil eye.

"Hope you can join me soon," I say and the man starts talking again before Mason can answer.

"I don't know how he does it," I mumble under my breath as I step around a herd of toddlers dressed up as various superheroes.

When I walk into the pub, it takes me a minute to find Tia and Jalena because the place is built like a shoe box, long and narrow. When I finally get back to where they are, I give them each a big hug and tell them how adorable they are in their pirate costumes.

"Wenches!" Jalena says. "We're wenches!"

"Not to be confused with witches!" Tia yells over the crowd.

I squeeze up to the bar and order a beer; then Tia asks if anyone needs to use the restroom. Since I'm waiting on a drink and Jalena's glass is almost full, Tia takes off by herself. I'm about to ask Jalena if she's seen Kevin when her eyes bug out and she points to the door and says, "Oh shit. Look who's here!"

I look up and see Kevin Jacobs walking in with three other guys. Hot guys.

"She wouldn't do it here," I say. "Would she?"

"She told me on the way over here that she's telling him as soon as she sees him, and she's been drinking since four o'clock." She leans over next to my ear. "Ace, you have to get him out of here," she says. "We can't let her do this to herself."

"What do you want me to do?" I ask. "Mason could be walking over here right now! Why can't you get him out of here?"

"We both know you could do it faster." Jalena looks around and points to the stage, which is currently unoccupied. "If you step behind that backdrop thing, there's a door that leads into the alley. Just tell him you want to talk to him, get him out there, and when Tia gets out of the bathroom I'll get her to leave and we can all go on about our business and hope we don't run into him again."

"What am I supposed to tell him?"

"I don't know," she says in a panic. "We just can't let this happen here." I think about Tia and how pitiful she was the night we stalked Kevin's house.

"Okay, stand here and wait for my drink and I'll go take care of this as fast as I can," I say and make my way over to Kevin Jacobs, who is wearing Mossy Oak camouflage from head to toe.

"Hey, Ace Jones!" he says when he sees me.

"Hi," I say. I glance back at Jalena, who gives me an impatient look. "Hey, I need to ask you something, but I can't ask you here." I point toward the stage. "Can you come with me?"

"Can I get a beer first?"

"No!" I say. "It's urgent." He raises his eyebrows and I can see that he's got the wrong idea. "Can you please come with me for a second?"

"Sure," he says. I start walking toward the stage, and he follows me. I step around the backdrop and out the door into the alley.

"Wow!" I say. "It's really loud in there." I look at him. "So what are you supposed to be? A tree trunk?"

"I just came outta the woods," he says, laughing.

Then he grins at me and I realize that I have made a terrible mistake. I think about all the time I spent giving him the wrong idea, and now I'm standing here in this alley with no time to clear that up.

"So," he says, taking a step closer to me. "What did you need to ask me?"

"Well, nothing really," I say, getting really nervous. "I just needed to get you out of there—"

"For what?" he says, taking another step closer and backing me against the wall.

"I don't know," I say and realize that my inability to articulate a clear answer is giving him more of the wrong idea than he already has. In the blink of an eye, he slides his arms around my waist and pulls me up close to him.

"I think I know what you want," he says and gently kisses me on the lips. "Is that it?"

"No," I squeak, but it's too late—his lips are on mine, and he proceeds to slobber all over my face. My mind is reeling with regret when I hear someone shouting my name.

"Ace? Ace! Is that you? What the hell are you doing?"

Kevin steps away from me, and I turn to see Mason stalking down the alley toward us. I mop my chin with the back of my hand.

"What the hell is this?" Mason shouts. "Jacobs, what the fuck, man? This is my fiancée. How do you not know that?"

Kevin takes another step back, and Mason glares at me.

"Ace, what the hell?" He points at Kevin. "What are you doing with this asshole?"

"Hey, man! She asked me to come out here," Kevin says.

Mason looks at him and says, "This would be a great time for you to shut the fuck up." And Kevin wastes no time getting back inside the bar.

"Mason, I swear to you that this is not what it looks like," I tell him. "I swear. I asked him to come out here because Tia was about to tell him that she was in love with him, and he's not in love with her, and Jalena and I were just trying to save her some embarrassment."

"So your solution was to bring him out in the alley and start making out?" he says sarcastically. "Great plan."

"Mason, no, I promise. Can we just go home and talk about this?"

"Right, let's just go home and sweep this under the rug like we did that shit you pulled at the charity ball. Wait, it seems like I remember you lying to me about something that night, too." He stares at me and I just stand there, saying nothing.

"I'm not cheating on you," I say.

"Yeah, I just saw that you weren't, Ace." He shakes his head. "Kevin Jacobs? Really? The same guy who's fucking your friend Tia? Hell, he's fucked everybody in the southeastern United States, so why not you, too?" He holds up his hand. "You know what? I'm done. I can't do this with you anymore."

"Mason, no, please, just let me explain."

"There's really nothing to explain, Ace, when you think about it."

He takes off, walking fast, and I follow him through a maze of alleys back to the truck. He says nothing on the drive home. When he pulls up in the driveway, he takes the keys out of the ignition and looks at me.

"I think you should go back to Bugtussle," he says. "Unless of course you have something else in mind, like moving in with Kevin Jacobs."

"Mason, please just let me explain."

"No, Ace. Let me explain something to you. I've been living down here by myself for over five years. Alone. Waiting on you to decide that you could trust me, and then you finally did, and now here we are—" He shakes his head. "After the way you acted about everything that happened before, who would've ever thought you'd be the one cheating on me."

"I am not cheating on you."

"Right. Like you didn't have anything to do with all that garbage at the charity ball?" he says, getting out of the truck. "Surely you don't expect me to believe that?" I get out and walk behind him up the steps to the door.

"Mason, please!" I say, following him into the kitchen, where he gets a beer out of the fridge.

"I don't want to hear it, Ace," he says, twisting the cap off the bottle.

"I was in the bar with Jalena and Tia and—"

"I said I don't want to hear it!" he yells, slamming his fist down on the bar. "You had to do something to make him think he could do that. Men don't walk up to random women on the street and start making out with them, Ace. It doesn't work that way. A woman has to give some indication or some kind of invitation to a man. If Tia or Jalena asked me to walk into a dark alley, do you think I would push them up against a wall and start kissing them?" He looks at me. "Do you?" I shake my head and he continues. "No! I wouldn't! So if you would like to explain something, please feel free to explain what might have led Kevin Jacobs, town whore, to think such behavior would be acceptable to you."

He looks at me and I look at the floor.

"Let's talk about logic," he says, putting his beer on the counter.

"Okay," I say, not looking up.

"Your defense against apologizing to Lenore Kennashaw, if I recall correctly, was that it's easy to be nice to nice people, but rather difficult to be nice to people who aren't, right?"

"Right," I say, and I'm almost sure this conversation isn't going to end well for me.

"That makes sense to me because I'm a logical guy, but here's the thing with logic: It can work for you or it can work against you. For example, the only logical conclusion I can draw from what happened tonight is that Kevin Jacobs would *not* have been all over you in that alley unless that was what you wanted." He picks up the beer. "Correct me if I'm wrong."

I want to say something, but words won't come. I bite my lip and feel the sting of tears.

"That's what I thought," he says. "I think you should leave." He walks out into the garage, where I can hear him banging stuff around. I go upstairs and start packing. Buster Loo creeps out from under the bed, and I pick him up and give him a hug.

"Mommy blew it, Buster Loo," I whisper to him. "I'm so sorry, little fellow."

After I load the last of my bags in my car, I go back in the kitchen and open the door to the garage. Mason is sitting in a lawn chair with his head in his hands.

"I'm sorry," I say. "I'm leaving now."

"Ace," he says, getting up.

"I'm so sorry," I say and bite my lip, but the tears start anyway.

"Please, don't do that," he says, wiping a tear off my cheek. "Listen, do you remember that day we were sitting in your grandma's swing under that big oak tree after your parents passed away, and I told you that I would always be around, no matter what?"

"Of course," I say. "I could never forget."

"Well, that promise still stands and it always will." I look up at him. "We tried, baby."

Mason kisses me on the cheek and I turn to go because I have to get out of there before I have a squalling nervous breakdown. He scoops up Buster Loo and tells him to be a good dog before handing him to me at the front door.

"Just go back to Bugtussle and think it all over," he says. "Who knows? You might decide to come back."

"Okay," I say, but we both know that's not going to happen. "Thank you so much, for everything." I walk out the door and don't look back.

I know I need to call Lilly, but I don't have the guts to tell her what happened. I decide to call her when I get to the Alabama state line. Then when I get to the Mississippi state line, I decide to call her when I get to Meridian. When I get to Meridian, I decide to call her when I get to Tupelo, and when I get to Tupelo, I know I have to do it.

"Happy Halloween!" she says cheerfully when she answers.

"Hey," I say, with a lump in my throat and a knot in my stomach. "Please don't ask me to explain right now—"

"Ace, what is it? What's going on?"

"Lilly, I'm coming home."

ACKNOWLEDGMENTS

Special thanks to Danielle Perez, Heidi Richter, Susanna Einstein, and Molly Reece.

And thanks to Joe McCay, Tonya LeMay, and the wonderful staff of Margaritaville Hotel in Pensacola Beach, as well as Ryan O'Keeley of O'Keeley Media in Pensacola, Tricia Foley, and TurnHere.

Thanks also to Kathy Patrick and the Pulpwood Queens of Jefferson, Texas; the BB Queens of Jackson, Mississippi; Emily Gatlin and the fine folks of Reed's Gum Tree Bookstore; Lyn Roberts of Square Books; Cat Blanco of the Book Exchange; Karen White; Echo Garrett; Angela Lee; Cynthia Callander at Vero Beach Book Center; Tom Warner of Litchfield Books; B. Bronson Tabler, P.A., of Tabler Law in Tupelo, Mississippi; Scott Thompson of the Ole Miss Alumni Association; Rhonda Keenum of Mississippi State University; Jordan Gann; Lelani Salter of *Town & Gown Magazine*; Brad Mooy of the Arkansas Literary Festival; Farris Yawn of Canton Festival of the Arts. And Barnes & Noble (Mississippi State), Booksellers at Laurelwood, Lemuria Books, Page & Palette, Capitol Book, Barnes & Noble (Pensacola), Orlando Public Library, Books Plus, and Blue Bicycle Books.

And thanks to Deirde Donahue of *USA Today*, Jennifer Brett of the

Atlanta Journal-Constitution, Barbara Hoffert of *Library Journal*, Sara Vilkomerson of *Entertainment Weekly*, Kristina Webb of TCPalm, Sam Grisham of the *Prentiss County Progress*, Brant Sappington of the *Banner-Independent/Daily Corinthian*, Cyrus Webb of Conversations Radio, the *Daily Journal* of Tupelo, Wendy Wax, Sophie Littlefield, Valerie Frankel, Rachael Herron, Deep South Magazine, Kindle Fever, Shelf Awareness, BlogHer, and everyone else who took the time to do an interview, book review, blog entry, and/or feature.

Finally, a big *muchas gracias* to Sandy Jackson and her aristocratic weenie dog, Buddy Chubz, Mandi Harris, Molly Wren, Melisa Depew, Jenny Little, Edgar Serrano, Michael Raines, Aaron Raines, Brent Raines, and Barry and Wanda Raines. Thanks also to all the rest of my family and friends. And, last but certainly not least, thanks to each and every person who is a fan of Ace Jones. There are no words to properly express my appreciation for all of your support.

Photo by Rachel Wade

Stephanie McAfee was born in Mississippi, and she now lives in Florida with her husband, young son, and chiweenie dog.